Anselm was remembering his dilemma—a dilemma familiar enough to surgeons. He could almost feel the cold sweat on his brow and the threatening panic inside his head, as though he were still in the operating room, desperately trying to think of something to do as his patient's blood pressure kept going down, down, down.

For the moment he had forgotten that Valerie was in the room. The sight of her relaxed him. "I want to tell you how glad I am to have you here," he said, filling two glasses with the wine she had brought.

"I'm glad to be here," she said. A feeling of protective affection overcame her. He was a good doctor, she thought. A good man—struggling against a system that had become corrupt.

But standing this close to him, Valerie felt more than affection . . . something she hadn't felt for a long time. . . .

DANGEROUS PRACTICES

DANGEROUS PRACTICES

Francis Roe

A SIGNET BOOK

SIGNET
Published by the Penguin Group
Penguin Books USA Inc., 375 Hudson Street,
New York, New York 10014, U.S.A.
Penguin Books Ltd, 27 Wrights Lane,
London W8 5TZ, England
Penguin Books Australia Ltd,
Victoria, Australia Ltd, Ringwood,
Penguin Books Canada Ltd, 10 Alcorn Avenue,
Toronto, Ontario, Canada M4V 3B2
Penguin Books (N.Z.) Ltd, 182-190 Wairau Road,
Auckland 10, New Zealand

Penguin Books Ltd, Registered Offices:
Harmondsworth, Middlesex, England

First published by Signet, an imprint of New American Library, a division of
Penguin Books USA Inc.

First Printing, September, 1993
10 9 8 7 6 5 4 3 2 1

PART
ONE

1

Shortly before seven in the morning, Dr. Anselm Harris swung his old blue Triumph sports car into the doctors' parking lot at the back of Glenport Hospital and pulled up some twenty yards past the emergency room entrance. He eased his long legs out and slammed the car door shut, noticing the newly green trees around him and the old pastel-colored wooden houses on the opposite side of Manitauk Avenue. The outlines of trees and houses were blurred and softened by the late April fog swirling in from the Sound.

Anselm walked toward the entrance; tall, well built, he had the smooth, easy gait of an athlete. A dark blue sweater was pulled over an open-collar plaid shirt, and his thick brown hair, worn longer than the old guard at the hospital felt appropriate for a professional man, was curled and ruffled by the open air and the humidity, making him look younger than his thirty-nine years, more like a college professor than a surgeon. Women often noticed Anselm's eyes first; gray-green and intense, they sparkled with enthusiasm or quiet amusement, and since his voice was usually quiet and controlled, they were often the only visible indicators of what he was feeling.

Behind Anselm, a bright red Lamborghini turned into the lot, jolted over the speed bump, passed him, and came to a smooth, power-laden halt in a parking space a few yards ahead.

Anselm reached the car just as his friend Peter Delafield stepped out. Peter, an internist and about the same age as Anselm, was casually dressed in a sports coat and slacks, silk tie, and brown Church shoes. With his regular features, wavy blond hair, and sea blue eyes, Peter had star-quality good looks and was not entirely unaware of it. In med school Peter, always more dashing than Anselm, had been nicknamed "Flash." Here, in the old Connecticut seafaring town of Glenport, the nurses called him "Mr. Cool."

"Glad I bumped into you," said Peter, closing his car door with respectful care. "I have a patient up on B3 I'd like you to see, if you have time."

"I thought you took Thursdays off," replied Anselm. "What happened? Did Susan sell your boat?"

"I think she'd like to," replied Peter, eyeing a couple of nurses coming out of the hospital. "Actually, I've got a bunch of discharge summaries to dictate." He sounded uncharacteristically tense, almost nervous, and Anselm wondered if he was having trouble with Susan. It wouldn't be the first time.

They were walking toward the emergency room entrance, the most convenient way of getting into the hospital, when they heard a slapping noise that rapidly reached window-rattling volume. A small military helicopter appeared over the trees and passed almost directly overhead, close enough to swirl the mist and kick up some of last year's dead leaves. It was heading over the water for Carver's Island, twelve miles offshore and home to the powerful and reclusive rich. The sound of the rotors briefly reminded Anselm of his childhood and the series of air force bases where he'd grown up.

"That must be Denton Bracknell going home for a long weekend," said Peter when the noise had receded. He shook his head and grinned. "I wouldn't mind that kind of life. A few days working in Washington, then back home to Carver's Island and a gorgeous wife."

"I'm surprised they're still flying in this fog," said Anselm. "It must be even worse out on the island."

"Yeah," said Peter with a curious inflection, staring after the disappearing 'copter, "it's getting real thick. An hour from now, even the seagulls'll be grounded."

They went in through the emergency room entrance, and passed the ER desk, where Dr. Bob North, the chief of surgery, was talking animatedly to Erica Barnes, the hospital's part-time public relations coordinator, while Pat Mooney, the head nurse, kept one eye on a chart and the other on Bob and Erica.

Erica looked up, excused herself, and hurried after Peter and Anselm. Bob North watched her walk away.

"Dr. Harris?"

The two men stopped and turned. Erica was worth stopping for; slim, elegant, with her carefully coiffed dark hair and big, almost black eyes that looked out of a smooth, oval face, she had a sophisticated attractiveness that made people wonder what she was doing in such a modest community hospital.

"Neil Gowan came by and wanted to be sure you'd see his mother," said Erica. "She's up on B3."

"That's the patient I want you to consult on, Anselm," said Peter, looking at Erica.

"Thanks," replied Anselm, "I'll be happy to see her." He had the kind of voice people listened to, quiet, with a hint of a midwestern accent.

"Would you call Mr. Gowan afterward, Dr. Harris?" Erica studiously avoided looking at Peter. "He said he'd be at the pharmacy all morning."

"Sure. I'll stop by on my way home."

Anselm and Peter continued along the corridor and

walked up the stairs toward the third floor of the old
medical wing, where Peter had most of his patients.

Two older doctors were coming down the stairs,
chatting to each other. They nodded to Peter but ignored Anselm altogether.

As they continued up, Anselm said nothing, but Peter was obviously uncomfortable by their colleagues'
evident hostility to Anselm.

"I'm sorry about that," he said as they walked up
the concrete steps. "Some of these old fuddy-duddies
really embarrass me."

"No skin off my nose," said Anselm, grinning.
"I'm used to trouble." And in fact, some of the things
he'd done since coming to Glenport a year before had
raised the hackles on some of his more conservative
colleagues.

"Yeah," said Peter, glancing at his friend. "You
always did thrive on it."

They reached the nurses' station, and Peter picked
a chart off the rack.

"I don't really know what's the matter with Florence," said Peter, tapping the chart. "Actually, Bob
North saw her yesterday, but he didn't think there was
much the matter with her."

Anselm said nothing. He knew Peter didn't think
much of North's professional skills, but there were political reasons why he would occasionally invite Bob
to consult on his patients.

"You know Florence is Neil Gowan's mother," Peter went on. He grinned. "And that fact, plus a buck
and a quarter, will get her on the subway." Like most
of the doctors, Peter didn't have much time for Neil
Gowan, the pharmacist. "Anyway, Gowan seems to
have a very high opinion of you, I can't imagine why."

"You want to know why?" said Anselm, giving Peter a gentle punch on the shoulder. "First . . ."

"Don't bother. Let me tell you about Florence.

She's a fifty-two-year-old married woman with two grown-up kids,'' he said, using the time-honored case-presentation format. "She developed acute nephritis about a year ago, and seemed to get better, the way they usually do. Then about six months ago she came to my officer with swollen ankles, pasty face, and was *this* close to being in congestive heart failure.'' Peter held up his thumb and forefinger, almost touching. "Her family doctor had been giving her aminophylline for her breathlessness . . .'' He shook his head. "Some of those guys, you wonder what they learned in medical school.''

Peter flipped through the pages of the chart, then passed it to Anselm. "You should know that Florence is a bit of a pain in the butt,'' he went on confidentially. "She's always complaining about something, so Bob North could be right, for once.''

They stopped outside Mrs. Gowan's room. "Yesterday she vomited a couple of times, and she hadn't done that before,'' Peter said, quietly enough not to be heard on the other side of the door. "She's on prednisone, and that usually makes her feel better, but now she's lethargic and has no appetite. . . .'' He put his hand on the doorknob. "Anyway, here we are,'' he said. "See for yourself.''

One look told Anselm that Mrs. Gowan was indeed seriously ill. Her breathing was shallow, she had a grayish look, and paid little attention to her visitors, aside from moving her eyes toward them when they came in.

"Florence, this is Dr. Anselm Harris,'' said Peter, taking her hand. "I've asked him to come and take a look at you.''

"I've heard about you from Neil,'' said Mrs. Gowan, her eyes lighting up with momentary interest. "He says you're the best surgeon here.''

Anselm gave her his professional smile, sat down at

her bedside, and pulled the top sheet back. Now he was all business; everything else went out of his head as he concentrated on his patient. Mrs. Gowan's belly was tense and swollen; Anselm put his hands on it, probing with a gentleness that surprised Peter. Then he listened to her abdomen with his stethoscope. It was silent, silent as a cave at midnight. Anselm moved the bell of the instrument around and listened for a few minutes to see if the pattern would change. It didn't.

Peter watched him. There was no question of Anselm's expertise, and Peter enjoyed seeing him work. Anselm was a born surgeon, and although it had been a tragic situation that had forced him to leave New York, it certainly had turned into a benefit for Peter and the rest of the Glenport community.

At that moment Mrs. Gowan grabbed a blue plastic kidney dish from the bedside table and vomited into it, a continuous, effortless stream that soon filled the dish and overflowed onto the sheets. Peter took the dish from her and Anselm called a nurse on the intercom, found a towel, and helped her to clean up. Mrs. Gowan lay back, exhausted, her eyes closed.

When the nurse arrived, Anselm gave him some instructions and motioned Peter outside.

"She has peritonitis," said Anselm when the door was closed. "She's perforated her gut, probably the large bowel."

Peter flushed, astonished. The possibility of peritonitis hadn't even occurred to him. "I knew she was sick. . . . That goddamn Bob North! That's the last time he's seeing any of my patients."

Anselm's expression didn't change. "It's possible that she perforated after Bob saw her," he said, "and of course the prednisone masks the symptoms."

Now that Anselm had pinpointed the cause of her illness, Peter knew that it had happened at least twenty-four hours before, and North had simply missed the diagnosis.

"So what now?"

"She's going to need surgery. I'll schedule the O.R. right now. Meanwhile we should check her 'lytes, start antibiotics, do the usual workup. Then we'll need to get the op permit signed. I'll go back in and tell her, if you like."

"I'll come with you," said Peter, now sounding seriously flustered. "And I'll need to call Neil, I suppose."

"I'll tell him," said Anselm, opening the door.

"Thanks, Anselm. I appreciate it. Meanwhile, I'll take care of Florence's medications."

Anselm's pager went off. Dr. Abruzzo, chief of the medical staff and responsible, among other things, for good order and discipline among the hospital doctors, wanted to see Anselm in his office as soon as possible.

2

Anselm took his time. After explaining to Florence Gowan what he was going to do, he made a detailed note in the chart before heading down the corridor. He knew why Frank Abruzzo wanted to see him.

Sitting at the desk of his small office, Dr. Abruzzo, who had been a surgeon at Glenport Hospital for the past forty years, was looking old and uncomfortable, but came straight to the point.

"Look, Anselm," he said, "you're causing some problems around here, and I'm concerned about your relationships with some of the docs on the medical staff here." He shook his head. "There's been some . . . well, a fair number of comments about you recently. I've decided to talk to you before things go any further."

"Thanks, Dr. Abruzzo," replied Anselm. "I've got some comments of my own," he said, thinking about Bob North, "but right now I'm keeping them to myself."

Dr. Abruzzo's dewlap quivered, but he went on. "Anselm, you have to realize that Glenport's a lot different from that New York hospital you were at, and not everybody here is as well trained as you. Some people are real sensitive about that, maybe even jealous, I suppose." He paused, his fingers drumming on the table. "You've been in practice here a year," he went on. "And you've made a few enemies . . ." Abruzzo held up both hands. "I know you've got some good friends too, but we all have to work together here, cooperate." Abruzzo stared blankly at Anselm for a second, then caught himself. "Right, cooperate . . . Specifically . . ." He held the piece of paper in his hand at arm's length and read from it. "I'm told you don't pay due attention to your colleagues' opinions," he said. He put the paper down. "Apparently you've even disagreed with some of your colleagues *in front of their patients*?" He stared at Anselm over his glasses.

"Are you saying I should always agree with their opinions?" asked Anselm, comfortably stretching his legs out in front of him.

"Well, no, of course not, but we're talking about professionalism, and we don't want to offend people."

"Professionalism? Is that agreeing with people when they're wrong?"

Dr. Abruzzo sighed. "Look, Anselm, I'm just trying to help you. If you plan on staying in this town, you'll have to learn to live with us. If enough of your colleagues don't like you, for whatever reason, they'll simply send their patients elsewhere and freeze you out."

"Thanks, Dr. Abruzzo," said Anselm. "Is that all?"

"*Do* you intend to stay practicing in Glenport?" persisted Abruzzo.

"Yes, I do," replied Anselm very definitely. "I'm here to stay, but that doesn't mean I have to agree with every backward medical attitude and half-assed opinion around here."

"Aside from all that," Abruzzo went on hurriedly, again referring to his piece of paper, "there's been complaints about your storefront clinic down on Bank

Street.'' He shook his head again. ''Bob North says you're trying to get free publicity, but in my opinion you're simply unwise to do things that most of the staff here don't approve of.''

He was getting tired, and his jaw trembled a little, but he was determined to finish. ''It's very noble of you to try to help those people, I suppose,'' he said. ''But those shiftless bums are responsible for most of the crime in this town. If we make them feel welcome here, they'll stay and attract others like them.''

Anselm stood up. ''Frank,'' he said quietly, ''we're supposed to have a tradition of helping the poor and the sick to the best of our ability. If you and the other docs here don't want to participate, that's on your conscience, not mine. Just don't get in my way when I'm doing the little I can, okay?''

Frank sighed again. ''Try to give your colleagues a bit more credit, Anselm,'' he said, making a final bid to get through to his difficult young colleague. ''Listen a bit more. Try to go along with them, even if it's only once in a while.''

Anselm walked back along the corridor feeling a little shaken, although Frank Abruzzo hadn't told him anything he didn't know. Anselm was well aware that he was controversial, but this was the first time that the nigglings of the small group of docs who felt threatened by him had come to the surface.

He went on up to the operating suite.

''Lucille, I want to schedule a case,'' he told the OR supervisor, a pale, stern, gray-eyed woman with a large nose. She sat very upright behind the desk, almost ostentatiously devoid of jewelry or makeup.

Lucille Heinz looked up at him. ''Today's Thursday, Dr. Harris.'' She never had any qualms about stating the obvious. ''And Thursday's the day we're always short-staffed. Can't this case wait until tomorrow, when I have a full crew?'' Her thin lips hardly moved, but her eyes were cold and aggressive. Anselm, who had had run-ins with Lucille almost from the day he came to Glenport, stared back, taking in her stiff, unyielding posture. The nicer among the OR staff called Lucille "the nun" behind her back, and the name fitted. She does belong in a convent, thought Anselm, or at least some place where she wouldn't have to deal with people on a daily basis.

"This is an urgent case, Lucille," he said with quiet emphasis. "And no, it can't wait until tomorrow. The patient has peritonitis." Anselm kept good control of his voice, and made himself remember that he was in the community hospital of Glenport, Connecticut, not back in his New York hospital, where speed and competence were taken for granted.

"We're already overbooked, Dr. Harris," said Lucille. "I don't think it's fair on the staff to add another case."

"Would you like me to speak to them?" asked Anselm, getting to the end of his patience. "Or should I just call Mr. Olson?" He knew there was little love lost between Stefan Olson, the hospital administrator, and Lucille.

Anselm reached through the window for the phone on her desk.

"That won't be necessary, Dr. Harris," she said. She put a hand on the phone. "I suppose we can have a room ready for you in about an hour. Dr. Burton is the anesthesiologist on call. You'll find him in the doctors' lounge." Her lips tightened and she stared at Anselm with undisguised hostility. She knew that Philip Burton was a friend of Bob North's, and not exactly a fan of Anselm's.

"I'll expect the patient to be up here in thirty minutes," said Anselm. At his last hospital, a supervisor with Lucille's attitude would have lasted maybe twenty minutes in the job. Anselm went off to tell Dr. Burton about the case.

During a pause in the action in the emergency room, Pat Mooney, the head nurse, took a coffee break with her student, a pale, blond young woman with watery-looking blue eyes named Emily Prosser. Pat had the admission book on her lap and was checking that the ER staff had filled in all the diagnoses for the past week.

"You were going to tell me about Dr. Harris," said Emily hopefully, putting Pat's mug on the counter beside her.

Pat's pencil stopped in midair at the mention of his name, and she looked up, smiling.

"Aside from the fact that he's so sexy and good-looking?"

Emily stared at her. From Pat, that was strong talk. "He's an old friend of Dr. Delafield," Pat went on. "They were in med school together. Peter was the one who got him to come here." She took a sip of coffee and stared thoughtfully at Emily. "Dr. Harris was in practice in New York. He was doing pretty well, then he was hit with a big malpractice suit."

"I thought just about every doctor had one of those at some time," said Emily.

"This one was a bit unusual," replied Pat. "Anyway, the patient was a big politician, and Dr. Harris got nailed. Then Peter wanted him to come here, but of course, a lot of our doctors were against it. Luckily, Peter Delafield carries quite a clout, and he fixed it so that Dr. Harris came."

"What did he do? I mean Dr. Harris." said Emily, her eyes round. "It must have been something pretty terrible."

Pat put down her mug and got up. "The patient died, but I don't know any of the details."

Emily's mouth opened slightly. "Oh dear," she said. "And he's so nice to work with." She clutched her mug, her eyes fixed on Pat. "Maybe the way he's nice and everything is just covering up how he really feels."

"His wife left him after the case was over," said Pat. "Peter says she was smart and beautiful, but flighty and sort of crazy, not what he needed at all."

"Peter tells you a lot, doesn't he? Did you ever go out with him?"

"Sure." Pat laughed. "Like everybody else."

"Erica Barnes seems to like Dr. Harris a lot, doesn't she?" Emily's eyes were glistening.

Pat shrugged. "A lot of women in this hospital like him a lot," she said. Her expression hardened. "Anyway, I think Erica's got something going with Peter. As far as men are concerned, that girl's out for what she can get, and she makes it pretty obvious. Dr. Harris is no dummy. I'm sure he knows the score."

"She's tough, though," murmured Emily. "Erica looks like somebody who always gets exactly what she wants."

"Not this time, I don't think," said Pat, smiling.

Emily took a sip of coffee. "Did you see the way she was looking at Dr. North? She really hates him, doesn't she?"

Pat hesitated for a second. "He did something very bad to a young woman Erica liked a lot," she replied, then stood up. "Anyway, that's enough gossip for today. We need to do a linen check."

"Please tell me," pleaded Emily. "We've still got five whole minutes."

Pat looked at the clock. It showed five minutes to ten. "Okay, I'll just give you the outlines. This nurse, whose name was Hermita Lopez, came from Mexico to work here. She was *very* pretty, a good nurse but not too smart. Bob North latched on to her within a day, and two months later she was pregnant. Meanwhile she'd made friends with Erica. Hermita was very Catholic, so there was no question of abortion and Bob never spoke to her after he knew she was pregnant. There wasn't much Erica could do. Hermita tried to cut her wrists, was taken to the psych unit in New Coventry, and was still there when she had her baby. Erica still goes to see her, but she's so severely depressed she can't even take care of her baby. That's why Erica hates Bob North. And now,'' said Pat, ''let's go. I'll get the inventory list and we can do it together.''

They came out of the lounge at the same moment Anselm was passing, and Emily, startled, couldn't suppress a giggle. He smiled at her, and they watched him as he left through the double doors.

''If I was ill,'' said Emily suddenly, ''I'd like it if Dr. Harris took care of me.''

''I'll be sure to tell him,'' said Pat. ''Now let's start with the draw sheets.''

Anselm was coming back from discussing Mrs. Gowan's case with the anesthesiologist when he saw Peter Delafield hurrying along the corridor toward him.

''I just got a call from Carver's Island,'' said Peter as he came up. ''You remember Denton Bracknell's helicopter coming over? Well, he's had some kind of a stroke over there, and they're bringing him here by boat. The fog's so thick that nothing's flying. It'll take them two or three hours to come over.'' Peter rattled a few coins in his pants pocket. ''Anselm, would you mind sticking around until he arrives?''

Anselm was mildly surprised but said, ''Sure thing.'' Treatment of a stroke was normally a medical problem, and therefore more in Peter's area of expertise. But he was looking anxious, and Anselm guessed that he was upset about missing the diagnosis on Florence Gowan and needed some moral support.

"Tell me about him," said Anselm curiously. "How did you happen to meet Denton Bracknell?"

"Sandy brought him to the office. Sandy's from around here and I knew her before they got married. That was about two years ago, when he'd just been appointed presidential adviser. He didn't like the Washington medical scene, was overworking and getting headaches, and a couple of times he had dizzy spells. We worked him up, but for a guy his age he was generally in pretty good shape."

Peter had been interested in Denton Bracknell at least in part because of his national importance, and was happy to tell Anselm about him. He described Bracknell as a large, heavily built, grizzled man, about six feet tall, not good-looking, for his nose had been injured in a student boxing tournament, but vastly intelligent and with a great reservoir of humor. Bracknell had been a professor of international relations at Georgetown, an intellectual heavyweight reputed to know more about European economic politics than many of Europe's own prime ministers and chancellors. He was now a familiar figure on television and a sought-out speaker. In the government he was said to have clout comparable with that of Henry Kissinger in his heyday.

He'd married Sandy, twenty-five years his junior, after a whirlwind romance. They had met on the ferry to Carver's Island; she had been in line in front of him, found that she'd left her purse at home, and had no money to pay for the trip.

As Peter talked about Bracknell, they walked slowly back toward the elevators.

"Did you tell Stefan Olson?" asked Anselm. "He'll want to know that a big-time VIP like Bracknell is getting admitted here."

"Right, of course. I'll call him." Peter looked pre-occupied. "You should be finished operating on Florence Gowan by the time Bracknell gets here," he said. "I'll page you as soon as he comes in."

Peter hurried toward the stairs, and Anselm continued toward the operating suite. Peter seemed excited and scared at the same time, and understandably so, thought Anselm. Denton Bracknell would be by far the most important patient who had ever been admitted to Glenport Memorial Hospital.

3

The operating room wasn't ready, so Anselm went up to the library. Two nurses were there talking quietly when he came in; they glanced at him and quickly put their heads back down into their books. The library was small and contained only a meager selection of volumes and journals, about half of which dealt with nursing topics.

He walked over to the new journals rack, flipped through the *JAMA,* looked for the *American Journal of Surgery,* but it wasn't there.

The phone by the library door rang, and one of the nurses got up to answer it. "It's for you, Dr. Harris," she said. "Dr. North."

Bob was furious; he had a naturally loud voice that got even louder when he was angry.

Anselm interrupted him. "If you want to discuss Florence Gowan," he said, "I'm in the library." He could feel his heart pounding; he didn't go out of his way to seek confrontations, but if they were necessary, he didn't avoid them either.

"Is that on the fourth floor?" asked Bob.

"Third," replied Anselm. "Turn right when you get off the elevator, it's at the end of the corridor. You can't miss it," he added with the faintest touch of sarcasm. It was hard to believe that Bob North didn't know where the hospital library was located.

It didn't take him long to find it, however, and he pushed past the nurses, who were just leaving, and slammed the door closed after them. Bob was rather short, pink-faced, and portly, with thinning black hair combed carefully over the top of his head. As he glowered up at Anselm, his short neck was tilted back and he looked like an angry, puffed-up turkey-cock.

"Florence Gowan has been my patient for years," he said in a loud, belligerent voice. "I operated on her husband a couple of years ago. I was up in the OR just now, and Lucille told me you have her scheduled for emergency surgery."

"Right," said Anselm. "She has peritonitis, probably from an intestinal perforation."

"She had nothing of the sort when I saw her yesterday," replied Bob, his eyes fixed aggressively on Anselm's. "She had some constipation, that was all."

"I agree she's constipated," said Anselm, stretching himself to his full height of six feet and looking down at Bob, "but that's because her bowel's paralyzed from the peritonitis." Anselm's voice was scrupulously polite, but Bob flushed at his tone.

"Well, I'll go up and see her again," said Bob. "As I said, she's my patient, and *I'll* decide what to do."

"She isn't," replied Anselm. "And you won't. She was admitted under Peter Delafield's care, and he asked me to see her. If you're really not too embarrassed about missing such an obvious diagnosis, I suggest you talk to Peter about it."

He opened the door to leave, then paused, his hand still on the doorknob. He turned to Bob, who was spluttering with fury. "By the way, I left a space on the chart for your consultation report," he said. "Meanwhile, I'm going to operate on Mrs. Gowan in about twenty minutes.'' He paused. ''If you want to assist me, you'll be most welcome.''

A couple of hours later, Anselm had just finished operating on Florence Gowan, and in the hospital's emergency room tension was mounting. The news about Denton Bracknell was already out, and the phone had been ringing off the hook with calls from AP, Reuter's, and the other wire services, the TV networks and stringers for the big dailies. Stefan Olson, the hospital administrator, had tried to set up a special line, but the phone company told him it would take three days at the earliest.

After accompanying Florence to the recovery room, Anselm came down to the ER to see what was going on.

Three young men appeared, an FBI agent and two Secret Service agents. They had been instructed from Washington to drop everything and get up to Glenport, and they had driven up through the fog from their regional offices in New Coventry. Anselm watched Pat Mooney check their IDs.

''Why don't you send them over to see Mr. Olson?'' he murmured to her. ''He'll want to know they're here.''

Pat did so, glad to have the responsibility off her shoulders. The FBI agent reappeared soon after and went outside to wait for the ambulance, while the Secret Service men gathered the hospital security guards together and gave them their instructions.

Anselm went back upstairs to check on Florence, and a few minutes later the ER staff heard the ambulance siren in the distance. Everybody was poised, waiting, and all normal work had come to a standstill. Two patients lay waiting in their cubicles, wondering what all the excitement was about and where everybody had gone.

The doors opened and Peter came in. He had gone down to the dock to meet the boat, examined Bracknell, and come back in his own car. Seconds later, the ambulance arrived, siren howling, its red-and-white flashing lights visible through the frosted glass of the ground-floor windows.

"Trauma room," called out Pat. The ambulance men knew where to go; the room was near the entrance and twice the size of the other cubicles. Sandy Bracknell came in with them, white-faced, holding tightly onto Denton's hand as the men hurried the stretcher along the corridor. Two reporters from a New Coventry TV station bustled in after them, one with a minicam trained on the stretcher, the other coming behind him holding the cable and shining a high-powered quartz light on the scene.

"Call Dr. Harris," said Peter to the woman in charge of the telephone. "Tell him to come down here right away."

"Sure, Dr. Delafield," she replied, thinking that Peter certainly wasn't Mr. Cool today. He hurried down the corridor toward the trauma room. There were people milling around the door of Room 5, and Peter shouted as he pushed through, "Everybody not directly involved in this case, leave! Get out of here! Beat it!" His voice was high, exasperated, and Pat, behind him, hustled the spectators away.

Inside the trauma room, a nurse was attaching EKG electrodes to Denton's arms and legs, and a technician was tying a piece of tubing around his upper arm preparatory to drawing blood and starting an IV.

Denton, who had been unconscious for most of the crossing, was now awake. He watched the proceedings without the panicky expression Peter had noted down at the dock, and it seemed that he had improved considerably even in the short time since he had come off the boat.

"How are you feeling, Denton?" asked Peter. "You're in the emergency room at Glenport Hospital."

"I know that," replied Denton. His voice was weak, and there was a trace of old-man shakiness in it. "Do I need all these things?" He raised his left arm, and the tech, who was about to stick a needle in it, said, "Don't move, please!"

Sandy, still holding Denton's hand, looked hard at Peter, as if willing him to get her husband better.

Peter took Denton's other hand. It was still cold as ice. The pulse was fast and thready, just as when he had come off the boat; Denton was obviously still in trouble, even though he seemed to have partially recovered some of his functions.

The door opened, and Anselm came in unobtrusively and stood beside Peter.

"This is Dr. Anselm Harris," said Peter to Denton and Sandy. "He's one of our surgeons," he went on, "and the best one we have, I might say. I've asked him to come in on consultation." He lowered his voice and addressed Anselm. "Mr. Bracknell seems to have a partial blockage in his right carotid artery, probably from a blood clot. I'd guess a piece of it broke off earlier today and went up into his brain." His voice came back to normal. "Anselm, I'd like you to meet Sandy and Denton Bracknell."

Anselm nodded. Even in her obvious anxiety, Sandy was a strikingly beautiful woman, with a fine figure and long blond hair tied up behind her head, and dark eyes slanted ever so slightly, as if there were some oriental blood somewhere in her family's past. Anselm asked Sandy to tell him exactly what had happened.

"Den had just come in from Washington on the helicopter," she said. "The fog was so thick I never thought they'd even try. Anyway, Den was looking really tired, and after a few minutes he said he felt dizzy, then developed a headache. That's happened before a few times, so I gave him a couple of headache pills, and he went upstairs to lie down for a while.''

She took a deep breath, tightened her grip on Denton's hand, and her voice shook ever so slightly as she went on. ''I came up an hour later to see if he wanted lunch, and I couldn't waken him. His eyes . . . they were sort of rolled up, and . . . Anyway, I called Rose, our housekeeper, then we got the island ambulance people because there was no way the helicopter could come back through that fog, so I packed a few things, called his office in Washington, then Alec Ponting took us over in his boat.''

At that moment a quiet voice right behind Anselm interrupted. ''Gentlemen, may I speak with you for a second?''

Anselm turned to see a thick-set young man with very pale blue eyes who was looking calmly at him and holding up a plastic ID card. ''I'm special agent Marlin Foster, from the FBI office in New Coventry.''

Peter started to say something, but Agent Foster said, ''Let's talk outside, gentlemen, if you don't mind, as soon as you're ready.''

''We'll need another five minutes,'' Anselm told him, turning back to Sandy.

He listened carefully to the rest of her account, noted her drawn face, felt the tightness and tension emanating from her, but mostly he watched Denton. He was a big man, restless, and now alert, very alert, his eyes slightly widened with apprehension. When Sandy finished her account, Anselm pulled his stethoscope out and placed the bell of the instrument very gently on the right side of Denton's neck.

''Excuse me, Mr. Bracknell,'' he murmured. He moved the bell slightly to cover the place where the right carotid artery divides into two major branches in the neck, knowing that if a clot had formed where

Peter thought it had, it would probably be there. The sound coming through his stethoscope was abnormal, there was no question of that; instead of the dull, regular faint pounding as the blood coursed along the vessel, there was a high-pitched, almost whistling noise as the blood sped fast and turbulently through the narrowed area. Anselm listened for a few moments, trying to exclude the other sounds in the room from his consciousness. Then he repeated the process, this time on the other side.

Finally he straightened up. "Not much question," he murmured to Peter. "That sounds like a pretty tight stenosis on the right side, but I think the artery's still open."

"He's had a mild stenosis there for at least a year," replied Peter, "but it hasn't given him any trouble until now."

"What's a stenosis?" asked Sandy.

"That's a narrowing of the artery, Mrs. Bracknell," replied Anselm in a particularly gentle voice. He put his stethoscope back in his pocket. Sandy was surprised by his compassion when he had first come in and Peter introduced him, her first impression had been that he seemed one of these cold, impersonal doctors interested only in diagnoses and fees.

"Do we have an ultrasound?" asked Anselm, turning to Peter.

"Yes. We did it about a year ago. It's in his X-ray chart. It shows a slight narrowing, as I said, but this"—he indicated Denton's neck—"this is new."

Both Denton and Sandy were watching the two doctors, waiting to hear what conclusions they had reached.

Peter turned to them. "We both think Denton has a blood clot on the right side, in the main artery going up to his head," he said. "A small piece of it broke off and went up into his brain. That's what caused his unconsciousness. But in all probability, most of the clot is still there. If Dr. Harris agrees with that diagnosis, he may want to operate to remove the rest of the clot. Otherwise, another, bigger piece could let go. . . .'' Peter looked away momentarily. ''And that would be likely to cause a very serious problem.''

Anselm, feeling that this scenario was a bit premature, interrupted. ''What Dr. Delafield described is certainly a major possibility,'' he said, ''but it's too early to make a definite diagnosis just yet. We'll need some more tests.'' He was aware of Peter's eyes boring into him, and turned to face him. ''Mr. Bracknell's stable right now, Peter, so why don't we talk some more about this outside?'' *Cooperate,* he thought, remembering Frank Abruzzo's warning. *You know that Peter is a good physician, so give him credit.*

Sandy turned to Peter. ''Will you let us know when you decide what you're going to do?''

''Sure thing, Sandy, of course.'' Peter put a reassuring hand on her arm, but she pulled away from him.

''Call the ultrasound lab, Pat,'' Anselm told the head nurse. ''I want a portable carotid scan done down here. I don't want to move him to the X-ray department unless we have to.''

Anselm looked at the monitor above Denton's head. It showed some tachycardia, a speeding up of the heart rate, but the rhythm was regular. Denton was still sweating, and although the room was warm, his hands were still icy cold. His eyes were moving anxiously around the room, and Anselm had a feeling that he was trying to recollect what had happened to him.

''Let's go,'' said Anselm to Peter, turning toward the door.

Agent Foster was waiting outside for them. ''I just want to let you know that I'm here, gentlemen,'' he said. ''We also have two Secret Service agents assigned to Mr. Bracknell. One of them will accompany him wherever he goes in the hospital, and the other will stay in his room. Nobody without a hospital ID will be allowed in. I've already talked to Mr. Olson and informed him of what we're doing.''

Peter followed Anselm into the small viewing room farther down the corridor.

''Don't you think the people in Washington will want to have him transferred?'' Anselm asked Peter. ''To Bethesda Naval, or maybe New Coventry?'' He opened the big yellow envelope that contained the old ultrasound films. ''I'm not sure that this is the best place to take care of a VIP with this kind of problem.''

Peter shook his head decisively, as if he also had been considering that possibility. ''No way. Absolutely not. He's far too sick. A trip in a helicopter or an ambulance could easily shake that clot loose and kill him. I'd veto any such suggestion.''

Although Anselm recognized the logic of Peter's statement, it was also clear that he was extraordinarily anxious to keep Denton Bracknell at Glenport Hospital. Anselm knew from long experience how ambitious, even egotistic his friend was, and now it was really showing. As the acknowledged physician of choice to the most important presidential adviser in a decade, Peter's local reputation would become unassailable. Anselm felt a touch of uneasiness and hoped that Peter's ambition wouldn't lead him to make any unwise decisions.

Anselm flipped the old ultrasound films of Bracknell's carotid arteries up on the viewing box. ''Not the best films I've ever seen,'' he said.

''Well, no,'' said Peter, ''but they're the best we can get here. Anyway, you can certainly see the narrowing . . . there.'' He pointed at the film.

''I don't suppose you ever got an arteriogram on him?'' asked Anselm.

Peter shook his head. ''That's a high-risk procedure—in this hospital, anyway,'' he replied. ''In any case, he wasn't having any symptoms, so no, we didn't.'' Peter glanced at the door. The noise in the corridor was increasing, and a few raised voices could be heard.

There was a knock on the door and Pat Mooney came in. ''Mr. Olson wants to see you both in his office,'' she said. ''He's expecting an important phone call any minute, and he wants both of you to be there.''

4

That same morning, attorney Valerie Morse was in the New Coventry District Courthouse, some fifty miles down the coast from Glenport. She sat at the attorneys' table, watching as Dr. Terence Kasper walked across to the witness stand. Dr. Kasper was a short, stocky, well-dressed middle-aged man with thin black hair, a heavy, flapping step, and an odd way of appearing to lean backward as he walked. In her mind Valerie went over the questions she was going to ask him. Normally she didn't hold any papers in her hand, but today she had a sheaf of them, and looked uncomfortable and unsure of herself.

After being sworn in, Dr. Kasper looked around the court as if it belonged to him, and nodded affably to the judge. Kasper had been there many times before and knew the ropes as well as anyone.

When the time came for her cross-examination, Valerie stood up. She was slim, of medium height, with a rather pale face, faint lipstick, and only a hint of mascara around her eyes. She didn't need much makeup; she had a flawless complexion, with dark eyes and almost black, luxuriant hair tied back with a clasp. For this case she had chosen a dark, well-fitting business suit with an almost invisibly thin pinstripe and a white silk shirt with a white jabot.

That morning there was a different feel in the court-room, and the clerks and secretaries and attorneys all recognized it; they'd felt it in other courts when Valerie had been working.

The court was almost empty, with only a few people lounging in the public seats; a few attorneys had seen her name on the docket and come in just to watch her, although this was only a routine insurance case with nothing particular to distinguish it.

"Dr. Kasper," said Valerie, shuffling her papers, "would you tell the court how long you have been in medical practice?"

"Twenty-five years," replied Kasper, his eyes moving appreciatively over Valerie. "Started in nineteen sixty-eight."

"Do you see a lot of back injury cases, Dr. Kasper?" Her voice sounded strained, as if she were aware that she was filling in the time with trivial questions.

"A few," replied Kasper, and there was a faint stirring of amusement in the court. Kasper was known to deal in little else but heavily insured back problems.

Valerie leafed through her papers, and there was silence in the courtroom for a few moments. "Do you remember a Mr. Ray Jones?"

"Of course I remember him," replied Kasper. He put his hands together; Valerie noticed they were small, and he wore a big ruby-centered gold class ring. Kasper grinned good-humoredly at the young and obviously very inexperienced attorney. "I remember every one of my patients," he said to her, glancing at the judge. "Judge Haynes can tell you that."

"Then you'll remember what Mr. Jones's complaints were?" asked Valerie. "You can use notes if you wish."

"I don't need notes," said Kasper. "I remember everything about him. Ray is a conscientious worker in the construction business who slipped on a wet patch of the floor at work, twisted his back as he went down, and strained the muscles in—''

''Just the complaints, please, Doctor, not the diagnosis.'' Valerie's voice was gentle, unaggressive.

''Sorry. When I saw him a few hours after the accident, Ray was in agony, complaining of severe lower back pain, occasionally radiating down his legs, made worse by walking or moving. He also complained of some weakness in both legs.''

''How did you proceed?''

''Well, we took a series of X rays to see if any bony damage had been done.''

''Was there any?''

''Some minimal changes,'' replied Kasper lightly. ''Luckily nothing serious, but you can't be too careful, can you?'' He glanced at Judge Haynes again, as if the two of them frequently consulted on such matters.

''So after the tests you were able to make a diagnosis, Doctor?'' Again uncertainty showed in Valerie's voice, and Kasper smiled encouragingly at her.

''Severe lumbar strain, possibly some torn spinal ligaments, sacrospinalis muscle spasm with resulting pressure on the intervertebral discs.'' Kasper put his palms together, fingers outstretched.

''Yes . . .'' Valerie shifted uncomfortably on her feet. ''I see. And what treatment did you prescribe, Dr. Kasper?''

He crossed his legs and glanced around the court. He'd been through this so many times his answers came almost reflexively. ''The treatment I prescribed for Ray was regular massage, vibromassage, hot baths, bed rest, traction, physiotherapy, and pain and sleep medication.''

''Over what period of time was the treatment, Doctor?'' asked Valerie.

''He's still getting it,'' said Kasper. ''He's not re-sponding too well, still getting a lot of muscle spasms although we're doing everything we can.''

"How long has he been having treatment?" asked Valerie. A piece of paper floated from her sheaf down to the floor and, visibly flustered, she bent down to pick it up.

"Twelve weeks," replied Kasper, grinning. "Maybe you should use a paper clip," he suggested, watching Valerie rearrange her papers. A faint murmur of amusement went through the courtroom.

"Is that the evaluation and treatment you prescribe for all such patients?" asked Valerie, gripping her papers tightly, as if trying to keep control of the situation.

"More or less," said Kasper. "It varies a bit according to the case, but generally, yes, that's the regime we find works best for this type of injury."

"Then basically, that's what you would recommend for someone with the same complaints that Ray Jones came in with."

"Yes, Counselor, I would." Kasper's grin was broad, and again his appreciation of Valerie's appearance showed in his eyes.

"Thank you, Doctor," said Valerie in a quiet voice. Then to the judge, she added, "I'd like to reserve the right to reexamine this witness."

The judge granted permission, to Dr. Kasper's annoyance, because that meant he had to wait. After a lackluster cross-examination of the patient, Ray Jones, who appeared on crutches and didn't make a particularly good impression on anybody, Valerie called a young man by the name of Ulf Anders, who was sworn in.

"Mr. Anders," started Valerie. She had put down her sheaf of papers, and suddenly she had a different look about her. "Mr. Anders, do you recognize Dr. Terence Kasper in this courtroom?"

Mr. Anders, a well-built young man with a small blond mustache and blue eyes, pointed at Dr. Kasper, who was now sitting in the front public seats and staring at Anders with a peculiar expression.

"When did you last see Dr. Kasper?" asked Valerie in a strong voice. The court seemed to be awakening, and the jury members were paying attention. Even the defending attorney looked up from his papers.

"Three weeks ago," replied Anders.

"Tell us about it," asked Valerie.

"First I saw his receptionist," said Anders. "I told her I'd slipped while walking in the park and twisted my back when I fell."

"What did she say?"

The defending attorney, Dick Stromberg, who had started to take an interest in the case, jumped to his feet.

"Hearsay!" he said loudly. "I object to the counselor's last question."

"Sustained," said the judge.

"At what point did you actually see Dr. Kasper?" Valerie asked Anders.

"Soon after. I told him my complaints, the severe pain in my back, passing down into my legs, the difficulty I was having walking—"

"Your Honor," said Stromberg, standing up and putting both hands on the table in front of him, "we're here to decide on the case of Ray Jones. Whatever problems this witness may have are totally irrelevant."

"Attorney Morse?" The judge, a small man with a round face and round glasses, looked questioningly at Valerie. "Would you address that question, please?"

"I wish to show that Dr. Kasper does *not* always treat his patients the same way, contrary to his sworn testimony," replied Valerie. "And since we're dealing with a protracted and very expensive illness, with weeks of lost work and a long course of treatment, this witness is most certainly relevant.''

"Proceed,'' said the judge, and sat back, almost disappearing into his chair.

"Mr. Anders,'' said Valerie, turning again to the witness box, "you were telling us about your complaints.''

"I told him exactly what you told me say,'' he said and Stromberg leaped to his feet again, outraged.

"Is Attorney Morse telling us that she *instructed* this man what to complain of?'' he said, his voice loud, threatening. "That she incited him to consult Dr. Kasper under false pretenses?''

Stromberg was red in the face with anger.

The judge sighed, but there was a flicker of something behind the round glasses when he addressed Valerie. "Would you care to explain the purpose of summoning this witness?'' he asked her.

"Certainly.'' There was nothing hesitant or unsure about Valerie's manner now. "My office hired Mr. Anders some weeks ago. He is an actor and, I believe, a very good one. Our premise is that Dr. Kasper is cheating the insurance company. We sent Mr. Anders with a list of every one of the complaints the patient Ray Jones said he was suffering from—''

"This is entrapment!'' cried Stromberg. "I move that this case be thrown out.''

"Motion denied, Mr. Stromberg. Please proceed, Counselor,'' said the judge courteously to Valerie.

She turned to Anders. "Tell the court what happened in Dr. Kasper's office,'' she said.

"I told him my symptoms, and he asked me if I had insurance. When I said no, he asked if I was quite certain I hadn't done it at work, and when I told him I hadn't, he seemed to lose interest.''

"Objection,'' said Stromberg, getting up again.

"The witness is telling us his impressions and not reporting facts."

"Stick to the facts, please, Mr. Anders," said the judge.

"Tell us what happened after that," said Valerie to the witness.

"He told me to take some aspirin, then he got up and said he had other patients to see."

"Did he take a complete medical history?"

The witness shook his head.

"Please answer yes or no, Mr. Anders," said the judge. "The court stenographer has to write down all your answers."

"Sorry. The answer is no, sir."

"Did he give you a physical examination?" Valerie's voice was taking on a relentless tone.

"No, ma'am."

"Did he make a return appointment for you?"

"No, ma'am, he did not."

"Did he say anything about physiotherapy?"

"No, ma'am. I tried to ask him on the way out, but he was too busy."

"Did he advise massage?"

"He did not."

"Did Dr. Kasper suggest traction, bed rest, heat lamps, sauna baths, or any other kind of treatment?"

"No, he did not. Oh, excuse me . . ." Anders stammered for a second. "Yes, he did offer me some advice."

"Please tell the court what that was," said Valerie.

"I was paying for the visit at the desk when he came by. He put his hand on my shoulder and said if I ever tripped and fell again, I should take care to do it on an insured property."

Everyone in the court laughed, and from that moment on the case was as good as over. Valerie had also brought an expert orthopedic witness who had examined Ray Jones and had found no demonstrable abnormality, as he put it, and shortly afterward the case was concluded, the judgment being in favor of the insurance company, the first time they had won in a long series of suits against Dr. Kasper.

Valerie happened to meet Judge Haynes later in the corridor, and he stopped and grinned up at her from behind his round lenses. "I'm going to miss Dr. Kasper," he said. "He'd become quite an institution around here."

5

On the way back to her office, Valerie heard on the car radio that Denton Bracknell, the president's senior adviser, had been admitted to Glenport Hospital in serious condition. She was concerned, because she knew Bracknell was one of the most capable and respected members of the administration, but she had a major problem at the office to think about, and soon forgot about him.

Late that afternoon, after the fog had lifted, Valerie drove over to Milford to see her brother, Patrick. He lived in a pleasant one-bedroom apartment on the ground floor of a converted mill. The complex was on a slight elevation, and from his bed Patrick could see a part of the harbor, a pier, and could also hear the clanking of rigging from the sailboats moored there.

She left her car in the parking lot and walked through the brick archway. Two young men passing through in the opposite direction turned to watch her. Carefully dressed and more than commonly attractive, Valerie had a confidence that radiated from her, and a purposeful but sexy way of walking that turned heads.

She had a key, of course, for Patrick couldn't come to open the door for her, and she let herself in.

Patrick was in bed, sitting up, grinning at her, and for some reason his cheerfulness irritated her.

"Tough day at the office?" he asked.

"Yes, as a matter of fact." Valerie looked around. There was a general untidiness about the place, nothing different from the usual, but today it set her teeth on edge. "You should get your girlfriends to tidy up here once in a while."

"I keep them otherwise engaged," replied Patrick. "And by the time I've finished with them, they don't have the energy to do housework."

Valerie went around the apartment, picking up newspapers, candy wrappers, an occasional small article of female apparel.

"Anything on the job market, Patrick?" she asked, pointing at a newspaper ad section. Several positions vacant had circles drawn around them.

"Nothing that actually beats what I'm doing now," replied Patrick. He glanced at the door.

Valerie came and sat on the end of the bed. "You know, Patrick," she said, her voice as firm as she could make it, "it would really help me if you could get a job. You can do your computer stuff just as well from here as in an office. We can get you whatever equipment you need, a fax machine, a printer, anything. You just have to try."

He shook his head. "I was talking to a colleague of yours today," he said. "He said he's heard about you."

"Patrick, I'm serious. I can't handle all these medical bills by myself. You *have* to start working again. You've had long enough, and I'm sure you know lots of people who could help you get started."

Patrick shrugged, and Valerie could see that she was in for an uphill battle, and decided to abandon the topic for now.

"Who was it you were talking to? An attorney? What were you talking to him about?" she asked, going back to Patrick's earlier comment.

"Joe Mellor. He was at school with me and practices up in Norwich. I'm thinking of starting a malpractice suit," said Patrick, watching her.

"Are you crazy? Against whom? Your doctors at New Coventry Medical Center?"

"Who else?" he asked. "They were the ones who fucked me over, and it's their bills that are giving you such a hard time." He grinned at her, the grin that had made countless women keel over like poleaxed sheep, but of course Valerie was immune. She took a deep breath. "So what did this attorney ask you?"

"You mean about the accident? Well, who was driving when it happened, what *did* happen, had I drunk any alcohol that day, stuff like that."

A year before, their parents had been killed in a small-plane crash near Sabattus, Maine, and Valerie and Patrick had driven up for the funeral. On the way back, they had almost reached New Coventry when they were involved in an accident on I-95. Patrick's neck was broken, but he wasn't paralyzed until an emergency room aide, trying to be helpful when he started to vomit, turned his head to one side. Unfortunately, no one had seen it happen, and the aide vigorously denied it. Patrick had spent several weeks in the New Coventry Medical Center Spinal Unit, but when he finally went home, after countless painful procedures, there had been only minimal improvement; he couldn't walk and needed a wheelchair to get around. In order to pay the medical bills, Valerie had given up her cherished but low-paying job at New Coventry Legal Aid to take a job with the prestigious firm of Collier, McDowell and Stern.

Valerie was annoyed that Patrick would consult an attorney without even mentioning it to her, but it was just like him to do that.

"I don't know anything about medical malpractice," she said, "but my guess is that you wouldn't have a hope in hell if you brought suit. For one thing, the damage was already done by the time you got to the Spinal Unit.''

''Yeah,'' said Patrick. ''that's what Joe Mellor said. He wouldn't touch it.'' He gave an exaggerated sigh. ''Such a pity. There I was with visions of a settlement in the millions, going on cruises around the world, with girls falling over themselves to get at me. . . .''

Although Patrick was talking with his usual insouciance, he was watching Valerie and could see that there was something seriously troubling his sister.

''What's up?'' he asked her. ''Did you lose your case this morning?''

''No,'' replied Valerie. ''Actually, I won *that* one. This afternoon didn't go so well, though.''

Patrick said nothing, and waited.

Valerie came and sat on the chair by his bed. ''I'm in a lot of trouble at the office, Patrick,'' she said. ''I was doing research on a real estate deal that Ralph Stern, one of the partners, set up, and it turns out that he stands to make millions in a related deal. . . . It's all very complicated, but there's a huge conflict of interest. Anyway, I called him on it this afternoon, and he was so pissed at me that I thought he was going to have a stroke. He's going to try to get me fired, for sure. In fact, he said so.''

''Ralph Stern?'' said Patrick thoughtfully. ''That name rings a bell. What are you going to do?''

''They'll have trouble firing me,'' replied Valerie. ''I've done a good job there, up to now, anyway, and my evaluations have been tops.''

''Better start revising your resumé,'' said Patrick with a grin. ''One of us has to have a job.''

Valerie got up and went through to the kitchen. ''Where's the coffee?'' she asked.

''I think it's all gone. You'll have to make do with instant. There's some on the counter.''

"Do you want some?"

"Sure. Strong and black. Which reminds me, wait till you meet Dixie."

When the coffee was made, Valerie came back with a mug in each hand. She was determined not to let her problems get the better of her. "So what else is up, Patrick? Is somebody coming to get you your supper?"

"It's Dixie's day. She should be here shortly. Actually, she came at lunchtime too."

Valerie straightened the bottom sheet and puffed up Patrick's pillows.

"She comes twice a day?" She wasn't paying attention or she wouldn't have said that, not to Patrick.

"Are you kidding? That girl can come twice in as many minutes. Physiotherapists are usually in good shape, and this one . . . Hey, I remember why Ralph Stern's name rang a bell. Do you remember Elliott Naughton? He visited here for a few days about a year ago?"

Valerie remembered Elliott well, a good-looking, clever, athletic young man, now in the State Department, and one of Patrick's vast retinue of friends. Elliott and Valerie had gone out together a couple of times. They had written, then lost touch when Elliott was transferred to Vienna.

"Elliott told me something weird about Ralph Stern a while ago," said Patrick, frowning with the effort of recollection. "Because there had been something in the paper about Stern trying for some elected office. . . . I don't really remember."

Valerie tried to jog his memory, but all she could get out of him was that Elliott Naughton was now in New York, on temporary assignment to the United Nations. It was quite obvious that Patrick's mind was elsewhere, and he kept looking at the door.

There was a faint sound from outside, then a key turned in the lock.

Dixie was a stunner, as even Valerie had to admit. Long, lithe, with flawless brown skin, she was dressed in a thin cotton dress with a bright red and green flower print on a white background. The close-fitting garment shimmered on her body like Clingwrap. She obviously wore no bra, and with a touch of unaccustomed envy, Valerie wondered if that insubstantial dress was all Dixie was wearing.

She came in, swinging her hips, rolled her big brown eyes briefly at Valerie but otherwise ignored her, and came straight over to Patrick's bed. "Hi, honey," she said, and leaned down to kiss him hard on the mouth. Sure enough, as she leaned forward, Valerie observed that there was no underwear in sight under the short dress, just a smooth, rounded, alluringly shapely behind.

"Meet my sister," said Patrick, his voice muffled.

Dixie straightened up and gave Valerie a big, friendly, unaffected smile.

"Hi," she said, turning toward Valerie and stuck out her hand. "I'm Dixie. I'm his therapist. Physio, that is."

"He's very lucky," said Valerie, smiling.

"Yeah, right. If he hadn't been in that car wreck, he'd have never met me." Her smile encompassed both of them, and Valerie suddenly felt pale, unhealthy, and generally lacking in liveliness and joie de vivre when contrasted with this vivacious, dazzling young woman.

While she was talking to Valerie, Dixie's left hand was behind her, idly stroking Patrick's thigh through the top sheet, and a tenting of the sheet nearby showed clearly that all was not dead below Patrick's waist.

"Well, I'll be off," said Valerie hurriedly. "Patrick, is there anything you need?"

"Nothing I'm not getting," he replied, breathing hard.

By the time Valerie closed the door behind her, Dixie had pulled back the sheet and was nuzzling down on him. Patrick's hand had disappeared under the skirt of her dress, and he was joyfully fondling Dixie's naked, rounded rump.

6

Stefan Olson, the administrator of Glenport Hospital, was a big, blond man with a wide face that seemed to be outlined in red, like a Van Gogh portrait. His almost white eyebrows and strong nose gave him a healthy, trustworthy Nordic look, and a pair of large, purposeful hands added to the solid, conservative image he presented.

Before coming to Glenport, Stefan had been assistant administrator in a big community hospital in Chicago, and since he was unmarried, the move had been logistically simple. He soon ran into problems at Glenport Hospital. The board of managers, who authorized the money to run the hospital, was quite happy with the status quo, and had a typical New England resistance to spending money even when it wasn't theirs. As a result, over the past few years the hospital hadn't kept up with modern developments, there was trouble with inadequate staffing, low salaries, rapid turnover, and inadequate equipment to the point where it had come to the attention of the JCAH, the joint commission that supervised hospitals throughout the country. Unless many changes and modernizations were in place within a year, they informed him, they would withdraw the hospital's accreditation, and that, as Stefan was well aware, and took pains to remind the board, would be the kiss of death for Glenport Hospital.

As it was, more and more doctors were sending their patients to New Coventry Medical Center, one hour away down the I-95, when they needed advanced tests and procedures not available in Glenport.

Farman Industries, the biggest employer in the area, was dissatisfied with the level of medical care available at Glenport Hospital, and was planning to set up a fully equipped alternative medical facility with its own doctors and nurses, which would serve all the Farman employees and their families. If that came to pass, it would make Glenport Hospital largely redundant.

When Stefan had first arrived, Farman had tried to cut a deal with him whereby the hospital would act as the company's insurer and provide complete medical care for the employees on a contract basis. At first sight it looked like an attractive proposition for the hospital, until the accountants pointed out that the hospital could go broke on it, for under the agreement it would shoulder the cost of tertiary care such as coronary bypass surgery that wasn't done in Glenport Hospital. The hospital board indignantly refused to negotiate, and that had been the trigger for Farman to start planning their own facility. The site had been chosen, and the company management, aware that its action would cause considerable upheaval and resentment in the community, was merely waiting for the right moment to start building.

And now Stefan was praying that nothing vital would break down in the hospital while Bracknell was a patient there. If it did, the hospital would be held up to public blame and ridicule, and Farman Industries would have the perfect excuse to go ahead with their project.

When Peter and Anselm entered the office, Stefan

was behind his desk, with Agent Foster facing him, sitting on the edge of a chair and holding onto a rather oddly shaped, bulky portable telephone, which he had placed, stubby antenna pointing up, on the wide expanse of the desk.

"Come in," said Stefan in his slow, deep voice. "We're waiting for a call, and I'm glad you're both here." And indeed, he looked mightily relieved.

"This is on a special frequency," said Foster, nodding at the instrument. "I can't get the volume up too high, so you'd better come close if you want to hear."

Peter and Anselm stood on either side of him. Foster looked at his watch. They waited. After a few minutes, Anselm asked whose call they they were waiting for. There was a moment's silence before Foster replied, "We're not sure, sir."

There was a hissing noise from the phone, then a voice said, "Testing this line, priority one, please confirm."

Agent Foster pressed a five-digit code on the set but said nothing.

"Please hold for Mr. Stennard," said the voice, then there was some more hissing.

"The president's chief of staff," said Foster in an undertone, his eyes fixed to his phone.

The hissing stopped. "Agent Foster?" asked a voice. The transmission was now crystal clear.

"Foster here, sir."

"Right, good. I have two people here with me, Foster, Admiral Graham Ellis, the medical officer in command of Bethesda Naval Hospital, and Marshall Forde of the FBI, whom I have no doubt you know."

"Yes sir, gentlemen. I'm in the office of the hospital administrator in Glenport. With me are Stefan Olson, the administrator, and"—Foster looked at the piece of paper in his hand—"Dr. Peter Delafield, the internist taking care of Mr. Bracknell, and Dr. Anselm Harris, a surgeon he's called in on the case.''

''Good,'' said Stennard. He had the kind of brisk voice used to giving orders. ''Dr. Delafield, would you bring us up to date on Mr. Bracknell's condition? The President is very concerned, and wants a full report from me as soon as possible.''

Peter outlined the situation, and as soon as he finished, Admiral Ellis broke in. ''Well, I only speak as a pediatrician, gentlemen, but it sounds to me as if y'all are doin' a great job,'' he drawled in a voice straight out of the deep South. ''An' we're ready, willin', and able to take him offa your hands right away. We can get a 'copter up there for him faster'n you can say Bethesda Naval—''

''He's too ill to move,'' said Peter. ''And in any case the fog's so thick up here that no helicopter could fly in.''

There was a brief silence. Then Stennard said, ''The President is anxious that Mr. Bracknell be treated in a facility that can offer him the most advanced care,'' he said smoothly. ''That's not to say that Glenport Hospital can't do that, but—''

Again Peter interrupted, his voice stubborn. ''We can take care of the problem here, Mr. Stennard. My professional opinion is that Mr. Bracknell's life would be placed in serious jeopardy if he underwent a helicopter flight at this time. I'm sure the admiral understands the medical rationale for this decision.'' He put a slight but unmistakable emphasis on the word *decision*.

Again there was a silence, broken only by the faint hissing that came from the portable phone when nobody was talking.

Admiral Ellis was the first to speak. ''Well,'' he said, ''that kina decision has to be made by the officer of the watch. An' that is you, I guess, Dr. Delafield.

However . . .'' There was some muffled talk at the other end, then his voice came on again. ''I'll be flying up to Glenport tomorrow, weather permitting, and I'll be bringing some special consultants appointed by the President,'' he went on, ''to evaluate the situation and to bring Mr. Bracknell back here with me if it seems medically appropriate.''

''Does that meet with your approval, Dr. Delafield?'' asked Stennard's clipped voice. He sounded put out.

''We'll be honored by the visit, sir,'' replied Peter.

''Y'all are not anticipatin' doing any surgery on him, are you?'' asked the admiral, then before there was time for a reply, he went on, a new authoritativeness in his voice replacing his previous relaxed, good-ole-boy tone. ''We would strongly advise against your doing anything beyond the usual basic diagnostic tests.''

''We're not planning on doing any surgery,'' replied Peter, leaning over and speaking directly into the mouthpiece. ''But if we're forced to by circumstances, sir, we can take care of it.'' He looked over at Anselm and grinned encouragingly.

''Good . . .'' The tone of the admiral's voice belied his words.

Stennard's voice came on again, the volume fluctuating as if he were very far away. ''The President asks that you pass on to Mr. Bracknell his best wishes for a speedy recovery.''

''We'll be happy to do that, sir,'' replied Peter.

There was a click, then a long silence, broken by Agent Foster, who switched the portable phone off and hooked it back onto his belt.

''I'll be keeping in touch, thank you, gentlemen,'' he said, then left the room.

The atmosphere in Stefan's office changed subtly after Agent Foster had gone, and the administrator felt himself back in command of the situation. He was slightly concerned by Peter's determination to keep Denton Bracknell as a patient in Glenport, and Anselm, who he felt was the cooler head of the two, so far hadn't said a word.

The door opened and Erica Barnes came in, apologized for being late, and sat down next to Anselm.

"What's happening with the media?" Stefan asked her.

Erica outlined her plans for dealing with the press and TV reporters, and when she finished, Stefan took a deep breath and looked at each man in turn. "Anselm, Peter, we need to do some hard-nosed thinking here. But first I need to make one thing quite clear. If Denton Bracknell is going to die, I don't want him to do it here in this hospital."

Anselm, watching him, was reminded that an administrator's view of medicine and hospitals was quite different from that of the physicians. Stefan was an executive running a business, and in addition, was being careful to protect his own interests.

"Second," Stefan went on, "I need to have statistics to help me make some decisions. We've got a crap game going here, and since I represent this hospital, I'm the banker." He leaned forward, hoping that he wouldn't have to spell out everything for them in detail.

"So, as banker, I need to know the odds," he said. "By which I mean the chances of Bracknell's survival." He looked at each man in turn, then held up one hand and ticked off the points on his fingers. "I also need to know his chances of leaving here with a permanent disability, like not being able to walk or talk, that kind of thing. Also, and I need your honest evaluation here, is this hospital capable of giving Bracknell the care he needs? Please think carefully before answering, because I am seriously concerned about his remaining here.''

Peter got red in the face and was about to interrupt, but Stefan raised his hand warningly. ''What I want you both to understand is that if the odds seem to be going against the bank, I will get Bracknell transferred to a bigger facility, whether you gentlemen wish it or not.''

There was no question that he was in earnest, although they all knew that if he transferred a patient against the advice of his own physicians, it would irreparably damage his relations with the medical staff. Stefan's hands were now flat on his desk, and he projected his personality across the desk with every speck of energy at his command.

He looked Peter straight in the eye. ''You know that as administrator, I have the authority to withdraw the hospital privileges of any member of the staff on an emergency basis, and I want you to know that if I am forced to, I won't hesitate to use that authority.''

Stefan's voice was not challenging; he was just making sure that the two doctors understood the facts as he saw them.

Peter, not as expert as Stefan in potentially hostile situations, had difficulty controlling the anger in his voice.

''Look, Stefan,'' he said, ''I don't appreciate being threatened, and nor, I'm sure, does Anselm here. Especially since it's not necessary.'' He took a deep breath and tried to get the emotion out of his voice. ''This is the situation, Stefan, as we see it. Bracknell is sick, no question, but at the present time, *he is recovering.*'' Peter glanced at Anselm, who had not opened his mouth during the entire exchange. ''Right now they're doing an ultrasound in the trauma room that will tell us more about his condition. Hopefully, he'll just keep on improving. If not, and we find that he does have a clot in his carotid, Anselm will remove it.'' Peter's eye gleamed suddenly. ''Look, Stefan, just think about Farman Industries for a second. If we show them we can take proper care of a guy as important as Denton Bracknell, they'll never even start building their medical facility. On the other hand, if we transfer him, they can point at us and say we can't handle any kind of tough medical problem.'' He paused and pointed a finger aggressively at the administrator. ''Getting Bracknell here is maybe the single best thing that ever happened to this hospital. Denton's a very strong man with a sound constitution, and one way or another, when he leaves this hospital, it'll be in a cloud of glory *in which you will share.*''

Peter emphasized the last words, and Stefan smiled ironically at him. Few of the doctors he'd ever dealt with had much subtlety about them, and Peter was no exception.

Stefan turned to Anselm, relieved that he didn't have to depend entirely on Peter's judgment, which some instinct told him contained other inputs besides the best interests of the patient and the hospital. ''You've been very quiet, Dr. Harris. Could we have the benefit of your opinion?''

''You wanted some statistics,'' said Anselm. ''If there *is* a clot narrowing the artery, and if we do nothing, he has a fifty percent chance of dying or getting a major stroke. If we can prove the diagnosis, surgery reduces that risk to around ten percent.''

''Sounds good,'' said Stefan slowly, after digesting the answer. ''The last question I had was about this hospital's ability to take care of him.''

''Of course we can,'' said Peter quickly. ''We take care of patients with this kind of problem every day.''

Stefan looked at Anselm, who nodded in agreement. Stefan let out a long, relieved breath.

''Okay, so right now let's assume that Bracknell's

going to be staying with us." He put his hands together and looked benignly across the desk, his bushy white eyebrows and square features giving him an air of integrity and strength. "Since you're both here, and while Erica's here, I want to mention one more thing," he went on. "There's going to be a lot of publicity over this case, and I'd appreciate it if both of you say nothing and I mean nothing whatever, to the press or the other media unless it's at a formal press conference at which I am present. I have already given similar instructions to the nurses and the rest of the hospital staff. Is that understood?"

Anselm nodded immediately, and after a moment's hesitation, so did Peter.

Anselm stood up. "We'll be in the E.R. until we can transfer Bracknell up to the medical floor," he said. "We'll keep you informed."

Peter followed Anselm out, glancing back once at Stefan with a curious, almost triumphant look.

7

Anselm and Peter walked back down the long corridor from the administrative offices toward the emergency room. Through the windows they could see the Sound; the fog had partially lifted, but a great impenetrable bank still lay about half a mile offshore.

"Do they have any kids?" asked Anselm out of curiosity.

"The Bracknells? No. And there weren't any from his previous marriage either. I know Sandy wanted children, but Denton had totally inactive sperm. We checked it twice. It was hard on them, particularly Sandy."

Back in the emergency room, Anselm glanced at Bracknell's monitor: everything seemed to be stable.

Denton, still obviously tense, licked his dry lips. "Dr. Harris," he asked, "have you dealt with this kind of problem before?" His voice was impersonal, as if he were asking a plumber if he knew how to join two pipes together.

"Yes, sir, I have," replied Anselm steadily.

"He's the best-trained surgeon here," interposed Peter quickly. "We're very lucky to have him with us."

"What do you think, hon?" asked Denton, not taking his eyes off Anselm.

"If Dr. Harris is okay with Peter, he's okay with us," replied Sandy, her eyes resting steadily on Anselm. "One hundred percent." She was standing up, one protective hand on Denton's shoulder.

While they were talking, the ultrasound tech had been setting up her equipment, applied the contact jelly to Bracknell's neck, and moved the sensor over the artery.

"Do this real gently," Anselm warned her softly. "We don't want to dislodge anything."

The green image on the screen came to life, changed, moved. "That's it," said Anselm, pointing at a section of the screen. "Go up the neck a bit, very gently."

Peter, who didn't know too much about ultrasound, watched from the other side. "Where?" he asked. Anselm pointed at a space between two green lines. "Common carotid," he said. "You see that parallel line, right next to it, fluttering a bit?" He glanced at Peter. "That's the vein that runs alongside it, the internal jugular." Anselm stared at the image. "That entire carotid artery looks narrower than on the old films," he said. "On both sides. Even the tributaries are narrowed, as if they're in spasm."

"I guess the technique's different," replied Peter rather vaguely. "There it is," he went on, trying to suppress the excitement in his voice. "That must be the clot, right there at the bifurcation." He pointed at a slightly denser green shadow on the screen.

Anselm hesitated. Peter might well be right, but to his more experienced eye, it wasn't quite as clear as Peter made it sound. He stared at the screen. "Take some films," he told the tech, and she pressed the switch that froze the picture on the screen, then photographed it. She did this several times, taking pictures on both sides until Anselm said, "I think that's enough, Mollie, thank you."

"Well, I think we can move him up to the floor now," said Peter to Anselm.

"Let's put him in the ICU," said Anselm. "We'll be able to keep a closer eye on him there."

"Good idea," said Peter. "Let's do just that."

Denton's heart rate was fast with occasional irregular beats, tiny beads of sweat were still around the top of his forehead, and his hands and feet were still as cold as ice. Anselm looked at the blood-pressure monitor and thought about the possible causes of such a big difference between his patient's systolic and diastolic pressures.

"We know he has a fair amount of arteriosclerosis," said Peter in Anselm's ear. "Certainly enough to explain such a high pulse pressure."

"What are my chances, Peter?" interrupted Denton quietly. Sandy gripped her husband's hand hard. "I mean chances of dying, or getting a big stroke?"

"Let's rather talk about your chances of survival, and your chances of walking out of here a well man," replied Peter. "In my opinion, those chances are excellent."

Denton didn't look entirely satisfied with that answer, but he lay back and stared at the ceiling. He didn't ask any more questions.

A few moments later, two transportation orderlies arrived, and Denton was wheeled up in his stretcher to the Intensive Care Unit.

Meanwhile, Anselm and Peter went to the X-ray department to examine the ultrasound films and review the chemical test results.

Peter scanned the lab readouts while Anselm stared at the ultrasound images on the screen.

Five minutes later, the phone rang.

"I'll take it," said Anselm. "Here, Peter, take a look at those films."

He picked up the phone and heard a breathless, panicky voice at the other end. "Dr. Harris? This is Nurse Edstrom in the ICU. Your patient Mr. Bracknell, who just arrived, I think he's convulsing. . . . We're calling a code on him now."

Anselm ran along the corridor toward the Intensive Care Unit, with Peter right behind him.

Inside the ICU, a crowd of people were milling about Bracknell's bed, and a nurse was wheeling a portable defibrillator across the unit from another cubicle. Three medical students from New Coventry Medical Center stood in a tight, scared cluster by the door, not knowing how to help. Jasmine Wu, the tiny head nurse, was hanging up a fresh bottle of intravenous fluid and telling another nurse to fetch two ampoules of calcium chloride from the emergency pack. Two techs from Respiratory Therapy were there, one putting an oxygen mask over Denton's face and the other adjusting the settings on the big pale green respirator on the left side of the bed.

"What happened?" Anselm asked Jasmine. Bracknell's eyes were closed, his face was a mottled red, and his left arm and leg were making jerky, twitching movements.

"He stopped breathing just after he got here," said Jasmine, wiping her hands on her hips. "His eyes turned up and he started to twitch like that."

"Any changes on the monitor?"

"No. We ran a strip on the EKG, but it looks okay, to me, anyway."

"Where is she? I mean his wife?" asked Peter, looking around.

"In the waiting room," replied Jasmine. "I asked her to leave. I drew some enzymes on him, if that's okay." She pointed at two blood-filled tubes on the small table.

''Good. Let's get them down to the lab. Now.'' Peter sounded flustered again.

Meanwhile, Anselm was checking the cardiac monitor for signs that Denton might have had a heart attack. It was unchanged, and the beat was regular, although still fast.

''Let's get a hard copy,'' said Peter, seeing what Anselm was doing. He pressed a button on the console, and the electrocardiogram paper spewed out in a long ribbon. Peter turned a switch every few seconds until the tracing contained readings from all of the leads, then he ripped off the paper and examined the tracings.

Anselm had his stethoscope out and was listening to Denton's neck. ''The sound's changed,'' he said to Peter a moment later. ''I think he's lost another piece of that clot, but not the whole thing.''

''Son of a bitch,'' said Peter, his voice almost a whisper. ''That figures.'' His gaze came up from the cardiogram strip. ''His heart's okay,'' he said to Anselm. ''If that's any comfort to you.'' He turned to the head nurse. ''Call Mr. Olson and tell him that Mr. Bracknell had a stroke and we'll get back to him as soon as things have stabilized.''

After completing their evaluation, Anselm and Peter retreated to the tiny dictation area.

''You're going to have to do something, Anselm,'' said Peter, sitting on the desk. ''We can't just leave him like this.'' His face was drawn; even though he now shared the responsibility for Denton Bracknell with Anselm, the strain was telling on him.

''Frankly, Peter,'' said Anselm, ''I'd still rather see him transferred to Bethesda. You know we're not really set up—''

''That is out of the question,'' said Peter loudly. ''And you know that too. God damn it, Anselm, I'm getting sick and tired of hearing everybody wanting to transfer him out. Just being moved into a helicopter could shake the rest of that clot loose, you know that as well as I do, and then he'd be paralyzed or dead, and all because we were too chicken to take care of him.'' Peter took a deep breath and looked at Anselm with an air of determination, almost of defiance. ''No, sir,'' he said, ''we're stuck with him, Anselm, and it's our job to take care of him the best we can right here.''

''That means we're going to have to operate on him, I suppose you know that,'' said Anselm heavily.

Peter got off the desk. ''Right. I entirely agree. Let's get going. I'll call Stefan Olson. He'll probably have a fit, but at this point we don't have any other option, do we?''

8

Tony Marino, chairman of the hospital's board of managers, was in his downtown office when Stefan Olson called to tell him about Bracknell's admission. Tony called his son-in-law, Bob North, and told him to meet him in fifteen minutes at the hospital, where he had a small office next to the boardroom.

Tony Marino was a big man, with a thick, jowly face and small, dark, heavy-lidded, aggressive eyes. He liked to wear large, loose-fitting suits, shiny brown shoes, and brightly colored ties. Thirty years before, as a young car salesman, Tony had affected a pompadour hairstyle, and he still wore a high pomaded wave on the top of his head. His hairline was low, leaving only a little expanse of forehead visible above his heavy eyebrows. Tony was quick, clever, and unscrupulous; he had made a lot of money since taking over an almost defunct local GM dealership some twenty years before. He had a wife, but nobody ever saw her; it was said that she was too fat to leave the house. His daughter, Maria, was a dark, ill-tempered, wide-hipped young woman who had inherited his thick black eyebrows and heavy nose but not his brains. Bob North had married Maria soon after Tony was elected to the hospital board, and thereafter Maria had emulated her mother, adopting a life-style that emphasized pasta, chocolate, plus lots of rest and television. Now she had become so large that she sweated and wheezed with the least exertion, and was an acute social embarrassment to Bob, but he was too intimidated by his father-in-law to say or do anything about it.

"How come you didn't get this case?" Tony asked Bob when he got to his office.

"Peter Delafield's decision," replied Bob. He passed a hand over his hair. "He can call whoever he likes."

"Bullshit." Tony shook his head. He used to think it was professional courtesy that prevented doctors from doing what any other businessman would have done, but he now knew it was just incompetence. "I went to the trouble of making you chief of surgery at this hospital," he went on. "Do I also have to explain to you how to get some benefit out of that position?"

"I don't want to get involved with the Bracknell case, Tony," said Bob. "It has nine chances out of ten of turning to shit, and I don't want to be holding the can when that happens."

Tony silently surveyed his son-in-law, and as usual, Bob cringed internally, although he managed to maintain his normal cocky expression.

"Then why don't you get him sent to Washington or wherever they send sick VIPs?" Tony bored in. "What you *don't* want is Harris getting the kudos if Bracknell does well, because it'll undermine your position here. If Harris comes out of this covered in glory, you'll lose whatever power you have now. Also he'll take over what's left of your practice. Surely you can insist on getting Bracknell transferred. Or would that be a breach of medical ethics or something?"

"Come on, Tony," said Bob, thoroughly uncomfortable. "Surely we have to put the patient's welfare first—"

"For Christ's sake, Bob," exploded Tony, "when

are you going to learn? Bracknell isn't just a patient. He's far too important. At this point he's a commodity, a liability, an asset, a bargaining chip, whatever, depending on who you are and where you're sitting. He's a lot of different things to different people."

"I suppose so," said Bob reluctantly. "But since he's not my patient there isn't much I can do, unless there's a serious breach of hospital rules, or improper treatment that can be documented. . . ."

Tony went over to the door, slammed it shut, and turned to face Bob. There was something in his stride, something fierce, street-wise, and determined about his father-in-law that frightened Bob.

"Look, you dumb asshole," said Tony, "if we play this right, Bracknell can be the key to a lot of things around here. Right now everybody in this goddamned hospital is trying to figure out how to cash in on him if he lives, and how to cover their asses if he dies. Stefan's going to use him to fight Farman Industries, Peter's hoping this'll cover him in glory and make him the leading doc in the area, and Harris, well, who knows what he wants out of it. What *you* had better start thinking about"—Tony took a step toward Bob, who instinctively moved back—"is how you can use this situation to consolidate your power base here. You better have a plan if Bracknell does well, another if he dies or is paralyzed or whatever. You know the hospital rules, so for God's sake use them."

Tony turned and sat down at his desk and reached for the phone. He looked at Bob briefly. "Now get the hell out of here," he told him. "I have a couple arms to twist."

By five o'clock, the operating room was being readied, the preoperative tests and other preparations were under way, and Anselm and Peter went to the waiting room to talk to Sandy Bracknell.

"I believe surgery is Denton's only chance," said Peter, putting a sympathetic hand on her arm.

Sandy fixed her gaze on Anselm; the strength of her character was beginning to show.

"Do you agree, Dr. Harris?"

Anselm nodded. On the basis of what he knew, there was no doubt that the surgery was necessary, but at the back of his mind a cautious voice was trying to speak up although the course of action had already been decided. But if he backed off now without a viable alternative treatment, he would destroy his credibility as a surgeon, not only with Peter but with the entire medical community.

"I'm afraid Peter's right. There's no real alternative, Mrs. Bracknell," he said. "But I have to tell you that there are substantial risks to the procedure." He went on to tell her a list of possible complications. "I have to go now," he said. "Peter can answer if you have any other questions."

Peter looked at Sandy, and his smile was almost inappropriately optimistic.

Walking along the corridor, Anselm considered who he would ask to assist him. Bob North was the obvious person, and was in the hospital. Somewhere at the back of Anselm's mind was the self-preserving thought that if things did go wrong, having the assistance of the chief of surgery during the operation might help to deflect any later criticism.

From the operating suite, he called the operator to page Dr. North. Bob heard the page and instantly figured what it was for. He thought for a moment and decided there was only one thing in it for him if he stayed to assist Anselm, and that was trouble. Better to get out, let Harris do his own thing, and then Bob could come back and pick up the pieces. He didn't even pause in his stride, and in a few moments he was out the doctors' entrance, into his BMW, and on his way home.

"I'm sorry, Dr. North did not respond," the operator told Anselm in her usual singsong voice a few minutes later. She checked the lights on the indicator board. "He is signed out of the hospital at this time."

Anselm decided to use Teresa Carling, one of the three physician's assistants who were hired to work in the operating rooms. Teresa would be as competent a helper as anybody.

In his office, Stefan Olson watched Marlin Foster, the FBI agent, punch a set of numbers into his bulky portable phone. The daylight was fading, and Stefan went to switch on the room lights. Foster paused, held the instrument up to his ear, listened, then punched in some more numbers. Stefan looked at the clock on his desk, and wondered about Foster's chances of raising anyone in Washington at this time of the evening.

But it only took a few seconds before Admiral Ellis was on the line. Foster introduced himself and passed the phone over to Stefan.

"There's been a change in Mr. Bracknell's condition, Admiral," said Stefan. "He appears to have taken a major turn for the worse. I understand he's had some kind of a severe stroke, and the two doctors you talked to earlier, Drs. Harris and Delafield, are very concerned about his condition."

Stefan grasped the phone tightly, expecting a tirade from the other end. There was a long silence, and Admiral Ellis asked if the president had been informed. Looking at Foster, Stefan told Ellis that no, that they would leave that up to him.

"I'm really concerned that you didn't decide to transfer him sooner, while he was still in reasonable condition," said the admiral stiffly, his folksy southern accent gone. "But we can't do much at this stage, I suppose. May I speak to Dr. Delafield or Dr. Harris?"

"They're both up in the ICU right now, as far as I know, sir," replied Stefan. His stomach was contracting, and he felt that events had really got away from him, that he had lost control over what was happening in his own hospital. "They have decided that Mr. Bracknell needs to be operated upon. . . ."

Admiral Ellis seemed to be carrying on another conversation with someone at his end, and Stefan wasn't sure if he had heard him. Then the admiral came back on the line. "Please keep us informed," he said. "We are at this time putting together a medical and surgical team to go up to Glenport to assist your own capable physicians. We'll be coming up by Medevac helicopter, one equipped to transport Mr. Bracknell if necessary. As soon as we have an ETA, we'll let you know."

"ETA?" asked Stefan.

"Estimated time of arrival," said the admiral. His voice was well controlled, but it was clear that he was angry. "Please tell your doctors to hold everything until we get there. Now please reconnect me to Agent Foster."

Stefan passed the instrument back to Marlin Foster, who listened for almost a minute without saying anything. Throughout, his pale eyes were fixed on Stefan. "Yes, sir," said Foster, then terminated the connection. He didn't look directly at Stefan, but as he was putting his equipment back in his briefcase, he murmured, "I sure hope things go well for Mr. Bracknell, Mr. Olson. The admiral sounded mad as hell."

Now that the die was cast, Anselm went calmly about the business of getting everything ready for Denton Bracknell's operation. He went over the instruments he would be using with the scrub tech, whose instinct was to have every single instrument available in case it was needed. Anselm had long ago submitted himself to the discipline of using only well-tried techniques he was comfortable with, so he knew exactly which instruments he would need for this case.

"Just those two Pott's scissors," he said, pointing at a pair of angled, sharp-pointed scissors in the tray of a dozen arterial scissors with blades of different sizes and shapes. He would use them to cut the wall of the carotid artery. "You can put the others away."

He smiled at the tech, who rather tremulously smiled back. At least it was going to be Dr. Harris doing this case, she told herself, not one of those other clowns like Dr. North.

Peter, with the help of Philip Burton, the on-call anesthesiologist, had taken the patient into the recovery room on a stretcher to get him ready for the operation, and Philip was busy putting in large-bore IV needles in both arms. Anselm wasn't entirely happy about having Philip do the case with him: Short, stocky, brusque, and bad-tempered, Philip wasn't the most competent anesthesiologist Anselm had ever met, and even worse, had a reputation for panicking when things got tough in the operating room.

Bracknell seemed to be waking up, but this time he wasn't recovering as well; his eyes were glassy, and he tried to speak, but the words were slurred and jumbled.

"Okay," said Philip to Teresa after the preoperative preparations were complete. He straightened up slowly, hurting from the arthritis that racked his leg joints. "Let's take him through. He's ready." He shook his head and glanced at Bracknell's bewildered face. "As ready as he'll ever be."

Anselm was waiting for them in the operating suite. "Stay with him," he told Teresa, indicating the patient. "Make sure he doesn't move his head around, and let me know when you're ready to position him on the table."

He went back to the doctors' lounge, made himself a cup of coffee, sat down, put his elbows on his knees, and considered the situation. This operation on Denton Bracknell was one he would have undertaken in New York without any hesitation, but there he had the staff, residents, and state-of-the-art facilities, the best in the world. Anselm was beginning to appreciate the degree to which he was dependent on those ancillary services, and an unpleasant thought occurred to him. Maybe he had overestimated his ability to overcome the limitations of this smaller and substantially less excellent hospital.

The wall phone by the door tinkled, and Anselm got up to answer it. Stefan Olson was on the line. His voice was heavy, and some of the residual Swedish accent was coming through. "I spoke with Admiral Ellis a few minutes ago, Anselm," he said. "He asks that you don't do anything until his team gets up here."

"I'm afraid that's too late," replied Anselm. "We're just about to start, and I don't think we should delay for any reason that isn't strictly medical."

There was a long pause, and Anselm could feel Stefan's anxiety coming through the wires. "Well, it's your decision, Dr. Harris," he said. "I hope everything goes well."

Stefan put the phone down slowly. He had been bombarded with calls after speaking with Admiral Ellis. The office of the president's chief of staff wanted the names of all the doctors involved in the care of Denton Bracknell, where they had trained and what their specialties were. The young man asking the questions was polite enough, but clearly regarded Glenport Hospital as some kind of medical backwater where no person of the importance of Denton Bracknell should ever have to undergo treatment.

Charles Kingston, the director of the New Coventry Medical Center, had called. Some White House staffer had phoned him to ask why the NCMC hadn't been able to accept Bracknell in transfer, since they were the nearest major referral center, and Kingston was furious.

"Your guys shouldn't be taking on this kind of case, Stefan," he said. "This is way beyond the capability of a community hospital, and really out of line."

Stefan responded by saying that the physicians involved were very competent, and Anselm Harris was a vascular surgeon with considerable experience in this type of case.

"From this point, Stefan, I'm going to be recording our conversation, for reasons that I'm sure are obvious to you." Stefan heard a faint beep before Kingston spoke again, now enunciating every word for the record.

"Stefan, I would like to repeat my offer to take your patient Denton Bracknell in transfer to the New Coventry Medical Center. We can have a fully equipped emergency vehicle in Glenport within an hour. The crew is on standby, waiting for the word to go. Also standing by is a medical team consisting of a senior neurologist, a neurosurgeon, and a vascular surgeon together with their technicians. Stefan, I urge you to think very carefully before you turn down this offer of help."

The phone beeped gently again, and Stefan felt that the whole world was on the line, listening and waiting for his reply.

"Thank you, Charles," he said carefully. "Your offer is appreciated, and I thank you. But at this point the situation is out of my hands. About a half hour ago, there was a major deterioration in Mr. Bracknell's condition, and his doctors felt that immediate surgery was indicated to save his life. Mr. Bracknell is at this moment in the operating room.''

After a curt goodbye, Charles Kingston hung up.

In the OR lounge, Anselm picked up the wall phone.

''We're ready to start your case, Dr. Harris,'' said Lucille.

9

"Right, Teresa, you can place the drapes now." Anselm stood behind the green sheet separating the operative field from the anesthesia equipment, holding Denton Bracknell's head, turning it very gently to the left.

Teresa held one end of the stretched iodoform-yellow adhesive drape while the scrub nurse held the other two corners, and slowly they deposited it on the patient's neck, sticky side down.

"Good," said Anselm. Teresa slid her gloved hand over the thin drape to eliminate the wrinkles while Anselm went next door to scrub. He put his foot on the small pedal by his feet, a thin brown jet of betadine solution squirted out into his cupped palm, and he went automatically into the routine. Anselm was grateful for the loud hissing of the water; he felt that in some way it insulated him from the outside world, from the pressures that he could sense building up out there.

Teresa put her head through the door. "We're ready when you are, Dr. Harris," she said in her soft Georgia accent. Anselm nodded, the door closed, and she went back into the OR.

Through the large window Anselm could see the preparations Philip Burton was making, drawing up medications in syringes, labeling them, making ad-

justments to the respirator. Denton was lying quietly
on his back, lightly anesthetized. Philip, bustling
around and obviously nervous, turned to speak to a
tech, who hurried out and headed off in the direction
of the blood bank.

Anselm turned the water off with his knee, and with
his hands and elbows dripping, he backed into the operating room.

Lucille was scrubbed, not something she did every
day, but this was an important case and she was on
call, so she couldn't get out of it. Helga, the regular
scrub tech, was doing the job of circulator, fetching
medications and generally coordinating what was going on.

Lucille gave Anselm a sterile towel to dry his hands,
then held the gown while he pushed his hands and
arms into the sleeves. While Helga tied the gown behind him, Lucille opened up his first glove between
her thumbs and held it out, but after he put his hand
into it, she pulled the cuff up so abruptly around his
wrist that it tore. She had to start all over again with
a new pair, and that made her blush with annoyance.

"No problem, Lucille," said Anselm, smiling. Under her mask Lucille gritted her teeth. He adjusted his
gloves, pushed the webs up between his fingers, then
went to the right side of the table and Teresa moved
over to make room.

The right side of Denton's neck was exposed, covered with betadine film, glowing yellow-brown in the
overhead lights that had been swung around to shine
directly on it. Anselm glanced up.

"Handles for the lights, Lucille, please." She had
forgotten to place the sterile handles that allowed the
surgeon to manipulate the lights during the operation.

She picked up the two ridged, hollow aluminum
handles and screwed them onto the sockets, avoiding
Helga's look. Lucille was flustered, there was no doubt

about that. Anselm glanced over the ether screen that walled off the operating area from the anesthesia zone.

"How is he?" he asked. Philip was putting strips of tape over Denton's eyelids to keep his eyes closed, and he didn't answer immediately.

"Okay . . . The sooner we get this over, the better," he replied. Philip sounded restless and there was a faint note of hostility in his voice. "I don't know how awake he is, so I'm not sure how much halothane to give him. I'm going to start real light, so don't be surprised if he moves."

"Vital signs?"

Philip shrugged and glanced at the monitor. "Okay so far."

Anselm could sense the nervousness in Philip's words, and it echoed the tension he felt building up inside himself. He knew that if the surgeon, the leader of the team, became nervous, it was invariably transmitted by some strange telepathic mechanism to the other people working in the operating room.

Teresa positioned herself at the table opposite Anselm. She was ready and knew her job well, but she too could feel a disembodied, free-floating anxiety permeating the room.

Anselm glanced at Philip, then at the monitor. Right now all seemed well. Anselm took a deep breath. This was the moment of truth. Even now he could still back off. . . .

"Scalpel." His voice was flat, free of inflection.

Lucille slapped it hard into his outstretched hand, and he turned his head toward her for a second. Everybody could see he was annoyed.

"If you'll just give it to me, Lucille, that'll do nicely." His voice was still flat, unemotional. Anselm put his left thumb and forefinger just below the patient's ear to tense the skin, and made a six-inch cut parallel to the long muscle in the neck. Teresa was there with the clamps and the suction, and from that point on, Anselm worked fast.

"Small Metz."

Lucille passed him the Metzenbaum scissors with just a second's delay, one long enough to interrupt the continuity, the steady momentum of the operation.

Anselm cut through a layer of fibrous tissue and exposed a big blue, thin-walled vein that seemed to flutter with the patient's respiration.

"Internal jugular?" asked Teresa very quietly.

"That's it. Now if you'd retract it very carefully along with the muscle, Teresa, I'll be able to get underneath it to the carotid."

Ten minutes later, Anselm had cleared about two inches of the artery, but although an onlooker would never have detected it, the operation was not going smoothly. When things are really going well in an operating room, there is a fluidity about every movement, a rhythm that depends on the efficiency and teamwork of everyone there. Lucille, out of practice, and never particularly competent in the operating room scene, kept breaking the rhythm, was late with instruments, kept asking the circulator in a penetrating whisper to bring her some saline, sutures, and other things she didn't need at the moment. She was giving everyone there the feeling that she was working at the outside limit of her abilities, and Anselm's patience was drawing thin.

The carotid artery, which to him seemed narrower than he'd expected, was about the thickness of an ordinary lead pencil. He had exposed it to the point where it divided into two big branches, one going upward to supply the face and scalp, the other diving deep into the skull to supply the brain.

"There's the plaque," he said to Teresa, pointing at the area just below the Y-shaped bifurcation. At that point the artery was as hard as a rock.

"Not much pulsation, is there?" asked Teresa, her voice a whisper from the tension.

Anselm agreed. This was going to be touch-and-go. If the artery was completely blocked, Denton Bracknell would be in very deep trouble. And, Anselm fully realized, so would he.

"Time to heparinize him, Philip." Anselm spoke softly, trying to transmit a sense of calm to the jittery anesthetist. Philip nodded and picked up a small syringe. "Two mg per kilo body weight, right?"

"Right."

The heparin, administered to prevent the blood from clotting, would take about a minute to mix in the circulation, after which it would be safe to open the artery.

"Give me a small right-angle."

Lucille passed the instrument, a clamp with a right-angled bend near the tip, and Anselm eased it gently under the artery. From this point he and Teresa were well aware that manipulating the artery presented a major risk of dislodging the clot inside it, and he worked with the greatest care and delicacy, all his concentration being focused on meticulously freeing the artery so that he could clamp it, then open it in safety.

"Tapes."

Lucille passed him a tape, one end fixed to the tip of a hemostat. Anselm was about to catch the end with the right-angle clamp when he noticed that the tape was dry. Pulling a dry tape under the artery would cause friction and catch the arterial wall, causing exactly the kind of problem he was trying to avoid.

He stopped.

"Lucille," he said, keeping his voice under firm control, "the tapes have to be wet, please."

"You didn't say so," she muttered, taking the tape back and dunking it in a bowl of saline.

A sudden wave of anger rose in Anselm's chest. "I

shouldn't have to tell you, Lucille," he said. "It's basic technique. If you don't know that, maybe you shouldn't be here."

The atmosphere in the room became electric, and Lucille's face blushed a blotchy, furious red under her mask. How dare he talk to her like that!

She passed the tapes again, this time soaked in saline.

Anselm slipped the tapes carefully under the exposed artery.

"Small-angled de Bakeys, please."

Anselm clamped the branch that didn't go to the brain. It was stiff, a very unhealthy artery. He examined the main carotid artery; it looked unusually narrow and constricted. The blood vessel had no resistance in it, and Anselm was beginning to feel sure that there was very little blood passing through it. A normal vessel would have a strong bounding pulse.

He stopped. "Now, everybody," he said, looking at Teresa but meaning Lucille, "we're going to have to work fast and accurately for the next few minutes. All the clamps, elevators, sutures, have to be ready the second I need them. Our result here will depend on how fast and accurate we can be. Okay?"

Nobody answered. Teresa's calm eyes rested on Anselm's, and he knew he could count on her.

He took a deep breath. "Angled vascular clamps," he said, and as soon as Lucille handed them to him, he placed them across the carotid, shutting off the blood supply to one half of the brain. From now on, the clock was ticking, and he had a lot to do within the next few minutes.

"Knife. Small blade," he added. Lucille had it ready, and he made an incision in the long axis of the artery. He could feel the blade grating against the calcified material inside the artery.

"Elevator." He took the instrument, which had a

rounded, dull-edged blade at each end, inserted the end between the wall of the artery and the solidified contents, gently separating them.

The tension continued to build. Everybody knew that this was the most crucial part of the entire procedure. It took a few moments for Anselm to tease out the blockage. The material he slowly took out of the artery was hard, brittle, like frozen toothpaste. He passed it to Lucille, who put it onto a small metal dish.

"We're going to check for back flow," he said. "Teresa, are you ready with the suction?"

She nodded.

Ever so gently, Anselm released the clamp at the top of the artery. Instead of the brisk flow he expected, only a very slight trickle of blood came back. Anselm suddenly felt beads of sweat run down his nose on the inside of his mask. This was a major complication; it showed that either there was a partial blockage farther up the artery, or the blood supply coming across from the other side was inadequate. Whichever was the cause, it was bad news.

"Dilator." Lucille, after a moment's hesitation, passed him a thin, stiff rubber tube with a little pearshaped bulb on the end. Anselm slipped the dilator into the open artery, able to insert it about an inch. When he brought it back, the bleeding was a bit brisker but still not normal.

"We'll check the forward flow now," he said, releasing the second clamp. A jet of blood shot out of the lower end of the carotid, and Anselm quickly shut the clamp again. He reviewed the situation rapidly. The blockage was removed, there was no doubt about that, and the flow from the lower end was excellent. Now all he needed to do was sew up the artery, open the clamps, and hope for the best.

He held out his hand. "Six-O Dexon." Lucille

promptly placed a needle holder in his hand. The tiny curved needle was caught in the jaws of the instrument, one-third the way along its length, just the way it was supposed to be, but pointing in the wrong direction. Anselm said nothing. Squinting at the tiny needle, he repositioned it and started to sew the cut edges of the artery together, working fast and accurately, but internally boiling with anger. It had been only a slight delay, but in this case, when time was so clearly of the essence, even a few seconds could make a big difference.

Anselm tested his repair by opening the lower clamp, and a fine jet of blood came through the line of stitches.

"It'll stop with pressure," he said to Teresa, who clearly expected him to put in another stitch. He opened the other clamp, allowing blood to flow again into that side of the brain. For a couple of minutes, while Anselm applied gentle pressure to the artery, there was almost complete silence in the operating room. Although the main part of the operation was completed, and his team was feeling a sense of relief, Anselm knew that it wasn't over. His fingers strained to feel a pulse under the gauze pad, and there was a growing awareness in his mind that things were not going well. He raced through the possibilities, the sequence of corrective action he might take, but that didn't help. He'd done everything he could, he'd taken the obstructing plaque out of the artery. . . .

"His pressure's going down," said Philip from the other side of the either screen. His voice was high, with a little quaver that showed he was on the brink of panic. There was a lot of activity going on behind the screen; Philip was injecting some drug into Bracknell's arm vein, his assistant was busy drawing medication up in a syringe, and the circulator was manually checking the blood pressure.

"What's it at?" Anselm's voice was cool, but he too could feel the early stirrings of panic.

"One hundred over forty," replied Philip, holding the cap of a syringe in his teeth. He stared at Anselm. "He dropped twenty points in the last couple of minutes."

Anselm was in a dilemma, familiar enough to most surgeons, but now, because of the importance of the patient and the ramifications of a wrong move would have at this moment, his apprehension was threatening to overwhelm him. He felt his brow cold with sweat, and inside his head it felt as if some kind of high-frequency jamming signal were swamping his ability to think clearly. Teresa was looking at him without expression, waiting for him to make a move, a decision. Lucille also was poised, one immobile hand holding a clamp, handle toward Anselm. She was watching, her vindictive eyes showing how well she understood and was enjoying his predicament. Philip, barely able to function because of his fear that the case was going to end badly and he would be held responsible, waited, watching Anselm over the top of the ether screen, obviously hoping that he would abort the case.

In the space of a moment all kinds of thoughts, sensations of color and sound, childhood recollections and smells, flashed through Anselm's mind; the strict gatekeeper of his brain, which regulated and controlled the thoughts he was permitted to consider at any one time, was inoperative, bombarded by the tension of the moment.

Meanwhile the pressure to do something, anything, was building fast. He couldn't just stand there and watch his patient's blood pressure keep on going down until he died.

Anselm forced his thoughts into some kind of order. The first decision he had to make was whether to close quickly and get the patient back to the recovery room, or to continue with the operation to make sure that blood was flowing properly into Denton Bracknell's brain.

He lifted the gauze off the carotid artery and examined it quickly. The vessel was tight, obviously full of blood, and for a second Anselm thought he could detect a pulse, but almost immediately he recognized that it was just wishful thinking. He was trying to *will* a pulse into that carotid.

"There's no pulse," he said finally, looking over at Philip. "I'm sorry, but I'm going to have to reopen."

"Jesus, Anselm!" Philip's voice was high with tension. "I don't know if I can maintain him. How about just closing and getting us and him the hell out of here?"

"Angled de Bakey clamps, Lucille, then the small Pott's scissors," said Anselm. Then he said to Philip, while he quickly clamped the artery again, "Sorry, Phil, if we close now he'll be paralyzed for sure. I'm going to give it another shot."

Anselm glanced up for a second and saw Philip's lips tighten in disapproval. "I can't guarantee . . ." he said, then muttered something and went on with his efforts.

Working as fast as he knew how, Anselm took the tiny scissors and cut through all the stitches he had so meticulously put in. Again he flushed the vessel out with saline from a small syringe. Then, holding his breath, he took off the top clamp, hoping against hope for a gush of bright red blood that would show that the channel to the brain was intact. Nothing happened. The vessel was as dry as a desert arroyo. Anselm felt his hands beginning to shake uncontrollably, and he stepped back from the table for a moment to regroup his thoughts. Nothing. No blood. That meant that there was a blockage farther up, inside Denton's skull.

"Close, close up and get out," said an urgent voice inside his head. "There's no point going on here."

"We'll give it one more shot," he said. "Lucille, give me the thinnest rubber catheter you've got. Let's see if we can get it through the blockage."

"I can't maintain him much longer," said Philip, his voice tight and accusatory.

"Three minutes," promised Anselm. He slid the rounded end of the catheter into the artery, twisted and manipulated it as carefully as he could, but wasn't able to get it in farther than about an inch. For a moment he thought of injecting saline under pressure to blow out the blockage, but that idea died at birth. It would simply reblock the artery a bit farther along, and would almost certainly do more harm than good.

"We're closing," he said finally, feeling a leaden weight coming up from his stomach to invade every part of him. "There's nothing more we can do."

Philip muttered something shut off the halothane, and turned up the oxygen concentration. At this point his chief concern was to get the patient off the table alive.

Anselm closed up the artery with is usual care, but his fingers flew; he knew what Philip was doing, and didn't want Bracknell to wake up and start struggling on the operating table before his neck was sewn up.

"Let's bypass the recovery room," said Philip. "And take him straight to the ICU."

"Fine with me," replied Anselm, not looking up.

"Call the ICU," said Philip to the circulator. "Tell them we'll need a respirator."

"Teresa, pick up the skin on both sides." Anselm was putting in the final skin clips. "Now you can let him wake up," he said to Philip.

"Thanks. I've been trying to wake him up for the last five minutes."

Anselm pulled off the plastic skin drape, then unclipped the green towel around the operative field. Philip had taken the tapes off Denton's eyes to look at the pupils; the lids were half closed and puffy.

"He's not breathing on his own," said Philip. "We'll have to bag him until we get him to the ICU." His voice was angry and he didn't look at Anselm.

He's blaming me for not closing earlier, thought Anselm as the stretcher was wheeled in and they got ready for the trip down the corridor to the ICU. He made a mental note to explain his actions to Philip as soon as they had settled their patient in the ICU. This was no time for hostility among the people taking care of Denton Bracknell.

10

Stefan Olson and Erica were waiting for Anselm by the desk of the operating suite, Stefan's well-disciplined, stolid face hiding his anxiety.

"How did it go?" he asked, moving out of the way as the stretcher came by, accompanied by Anselm, Teresa, and at the head of the stretcher, Philip rhythmically squeezing air into Bracknell's lungs from a black ventilator bag.

"Not now," said Anselm abruptly as they hurried past. "Sorry, but right now . . . you can see . . . Look, I'll talk to you in the ICU in about ten minutes, okay?"

Stefan flushed, annoyed, but said he'd be there. He turned to Erica.

"You can tell the media that the operation is over, and Bracknell's in the ICU," he told her. "No other details are available at this time."

Anselm hurried on with the stretcher, holding onto the IV bags to keep them from swinging off the pole. He hadn't stopped to give Stefan the information he wanted because he didn't know what to tell him. Until Bracknell recovered consciousness and they were able to test his arms and legs for function, to evaluate whether any brain damage had occurred, there was no way of telling what his condition was.

The doors to the ICU opened automatically as soon as the stretcher approached. "First booth," called out Jasmine Wu. Within a minute Bracknell had been transferred to the bed, the IVs were hooked up to a pole by the bed, chest electrodes were connected to the wall monitor above the bed, and his endotracheal tube had been attached to the respirator.

Peter joined them and was soon deep in a whispered conversation with Anselm. His face fell as he listened.

"Okay, let's check him out," muttered Philip. Obviously still angry, he opened one of Bracknell's eyes, shone a light into it, then did the same with the other. He straightened up, then looked around for Anselm. When he saw Peter, he addressed him instead. "Nonreactive pupils," he said. "Do you want to take a look at his fundi?"

Peter took the ophthalmoscope, turned it to the correct aperture, held Bracknell's eye open with one finger, leaned forward, and looked through the pupil into the back of his eye. "Nothing much here," he said after checking the retina and the blood vessels radiating out from its center. He went to the other eye, and after a few moments he shook his head and gave the instrument back to Philip.

"Maybe there's a little less tension in the vessels on the right side," he said. "Aside from that, I can't see much."

"You want to give him some Nalorphin or something like that? Maybe that would jolt him awake," said Anselm.

"I already did," replied Philip. He turned on Anselm angrily. "I'm going to have to put in a report," he said. "You should have terminated the case as soon as his pressure started to drop."

"Go ahead," replied Anselm. "Write your report. But I want you to know that at that time there was still a chance to open up that artery, and I decided to take it.''

"Well, did you open it?'' Philip's voice was sharp, sarcastic.

"No,'' replied Anselm. "I wasn't able to.''

Philip glanced around and lowered his voice so that only Anselm and Peter could hear. His face was red and furious. "So now we're left with a guy who isn't waking up, and who'll probably be a vegetable when he does. Good work, Harris!'' He put his stethoscope to his ears and started to take the blood pressure on Bracknell's arm.

Peter and Anselm looked at each other, then Anselm shrugged. He'd done the best possible job he could, he was quite certain of that.

"Peter, I'm not in a business where I can guarantee results,'' he said. They went toward the small conference area. "Don't worry about Philip,'' he went on. "He's like that. He doesn't respond very well to stress. Here, let's get us a cup of coffee.''

The automatic doors opened, and Stefan and Erica came into the ICU. Stefan looked stiff-jawed and concerned, but Erica looked as fresh as if she was just coming to work instead of having been on the job for almost sixteen hours. She smiled at Anselm, a smile that both Peter and Stefan would have killed for, but Anselm didn't react.

"The media's waiting for you in the main conference room,'' she told him. "They want to talk to you as soon as the operation was over.''

"I don't think that's a good idea,'' said Anselm sharply, and Erica was startled by his tone. Men just didn't talk to her like that. "At this point I can't really tell them anything. Let's wait for maybe a half hour. A little more waiting shouldn't make any difference to them.'' His hands were sweating, and he brushed the palms down the side of his white coat.

"They already know you're out of the operating room," said Stefan. "So if there's a delay, they're going to assume the worst."

"Well, damn it," burst out Anselm, "who told them we were finished? What the hell's going on around here?"

"Take it easy," said Stefan. "Erica told them. She's just doing her job."

"It isn't her job to give me additional problems," snapped Anselm, all the frustration of the last hours coming to the surface. "You guys are putting me in a jam. If I go out there and tell the media that Bracknell's still unconscious, they're going to say we screwed up, and if we wait a half hour, they're going to say we're withholding information."

Anselm looked at Erica; to his surprise her lip was trembling and her eyes were full of angry tears. At the same moment they all heard the low-pitched, thudding noise of a large helicopter approaching, and for a couple of seconds the windows of the unit vibrated. Then the noise diminished and was gone.

"That must be the team from Washington," said Stefan quickly. "I was about to tell you—"

"What team?" asked Peter, a sudden anger in his voice. "The navy people? They said they were coming tomorrow. What happened?" He stared suspiciously at Stefan.

"They decided to come sooner," he said calmly. "What's more, they're here on the president's direct orders." His voice was firm and, though less loud, carried over Peter's raised tones. "The admiral's bringing a team of medical experts to assist you in Bracknell's care."

"Assist? Jesus Christ, man," said Peter, "don't you know what they're going to do? They're going to try to take over the case, take credit if things go well, and pour shit on all of us if it doesn't.'' He took a deep breath and checked himself.

Philip came out of Bracknell's booth, looking tired and dejected.

Philip nodded to Stefan, then turned with an unmistakably hostile expression to Anselm. ''He's not doing well. He's totally unresponsive. I can hardly get any reflexes out of him. Also . . .'' he said, glowering, ''he's totally dependent on the ventilator, and he's not able to make any breathing effort on his own.''

''What does all that mean?'' asked Stefan.

''It means that in my opinion, Denton Bracknell has suffered major brain damage during the operation, and that unless things change dramatically, he's in the deepest trouble.''

Philip looked at Anselm, challenging him to say something, but Anselm remained silent. ''And another thing,'' Philip went on, swinging around to face Stefan, ''you're going to get a detailed report from me concerning the way this case has been managed.'' He turned and walked back into the ICU.

Stefan looked at Anselm and then at Peter. ''We're going down to the helipad now to meet the navy people,'' he said. ''I guess their arrival has taken you guys off the hook with the media for a while. I'll see you both in the conference room when you can come down. Take your time.''

Anselm and Peter watched Stefan and Erica leave the unit. ''Okay, Anselm,'' said Peter urgently, ''we'd better get our act together before those Washington guys come on the scene. Now, tell me exactly what happened back there in the operating room.''

Erica was still mad at Anselm as she and Stefan hurried along the corridor, and her heels clicked angrily on the tiled floor. She'd been interested in Dr. Harris from the time he came to Glenport, they'd gone out a couple of times together, but Anselm had gently resisted her efforts to deepen the relationship. Peter had seen what she was up to and was understandably annoyed. He told her to lay off, that anyway Anselm wasn't ready, was still hurting from his divorce. But then, Peter had his own agenda. Tonight, however, there was something in the way Anselm had looked at her that told Erica there was no point in trying.

They reached the elevator, and while they waited Stefan gazed at her out of the corner of his eye. He knew what was going on in Erica's life and was quite prepared to bide his time. When they got out to the helipad, there was a small crowd of people around the helicopter. Its twin rotors were still turning, and Erica noticed that the craft was huge, much bigger than the helicopter that occasionally transported patients from the hospital to New Coventry. Four men, all in civilian clothes, came down the ramp, led by a slim, serious-looking black-haired man who looked in his late forties, and Stefan stepped forward to greet them.

"Hi," said the first man, unsmiling. "I'm Admiral Ellis." As soon as they were out of the draft from the rotors, he turned to introduce his companions: Dr. Neville Sachs, a completely bald, middle-aged man wearing granny glasses, who was, Ellis said, a neurologist from Georgetown who did consulting work for the navy. To his right was Dr. Simon Faber, a young, crew-cut naval neurosurgeon wearing thick horn-rimmed glasses, and last, a small, round man with thin blond hair whose overly large raincoat blew about him. He was Dr. Marcus Poynter, an intensive-care specialist.

"Let's go up to my office," said Stefan, opening the door for the visitors.

"We'd like to see the patient first, if that's okay with you," replied the admiral without breaking step.

"Maybe the doctors in charge of Mr. Bracknell can brief us on the way up."

"I don't know." Stefan sounded uncharacteristically flustered. "Dr. Harris is with the patient in the ICU, and—"

The admiral stopped, more because of the tone of Stefan's voice than what he said. "Dr. Harris is the surgeon, right?"

"Yes. As I mentioned to you on the phone, Dr. Harris and Dr. Delafield decided that since the patient's condition was worsening, they would have to operate."

The admiral started to shake his head emphatically, but caught himself and said with a forced joviality, "Well, luckily we have the country's top neuro people here with us. They'll be glad to help your doctors decide."

Stefan took a deep breath. "They already decided. Dr. Harris performed the surgery about an hour ago."

There was a long silence, broken only by the slapping noise of shoes on the plastic floor tiles as the group marched toward the elevator. The doctors walking behind Stefan and the admiral exchanged glances.

"Okay," said the admiral as they crowded into the elevator. His lips were tightly compressed, and Stefan could see that he was having trouble containing his anger. "That certainly changes the picture. I thought . . ." Stefan was expecting an explosion, but the admiral bit his lip and said no more until they reached the third floor.

"Turn left," said Stefan when the doors opened. Erica hurried down the corridor ahead of them to open the ICU door. The guard took one look at the solid phalanx of men advancing on him and almost jumped out of the way.

Anselm was standing by the patient's bed when they came in. After brief introductions, Dr. Poynter, the intensivist, took off his coat and busied himself with the patient, checking the IVs, the medications, the respirator settings, while Anselm and the others went into the staff room.

"So you decided to operate," said Admiral Ellis, looking at Anselm through bright blue eyes. His voice was polite, chilly. "Perhaps you'd like to tell us the events that forced you to make that decision."

While Anselm told them, Stefan drifted off toward the entrance, and Erica, who had been on the phone, followed him.

"The media people are waiting," she said, still sounding as calm and efficient as ever. "They want to know who all these new arrivals are."

"Well, they'll just have to wait," replied Stefan. At this moment his main concern was how to keep the admiral from venting his anger by lowering the boom on the hospital when he went back to Washington.

In the Intensive Care Unit, gently but remorselessly, Admiral Ellis and his colleagues were backing Anselm up against the wall.

"I assume you got a neurosurgical opinion before deciding to operate," asked Simon Faber, the neurosurgeon. He was brisk and businesslike, obviously not comfortable with having to interrogate a colleague this way.

"We didn't," replied Anselm. He didn't mention that the only neurosurgeon in town was a sick man who'd had a triple bypass a year before and gone religious. Most of the doctors kept professionally very clear of him now.

"Actually, there are two of us with vascular training here," he replied, "and between us we do most of the carotids."

Dr. Poynter came into the room, and the conversation stopped.

"He's in real bad shape, sir," said Poynter, addressing the admiral. "I'd like Dr. Faber and Dr. Sachs to take a look at him, but I think we should plan on getting him out of here"—his gaze fell on Anselm for a second—"as fast as possible."

While the final preparations were being made for Bracknell's transfer, Peter and Anselm went to the ICU waiting room to tell Sandy what was happening. She was pale but took the news without flinching.

"I'm going with him," she said.

11

"Okay, Teresa, I want you to hold his head and keep it steady while we get him onto the stretcher," said Dr. Poynter, getting everything ready. "I'll bag him until we get him into the helicopter." He had taken charge of the patient immediately, and his competence was obvious. Even Peter had to admit that he was good; very methodically, Poynter had made sure that every eventuality was covered. At the end of the stretcher he had placed a box containing labeled and pre-filled syringes of various emergency medicines, and he had put a separate IV into Bracknell's arm specifically for the administration of medication.

Teresa watched while Poynter went to the respirator and turned up the oxygen concentration and increased the depth of Bracknell's respiration.

"I want to hyperventilate him a bit before the transfer," he explained, seeing her unspoken query. "Then we have a bit of leeway if there's a problem between here and the 'copter."

Teresa nodded. "I'll take an extra bag down with us," she said, indicating a spherical black respirator bag she had taken from the department of anesthesiology.

"Good. Meanwhile, hold the monitor out of the way while we get him onto the stretcher."

One of the nurses took the IV bags and hung them on the pole attached to the stretcher, and now everything seemed to be ready for the transfer.

"Right, everybody," said Poynter, glancing around at the nurses and aides, then momentarily at Bracknell, lying immobile except for his chest, which went up and down with each breath from the respirator beside him. "On the count of three, okay?" He quickly detached the plastic tube in Bracknell's throat from the respirator and attached the manually operated breathing bag. "You have his head, Teresa? Okay, then, one, two . . ." On "three" the aides and nurses around the bed lifted the part of the lower sheet they were next to, and Bracknell sailed up and onto the stretcher drawn up next to the bed.

"Right, let's go." Poynter, for all his tubbiness, moved fast.

The stretcher trundled rapidly through the open doors of the ICU and headed down the corridor. Peter, Anselm, and Sandy joined the procession at the door. Poynter had detailed one of the security guards to hold the elevator, and while the guard held the doors open, the stretcher was hurried in, with Poynter at the head, rhythmically compressing the black respirator bag to inflate Bracknell's paralyzed lungs.

On the ground floor, they pushed the stretcher fast along the corridor, everyone feeling the same sense of urgency. They had to get Bracknell into the helicopter, with its sophisticated equipment, quickly. If anything happened to him in transit, such as a convulsion or a cardiac arrest, his chances of survival would be dramatically reduced.

The people they passed in the corridor, nurses, visitors, held themselves against the wall out of the way, but they all tried to get a glimpse of the famous patient's face.

The accident happened as they were turning the corner toward the main hospital entrance. Dr. Poynter, trotting along beside the stretcher, compressing the ventilating balloon by hand every five or six seconds, was on the inside of the curve. The leading wheel caught his foot, he tripped, made an attempt to recover himself, but fell flat, still clutching the balloon. As it was attached to the endotracheal tube in Bracknell's windpipe, it jerked the tube out, in spite of the adhesive tape that had been applied to retain it.

Poynter scrambled quickly to his feet, panting, still holding the bag with the tube attached to it. The stretcher had stopped a few feet farther along. This was the only eventuality he hadn't foreseen, and he lost his cool altogether. "Teresa, run, get me a laryngoscope!" he screamed, and Teresa took off running back along the corridor, hoping that the elevator was still there. But she knew that the play would probably be over by the time she got back.

Anselm, Sandy, and Peter had been walking several yards behind the procession. Sandy could see that something terrible had happened. It was too much for her, and she turned her face to the wall and closed her eyes.

As soon as Anselm saw Poynter fall, he started forward to help, but Peter instantly put a restraining hand on his arm. "Stay out of this," he whispered urgently. "Poynter may just accidentally have saved our skins."

Astonished, not understanding what Peter was talking about, Anselm shook him off and hurried forward. But there wasn't much he could do beyond deflating the balloon on the endotracheal tube so that Poynter could get it back in once he had a laryngoscope to position it.

Poynter could see that Bracknell showed no sign of spontaneous breathing, and ignoring the blood around the patient's nose and mouth, he put a hand behind his neck and started to give Bracknell mouth-to-mouth resuscitation, while Dr. Sachs, who had decided to accompany the patient, checked the heart rate and pattern on the portable monitor, ready to administer manual cardiac compression if that became necessary.

Dr. Sachs took over the mouth-to-mouth breathing from Poynter after a couple of minutes. Then they heard Teresa running back down the corridor toward them. Out of breath, she held out the laryngoscope to Dr. Poynter. He glanced at it in disgust; it was an old-fashioned model with a straight, right-angled blade. He switched the light on; the batteries were weak and the light flickered, but he didn't have any choice, so he put one hand behind Bracknell's neck, angling it upward, and put the laryngoscope in his mouth. All Poynter needed was one glimpse of the vocal cords so that he could slip the tube between them into the trachea. Anselm held out the tube, and Poynter snatched it, his hand shaking. He was lucky and got it in on the first try.

Within a few moments the procession was on its way again, with Dr. Sachs pumping the balloon to reinflate Bracknell's lungs.

Peter came alongside, walking fast. "You see why I didn't want him transferred?" he snarled at Poynter, who was limping along. "You probably did irreparable damage to Mr. Bracknell just then." Peter's voice was loud; he wanted everybody around to hear and remember what he'd said.

Poynter didn't reply; he was out of breath, his ankle was hurting, but he glanced angrily around at Peter.

Dr. Sachs, the peacemaker, said, "No problem, Dr. Delafield. Bracknell's heart didn't miss a beat throughout that episode. I don't think we lost any ground with him."

But Sachs and Poynter were already thinking in terms of damage control, and how they could minimize the impact of this nearly fatal accident when the press got to hear about it.

And Peter, walking along, holding Sandy's arm, was quickly going over the various ways he could use the incident to his own advantage.

A minute later, the stretcher was being hoisted on board the stretcher under the bright lights of the TV cameras. Sandy and Admiral Ellis clambered up the ramp, and the rotors started to turn even before the doors were closed.

Anselm, Peter, and Stefan started to walk back together into the hospital as soon as the helicopter had taken off, while Erica, who had had a piece of dust blown into her eye during the takeoff, was swallowed up by a crowd of media people, who all shouted at her simultaneously, demanding to know what was happening.

"Well, thank God that's over and done with," said Peter in a heartfelt voice when the helicopter noise had diminished enough for him to be heard.

Stefan stopped with his hand on the door and looked back at him with an incredulous expression. "Over? Dr. Delafield, are you serious?" He shook his head. "Let me tell you," he said, "this whole sorry mess isn't over. It's just beginning. And the first thing I suggest you do, both of you" he looked from Peter to Anselm—"is to contact your malpractice insurance carriers."

Irritably he went on when he saw Peter was about to interrupt. "I've already left a message for our hospital lawyer, and another for the hospital's insurers, and both of you should do the same. It's not that you're necessarily going to be sued," he told them. "The insurers have to be informed if there's even a possibility. You'll find that provision in your contract." Stefan's snide next comment showed how stressed out he was. "Ask Anselm," he said to Peter. "He knows all about that stuff."

Anselm went back up to the third floor to finish dictating his consultation and operative report on Denton Bracknell, and weariness hit him so hard that he had to pause from time to time, then play his words back on the machine so that he wouldn't lose track of what he'd been saying. It reminded him of his residency days, when he was so chronically tired that he functioned on automatic pilot for days, even weeks at a time.

Peter had gone home, and after Anselm made his last call into the ICU to check on Florence Gowan, who was stable and sleeping, he headed toward the emergency room. Walking through the deserted, dimly lit corridors, making a conscious effort to make as little noise as possible, he was aware of the early morning stillness of the hospital, and marveled at the weird contrast with the frantic activity there only a few hours before.

Thoughts that he was normally able to keep at bay kept flashing out of the dark at him, like enemy fighters in an arcade game. Thoughts about his childhood, life in New York, his former wife, thoughts that had been put down so many times they didn't usually bother to surface. Anselm had been an air force brat whose father was a pilot good enough to be in the Thunderbirds aerobatic team, and whose mother was a saddened, unsmiling elementary school teacher. For years they had moved from base to base, different schools every couple of years. Anselm hadn't minded, not that it would have mattered if he had. He had a vision of his father, like a snapshot inside his head, of an easygoing, loving, playful man, as good-looking and dashing as any Tolstoyan cavalry officer. His mother didn't appreciate the dashing bit, though, and they often had rows that lasted long after Anselm had gone to sleep, but he never knew exactly what or who they were about. The morning after one row, Anselm, aged ten, was out with his mother watching his father's team as they flew in practice over the airfield. The four planes roared past in formation as if glued together on an invisible blackboard, then went straight up in the air, glistening in the sunlight, the two outside planes swooping out in a fleur-de-lys, to rejoin and come hurtling soundlessly just above the main runway at close to the speed of sound, followed by the thundering roar of their afterburners, then up again, vertically, like four incredibly swift arrows piercing the sky. The next maneuver was a loop in tight formation, and the four aircraft, high silvery specks upside down in the sky, started to come down, getting bigger and bigger as they approached, swinging in a wide arc whose perigee was calculated to be over the center of the field. As the planes came diving out of the sky, getting closer and closer, Anselm could feel the tension in his mother as clearly as if she were screaming out loud. Then it happened. At the bottom of the loop, one of the aircraft disappeared. A great cloud of black smoke shot up from the ground, while the three remaining aircraft went vertically up into the sky again, still free, still alive. Anselm knew instantly that his father was gone, and a moment later they heard the sound of it, a deep thud that shook the ground, and Anselm felt his father's spirit leave this earth with it. His mother, holding his shoulder like a claw, said, "You'd better go inside, dear."

Anselm pushed that visceral remembrance from him, but the sound of his father's departing soul resounded in his brain, reverberating and echoing like a soft gong in the center of mirrors of sound.

Outside the hospital, the smell of the helicopter's kerosene was still in the air, hanging in invisible wisps around the landing pad, and Anselm headed for his car, thinking about the many times he'd left the hospital late when he was in New York, and remembered the wariness, the fear of muggings, that he had simply absorbed as part of his existence.

Latterly, he had been getting quite successful in his career there, with a smart office in Queens, an appointment at a prestigious hospital, and a beautiful wife. Mariana was a high-flying advertising exec with one of the Big Five agencies: dashing, imaginative, infuriating, unpredictable. They had met when a taxi driver had slammed her hand in the door of his vehicle, and in a panic took her to the emergency room at Bellevue Hospital, where Anselm happened to be working. Mariana came into that sordid and miserable place like a goddess visiting the nether regions, with blood coming through a silk Hermès scarf around her hand. Anselm had been entranced with her, partly because of the contrast she made with the bums and drunks that made up the usual clientele of that establishment. She, in turn, was enchanted with the handsome surgeon who took such good care of her, and she invited him to a party at her Madison Avenue office the next week. One thing led to another, and within a few weeks they were married, in spite of insistent warnings by Anselm's friends, including Peter. She's not for you, they said. She's flighty, self-engrossed, basically nuttier than a Bloomingdale's fruitcake, and certainly not a wife for an up-and-coming surgeon. Anselm found that life with Mariana was like being on a roller coaster running at five times the normal speed. About six months after they were married, he came home to their comfortable apartment to find it completely bare, without a stick of furniture on the shiny parquet floors. Mariana was sitting naked and cross-legged in the middle of the floor, meditating. Speechless, Anselm went to his study, which was also bare. Everything was gone, files, framed photographs, his desk, computer, and the Kashan rug his grandparents had given him when he finished his residency. It turned out that Mariana had decided their life needed a new start, so everything had to be changed, clothes, habits, everything. A truck had come from the Salvation Army and taken everything. The new furniture would be bamboo and leather, she said, and should arrive later in the week. In spite of such occasional seismic upheavals, Mariana was not insane—far from it. She was very successful in an extremely demanding job; it was simply that when she decided that something needed to be done, there were no half measures, and she would follow through to the logical conclusion, or sometimes beyond.

Anselm had wanted children, and at first Mariana thought it was a great idea. Then she changed her mind, saying that the demands of her job would make that quite impossible for several years, anyway.

Then, without warning, Anselm's life shattered and fell about him in tatters. All the support systems he'd either known about or expected to be there vanished, the hospital staff, his local medical society, his friends, even his wife.

Mariana quickly decided that all the adverse publicity surrounding Anselm's lawsuit was harming her career. When the leading tabloid ran a headline of DOCTOR DEATH with Anselm's photo filling the rest of the front page, Mariana moved out, went to live in her parents' East Side apartment, and didn't return his calls. The next he heard was from her lawyer, and he didn't contest the divorce. After the final hearing, when he was leaving the court, she came over to him and put her arms around his neck, kissed him, and said, "It was all for the best, darling, really. Of course I still love you."

She called a week later, complaining that he'd thrown her off so roughly on the steps of the courthouse that the bruises still hadn't healed.

Even now Mariana would call at the oddest times, sometimes from a party, or when she couldn't sleep. Once, when she had obviously drunk too much, she'd called to say she was coming back to him and was on her way up to Glenport, but she never showed up. Anselm knew Mariana had occasional men friends, but her job took up most of her time and energy. And from time to time the vision of Mariana's elegant person, long-legged and model-slim, would come unbidden to disturb him. But her calls were getting weirder each time, and Anselm wondered how she still managed to do her job.

For a couple of minutes he sat immobile in the bucket seat of his Triumph, bone-tired and rattled by the events of the evening. Then he started the engine and drove home.

When he had first come to Glenport, Anselm had rented an apartment for a few weeks, then bought a small house not too far from the hospital. He collected a few pieces of furniture here and there, a bed, a table, a desk, two lamps, and a couple of filing cabinets. Later, he bought three rugs at a going-out-of-business sale at Touloukian's, a Kashan and two Afghans. He went to an auction with Peter and Susan, and came home with a few colorful, ready-framed prints of local scenes. It was the kind of house that brought to the boil all the motherly and homemaking instincts in women, but he liked its simple, almost monastic atmosphere, and resisted several efforts at turning it into a home "that he would be more comfortable in."

And now his house felt cold, dark, and empty, just like his life had become. He wondered how Denton Bracknell was faring, but his clinical experience and instincts told him that it would be a rocky course at best.

He looked at the telephone for a long moment, thinking about Mariana and wondering if he would ever really get over her, then went to bed.

12

Admiral Ellis took Sandy directly into the passenger seating area in the helicopter's small rear compartment, which was separated from the main forward area by a bulkhead and a doorway covered by a faded green curtain. Ellis helped her fasten the canvas safety straps around her waist, then sat down in the seat next to her. He put on a pair of earphones plugged into a wall socket next to him, and pulled out a magazine, as if he did this kind of thing every day.

The main door closed with a thump, and a moment later the craft vibrated, the engine noise swelled to a howl, and Sandy felt the pressure rise in her ears. The front of the helicopter came up and they were off the ground. Through the small window Sandy got a brief glimpse of faces gazing up, the illuminated hospital buildings, the sharp shadows from the floodlights, and then it was dark.

At fifteen hundred feet, the front of the ship tilted down slightly, and they were on their way, heading along the Connecticut coast, destination Bethesda Naval Hospital, Maryland.

Sandy shivered in the chilly cabin. Admiral Ellis stopped reading and stared into space, listening to something that was being said into his earphones. Then he hung the phones on a hook next to the socket, undid his seat belt, and went forward. When he parted the curtains, Sandy got a quick glimpse of the forward compartment, which seemed huge compared with the cramped space at the back, but that was all she saw.

Ellis went up to Dr. Poynter, who was looking nervous and upset. He was injecting something into Bracknell's IV port, and Ellis noted that the patient was sweating, a little line of beads just below the hairline.

"He's just had a run of tachycardia," said Poynter, nodding at the monitor. The electrocardiogram tracing showed that Bracknell's heart rate was fast, with a suddenly irregular heart pattern every few seconds. "I've just given him some propranolol. That should control it."

Ellis went to the stretcher and opened Bracknell's right eye with his index finger. The eye was turned up, and only the white showed. Ellis opened it more to get a look at the pupil. "It's contracted," he said, and Poynter nodded. "The other one's the same," he said. "He's showed no sign of consciousness so far."

One of the corpsmen who had been busy at a piece of lab equipment situated on a bench a few feet forward came back with a printout in his hand.

"Patient's blood gases, sir. His oxygen saturation's down again, and his CO_2's climbing."

Poynter took the sheet, scanned it, then passed it to Ellis. "He's getting acidotic," he said, knowing that Ellis wasn't too familiar with this kind of problem. He stuck a finger on the sheet. "See, his bicarb's down."

"Sir," said the corpsman, a slim young man with crewcut blond hair. He pointed at the monitor screen. Poynter looked up. Bracknell's heart rate had suddenly accelerated and was now running at 174 beats per minute.

"God damn," said Poynter, staring at the screen and trying to make out what kind of tachycardia

Bracknell had been struck with this time. "That's just what we needed right now."

"Is that supraventricular, sir?" asked the corpsman.

"Probably, yes, I think so." The rate was so fast that it was difficult to be sure. "Get a printout, and let's give him some more propranolol."

"His pressure's up," said Ellis. The indicator was showing 210/155, a dangerously high blood pressure. A few moments later, just when the corpsman was sticking the needle of the syringe into the IV port, Bracknell's heart rate suddenly went back to normal.

Poynter sighed with relief. "You see," he said to the corpsman, pointing at his syringe, "if you'd injected that one minute earlier, we'd all have said what great stuff propranolol is."

They watched their patient for a few more minutes, while the other corpsman checked the blood pressure manually.

The curtain moved, and Dr. Sachs appeared from the rear compartment.

"How's it going?" he asked.

"Nothing much in your area of interest," Poynter told him. "Do you want to check his pupils?" he asked, deferring to the neurologist.

Sachs shrugged. "Not really," he said.

"Funny, isn't it?" said Poynter, relaxing momentarily. "If this was just anybody, he'd have probably been made DNR yesterday, and he'd be dead by now."

"Nobody this important ever gets made Do Not Resuscitate," replied Sachs, becoming philosophical. "The more important you get, the less likely you are to die in peace."

"Oh, Jesus," said Poynter, who was looking at the monitor, and the same moment the monitor alarm went off. "He's in V-tach," he shouted at Ellis, although the admiral could see for himself the frighteningly fast heart rate of ventricular tachycardia, a herald of ventricular fibrillation, a potentially fatal disorder of the heart's action.

"We're going to use the defibrillator," Poynter shouted at the corpsman over the noise of the engine. He pulled the flat round metal paddles down from their niche by the defibrillator. "Check the charge."

The corpsman peered up at the small dial on the instrument. "Fully charged, sir."

Ellis found a tube of electrode jelly and put a big blob on each side of Bracknell's white chest.

Poynter held the paddles out. "Put some on these."

Admiral Ellis did so, then backed out of the way. The alarm was still making the high-pitched howl that put his teeth on edge; Bracknell's heart rate was now 220 ineffective beats per minute.

"Stand back, everybody!" Poynter put one of the flat metal paddles on each side of Bracknell's chest, and everybody stood away from the metal parts of the stretcher.

Gritting his teeth, Poynter pressed the red button, and Bracknell's entire body jerked as the current shot through his chest. A moment later, the defibrillator started to make a high, whining sound as the capacitors recharged.

Everybody looked at the monitor. During the fraction of a second when the current had been passing through Bracknell, the line of the EKG had blown right off the screen, and it took a few moments to come back.

The heart rate was extremely irregular now, with abnormal extra beats every few moments.

"He's still in V-tach," said Sachs.

"I'm going to shock him again," said Poynter. "For God's sake, somebody switch off that alarm!" He had to wait a few moments longer for the recharge current to build up. The ready light went on. There were two round red marks on Bracknell's chest where the electrodes had been placed, and Poynter chose two different locations. He didn't want Bracknell to have to cope with second-degree burns on top of everything else.

The second shock resulted in another, weaker convulsion, and the wait for the EKG to come back on the monitor seemed to last forever.

"We have a straight line," reported Dr. Sachs, who could see the monitor better than Poynter.

Poynter was sweating hard now.

"Adrenalin," he said. "with the long intracardiac needle."

The corpsman handed him a large syringe with a needle about six inches long. Poynter, a Catholic, resisted a strong urge to cross himself, and pushed the needle up and under Bracknell's ribs, aiming for the left ventricle of the heart. He pulled on the plunger of the syringe, and dark blood came back easily.

"I'm in!" Poynter took a deep breath and injected the Adrenalin straight into Bracknell's heart.

Realistically this was their last shot, the very last thing they could do to salvage their patient.

While they waited for the medication to work, Poynter and Sachs watched the monitor. At this point there was nothing else for them to do.

Admiral Ellis, who had stayed out of the way for most of the resuscitation attempt, came forward, and Poynter turned to him.

"We're in very deep trouble here, sir," he said, his voice harsh with fatigue. Keeping an eye on the monitor, he explained the events of the last few minutes.

They tried one more time to revive him with external cardiac compression, but twelve minutes later it was decided finally to abandon the struggle. At 0213 Eastern Standard Time, Friday the 29th of April, Dr. Poynter pronounced Denton Bracknell dead.

"I'll call the White House," said Ellis, glancing at the communications center behind the pilot's cabin. Then, reluctantly, he added, "I guess I'll have to go back there and tell his wife too."

PART
TWO

13

Anselm was wakened at just after four on that Friday morning by Stefan Olson, who wearily informed him that Denton Bracknell had died on the way to Bethesda. After that, Anselm lay awake in bed, thinking and turning over every aspect of the case. He had seen and taken care of many patients with the same general kind of problem, but certain aspects of Denton's illness confused him. Could Bracknell have been suffering from some undiscovered additional condition, or had there been some sort of complication that he had missed? Anselm remembered William Casey, the former head of the CIA, whose fatal brain tumor had gone unnoticed for months, maybe years; Casey's secretaries had known he was sick before his doctors did. There were plenty of other cases Anselm knew about in which patients had an obvious condition that masked another, often more serious disease.

But Anselm had gone over Bracknell as carefully as he could, and Peter had known and taken care of him for years, so it seemed unlikely that they could have both missed something important.

Anselm finally got out of bed feeling anxious, irritable, and expecting serious repercussions from Bracknell's death. Not that it could turn into the kind of nightmare that the Andy Panneterio case in New

York had been, because the mob had controlled every
aspect of that case, although of course Anselm hadn't
known it at the time. Thinking about that, Anselm
called his medical malpractice insurance agent and left
a message in his voice mail.

Anselm arrived at the hospital just as the sun came
up over the Sound, and it looked red, baleful, and
foreboding.

It was obvious that everybody already knew what
had happened. In the emergency room, he ran into Pat
Mooney, who offered him a cup of coffee, which he
was happy to accept, and followed her into the lounge.
Emily Prosser, the student nurse, was sitting there.
She gulped down the coffee she'd been drinking, gave
Anselm a scared, wide-eyed look, and almost ran out
of the room.

"Everybody's upset about what happened last
night," explained Pat. "I'm really sorry. We all know
that you did everything you could. Like they say, you
can't win them all."

"We all did what we had to do," said Anselm.
"And everybody here in the ER did a great job." He
put a reassuring hand on Pat's elbow. "Don't worry,
everything's going to be just fine," Even to himself,
his voice lacked conviction.

"I had breakfast with a bunch of other nurses," said
Pat. "Most of them, the ones who've worked with you,
were on your side. It may not be much comfort to you,
but I just wanted to mention it."

"Let me tell you what actually happened," said Anselm, suspecting that all kinds of rumors were floating
around the hospital. "Mr. Bracknell's problem was
simply too far advanced for us to be able to save him.
We operated on him because we didn't have any option. I'm sure you know that this kind of situation crops
up from time to time, and there's nothing we can do

to foresee it. The only real difference is that this guy happened to be a very important person.''

The door opened and a nurse poked her head in to tell Pat she was needed in one of the cubicles.

''That's what we figured, Dr. Harris.'' Pat started to move toward the door. ''Lucille was there, and she said there was a great fight in the OR between you and Dr. Burton, but nobody believed her. Anyway. if there's anything I can do, let me know.''

In the doctors' lounge, Dr. Burton was talking animatedly to a group of physicians gathered around him, but fell silent when Anselm walked by.

Then Anselm's beeper went off; Stefan Olson wanted to see him in his office as soon as possible.

Stefan looked ten years older than the day before, and he hadn't shaved, which didn't help matters. But he sounded wide awake and in control. ''Dr. Harris, I'm asking everyone involved in the Bracknell case to put in a detailed report,'' he said. ''And that goes for you and Dr. Delafield too, of course.''

''Everything I've got to say is already dictated,'' replied Anselm. ''The consultation report, progress notes, pre-op note, operation notes, everything.''

''Good,'' said Stefan. ''I'll tell the records people to type them up as a top priority.'' He hesitated for a second. ''Do you want to . . . review or possibly re-dictate any of that material? I mean, in the light of everything that's happened?''

''No, I don't.'' Anselm stared at Stefan. ''And if I did, somebody would be sure to find the original, and as they say, that would lead to one whole lot of trouble in the OK Corral.''

Stefan shrugged. ''Whatever you say. Everybody was tired and under a great deal of stress yesterday, so things could have got said and written that might come out sounding different today, or not truly reflecting the state of affairs at the time.''

"Tell that to Philip Burton," said Anselm.

"I have his report right here," said Stefan wearily, touching a folder on his desk. "It's all typed up already, so there's not much I can do about that."

Anselm took the elevator to the ICU, his mind turning to Florence Gowan. So far she'd done well, although she was far from out of the woods.

His pager went off again. This time it was his insurance agent returning his call. Anselm told him briefly what had happened. No, he hadn't received any subpoena, he said, he was just telling him about the possibility of a suit, as required in the insurance policy. As he spoke, he felt he was wasting his time; he hadn't made any errors and the chances of any malpractice suit based on Bracknell's treatment seemed so remote as to be laughable. But Stefan hadn't seemed to think so, and neither did the agent. He'd let the appropriate people know, he said, and asked Anselm meanwhile not to discuss the case with anyone.

The ICU was unusually quiet; only a third of the curtained cubicles were occupied. Anselm smiled at the two nurses sitting at the long desk facing the cubicles, crossed the room, and pulled the curtain on Cubicle 3, where Florence lay in the bed, her eyes closed. A plastic tube in her nose made an occasional gurgling noise when the automatic suction system activated, and the green oxygen mask sat slightly askew on her face, making a faint hissing.

Coming quietly into the cubicle, Anselm checked the containers at the foot of the bed, then went up to the head and gently adjusted the oxygen mask.

Florence opened her eyes. Anselm smiled, sat down in the chair next to the head of the bed, and took her hand, taking care not to disturb the IV needle taped to her wrist. Her hand was puffy, and Anselm noticed that her face was very puffy too.

Almost instinctively he checked her pulse: it was

fast and thready. He looked up at the IV pole and the clear IV tubing running down from the bottle. The control was wide open, and the solution was running in very fast. The monitor behind the bed confirmed that her pulse rate was higher than he had expected.

A sixth sense told him that Florence was in imminent danger, and he hesitated, because right now he didn't know from what. They had already taken the blood-pressure catheter out of the artery in her arm, so Anselm grabbed a cuff, wrapped it around Florence's forearm, and checked the pressure. It was 80 over 25. Anselm stared at the mercury column for a moment, trying to figure out what it all meant, then it hit him. Leaving the cuff where it was, he took the stethoscope out of his pocket and listened quickly to her chest. Sure enough, he heard telltale crackling sounds on both sides of her lungs. Anselm shut down the IV to the barest trickle, got up, still very quietly, smiled at Florence, who smiled back uncertainly, perhaps feeling the urgency about his movements.

"I'll be right back," he said.

Jasmine Wu, the tiny head nurse, was seated at the long counter, working on the next month's on-call schedule.

"Florence's blood pressure is way down," said Anselm very calmly.

"Right." Jasmine looked up for a second. "Dr. Delafield was in a half hour ago. He noticed her low pressure and said to push her IV fluids. We're giving her a quick thousand mls of Ringer's lactate to bring her pressure up again, then we'll cut back on the rate."

Anselm turned to pick up Florence's aluminum-covered chart from the rack and started to thumb quickly through the medications section, paying particular attention to the medications Florence had received before and after the operation and to the urine output during the same period.

"Damn," he said quietly.

Jasmine stared at him.

"Florence is about to go into shock," he told her. "She was on high doses of steroids when she came in, and according to this"—he tapped the chart—"she hasn't had any since. Can you confirm that?"

"There certainly hasn't been any ordered since she came in here, Dr. Harris," said Jasmine, her face getting paler.

"Give her four hundred milligrams of IV hydrocortisone *immediately*," he said. His voice was still very quiet, but there was no mistaking the urgency in it. Jasmine practically flew off her stool to the drug closet, and came back with a small syringe and an ampoule of clear fluid. Her hand was shaking because she understood the implications of what Dr. Harris was saying; when Florence had come into the hospital, she had been taking high doses of steroids, which had been discontinued before her surgery, precisely the time when her requirements for the drug would increase.

"Here, give it to me." Anselm's calm, take-charge attitude reassured Jasmine, and she handed him the syringe and ampoule, and watched as he drew up the medication into the barrel of the syringe.

"I've almost shut down her IV fluids," he said. "It's set at keep-open. Right now she's on the brink of going into congestive heart failure because there's about three liters of excess fluid swilling around inside her."

"Oh, my" was all Jasmine could say.

"So as soon as you've put this in," he said, "we'll start her on a mannitol infusion to get her urine output back up before she goes into kidney failure," he said, handing her the syringe. "We don't need that extra complication."

Jasmine got one of the other nurses to help her set up the mannitol infusion, a powerful diuretic used to increase kidney function. Then, in his usual unhurried way, he went back to Cubicle 3 and sat down on the chair while Jasmine emptied the first syringe into one of the IV ports.

"What's happening?" Florence whispered.

"Right now we're giving you a shot of hydrocortisone, and that's going to make you feel better," he replied. "And also you've got too much fluid on board, so we're going to give you a diuretic that'll make you pee it out."

"But I can't get up to go," said Florence, alarmed.

"There's a catheter in your bladder," replied Anselm, smiling. "So there'll be no effort required on your part."

He sat with Florence for over an hour, talking to her quietly from time to time, waiting until he was sure the medications were taking effect. She fell asleep after a while, her blood pressure started gradually to return to normal, and the urine collector hanging from the end of the bed filled rapidly and had to be changed.

But when Anselm finally stood up and tiptoed out to the desk, intending to write instructions for Florence's future medications, his expression hardened. When it was first decided that Florence needed surgery, Peter had clearly said he'd take care of all her medications, a normal responsibility for the attending internist to take. He had carelessly omitted to order her most important medication, hydrocortisone, and because of that Florence had almost died.

Anselm paused, his hand on the ICU telephone, thinking how best to deal with the situation. If it had been anyone else, he knew he would haul that physician mercilessly over the coals, but with Peter . . . Anselm decided not to use the telephone; he'd find Peter and have it out with him in person.

14

The next day, in the twentieth-floor offices of Collier, McDowell and Stern, Valerie came into the office and had barely taken off her coat when she was summoned to the boardroom by Andrew Collier's secretary. Collier was the firm's founder and senior partner.

"This is it," thought Valerie, wondering how she would be able to take actually being fired. She could feel her heart beating fast as she went along the corridor and quickly reviewed in her mind the crucial conversation she'd had with Elliott Naughton, Patrick's old buddy from the State Department. Valerie had tracked him down to his office in the U.N. building in New York, and Elliott was delighted to hear from her. After exchanging their news, Valerie coaxed him into giving her the information she wanted on Ralph Stern, but first she had to explain the urgency of the matter.

Neil McDowell and Ralph Stern were sitting together at the long table in the boardroom. Neil was looking very grim, and unsmilingly watched Valerie approach. Ralph stared straight ahead of him and said nothing.

"Andrew should be back in a few moments, Miss Morse." Neil's voice was curt. "He had to take a telephone call."

"Good," said Valerie, looking not at all put out by

their frosty demeanor. "That gives the three of us a couple of moments to talk."

Ralph looked up, surprised at her cheerful tone. Surely the woman knew that they were about to make her walk the plank.

Valerie didn't know how long she had, so she went directly to the heart of the matter. "I was just now talking to an old friend of yours," she said to Ralph. He didn't respond, so she went on, sounding relaxed and conversational. "Elliott Naughton, in New York. I'm sure you remember him. He sends you his regards."

"I don't think I know anyone of that name," replied Ralph stiffly. He shuffled some papers in his hand and looked at the door, wishing that Andrew would hurry up and put an end to this uncomfortable business.

"Oh, of course you do," said Valerie with a laugh, but her voice was sharp and insistent. "How could you possibly forget him? He was second secretary at the embassy in London when you . . . ran into him."

Ralph turned toward her, and a blotchy flush appeared on his cheeks. The left corner of his mouth started to twitch. "You know him?" he said. His voice was strained, and he licked his lips and stared at Valerie as if she were some sort of witch from Hell.

"He's coming up to spend a few days of R and R here," went on Valerie blithely. She knew that she had only a few moments to ram her message home quickly and effectively before Andrew came back. "He said he'll fill me in on the details of the story then." She gazed fixedly at Ralph to let him know that she already knew the broad outlines, and was prepared to divulge them if necessary.

Neil was looking interestedly from Ralph to Valerie and back, sensing a major clash between them, and also observing that Valerie was winning. Ralph was tensed in his chair, and he glowered silently at Valerie as if unable to decide whether to physically attack her or throw up. He moistened his lips again and started to say something, but at that moment Andrew came in, dressed as usual in a conservative pinstripe suit made for him in London's Savile Row. He nodded politely at Valerie, then sat down at the head of the table.

"All right, then," said Andrew, speaking rather abruptly to Ralph, "let's go on with it. You had a major problem with some work that Miss Morse did for you, is that right?"

Ralph could barely disguise his fury and frustration, but under Andrew's eye and Valerie's cool stare, he had to say something.

"Actually, there's been a mistake," he muttered, his eyes shifting to the papers on the table in front of him. "I was under the impression that . . . Well, I didn't get all the papers, and I thought that a lot of material hadn't been done, but in fact . . ." Ralph swallowed. "It had been done, but I didn't find that out until . . . just a short time ago."

Andrew frowned and stared at Ralph. "You mean that you don't have a complaint after all?" His voice became acid. "Yet you called this special meeting?" He caught himself and looked hard at the three of them, one after the other. Andrew was a very smart lawyer and could see that in some way Ralph had been bested, and probably by Valerie herself. "I see. Can I assume then that you are now quite satisfied with Attorney Morse's work?"

"Yes," mumbled Ralph, in torment.

"Was the work done well, would you say?" asked Andrew, rubbing it in. "How would you assess it? Since you called this meeting, Ralph, it's only fair to Miss Morse that you give the evaluation in her presence. Was her work fair, good, or exceptional?"

There was a long pause, during which Valerie thought Ralph was going to cough up blood.

"I have to say exceptional," he said in a low voice. "Really very good, indeed."

"Good," replied Andrew. "Then we can use this occasion to compliment Attorney Morse. Ever since she joined us her work has been recognized to be excellent, wouldn't you say, Neil?"

Neil McDowell's eyes flicked at Ralph, then at Valerie. He grinned mischievously and stretched his long legs under the table. "Absolutely," he said. "Valerie's a star."

"Was there anything else you wished to discuss?" asked Andrew.

The two men shook their heads in unison.

"Then this meeting is adjourned *sine die,* said Andrew. He stood up and turned to Valerie. "Miss Morse," he said, "There's a matter I'd like to discuss with you in my office, if you have a few moments, please."

Andrew had the best-situated office in the suite, located on the southeast corner of the building, with a splendid prospect of the university campus on one side and the harbor and the Sound on the other.

"Do sit down, Miss Morse," he said in his studied, formal way. He had a wide reputation as a tenacious and aggressive corporate lawyer, but now he looked more like an ambassador, with his starched French cuffs, his thick, carefully styled white hair, and immaculately manicured hands.

"I was talking earlier with Judge Haynes, and he told me how well you handled the Kasper case. Well done."

Andrew hesitated for a second and glanced at a pad in front of him. "This morning I received a call from Paul Arrow, at Professional Insurers. No doubt you've read in the papers about what they're now calling the Bracknell case. PI is the insurance carrier for the Glenport surgeon involved, a Dr. Anselm Harris, and he has informed them that the case had a number of serious complications. That's a routine early warning system in their contract; it doesn't necessarily mean a suit will be filed.'' He gazed thoughtfully out the window for a moment, as if making up his mind. ''You may know that we're under contract to PI, and if the case materializes, I'd like you to handle it.''

Andrew held up his hand when he saw Valerie about to protest. ''I know what you're going to say. You're not an expert in medical malpractice. I know that, although you handled yourself very well with the Kasper case. I don't want you to feel we're throwing you to the wolves either,'' he went on, apparently reading her thoughts. ''I've already spoken to Dexter Milne, who as you know handles most of our malpractice litigation, and he assured me he'll be happy to give you a guiding hand if and when you need one.''

Andrew waited for Valerie to say something, but she decided to keep quiet until she had a chance to talk to Milne about the case. Dexter was a friend of hers, and a good lawyer who would give her solid advice.

''So I want you to be ready if this case does materialize,'' said Andrew. ''Paul is sending all the information by messenger, so you should have it some time today.''

Valerie watched her boss, a slight frown on her face, wondering why he had selected her for this case. Medical malpractice was not an area in which she had expertise, and she knew that if she took the case, she'd be going up against a team of crackerjack plaintiff's attorneys, part of whose task would be to eat her alive.

''Thanks, Mr. Collier,'' she said, not wishing to commit herself until she'd had a chance to think about it. ''I'll certainly be happy to go over the papers.''

A few moments later, Valerie was heading back to her office. She knew that Andrew would prefer his firm to prosecute rather than defend a malpractice suit, but a prosecution would have gone to a much more experienced senior attorney, because there would have been much more money at stake. Defending a malpractice suit was another matter; the insurance company paid the attorneys by the hour. There was no fat settlement or judgment to be shared with the plaintiff when it was all over, so law firms rarely put their most experienced and highest-priced attorneys on the case.

In the back of her mind, Valerie had a disquieting question; although Ralph had backed down at the meeting, Andrew surely knew that Ralph wanted her out of the firm, and Ralph was obviously far more important to them than she was. So why had she been put in charge of defending what looked like a major malpractice suit?

Sandy Bracknell stayed with friends in Georgetown and returned to Glenport on Monday. She refused the president's personal offer to have her flown back by helicopter. No, thank you, she said firmly, thinking it would be a terrible waste of public money.

Her parents drove up to meet her at the airport, and Sandy recognized the car first; they had brought her own yellow Toyota.

"The reporters have been a real nuisance," said Beth, Sandy's mother, as she drove out through the terminal exit. "They were here on Friday, knocking at the door, pretending to deliver stuff and shouting questions at us from the street." She was really offended; when Denton had been made a special presidential adviser with some fanfare two years before, the reporters had come to talk to them, but their attitude at that time had been deferential and polite.

"They'll be gone by tomorrow," said Sandy, who knew the ways of the media. "And it'll be just photographers at the funeral."

"Where's Denton?" asked her father suddenly from

the backseat. His clear blue eyes were vacant, and he looked at Sandy as if he were surprised to hear the words that had come out of his mouth.

"He's dead, Daddy," replied Sandy quietly. She turned around to look at her father. "He died early on Friday morning."

But he wasn't listening; he was looking out the window at the sumac bushes sliding past on the side of the road as the car drove along. The leaves were just beginning to appear.

"Dad's no better," said Beth in a quiet voice. "We . . . I was so shocked . . . Do you know what happened? I mean about Denton?"

"He had a cardiac arrest in the helicopter," said Sandy. "The navy doctors were very nice . . ." She hesitated.

Beth glanced over at her questioningly.

"They said they'd come on the scene too late to save him," said Sandy slowly.

"Oh dear," said Beth. "I had a bad feeling about Denton going to Glenport Hospital. What else did they say?"

"One of them, Admiral Ellis, said that the damage had already been done before his team got there, and that maybe if they'd got to him earlier they could have done something. But he was very upset with Denton dying, and—"

"Damage? The damage had already been done? Did he mean from his illness, or do you think he meant damage from the surgery? Because—"

"I don't know, Mom. He said they would be doing an autopsy, and they'd have a better idea after that."

There was a silence for a few moments. Beth's lips gradually compressed as various possibilities passed through her mind. Like a goodly number of other citizens of Glenport, Beth had her doubts about the level of care people could expect at the hands of the doctors who worked at their local hospital.

"Sandy, I think you should see a lawyer," she said firmly.

Sandy stared out the window for a long time. "I was just thinking about that, Mom."

"Have you made any decisions about the funeral?" asked Beth.

"Well, it's not going to be Arlington, I can tell you that," replied Sandy.

That had been the president's suggestion; he'd tactfully indicated that if that was what she wanted, she wouldn't have to be concerned with funeral directors or any of the other arrangements.

Her father started to hum quietly, but there was no recognizable tune to it.

"We'll bury him on the island," said Sandy, making up her mind. "He liked the wind and the solitude, and the cemetery faces the ocean."

After they got back to her parents' home, a green two-story wooden house near the center of Glenport, Sandy made a few phone calls, then sat with a legal pad at the dining room table. She felt overwhelmed by everything that had been happening, and had trouble concentrating on her task. Her tired mind was like a kaleidoscope, and her thoughts flitted about, touching down on different moments of her life, the people she'd known before and after she met Denton, her home on the island.

She saw the house clearly in her mind's eye, a discreet, comfortably luxurious home built on the edge of a sheet of smooth rock that sloped gently down to the water's edge, where their sloop was moored to a red buoy twenty yards from the shore. On the opposite side of the house, a curved pool was separated from the house by a wide, paved patio, overlooked by the windows of her studio.

The day that Denton had been taken ill, she'd watched him climb down from the helicopter and stump the fifty yards to the house, looking like a tank barreling toward her through the fog. At the door he put down his bag and hugged her in his bear-like grip, downed a quick shot of scotch, and asked how her painting was progressing. They'd gone upstairs together, arm in arm, through the master bedroom into the studio, where a heavy, paint-splattered tarpaulin covered most of the floor. They went over to her old wooden easel in the middle of the bright, sunlit room, and Denton looked at the painting for a long time, taking in the mermaid sitting on a partially submerged rock, her gaze fixed longingly on a distant, bright, crowded promenade, an arm placed protectively around her two merchildren, a boy and a girl. The painting, Denton said after a while, reminded him of Marc Chagall, but with the kind of tougher, decisive overtones of a Diego Rivera. Sandy was pleased that he liked it, but Denton fell rather silent afterward, no doubt because his headache was already starting to bother him.

Sandy's mother came in carrying a mug of coffee and a danish on a flowery plate that she placed in front of Sandy.

"Did you decide what to do?"

"I called a lawyer in Hartford. He specializes in medical malpractice cases."

"Oh, yes? Who is it?"

"His name's Norman Hartman."

"You know this man?" Beth looked curiously at her daughter.

"No, I got his name from a friend."

"When's your appointment?" she asked.

"Two o'clock," replied Sandy. "He wants to see me today."

"You know how to get there?" asked her mother.

"Sure. It's in downtown Hartford. I even know the office building."

"I hope he can do something," said Beth.

Sandy nodded and looked at the list on her pad.

"Are you leaving now?" asked her mother.

"I have a couple of things to do first. For one thing, I need to go down and talk to Peter," she said in what her mother thought was a strange voice.

"Why?"

Sandy shrugged.

"Peter, Peter, Peter," said her mother, without heat but with an undercurrent of annoyance. "Everything always comes back to Peter. You've never got over him, have you?" She went into the kitchen. "Do you want any more coffee?" she called out. "I'm making some for your father."

"No, thanks. Maybe I should phone first . . ." She looked at her watch and changed her mind. "He should be in his office by now, I'll just go there." She was speaking almost to herself, but Beth heard her.

"Do you think that's a good idea?" she asked, coming back in from the kitchen. She wiped her hands on her apron. "I mean, going down there. Everybody knew about him and you."

"They also know I've been married for years," replied Sandy sharply. She stood up. "Anyway, all I want from him is some answers about what happened to Den."

Rose Beckwith, Peter's receptionist, called through when Sandy arrived, and a moment later Peter hurried out of one of the examining rooms. He took Sandy's arm and led her into his office. Sandy stayed there about ten minutes, and they both looked very grim when they emerged. Peter's goodbye was curt, and Sandy didn't reply.

15

Denton Bracknell's autopsy was carried out in the pathology department of Bethesda Naval Hospital on Monday afternoon. The routine for VIP autopsies was to have two pathologists of equal seniority present. Both would sign the report, and any disagreement on the findings would be referred to a third pathologist for mediation.

The room was huge, almost too brightly lit by flat panel lights that covered most of the ceiling. The walls were white, spotless, as impersonal as an empty refrigerator. A row of eight stainless steel tables stretched down the middle of the room, each with its draining channels around the pedestal, its water hose, sinks, sound-activated microphone, and video camera suspended from a ceiling mount.

There was only one table occupied, the one nearest the main entrance door. The two pathologists, both senior navy captains, were talking together in low tones next to a large glass-enclosed instrument closet, discussing the detailed technique they would use for this case.

"I'd really like to get both carotids out in one piece," said Jay Penn, who was older but slightly junior in rank to his colleague, Barry Herkheimer. Dr. Penn had a pale, round, academic-looking face, thin black hair, and thick black-rimmed glasses that magnified his eyes and gave him a staring look. "But it's technically such a problem, I don't know if we can do it."

"We developed a method for doing that a few years back," replied Herkheimer, an intense, sallow-skinned man who also wore heavy glasses, "but we rarely need to use it. The tech enlarges the carotid opening with a small electric saw, and then you can pull the entire carotid arterial system through with it when you lift the brain out."

"Okay," said Jay doubtfully. "As long as he doesn't mess up the artery with his saw. He'll be right next to it."

"Arno knows what he's doing," replied Herkheimer confidently. "I trained him myself."

They turned to look at the body. Denton Bracknell was lying naked on his back, both arms slightly flexed, as were both knees. The IVs and tapes were still in the arms, the tubing having been cut a couple of inches from the cannulas. Early post-mortem changes had already occurred: the skin in the back and posterior thighs had a purplish discoloration where the blood had pooled in the small capillary vessels of the skin.

The swing doors opened, and Arno, the technician, came in, wearing a long white rubber apron and boots. He was a thin, grizzled man of about sixty, slightly bent, with a gray crewcut showing around his white cap.

Herkheimer looked at the clock. "Ready?" he asked.

"Yes, sir," replied Arno. "Commander Fox is out there keeping the media at bay. You wanna start with the abdomen and chest?"

"Yes. When you're done with that we need the carotids out in one piece, so we'll do the head and neck last, after we're done with the rest, okay?"

Arno nodded and went over to his instrument table.

"You want to do the external appearances?" Herkheimer asked Penn.

"Sure." He went up to the microphone, keeping his eyes on Bracknell's body, scanning it. "The body has been previously identified as that of Denton Bracknell, a federal employee," he said, speaking into the mike. "It is that of a male subject who looks approximately the stated age. Two circular areas, each approximately three inches across, of second-degree burns are noted on the anterior and left lateral chest wall, consistent with the recent use of defibrillator electrodes. A recent surgical incision is noted in the right neck. Sutures are intact . . ."

While Penn was dictating in the time-honored monotone used on these occasions, Arno pulled on a pair of thick rubber gloves, placed a wooden cutting board on the edge of the sink, and started to arrange his instruments tidily on it. A long-handled scalpel with a large blade was placed next to a set of three bone cutters of different sizes, an electric saw with a series of blades, a giant pair of black-handled scissors attached with a metal chain to the autopsy table, and a selection of clamps and forceps almost as impressive as those in an operating room. Arno then stood back impassively and listened while Penn went on with his careful description of the body's external appearance. Arno wasn't permitted to touch the body until this essential part of the autopsy had been completed.

As soon as Penn finished, he stood away from the table and Arno moved in. He picked up a heavy scalpel and started at the notch at the top of Bracknell's breastbone and made a long incision down the front of the chest, straight down to the lower end of the abdomen. A small red light on the video camera above them showed that it was recording the entire procedure.

Using the same scalpel, Arno undermined the skin on the chest wall and swiftly peeled it back, first on one side, then the other, until the red muscles and yellow-white ribs and knuckles of cartilage were visible. When he had exposed enough tissue, Arno turned to pick up a long-handled bone cutter that looked somewhat like garden shears, then cut the ribs on both sides, and opened the chest by removing the breastbone with the attached rib segments. He was careful to separate the delicate underlying tissues and blood vessels, which could easily be torn by a clumsy movement. Arno placed the removed section of ribs on the side of the table, leaning it against the body.

Turning his attention to the abdomen, Arno deepened the central cut, then looked up at Herkheimer, who nodded and pulled on his own pair of gloves before taking over. With the heavy scissors Herkheimer deepened Arno's incision, made an opening in the midline just big enough to take two fingers. Holding the front wall of the abdomen up with two fingers of his left hand, Herkheimer cut along the tissues, opening up the entire abdomen from the chest to the top of the pubic bone.

Without a word, for they had done this many times together in the past, Arno and Herkheimer put ties around the gray, floppy intestine below the stomach and at the rectum, then cut it before removing it in its entirety to the draining board.

"Hard as a rock," said Herkheimer, looking over at Penn. He was feeling the cut edge of the main artery to the intestine where he had severed it close to the duodenum. "Take a look at this."

Penn looked into the body cavity. The artery, normally soft and rubbery, was thickened and as stiff as a pencil, and the central cavity was narrowed to a fraction of its normal width.

"The aorta's almost as bad," reported Penn after

feeling around for a few moments. He pressed a button to inactivate the microphone for a moment. "Look at this," he said to Herkheimer, pointing at the series of stiff, thickened arteries coming off the aorta. "This guy was arteriosclerotic from one end of his body to the other."

Arno came back from the sink, where he had been draining the intestine of its contents. They were all so inured to the smell of this procedure that none of them even noticed.

"Ready?" asked Arno.

Penn nodded and stepped back. Arno slipped a hand between the diaphragm and the liver and pulled it down, while he cut the retaining ligaments with a knife in the other hand. The liver came out with a loud slurping noise, and Arno put it on the draining board, watched by Penn and Herkheimer.

"Big, huh?" said Penn, looking at the large, stiff-looking organ.

"FBI says he drank a bit," said Herkheimer. "About a bottle of scotch over a weekend."

Penn shrugged but didn't say anything.

Arno was back at the table with his knife, carefully cutting the hardened arteries an inch above the aorta. Then he reached up into the neck and cut the windpipe and esophagus under the skin.

Grasping the lower cut ends with his gloved hands, Arno eased the heart and lungs out of the chest, all in one practiced, effortless movement, snip-snipping with his scissors at strands of tissues that resisted this forcible extrusion.

"The externally visible coronary arteries are encased in fatty tissue," dictated Herkheimer a few minutes later as, with Bracknell's heart in his hand, he examined the vessels coursing around the outside of the organ. He turned the heart around in his hand. "There are no outward signs of myocardial infarction,'' he went on, after checking for any softness and discoloration in the heart muscle that would have signaled that Bracknell had suffered a heart attack.

Meanwhile, Arno made an incision in the scalp from behind the ear all the way around the back to the other ear, and pulled the scalp and hair over the top of the skull so that it finished covering his face and leaving the skull bare. When they heard the high-pitched whine of the saw, the pathologists knew that Arno was busy cutting the top off the skull. Soon the brain would be out, with the attached arteries coming out with it. That was the moment they were both waiting for; all the other stuff, unless something really surprising turned up, like discovering an unsuspected tumor somewhere in the body, was merely setting the scene.

Before leaving Glenport, Bracknell's entire chart had been Xeroxed and lay, with copies of the ultrasound tests, in a tan-colored government manila folder on a desk near the door. A copy of Anselm's dictated and hastily typed operative report had been faxed to Bethesda, and the stack of curling papers was now clipped to the outside of Bracknell's chart.

While Arno was working, Herkheimer went over to check something in the operative report, and Penn followed him. Herkheimer's tapping fingers left bloody smears on the edge of the paper.

''Those guys up in Glenport could be in really deep trouble,'' he said. ''If our guys had operated on Bracknell here and screwed up, they could have probably covered it up and got away with it, but if they screwed up in Glenport, Connecticut, that'll put them in the fifth circle in no time.''

There was a pause while Penn looked questioningly at Herkheimer with his dark, quick eyes. ''The fifth circle?'' he asked.

Herkheimer grinned, a touch of condescension on

his lips. "The fifth circle of Hell, my boy," he replied. "Haven't you read Dante?"

Penn shook his head, annoyed. "No, I haven't," he replied. "It wasn't required reading where I went to medical school."

"I'm sure you'd enjoy him," said Herkheimer, glancing back at the table. Arno was almost done. "The fifth circle is reserved for the wrathful and the morose. They tear each other to pieces, and all the time they're wallowing in shit up to their nostrils."

"Sounds like Washington politics," said Penn.

"Or maybe what happens to small-town surgeons who take on more than they can handle," replied Herkheimer.

"Ready," said Arno, looking around at them.

The two men walked back to the table, and Herkheimer slid a gloved hand under the front of the brain and carefully started to cut the various attached nerves that held it in place. Within five minutes, and with some help from Dr. Penn, who freed up the arteries in the neck, Herkheimer had the brain and the arteries that supplied it cupped in his hands.

Together they looked at the specimen: both carotid arteries were stiff and narrowed. The right carotid artery showed the surgical incision that Anselm had made. Penn laid the brain on the wooden cutting surface and carefully opened the artery. It was completely blocked for a distance of about two inches.

When they later examined the brain, they found a softening extending throughout much of the right side, indicating that the patient had suffered a major stroke as a result of the carotid blockage.

"Those guys are in deep shit, for sure," said Herkheimer, straightening up from the cutting table. "Bracknell was riddled with arteriosclerosis. They should never have operated on him."

"That carotid looks as if it had contracted around

the blockage,'' said Penn, looking carefully at the specimen. ''Maybe he got an arterial spasm, and for some reason that triggered the whole sequence of events.''

''Yeah, certainly could be,'' said Herkheimer, nodding. ''We should put that in the report.''

Behind them, Arno was sewing up Denton Bracknell's empty body cavity with a length of thick thread attached to a wicked-looking curved needle. On the stainless steel table beside him was a series of large glass jars containing Bracknell's brain, liver, and other organs, already carefully labeled. These would be retained for further microscopic examination in the lab.

''I'll call Admiral Ellis,'' said Herkheimer. ''He's waiting to hear what we found.''

''I'll bet he is,'' replied Penn.

They both grinned. They'd been around long enough to know the score; their report would be completely accurate and factual, but would be couched in terms which would be favorable to the admiral and his team if the document ever saw the light of day in court. And by now everybody was assuming that it would.

16

An hour and a half after leaving Peter's office, Sandy Bracknell found a parking place near the offices of Bowie and Hartman, a small, high-powered firm that dealt almost exclusively with medical and legal malpractice and product liability.

The office had an efficient, no-nonsense atmosphere. The decor and furnishings were of the best quality, solid, made to keep looking good for years. The receptionist was attractive, friendly, and competent, and showed Sandy directly into Norman Hartman's office. The room was large, rather dark in spite of a big window, and unadorned, with plain but expensive gray wall-to-wall carpeting; to the right of the door, a big plain oak desk and chair stood before a few black-framed diplomas on the wall. Over by the window was an oval rosewood conference table with glasses and a large pitcher of water on its polished surface, surrounded by a half dozen comfortable-looking black leather chairs.

Norm Hartman got up from his desk, shook hands with Sandy, and led her to the table with deferential courtesy. He was tall, thin, with bright, dark eyes and black hair slicked back over his head. He pulled a chair out for her and sat himself at the head of the table, carefully arranging a yellow pad and a pencil in front of him. Then he sat back and looked at his visitor, his head tilted to one side like an attentive raven.

Without any preliminaries he asked Sandy about Denton's previous health, then about the medical care he'd received.

"Didn't he ever see a government doctor, get tests or a physical exam when he first went to Washington?"

"No. Denton was always healthy. He told me that aside from seeing Dr. Delafield on a couple of occasions, the last time he had a full medical exam was for a life insurance policy about fifteen years ago."

In spite of herself Sandy gave a small smile, which Norm, who rarely missed a trick, noticed. He didn't say anything but raised his eyebrows questioningly.

"He told me about it," said Sandy, slightly embarrassed. "I mean the physical exam. Denton said he'd never let anybody stick a finger up his butt ever again, because he felt it for a week afterward."

"I can sympathize with that," was all that Norm replied, but somehow his words, or the way he said them, gave Sandy a sense that Norm Hartman was a caring and considerate person, and she felt able to relax just a little.

Norm paid a lot of attention to how Anselm Harris had come into the picture. "How did Dr. Delafield introduce Dr. Harris to you and Mr. Bracknell?" he asked.

Sandy thought for a moment. "Peter brought him into the room and said something about him being the best surgeon in the hospital," she replied. "But quite honestly, my head wasn't exactly clear at the time, so he might have mentioned some other things about him."

"Of course." Norm fixed Sandy with a pay-close-attention-to-me look. "Now, Mrs. Bracknell," he said, enunciating his words carefully, "at this point I want you to know that I have no solid basis as yet for the following, but I have heard a rumor that Dr. Harris was involved in a major malpractice case in New York. My question to you, Mrs. Bracknell, is: Did Dr. Delafield ever at any time mention anything, anything at all, to you about any previous malpractice case that Dr. Harris might have been involved in?''

''No. Not at any time,'' replied Sandy.

''Did he inform you that if you wished, you had the right to choose another surgeon to come in to consult?''

''Well, no. Naturally I trusted Peter's judgment. Whoever he chose was—''

Norm interrupted, so smoothly it didn't seem like an interruption. ''Mrs. Bracknell, if you had known or even suspected *at that time* that Dr. Harris had had a recent major malpractice judgment against him, and that his medical competence was in serious doubt, would you have allowed him to take care of your husband?''

''No, of course not,'' answered Sandy reluctantly, ''but . . .''

''Naturally,'' murmured Norm, making a notation on his pad. ''I didn't think so. Now,'' he went on, ''when Dr. Harris had made the decision to operate on your husband, did he tell you what he was going to do?''

''Yes, of course,'' replied Sandy. ''Then he asked me to sign a consent form, which I did.''

Norm leaned forward suddenly, and she was startled by the intensity of his expression. ''Mrs. Bracknell,'' he said, ''what *exactly* did Dr. Harris tell you he was going to do?''

Sandy hesitated. ''I'm not really sure, now you mention it. They'd been saying something about a blockage, and Dr. Harris was going to unblock it.''

''Did he tell you exactly where this blockage was?

Did he tell you which blood vessels were involved? Did he draw any kind of diagram for you or show you a video of the kind of procedure he was talking about?''

Sandy was taken aback by his rapid-fire questions. ''No, not in such detail. He just told me about the blockage. . . .'' She shook her head.

''Mrs. Bracknell, I'd like you to think very carefully about the question I'm about to ask you. On the basis of what Dr. Harris told you, could you explain to me the operation that he performed on your husband?'' He pushed the pad and the pencil toward her. ''You can draw a diagram if you want.''

Sandy stared at him. ''I don't know,'' she said. ''I wouldn't know where to start. I'm not a . . .''

''So then, Mrs. Bracknell, although Dr. Harris did tell you something about the proposed operation, neither you nor Mr Bracknell ever really understood exactly what he was going to do, is that correct?''

Sandy paused for a moment, realizing that this was a very important question and she had to answer it carefully. She looked straight at Norm. ''Yes, that is correct,'' she said. ''Quite honestly, I only had a very vague idea of what he was going to do.''

Norm nodded, satisfied, and wrote a few words on the yellow pad. ''Now, Mrs. Bracknell,'' he said, still as formal as ever, ''an operation of this sort is obviously very risky. Did Dr. Harris spell out precisely what the risks were?''

''He said . . . well, he said that it was the only thing they could do to save Denton's life.''

''Did he spell out the precise risks? Did he tell you what percentage chance Mr. Bracknell had of being paralyzed as a result of the operation, of being mentally impaired, of dying?''

Sandy sat back, feeling the pressure of the relentless questioning. ''Not exactly,'' she said. ''It was more an impression he gave that Denton was in serious trouble.''

"You're saying he did not spell out the exact risks?" asked Norm, his eyes fixed unblinkingly on hers.

"Yes," replied Sandy, trying to remember, but much of what had happened on that dreadful day was just a jumble of impressions and vague recollections. She sat back, suddenly feeling very tired.

The interview lasted about a half hour longer. Norm probed into all the aspects of the transfer to the naval doctors. "Did Dr. Harris formally tell you that the care and responsibility for Mr. Bracknell would be transferred to a specific member of the navy team?" he asked, and wearily Sandy replied that no, he had not done so. The transfer just seemed to happen, she said, although Admiral Ellis seemed in overall charge of the navy doctors.

Finally Norm stood up, and his tough, uncompromising attitude slid off him like a wet raincoat. He smiled and took her hand in both of his. "I really have to compliment you, Mrs. Bracknell," he said, the admiration clear in his eyes. "You stood up wonderfully to my questioning, and I apologize if it seemed rather harsh." He let the kindness and compassion of his personality radiate over her for a moment. "And yes, Mrs. Bracknell, I will take on this case. I think that there are very clear indications that a most serious degree of malpractice has occurred here, and from my long experience in this field I feel very confident about the outcome."

Before she left, he gave her a little printed booklet that explained his firm's policy on malpractice cases, and the terms and conditions they worked under. He would get to work immediately, he said, and the first subpoenas would go out the next day.

Sandy, feeling relieved but weak, as if she'd been put through a wringer, shook his hand and said in a heartfelt voice, "Mr. Hartman, I must tell you, I'm very glad you're on my side."

After seeing Sandy to the elevator, Norm went back to his office, checked a number on his phone file, and dialed the New Coventry number of the detective agency he used for almost every case he was involved in. "Terry?" he asked. "Listen, there's two people I need you to check out." He gave the detective Anselm's and Peter's names, addresses, and phone numbers. "The full treatment," he went on. "I want to know more about them than their mothers or wives ever suspected. Right, everything from their school days up." Norm listened for a few seconds. "I want you to pay particular attention to Dr. Harris. He may have been involved in a malpractice case about a year ago in New York, I can't tell you which borough. My computer here is down, otherwise I could have found it myself. You can get all the papers and a transcript from whichever district court it was in. For the other stuff, a good place to start is the *Index of Medical Specialists*. There'll be a paragraph about each of them, like in *Who's Who*. Yeah, right, you can go back from there. Terry, I want this on the front burner. If you need to hire more people, go ahead. I need a full report just as soon as you can get it to me."

After hanging up, Norm got busy. There was a lot to do, from issuing subpoenas for hospital records to finding the names of every single nurse, technician, and hospital staff member who had seen Denton Bracknell during his brief stay in the hospital. And throughout, he smiled to himself. Every instinct told him that he was on to a winner, the biggest in his long and successful career as a plaintiff's attorney.

17

Anselm didn't get to talk privately to Peter until several days after the incident with Florence Gowan, which was just as well, because it gave him an opportunity to cool off. He called Peter at his office and suggested they go for a walk along the city beach after office hours. Peter of course knew what had happened with Florence, and sensing a row, tried to find an excuse, but Anselm wouldn't let him off the hook.

They met in the parking lot at five in the afternoon. There weren't many people around, although it was unseasonably warm. They walked in silence past the bandstand, past the skeletonized fun fair, past the flag-rimmed public swimming pool, empty for over a year while different groups fought for a share of the payoffs, and onto the wide deck that led to the half-mile boardwalk.

"What's on your mind?" asked Peter, looking straight ahead.

"Florence Gowan," replied Anselm. "She's on my mind because she almost died after her operation."

"She's doing very well now," replied Peter, staring out over the water. "She told me today she was going home."

Anselm stopped and faced Peter. Now he felt more concerned than angry. "She almost died because you didn't reorder her prednisone," he said. "Peter, what the hell is the matter with you? What's going on? That was twice you missed a diagnosis on a single patient. First when Florence had peritonitis and then the prednisone thing. Are you okay? You never used to miss things like this, not even when we were in med school."

"I'm sorry," said Peter. "I guess I had a lot on my mind, and some stuff just slipped away from me." He started to walk on, but Anselm called him back.

"That just won't do," he said. "Look, Peter, we've been friends for years, and right now there's enough trouble flying around without any getting between you and me." Anselm folded his arms. "I know that there's something going on with you, and whatever it is, it's seriously affecting your work. What's happening? Is it something to do with Susan?"

Peter laughed. "I can't say that things are great with her, but that's hardly new. No, I suppose all that business with Bracknell, and well . . ." He hesitated. "I've got a few problems of my own, I guess, and maybe . . . Anyway, they're things I have to straighten out myself." Peter seemed to be searching for something to say that would stop Anselm from probing him. "By the way," he said, "have you called your malpractice insurance agent? Sandy Bracknell was kind enough to tell me she was going to see an attorney."

"Sure." Anselm grinned wryly. "I called him. Remember, I'm vastly experienced in this kind of thing."

They continued their walk along the boardwalk. The sun was beginning to go down over the trees, many of which were still bare of leaves. A sudden breeze came up from the Sound, and they both felt chilled.

"Let's run," said Anselm, realizing that Peter wasn't about to say what was troubling him. They were both in good shape, and even though they wore ordinary shoes, they had a good run, up to the end of the

boardwalk, dislodging a pair of seagulls that flew off
with a raucous cry from the railing, went in a circle,
and landed precisely where they had started. Anselm
and Peter turned without stopping and jogged back to
their cars.

"Wow," said Peter, out of breath, leaning against
the roof of his glistening Lamborghini. "We should
do this more often."

"Any time, Peter," said Anselm, who had barely
raised a sweat. "Is it that you're worried about getting
sued?" he asked still concerned, his eyes on his friend.

"No. I'm okay, Anselm, really."

"You're not worried?" Anselm shook his head. "I
can tell you, I am. All I need is another suit like that
last one. Have you ever been sued?"

"Sure," replied Peter. "Twice. They settled both
times. But honestly, when it comes down to it, I don't
think Sandy will sue us. She knows we all did the best
we could for Denton."

Anselm shook his head. "We'll see, but I wouldn't
be so sure. If I were Sandy Bracknell's attorney, I'd sure
as hell go for it. There's plenty of stuff he could make
a meal of, like the hospital's antique equipment, the fact
we didn't transfer Bracknell when we could . . ."

Peter got into his car, obviously anxious to end the
conversation. He wound down the window. "Look,
Anselm," he said, "there's no point in getting too
excited about something that may never happen. If we
get sued, okay, then we'll deal with it. Actually, right
now I'm more concerned about getting my boat in the
water. I have to put a couple of coats of anti-fouling
paint on the bottom this weekend, and that's a bitch."

Anselm watched him leave. He remembered feeling
the same way at one time in his career, that nothing
really bad could ever happen to him. And he also had
a sense that there was something major going on in
Peter's life that he wasn't talking about. Maybe Susan

was giving him a hard time about his girlfriends. He thought about Erica Barnes, who was known to be interested in Peter. Beautiful as she was, it was quite possible that Peter had something serious going on with her, maybe even serious enough for him to leave Susan. Anselm hoped not; he liked Susan, and had known her for a long time.

It was almost dark when Anselm got back to his office. Melanie, his secretary, was still there.

"Any messages?" he asked.

"Yes. Mr. Lanier called, asking when you'd be in."

"Sheriff Lanier?"

"That's the one." Melanie looked up at the clock. "He should be here any minute now."

"Anything else?"

"No. Everything's as quiet as the grave. A couple of patients canceled, though." Melanie, inappropriately named, had short carrot-red hair and light, freckled skin. She had got the job with Anselm through her sister, who was a nurse at the hospital.

The front door opened, and Deputy Sheriff Armand Lanier came in, as usual in civilian clothes. He had a large envelope and a clipboard in his hand.

"Hi, doc," he said jovially. "I've got something for you here." He held out the envelope, then the clipboard. "This one came express delivery," he said, eyeing Anselm without curiosity. "If you'll sign on the bottom line, please, we'll be all shipshape and correct, and I can collect my fee. Thank you, sir, and a good day to you."

Lanier touched his forehead in salute, winked at Melanie, and walked out.

A feeling of dread enveloped Anselm as he stared at the thick legal-sized envelope. From time to time he had received summons to appear in court on behalf of a patient, but he was pretty sure he knew what this was, although it had come much sooner than he expected.

Holding the unopened envelope in his hand as if it were radioactive, he walked into his office, closed the door, and tore the envelope open.

He read the first page of the long legal document, and sat down heavily at his desk. He could feel his stomach contracting and his palms sweating as he forced himself to read the rest of it.

When he finished reading the document, he felt his mood change rapidly to one of relief. Knowing was better than waiting, and now that he knew, there was a lot to be done. First he called his insurance agent to tell him that the suit had been filed.

"Yeah," said the agent, unsurprised. There was a hint of insolence in his voice that Anselm hadn't heard before. "That's what we all figured here. You'll be hearing from Attorney . . . wait just a second while I find the file. Right. Here we are. Collier, McDowell and Stern in New Coventry. They're a good outfit. The attorney they'll be sending is named V. Morse."

Melanie came in a few moments later, with her coat on. She'd be leaving, she told him, at the end of the week. Her mother lived in Minnesota and was about to have surgery, and there was nobody else to look after her. Melanie hoped she could come back in a couple of weeks, but she wasn't sure.

18

The papers notifying the hospital that they were defendants in a lawsuit arrived on Stefan Olson's desk about the same time as Anselm received his subpoena.

Stefan signed for the papers, waited until the deputy sheriff had gone, then reached for the phone. First he called Tony Marino, then the hospital's insurance agent, and finally John Kestler, the hospital's lawyer.

"I'm sorry, Mr. Kestler's in conference," the secretary told him.

"Then get him out of conference," snapped Stefan. He knew that John's conferences were often with a golf ball on the roll-up putting surface he kept at the end of his office.

A minute or two later, Kestler came on the phone. His voice was brusque, as if he'd been wakened from a nap rather than interrupted in match play. "Yes, Stefan, what can I do for you?"

"The hospital's been named in a lawsuit by Denton Bracknell's widow," said Stefan. "Not entirely unexpected, but the papers just came in. We need to get together on this as soon as possible."

"Have you told the insurance people?"

"Of course. When can you and I meet to go over this?"

"Take it easy, Stefan," said John. "I'll need to read

the subpoena first. There's no point jumping the gun, is there?''

''I'm sending you a copy right away by messenger,'' said Stefan, who knew he had to be careful with John. A few months after coming to Glenport, Stefan had tried to replace him with a bright young attorney who had trained in New Coventry, and the reaction had been fierce. Kestler, incompetent but locally well-liked and very social, was kept on by unanimous vote of the board, although not a single one of them would have dreamed of using him as their own attorney. The end result was that Stefan's own position as hospital CEO had become noticeably less secure. At this point Stefan knew John would do a leisurely job, working just hard enough to keep himself out of trouble, but certainly without any sense of dedication or even goodwill.

''Good,'' said John. ''I'll read it as soon as I can get to it.''

''John, I don't have to tell you that this is a very important matter, and it can't wait in line with all the other stuff you have to do.''

''Stefan, take it easy,'' said John again in his mellifluous voice, a shade raspy these days from years of immersing his vocal cords in Dimple Haig. ''Let me tell you something. Lawsuits take a long time. There's no emergency here, take it from me.''

''There are other things we have to consider in the light of this suit,'' said Stefan, careful to keep the impatience out of his voice. ''The Farman medical clinic, for instance, and there's the problem of how the hospital should deal with Dr. Harris, who's the principal defendant in this suit. Also we're expecting some really adverse publicity in the wake of this case . . .''

''Yes, right, I was thinking about that, Stefan.'' There was a pause while John thought about it. ''I think we should hire a public relations company to deal with that part of the problem," he said. "It's a very specialized business these days, like image building, that kind of stuff." He was sounding vague, as if he had no idea of what public relations was really about. "There's a good firm down in New Coventry," he went on, "the one that handled that research scandal for Yale medical school, do you remember?"

"John, right now this is going to be something we have to deal with ourselves. For one thing, the board won't appropriate additional funds for any public relations effort, you can be certain of that," said Stefan. "Second, time is of the essence here, and we don't have time to brief people who don't know anything about the situation."

"What about that pretty Erica Barnes? She's a smart little cookie. She's your public relations person, isn't she? Wouldn't she normally handle something like this?"

"Basically Erica's the voice of the hospital," replied Stefan, wondering if John's vocabulary was ever going to emerge into the 1990s. "But *we* have to decide what that voice says."

"Stefan, I went to law school, and they didn't teach us that kind of stuff there. But of course I'll be happy to read your press releases and check them out from the legal standpoint."

Frustrated, Stefan put the phone down a few minutes later, just as Tony Marino came into his office. Tony had an unusual walk, fast but with shorter steps one would expect from a man his size. Tony was wearing a lightweight green suit with a wide pink and mauve flowered tie, and he looked angry.

He stood, legs apart, in front of Stefan's desk. "Who else is named in this suit?" he asked brusquely. Tony had his own problems to deal with, and other things to do besides getting involved in a lawsuit that should never have happened.

Stefan had dealt with Tony long enough not to be too intimidated, but his voice, always deep and slow, took on an extra Nordic resonance when he answered. "Well, Mr. Marino, Dr. Harris is first, of course, then Dr. Delafield, three of the ICU nurses, Pat Mooney—"

"Who's she?"

"She's the emergency room supervisor. She was there when Bracknell was admitted."

The door opened again and Bob North came in, looking chubby and smug in an impeccably tailored white coat, his thinning black hair carefully combed over the top of his head. He was followed by Erica, elegant and well turned out in a dark skirt and pink silk blouse. Tony looked suspiciously at both of them before turning back to Stefan.

"Who else?"

"I'm telling Mr. Marino the names of the defendants in the Bracknell suit," explained Stefan to the new arrivals. "There's a whole list of others, Mr. Marino. There's Dr. Burton, who gave the anesthetic, the ICU supervisor, the head of respiratory therapy . . ."

"The shotgun approach, huh," said Bob, relieved that his name wasn't on the list. "That's a common tactic among lawyers."

Stefan and Tony ignored him.

"Have you called John Kestler?" asked Tony.

"Yes, I just talked to him." The tone of Stefan's voice made Tony glance sharply at him.

"Busy improving his golf game, I bet," said Tony. "In any case, we're going to need more help than he can give us."

"Right." Stefan paused. "I've also called the insurers. Their attorney's supposed to get in touch with me some time today."

"Yeah. Well, meanwhile I suppose we'd better think about developing some defensive strategy here." Tony pulled out a cigar, looked at it for a long moment, and put it back in his pocket. "First, is there anything solid they can get us on?"

"I'm not a lawyer," said Stefan carefully, "but I would guess their approach will be that we weren't equipped and staffed to take proper care of this type of case, and we should have sent Bracknell immediately to a tertiary-care center."

"That's just nonsense," said Bob angrily. "We can take care of any kind of patient in this hospital, short of open-heart surgery."

"Can you defend that position?" Tony asked Stefan.

Stefan shrugged. "Sure. Like Bob said, we've been dealing with patients with those kinds of conditions for years."

"Well, the navy people didn't think so, and the people at New Coventry Medical Center didn't think so." Tony stared belligerently at Stefan. "For God's sake, Stefan, even your own staff anesthesia man—what's his name, Burton—he's put in an adverse report on the way the case was handled."

"That was about the way *Harris* handled the case," said Bob. "There was no problem with the hospital's function. In fact, the responsibility for this whole screw-up belongs to Harris. The hospital shouldn't even be named in that lawsuit."

"The plaintiff's attorney is going to make a big thing about the hospital, you can be sure of that," said Stefan, looking from Tony to Bob. "As soon as they start looking, they'll find that the hospital's already in trouble. We're on a probationary basis with the JCAH because of deficiencies in equipment, we have staffing problems—"

"This particular case still boils down to Anselm Harris," interrupted Bob, his voice stubborn. "If he'd done his job properly, we wouldn't be sitting here being sued."

"Bob, in this kind of situation it isn't so much a question of who's right and who's wrong," explained Stefan patiently. "The plaintiff's attorneys are interested in who has the deep pockets. We have the deep pockets, or rather our insurance company does, and that's why we're on the firing line."

Erica sat in her seat listening, taking notes, but saying nothing. She liked Anselm Harris and despised Bob North, but also was very much aware of which side her bread was buttered.

Bob was looking at her legs, then smiled at her before going back to his favorite topic.

"There's a lot of docs on the staff who think we should get rid of Harris," he said. "And that's regardless of the lawsuit."

"That's not what we're here for, Bob," snapped Tony. "We have a major lawsuit on our hands, and we need to take care of that; we don't need to hear about your personal vendettas."

"On the other hand, Tony," said Stefan carefully, "I think the whole topic of Anselm Harris may blow up in our faces, and if that happens, it will have a major impact on the outcome of this lawsuit. I think that our attitude and relationship to Dr. Harris is certainly something we'll need to discuss." Stefan splayed his large hands out in front of him on the desk. There was something very solid and reliable about his presence, about the heavy tweed jacket and conservative tie he wore, and above all, about the slow, determined precision of his speech and movements.

Tony thought for a minute about what Stefan had just said, then nodded slowly in agreement, while Bob smiled broadly and winked surreptitiously at Erica. Tony took out his cigar again, and this time he lit it.

19

Denton Bracknell was buried on Carver's Island, in the grassy old cemetery that sloped down to the Sound. Because of the difficulty in getting over to the island and the limited facilities there, it was decided to hold a memorial service a week later in the Presbyterian church in Glenport, the biggest church in the town.

All morning on the day of the service, cars and limousines had been coming up I-95 from New York and Washington, and there was a big stir when the word got around that a large Boeing with air force markings and the presidential seal had flown into the local airport. Special clearance had been obtained for landing, and local air traffic was diverted or put in a holding pattern for fifteen minutes before the aircraft's estimated time of arrival. The plane parked on the opposite side of the airport from the terminal, and the rumor flew around the town that the president himself had come to pay his respects to his most trusted adviser. However, to general disappointment it turned out to be only the secretary of state with several cabinet colleagues and other senior members of the government who came down the steps from the plane into waiting limousines. Within minutes the motorcade swept out of the airport gates, led and followed by a motorcycle escort of state troopers, lights flashing and sirens coming to howling life when they came to an intersection.

The church was crowded, and long before the service was due to start, several dozen curious sightseers had gathered around the entrance. The limousines were parked on the opposite side of the road, and small children came and stood enthralled, checking out the strange license plates and watching the uniformed chauffeurs lounging against their vehicles, smoking and chatting among themselves. Never before had the town of Glenport been host to such an event.

Sandy Bracknell, wearing a simple black dress and only a minimum of carefully applied makeup on her pale face, sat in the front row of the church, surrounded by her parents and members of Denton's family. Denton's brother Grant, a tall, grizzled lawyer from Atlanta, sat beside her, wearing a large ornate bolo with an irregularly shaped turquoise set in silver. He had flown up two days before, and already had gone through Denton's investments with Sandy, dealt with the will, arranged for the legal transfer of assets, and generally helped Sandy find out how she stood with regard to her late husband's financial affairs. Grant was a model of helpfulness, but his slow-moving, deliberate way of working made her impatient; Grant seemed to have made an entire profession out of simple courtesy. Before the funeral he revealed to her that Denton's expertise had not extended to domestic financial matters, and she could count on only a very modest legacy. That came as no surprise; Denton's lack of competence with money was something she had long known but had been unable to do anything about.

Grant sat on the pew next to Sandy, talking in a low voice over his shoulder with Norm Hartman, the trial attorney Sandy had hired. Tall, thin, sallow-skinned, and lugubrious-looking in his dark suit, Norm looked as if he should be driving the hearse rather than sitting in the pew behind the family, but there he was discussing legal strategy in low tones with Grant even at this moment of reflection and sorrow.

Peter came into the church behind a delegation of a half dozen senior people from the hospital that included Stefan Olson, a couple of junior administrators, the head nurses of the ICU and ER, and Lucille Heinz. Peter sat down at the end of the pew, his long legs sticking out into the aisle. Tony Marino and Bob North were in the church too, sitting with their enormous wives nearer the front.

Anselm slipped in when the service was about to start, and stood unobtrusively at the back with other latecomers who had been unable to find a seat. He felt dissociated and confused; he hadn't really wanted to attend the service, but something within impelled him to go; maybe it was a need to appear in public, to defuse his own sense of guilt, and to show that he hadn't gone into hiding. On one hand, he knew that nothing he could have done differently would have saved Denton Bracknell, but on the other hand a huge weight of undifferentiated, self-imposed blame weighed on him, making him feel unworthy to be responsible for the lives of his patients. He felt alone, separated from his colleagues and the rest of the world, the only one who deserved the blame for what had happened, and in his self-disgust he likened himself to a murderer coming back to watch the funeral of his victim.

The service lasted an hour, including several eulogies and a recital of Denton's favorite music, which ranged from Bach to Gershwin, which sounded strange and ponderous on the organ. It's incongruous, like an elephant dancing, thought Anselm, listening to a selection from *Girl Crazy*. He watched the crowd from the back of the church in a sad, detached way.

He was the first out, leaving just as the organ started to peal out the opening bars of Berlioz's *Roman Carnival* overture, and he dodged around the back and through the side gate to avoid the TV cameras and reporters clustered in the street outside the main entrance.

Thus Anselm missed seeing the family pass down the central aisle on the way out. Sandy could hardly avoid seeing Peter, seated on the aisle, but she ignored him completely, nodding instead to Stefan, who was sitting next to him. Anselm also missed Norm Hartman's tight-lipped comment when he was cornered by TV reporters outside the church.

''This is a very sad day,'' he said, standing in front of the cameras, ''not only for Denton Bracknell's grieving widow, but for all of America, which has lost a dedicated and brilliant public servant.'' Then in the kind of aside for which he was famous, he added over his shoulder, ''The worst part of this tragedy is that it needn't have happened.''

Anselm had left his car parked down a side street a couple of blocks away, and he walked quickly toward it, thinking about Denton, the man he had never seen in health. Even after making allowance for the hyperbole of the eulogies, by all accounts Denton Bracknell must have been an unusual man, clever, hardworking, and above all a wily negotiator in the mine fields of international politics. Anselm felt terrible; for the thousandth time since Denton's death, he wondered if he had been correct in his diagnosis and treatment, and whether at each step he had made the right decision. He had lain awake night after night going over alternative approaches he might have used. Should he have overridden Peter right at the start and insisted that Denton be transferred? But at that time Peter was in charge, and Anselm knew that if he had spoken up,

Peter would simply have found another surgeon to take his place, and the end result would have been the same.

Should he have waited? Should he have tried medication to open up the artery? Had he relied too much on the hospital's outmoded equipment? These and countless other questions raced through his mind until he couldn't think straight.

He drove slowly back past the church. Sandy, just getting into a limousine, looked up and saw him. She stared directly at him for a moment, then looked away without a change of expression. In spite of himself Anselm felt his heart contract. She must really be certain that I was careless or neglectful with her husband, he thought, and she must be convinced that I caused his death. Anselm thought about how much he would hate the person who was responsible for the death of someone he loved.

Anger welled up inside him, an undirected, unstructured anger, aimed at nobody and everybody, and it was mixed with feelings of fear and insecurity. Suppose the case didn't get settled out of court, and it came to a trial and he was found guilty of malpractice? Would he ever be able to find work as a surgeon again? Would he be able to face the final collapse of his career? He would certainly be hounded out of Glenport, he was sure of that. The image of Bob North's triumphant face appeared, almost as clearly as if he was sitting in the car with him.

When Anselm got home, he sat looking at the telephone, a hairsbreadth from calling Mariana and asking her to come to Glenport. He dialed her number, all but the last digit, then put the phone down. He had never felt so alone in his life.

PART
THREE

20

Michael Parrett, dispatched from the office of the *New Coventry Herald,* arrived in Glenport the day after Denton Bracknell's funeral service, with instructions to get material for a feature story about the death of the late presidential adviser. "Get the background info on the nurses and the doctors who took care of him," his editor told him, "you know, personal stuff; you're good at that." Michael knew exactly what he meant; there's always dirt to be dug up in this kind of case, so go find it, boy.

Michael was the proud possessor of a Porsche 944, which made an exciting adventure out of the normally tedious drive up the Connecticut Turnpike. Michael had the habit, when riding the expressways, of checking out cars driven by women. If the vehicle was driven by a young, attractive female, he'd drive alongside in the next lane, smile and signal to her, then pull off at the next roadside McDonald's. According to the statistics he kept, twenty-seven percent of the time they followed him in.

Not today, he said to himself as he swept by a pretty woman driving a big Mercedes, not today. Michael was thirty-one years old, in a hurry both for the moment and for his career, and was tired of the kind of assignment that he'd been getting. He wanted to leave his job with the provincial *Herald* and become an investigative reporter for a big-city paper. He was tired of all the little scrappy stories he'd been writing for the past two years, marginal stories, cute stories, storm-and-flood stories complete with human interest, gossip. His editor had recently been pushing him in the latter direction, because he had a knack for getting stories out of women, even if, as the editor suspected, he had to get his contributors between the sheets first.

Michael had sent resumés to *USA Today,* to the *Miami Herald,* the *L.A. Times,* and several other national dailies, but without success. At his interviews, when he got one, a senior editor would flip through his portfolio of reports and articles and say, "Mr. Parrett, this is all very nice, but you simply don't have any big stories here. You may be the man for this job, but we need more proof. Sorry."

Proof, said Michael to himself as he negotiated the dangerous I-91 interchange in New Coventry. They wanted proof that he could handle a big story and make the most of it. Well, this one might be his big break; from what his editor had told him, it certainly had the makings of a big story. Denton Bracknell, internationally renowned political economist, chief advisor to the president, had been taken ill on Carver's Island, transported at death's door to Glenport Hospital, operated on there, and died in transit to Bethesda Naval Hospital.

Michael started to think ahead about whom he would need to interview at the hospital. But if he was going to make this a big story, scoop the competition, he knew he would have to get access to inside information, the kind of stuff even the local media insiders didn't have. He grinned to himself, put his foot down, and zoomed past a semi as if it weren't even moving. That, my boy, he said out loud over the noise of the engine, is what investigative reporting is all about.

At the hospital, security had been relaxed to its pre-Bracknell level, and Michael got past the guard by the simple device of wearing the photo-bearing plastic ID tag that his newspaper had issued him, wishing the guard an authoritative, preoccupied good morning, and looking as if he were in a hurry and wouldn't take kindly to being stopped.

Walking quickly through the lobby, Michael followed the corridor arrows to the ICU, thinking he might as well start there. But there was a security guard posted outside the ICU, younger and of a different mettle from the one in the lobby, as he could see from the way the man watched him approach.

Michael had no wish to get involved in any argument or risk getting thrown out, so he turned away and walked back down the corridor, toward the operating suite. A cleaning woman was working in the corridor between two yellow signs that said BE CAREFUL, FLOOR WET. The woman was on her knees, pulling on the handle of her galvanized bucket, trying to wring out a mop without getting up. She watched while Michael came toward her. He considered going down to the flower shop for a bouquet and bringing it back to the ICU masquerading as a delivery boy, but whatever he did, he knew he'd better do it fast, before somebody challenged his presence in the hospital. Michael didn't notice the cautionary signs and slipped on a wet patch just outside the entrance to the OR. He fell with a crash against one of the signs just as the door opened and Lucille Heinz came out.

"Oh, my goodness," she said, and went to help him. She noticed instantly how good-looking he was, that he was wearing a very nice suit with a button-down pale blue shirt and a dark red silk tie. With the help of the cleaning woman, Lucille helped the young man to sit up, but he was obviously in pain. "I think

I twisted my ankle,'' he said with a crinkly smile that set Lucille's heart pounding.

"Let's get you in there,'' said Lucille, now all concern and attention. "You can sit for a while till you feel better.''

Michael saw that this stocky, unattractive, middle-aged woman had an air of authority about her, and also noticed that the cleaning woman seemed afraid of her.

"Thank you so much,'' he said to Lucille, feeling perfectly able to stand up and walk away, but he did no such thing. He allowed the two women to help him up, then he hopped through the doorway held open for him by the still scared cleaning woman.

Michael smiled gratefully at Lucille, who was now holding his arm with both hands, supporting him until he sat down with a gasp of simulated pain in one of the chairs in the waiting area of the deserted operating suite.

Maybe, just the faintest of maybes, he thought, this woman might be a gift sent straight from heaven.

Bending over him, Lucille looked at the name tag on his lapel and smiled. "I didn't think you worked here,'' she said. "Now, let's take a look at that ankle. . . .'' She gave him a sharp look. "Do you know anyone in this hospital? I mean, were you visiting a patient?''

Michael shook his head, instinctively understanding what she was saying. "No. I don't know a soul here. I work for the New Coventry paper, and I was sent to cover the Bracknell story. I just got here.''

"That stupid cleaner out there, she always puts those signs where nobody can see them.'' Lucille was thinking fast and didn't take her eyes off him. She came to an instant decision, then bent down and quickly removed his shoe, noticing that it was an expensive Italian loafer with a paper-thin leather sole, then gently slipped off his sock. Lucille had never seen a man's silk sock before, and held it for a second, enjoying its sensual softness. Even its faint odor excited her.

"It doesn't look too bad," she said, still bending down and gently rubbing Michael's ankle. She took pains to make her voice sound clinical and disengaged. "It's a little swollen, but I don't think you broke anything. It's probably just a sprain."

"That's a comfort, thank you so much, Nurse . . ." He squinted at the ID pinned to her uniform. ". . . L. Heinz." Michael put every ounce of horsepower into his smile, then set his foot gingerly on the ground and winced realistically. "Boy," he said, "am I glad I fell outside *your* door."

"Can I get you anything?" Lucille eyed him greedily.

"A glass of water?" asked Michael. Somehow he had to string this out a bit longer, or in two minutes he'd be hobbling out of the suite having accomplished nothing.

Lucille was back in a moment with a paper cup.

"Here," she said, then knelt beside him. "How does it feel now?" She took his foot in both hands and looked up at him.

Michael smiled again, forcing himself to look her straight in the eye. In the corridor he had instantly noted her squat figure, her short legs and shapeless body, but now, close up, he could see her long nose and the open pores around its base, plus the small gray eyes that roamed over him with a growing possessiveness. At this close range he became aware of her acrid body odor. Faint as it was, it put Michael off more than anything else he'd so far noticed about her.

He put a hand on her shoulder, and Lucille couldn't prevent herself from quivering at his touch. "May I ask what your first name is?" he asked.

"Lucille," she replied. "Lucille Heinz. I'm in charge of the operating rooms here."

"Wow," said Michael, sounding suitably impressed. "Listen, you've been very nice to me, and for some reason, although we've just met, I feel as if I've known you for ages. I hope you won't think I'm being fresh if I ask you something?"

Lucille picked up Michael's sock and rubbed it between her fingers.

"Try me," she said, smiling, and Michael had the feeling that he could have said anything, anything at all, and she would have agreed and gone on smiling that fatuous, silly smile into his eyes.

Michael took a deep breath. "What do you say we go out to dinner tonight?"

"I'd love to," said Lucille without hesitation, "but I'm not sure when I'll be finished here."

"That's all right," he said. "I'm staying at the Hilton. Here." He pulled out a slim alligator-skin wallet and extracted a card. He wrote something on the back of it. "I'm in Room 505. I'll just wait there until you call."

"All right," she said breathlessly. "Promise you won't kill me if I'm late."

Michael slipped on his shoes and stood up. "I'd better let you get on with your work. I'll see you later, right? Don't forget."

"I won't," said Lucille.

There was no sign of a limp as Michael walked out. Lucille smiled fondly as she watched the door close behind him. What a stroke of pure luck! To find this devastatingly attractive man, young, obviously wealthy, and best of all, who didn't have any association whatever with the hospital. And he was clearly fascinated, overwhelmed by her.

It was the thought of being talked about in the hospital corridors that had for years kept her from socializing with other members of the hospital staff, although she had certainly broken that rule when Anselm Harris had come to town. It was the way Anselm had turned her down that had made her hate him so powerfully. Once, after he'd been at the hospital only a week or so, she had got him alone in the instrument room on the pretext of checking out the instruments he wanted for a case the next day. Lucille was convinced that Anselm would snatch her into his arms if only he had the opportunity, and if she showed him clearly how fascinated she was by him.

She put all the instruments out on the long steel table, and, a little puzzled, Anselm sat down to select the ones he wanted. Normally the scrub tech would find the surgeon before an operation and ask if there was anything special he needed, but apparently they did things a bit differently here. Lucille stood behind his chair, and when she reached forward to point at an instrument, her breasts pressed into his back and shoulder. Her breathing was getting heavy and she could feel the excited, throbbing heat in her breasts and between her legs.

Finally Anselm, having calmly selected the instruments he would need, stood up.

"I suggest you go and take a cold shower, Lucille," he said, smiling, but there was a chill in his smile that stabbed her through the heart. "If you're looking for a romance with me, just forget it. I'm not interested, period. Do you understand what I'm saying, or would you like it in writing?"

After that, Lucille had told a few people how Anselm had cornered her in the instrument room and practically raped her, but the only response she got was hoots of disbelieving laughter. Even now a quiver of cold rage went through her when she thought about it.

But with Michael it was different, she was quite, quite sure about that. He had nothing to do with the hospital, so she wouldn't suffer the humiliation of gossip, at least not until the time came when she could make the relationship public.

She imagined herself first making the announcement to her staff, and watching the expressions on their envious faces, then she'd sweep off to the office of the head of nursing. But for that occasion she would bring Michael with her, and that would really put Marge Taylor's eye out.

"Marge, I'd like you to meet my husband-to-be, Mr. Michael Parrett. Yes, we're getting married in a few weeks, so I'll be leaving here at the end of the month. . . ." Lucille sighed happily and sat down with her Rolodex file and started to put together the next month's on-call list.

Things didn't work out the way she'd hoped, however. Early that evening an auto crash on I-95 brought in three seriously injured victims, and two of them had to be taken to the operating room. She had just time to call Michael to cancel the dinner date, and he was not pleased.

"Could we do it tomorrow?" asked Lucille, who didn't even try to disguise the pleading tone of her voice.

"I'm afraid I'll be back in New Coventry," he replied, his voice cold, and Lucille saw her dream fading before her eyes.

"I have so much to tell you," she said desperately. "About the Bracknell case and especially about Dr. Harris. I was there when he operated on him."

Michael thought fast. It was only an hour's drive from New Coventry, and the story could wait a day if she really had something good to tell him.

"Okay," he said. "I'll stay over. You're sure there won't be a problem tomorrow?"

"Oh no," said Lucille breathlessly. "You see, Michael, I'm on call today. Tomorrow I can guarantee I'll be there.''

"Fantastic," replied Michael, trying to infuse some enthusiasm into his voice. "I'll see you around seven tomorrow, then, at the hotel.''

21

When the papers on the Bracknell case arrived at the offices of Collier, McDowell and Stern, Valerie went over them carefully, making notations on a legal pad. The plaintiff alleged that Dr. Anselm Harris had been guilty of negligence, improper treatment, inadequate preoperative evaluation, and a host of other errors both of omission and commission. The medical terms and language used in the documents were unfamiliar to Valerie, and even with *Taber's* medical dictionary on the desk beside her, she found it difficult to understand what Denton Bracknell had been suffering from, what they had done for him at the hospital, what the operation was that Dr. Harris had carried out, or why the patient hadn't wakened up from the anesthetic.

The information she had on her client wasn't too encouraging either. Anselm Harris had gone to a state medical school in New Jersey. Valerie tapped her pencil on the paper. She knew that it wasn't exactly top-of-the-line, but nothing to be ashamed of either, especially since he'd done pretty well in med school. From there he had entered a surgical residency program in Bridgeport, Connecticut, and fortunately seemed to have done well there too. Valerie made a notation to get in touch with the program director in Bridgeport; she'd get some insight into both what Harris's teachers thought of him and what sort of a doctor he had been at that time.

Working her way through the file, Valerie found that after finishing his residency, Harris had worked first at Bellevue Hospital in Manhattan, then with a semi-retired surgeon in Queens. The next piece of information made Valerie sigh, and she leaned back in her chair and stared at the ceiling for a few moments before going back to the papers in front of her. There had been a malpractice suit involving Harris and the hospital where he was working, and the case had resulted in a large judgment for the plaintiff.

Valerie checked which court had handed down the judgment and made a note to herself to get the docket number and pull the papers on the case. A malpractice suit didn't always mean the doctor was negligent, even if the judgment went against him. But still, unless she was very careful not to let them admit it into evidence, it was something the plaintiff's attorneys could make a meal out of if they wanted to, and they would, for sure. By the time Valerie had read once through the papers, she was already feeling discouraged, and beginning to wonder why Collier had given her the case when there were others in the firm who had more expertise and experience in this very specialized type of work.

Feeling over her head, Valerie called Dexter Milne, the firm's medical malpractice expert, and went down the corridor to his office. Setting aside his own work, Milne went over the entire case with her, concentrating on Bracknell's operation. With *Gray's Anatomy* open on his desk, he showed her the disposition of the blood vessels in the neck, then went to the bookcase for Eastcott's *Vascular Surgery* and Denton Cooley's *Techniques in Vascular Surgery*, and explained how the carotid arteries could be exposed during surgery. He went into some detail discussing the kind of operation Dr. Harris had done.

Valerie was impressed. "You sound like a doctor yourself, Dexter," she said. "It's amazing. I don't see how I can ever learn all that stuff."

Milne smiled gently at her. He was a slender, thoughtful-looking man in his late fifties, much less aggressive and macho than most of his colleagues, but renowned as a fearsome opponent and utterly relentless in a courtroom.

"I was an internist, as a matter of fact," he replied. "I dealt with allergies and pulmonary diseases for many years, but eventually I got disgusted with it all." He hesitated, watching Valerie with his careful blue eyes, and almost started to tell her about it. Instead he turned back to his desk, opening the Harris file that Valerie had brought with her and explained to her how the patients' charts were organized.

"The hospital chart is always the key," he said. "If you know how to extract the information you need, your entire case can and should be built on it."

Dexter showed her what to look for, discrepancies between the nurse's notes and the doctor's notes, gaps in the progress notes, places where the writing was crammed into small spaces, suggesting that the doctor might have written the notes retrospectively, and how differences between the original and copies could show that the original had been tampered with. That, he told her, was a particularly stupid error that a competent attorney could use to destroy the doctor's credibility.

"I'm on the defending side," Valerie reminded him.

"Doesn't matter," replied Dexter. "The more you know, the better you can defend him. And if your client *is* doing stuff like that, you need to know about it and figure out a way of explaining it to a jury."

While Valerie packed her papers back into her briefcase, Dexter watched her as if something was puzzling him. "Andrew must have a lot of confidence in you," he said. "You've pulled a real tough case. Do you know Mrs. Harris's attorney?"

"All I know is his name," she said.

"Norm Hartman is a very competent attorney," said Dexter in his precise way. "He's knowledgeable, careful, and very hungry. I've heard people call him the No Heart Man."

"That's encouraging," said Valerie.

"You'll be all right as long as you don't take any chances with him," said Dexter. "He's completely honest, I can tell you that. He won't hide stuff from you, and if he doesn't think the client has a really good case, he won't take it."

"He took this one," said Valerie.

"That's true," replied Dexter, smiling. "But Norm's no more infallible than the rest of us, and from the scuttlebutt I hear around this place, you're a pretty sharp attorney yourself."

Valerie could see that something was troubling Dexter about the case and her involvement in it, and she wondered if he was just trying to make her feel better about being thrown into the malpractice snakepit.

Dexter heaved the big *Gray's Anatomy* back on the shelf. "As Andrew always says," he said, not looking at her, "you can't win them all." He paused, then turned to face her. He grinned a slightly lopsided but attractive grin at Valerie. "But he also says you'd better have a damn good explanation for the ones you lose."

As Valerie was preparing to leave, Dexter watched her and coughed nervously as if he were trying to make up his mind to say something.

"Okay, Dexter, out with it," said Valerie, smiling. "You've been trying to tell me something all evening."

"I was just wondering what you did to get Ralph so

mad at you," said Dexter, his voice somber. "He con-
vened a special partners' meeting just to get you
fired."

"I know," replied Valerie. "I was there." She
smiled. "Not because they made me a partner, you
understand. Only to defend myself."

Dexter stared at her. "You were there?" he repeated
slowly. "So what happened?"

Valerie's mischievous grin lit up her whole face, and
Dexter couldn't help smiling with her. "Oh, something must have happened," she replied demurely,
"because all of a sudden Ralph changed his mind and
decided not to press the issue." Valerie watched Dexter, trying to figure out how much he already knew.

Dexter shook his head. "I can't imagine how you
pulled that off," he said. After a pause, when it became clear that Valerie was not about to enlighten him,
he went on. "Ralph is mean," he said, "not just ordinary mean but deep-down mean. He doesn't forgive
and he doesn't forget, and on top of that, as you probably know, he hates women. I don't know what you
did to make him change his mind, but my guess is that
he didn't do it willingly. If you're interested in staying
with this firm, and I hope you are, I suggest you make
a serious effort to placate him."

"Any suggestions?"

A tiny grin crept over Dexter's face, then he shook
his head. "No," he said, "what I was thinking of
wouldn't work, not with him."

The next morning, Valerie got up early, fixed herself
a quick breakfast, and decided to drive up I-95 to
Glenport rather than take the Amtrak. A light rain had
fallen during the night and left a thin, ice-like sheen
on the surface of the road. Most of the vehicles still
had their lights on, and as she drove up the ramp to
I-95, she remembered the day Patrick had had his ac-

cident. Almost reflexively she tightened her seat belt, at the same time deciding that when she could afford a new car, it would have air bags and anti-skid brakes.

She tried to concentrate on the Bracknell case, but her confrontation with Ralph Stern kept creeping back into her consciousness. She knew that Dexter was right, and there would be lots of trouble in the days and weeks ahead. Ralph was an implacable enemy who would be gunning for her, waiting for her to make a mistake in her job, and of course, sooner or later she would make one, just like everyone else. Valerie knew that at this stage in her career she wasn't particularly important to the firm of Collier, McDowell and Stern; if they decided she was a liability, she would be dismissed without hesitation. There were plenty of talented young lawyers out there waiting for her job. Valerie forced her mind back to Bracknell and Dr Harris, afraid that her ignorance of medical matters would soon become very apparent to everybody on the case, including her client.

It took Valerie just over an hour to get to Glenport, and another ten minutes to find Dr. Harris's office, located a half mile down from the hospital on Manitauk Avenue, within sight of the water.

There was an old sports car occupying the driveway, so Valerie turned at the next intersection, came back, and parked in the small lot opposite. The office was one of a row of unassuming two-story residential houses, with a sign outside that said ANSELM HARRIS, M.D., GENERAL AND VASCULAR SURGERY. Valerie hadn't thought about what kind of car the doctor would have, but the old dark blue Triumph surprised her. She got out, taking her big briefcase with her, and crossed the street.

Inside, the office was nice enough, cozy, with comfortable brown chairs and pictures of snow-covered mountains on the walls. A freckled young woman with bright red hair was sitting in a little office facing the outside door. She smiled at Valerie, who smiled back, introduced herself, and handed her card through the window.

"Hi, I'm Melanie," said the young woman. "I'll tell Dr. Harris you're here." She got up and went toward an inner office, holding the card and motioning to Valerie to follow her.

Dr. Harris was sitting back in a chair, talking on the phone. He looked surprised, then smiled at her and pointed at the chair opposite the desk. Valerie put her briefcase on the floor by the chair and sat down. The room gave the impression of having been subdivided from a much larger room, but it was not so small as to be cramped. The paneled wall behind the desk held four framed diplomas, including one from Bellevue Hospital. To the left of the desk a glass-fronted bookcase held a collection of reference books and several piles of journals. The oriental rug had a soft, floppy look that made Valerie think it had originated in Belgium rather than Iran. On the opposite side of the room were two closed doors that presumably led to examining rooms.

Valerie looked at Dr. Harris with interest. He seemed in his late thirties, good-looking, a bit rumpled and unconventional, with hair down to his collar, but strong-looking, with a smooth, tanned skin she instinctively wanted to touch. There was something about the line of his jaw, stubbornness perhaps, but his eyes seemed thoughtful and gentle, maybe even a bit too trustful. He was not at all what she'd expected from reading the charts and other documents, although she couldn't remember exactly what she had expected. Valerie caught herself; here she was again, forming opinions about someone merely on the basis of superficial appearances. With her training and experience, she knew better.

He put the phone down. "I'm sorry," he said. "You're the attorney from the insurance company?"

Valerie introduced herself.

Anselm grinned. "I don't know why, but I was expecting to see a man," he said. "I guess I must have looked surprised when you came in."

"Well, I guess you just lucked out," replied Valerie, smiling back at him. She took a deep breath, conscious of his eyes on her. Could he see what a novice she was in this business? Could he see that all she knew about medicine was what she'd learned when Patrick was in the hospital, and a bit from Dexter Milne?

"Anyway," she went on, "here we are. My job will be to defend you in the case that Mrs. Bracknell has brought against you."

"Right." Anselm shifted in his chair and folded his arms across his chest. Watching him, Valerie could almost see the defensiveness growing in his eyes, and wondered how difficult he was going to be to deal with. She detected something else in his look; it hadn't occurred to her that it would hurt to be the defendant in a malpractice suit, and of course for Dr. Harris this was the second time.

Valerie opened her briefcase, took out a yellow legal pad, and put it on her knee.

"I know you've been through all this before," she said, "but I'd like to make sure you understand how this case will be conducted."

Looking at Anselm, Valerie realized that she must have said something wrong, although the change in his expression was almost imperceptible. Surely, she thought, he must be aware that she'd know about his previous malpractice case.

She went on to tell him about the depositions that both she and the plaintiff's attorney would be requesting, and how these would be conducted.

"Before you do any depositions," she said, "you and I will go over every possible aspect of the case. I don't want you to have to deal with any questions we don't have a prepared answer for."

Anselm watched her, sitting back in his chair, arms still folded across his chest. Valerie noticed that the door had been left ajar and got up to close it.

"I'd like to get to know something about you," she went on, coming back to her chair.

He answered her questions briefly but without hesitation. She asked him about his training, his surgical teachers, which of them he'd liked, and whether he had gathered any awards or academic distinctions. Then she asked about his personal life, his hobbies, was he married, were there children. When the questions took that direction, his answers became brief, and although he remained polite, he couldn't hide the irritation in his voice.

Finally Valerie put down her pencil and said, "Look, Dr. Harris, I'm not asking you these questions to pry into your personal life. As your attorney, I need to know everything I can about you so that I can defend this case as well as possible. You can be sure that by trial time, Mrs. Bracknell's attorneys will know more about you than you know yourself."

Anselm grinned suddenly, and Valerie had a momentary glimpse of an entirely different person sitting opposite her. "Would you answer these same questions if I asked them?" he asked.

"I would if it were necessary," she replied coolly. "But you're not defending me, so it doesn't matter to you whether I'm married or have children."

Anselm glanced at her left hand, which was innocent of rings, and smiled at her. "As a trained observer," he said, "there are some questions I don't need to ask."

"That's just *one* of the differences between us," she

replied, slightly nettled by his inference that she was not a trained observer, but she wanted to go along with the apparent lightening of his mood. Valerie certainly wasn't being flirtatious, she simply wanted this uptight doctor to ease off a bit.

Anselm must have misunderstood her because his expression hardened, and instantly the barriers were back up and his hostility was more obvious than ever. He looked at the small clock on his desk.

"Ms. Morse," he said in an icy voice, "I need to explain a couple of things to you. Up to this time, every experience I've had with lawyers has been a bad one. The lawyer who dealt with my father's estate was a thief. The attorney who defended me in my New York malpractice case was alcoholic to the point that most of the time he couldn't see straight. In addition, he was corrupt, or so I've been told since. My former wife's divorce lawyer was a liar, and my divorce attorney finished up the case by having an affair with her. For other matters, lawyers I've dealt with have been too hungry and too busy to pay attention to details, or else they're trying to get something else out of the case besides winning it, like more money, or boosting their reputation and their own egos. So you can understand why I'm not enthusiastic about this interview."

"You've just had bad luck," answered Valerie simply. "Not all lawyers are thieves or drunks, just like all doctors aren't greedy or incompetent. Maybe it would help if I told you that personally I take maybe a couple of drinks a week, that I used to work for Legal Aid and still would if I didn't need to make more money, I'm considered to be above average competent, and I don't have more ego problems than anybody else who works real hard for a living."

Valerie was angry. She was tempted to stand up, tell this doctor to cram his case wherever he could find a place it would fit, then leave him to figure out his own defense.

"You didn't mention how much experience you'd had in this field, Ms. Morse, so I've had to draw my own conclusions," said Anselm relentlessly. "Now I have to decide whether I need an attorney who's good and careful and as hardworking as you say you are, or one who has lots of experience. I guess it would be too much to hope to find one with both."

"That's probably correct," said Valerie coldly. "Of course, you could hire your own lawyer. Then you can get whoever you like."

"Thanks for the information," said Anselm, aware that he was sounding stuffy and pompous, and angry at himself for it. The fact was, his experiences had made him allergic to lawyers, and at this point it didn't seem to matter how dedicated and competent they were. "Meanwhile, let's get back to the case. If you have any more *relevant* questions, I'll do my best to answer them."

Valerie took a deep breath and shuffled papers for a moment to regain her composure. The thought went through her head that Andrew Collier might have given her this case as a punishment.

"I need to know how many cases you've done similar to the one you performed on Denton Bracknell," she said.

"Maybe sixty," he said. "Maybe a few more."

"Can you find the exact numbers for me?" asked Valerie. "The prosecuting attorneys will ask you that question, and they could give you a hard time if you don't have a precise number."

"I can't tell you right now, but I can tell you exactly next time I see you," replied Anselm. "I'll need to go through my records." He made a note on the pad in front of him.

"I'll also need to know the success rate you've

had," Valerie went on, "and how it compares with figures from other surgeons who do this kind of case."

"I can tell you that," replied Anselm. "I've had one death on the table from anesthetic complications, another from a heart attack the day after surgery. Four others had strokes within a year. The others, as far as I can tell you, have done well."

"Is that approximately the same kind of results that other surgeons get? I'm talking about surgeons with the same kind of training and experience."

Anselm turned and pulled a recent copy of the *Journal of Surgery* from the shelves. "Here," he said, opening it and giving it to her, "that's the result of a big study at the Mayo Clinic." He smiled. "On average, they didn't do any better."

"Good." Valerie was pleased. "Can you make me a copy of the paper?"

"Sure." He stood up and took the journal with him into the outer office, and a few minutes later Melanie brought the copy back.

Valerie spent another hour with him, and by the time she was ready to go, Anselm was reluctantly impressed with her methodical approach. She had shown that she wasn't one to gloss over things or leave them to chance, even at the risk of upsetting her client. In his mind he contrasted the way she was handling the case with the casual and careless attitude of his previous malpractice attorney.

Before she left, she told Anselm that on their next visit they would review Denton Bracknell's entire hospital course, then go over the hospital chart, the navy report, and the report from the anesthetist, Dr. Burton. After they'd done that, she said, she would need to go over the entire management of the case with Dr. Delafield.

Anselm stood up and put out his hand in an oddly conciliatory gesture. "Counselor, thank you," he said simply. But his voice told Valerie that his hostility had been replaced by a wary respect, and she herself felt the faintest flicker of liking for this surgeon who had obviously survived some very difficult times in the past and in spite of his bad experiences with lawyers, was doing his best to cooperate with her.

22

The morning after Valerie's visit, Anselm went to the hospital to do rounds, full of energy and ready to do battle. His interview with her had somehow raised his spirits, and for a second he saw her in his mind's eye, her alert look and confident step when she had come into his office, the ease with which she swung her heavy briefcase, and the way she watched him with those clear eyes of hers. At that moment his impression of her had been purely physical, and it had stopped him dead. Then she told him who she was and why she was there, and instantly, as a person, she disappeared. Only after she had gone did she reappear in his mind, and now he had a surprisingly clear impression of her: not just attractive but smart, hard-working, tough, a woman who could be a formidable ally. His mind slid from Valerie to Mariana. Early on in his marriage, very early on, he'd hoped Mariana would be such an ally, in spite of what his friends had told him. Some ally she had turned out to be.

Walking along the corridor, Anselm thought about Valerie's strange disappearance as a person, and realized that had trained himself to do that when he was involved in a professional relationship with women. Even with the most attractive women patients, at the time he was examining them he was able to put away all feelings except those related to his diagnosis and treatment, although he did occasionally later relive the physical examination with more of an artist's eye.

Quite aside from her appearance, he recognized now, Valerie had that distinctive quality, that aura of confident femininity that had nothing weak or submissive about it, which he found so attractive. A real woman of the nineties was Valerie, he thought, cool, balanced, confident, totally unlike Mariana, who was certainly competent at her job but who carried an entirely different aura of unpredictable willfulness, seductiveness, and an explosive bad temper.

"Dr. Harris, do you have a minute?" He turned to see Erica Barnes, bright and elegant in a tight red skirt and white bouffant silk blouse. Still immersed in his thoughts, he stared at her for a second, then laughed. "I'm sorry, Erica, I was far away. . . ."

"I have a package for you in my office," she said, smiling back at him and wondering what or whom he'd been thinking about so intently. "It arrived from Washington this morning."

Anselm had a pretty good idea what was in the package. He turned and walked back along the corridor with Erica, her heels click-clicking beside him on the tiled floor. He liked Erica, found her attractive, but for some reason he could never think of anything to say to her that wasn't strictly about business. Anselm pushed open the door of her office and followed her in.

"Here it is." Erica reached down and picked a parcel with a Federal Express label off the floor. She stood up, close enough to him that he could smell the faint odor of her perfume, and proffered the package but held on so they were both holding it. Her dark eyes looked up at him with a curious, almost anxious expression. "Dr. Harris," she said, sounding very formal, "I'd love it if you'd let me take you out to dinner sometime."

Anselm hesitated, surprised, and Erica took a little step back, watching his face.

"That's a lovely idea, Erica," he said carefully, "and thank you. But quite honestly, right now I'm really caught up with all the Bracknell business and all that's going along with it." He tapped the package. "So at this point I don't think I'd be great company for you."

Two little spots of color appeared on her cheeks. She wanted to say that it didn't really matter to her even if he just sat there all evening and said nothing, she just wanted to spend some time getting to know him a bit, but instead she said, "Well, perhaps when that's all over and done with . . ."

At the same moment she knew that it wouldn't happen, and felt simultaneously embarrassed and sad. It wasn't often that she made the first move, and it was even less often that she got turned down.

Anselm took the package and left. Erica stared at the closed door for a moment, then shrugged. His response had not been totally unexpected, but it had been worth the try, and worse things had happened to her in her life than being turned down by a guy she liked. She had a sudden vision of her husband's funeral two years before, after his death from alcoholic cirrhosis of the liver. On that day the rain had poured relentlessly down, making rivulets in the muddy earth around the grave. The rain had been a metaphor for her utter desolation, and it had seeped through her clothes and flesh into her very bones.

Erica sat at her desk and cupped her chin in her hand. She had got a lot tougher since Don's death, and knew she never wanted to be poor or alone ever again. No, Anselm Harris wasn't the only fish in the ocean, not by any means. There were plenty of attractive men around, men who would be only too happy if she even looked in their direction. And there were other relationships she could revive, not just for fun this time, but with matrimony and lifetime security in mind. Still thinking along those lines, she went back along the corridor and happened to run into Peter Delafield, who was waiting by the elevator.

Anselm finished his rounds, came out through the ER entrance, sniffed the salty sea air coming off the water, and decided to walk to his office, three-quarters of a mile along Manitauk Avenue. He strode briskly past the carefully tended front yards with daffodils and primroses making their first demure appearance, and here and there the first yellow flashes of forsythia glinted on the bushes. A few hardy sailors were already out in the Sound, their white-sailed sloops heeling hard in the stiff May breeze. Caught up in the feeling of spring, Anselm ran the last half mile and passed a couple of surprised pedestrians who looked at him trotting by in his professorial sweater and chinos, no doubt wondering what class he was running away from.

"The employment agency doesn't have anybody to send over next week when I'm gone," Melanie told him, worried. "I asked around a few of the doctors' offices, but I couldn't find anybody to take over. The agency said they'd maybe have somebody the week after."

"Don't worry, Melanie," replied Anselm. "There isn't that much to do right now, and I'm sure I can manage for a week."

He sat at his desk, feeling that things were not nearly as grim as they'd seemed only a few days before. He had a few good people on his side, including a fair number of the hospital nurses, a capable lawyer, and best of all his conscience was entirely clear. He had done the best he could with Denton Bracknell, and he felt strongly that a jury, which after all was usually composed of solid, sensible people, would not find against him. In any case, Anselm was well aware that most malpractice cases never got to a jury and were settled out of court, but he also knew that this one was different, as the case of Andy Panneterio had been different, but for entirely other reasons.

Meanwhile, he had to start preparing his case. Valerie was new at this game, and although she seemed to know her way around the legal side of things, Anselm would have to translate a lot of the medical terminology and jargon into English for her, and make sure she really understood the techniques and procedures involved.

Anselm opened the cardboard mail pack Erica had given him and pulled out a bound volume with the seal of the United States in gold on the front. It was the autopsy report on Denton Bracknell, as he had expected. He spent the next two hours reading it, and he made several notes on points that weren't entirely clear to him. Then he closed it, sat back in his chair, and thought about the overall picture that the report presented and the conclusions the navy doctors had reached.

Anselm was mildly surprised at the extensiveness of the arteriosclerosis the pathologists had found in Bracknell's body. Several major arteries had been partially blocked, including the ones to the liver, the intestines, and the lower parts of the body. These problems would have been impossible to detect under the emergency conditions that had existed, but Anselm was surprised that Peter, who had known Denton for several years, hadn't recognized the degree of severity of the problem. But of course, Peter hadn't seen what was happening with Florence Gowan either, before or after her surgery, and Anselm wondered again what was going on with him. He felt dismayed that Peter hadn't told him what was bothering him; they had been best friends for years, and until now they'd always told each other what was on their minds. They hadn't spoken since their conversation at the boardwalk.

The phone rang, and he picked it up. It was Peter.

"Did you get the autopsy report?" he asked.

"Just finished reading it," answered Anselm, feeling glad that Peter had called. "I'm never going to eat bacon and eggs again."

"It's not going to be much help to us, is it?" Peter's voice was cool; he was letting Anselm know that he hadn't forgotten or forgiven Anselm's criticisms about Florence Gowan.

"I don't see it should make a whole lot of difference," replied Anselm. "We had to try to clear Bracknell's artery, regardless of the amount of arteriosclerosis, because he would have died for sure if we'd just left it the way it was."

"I'm not so sure now, to tell you the truth," said Peter, and the tone of his voice made Anselm suddenly uncomfortable. "When Sandy's attorney reads this, he'll get his medical-expert witnesses to say that it was surgically a hopeless situation, and we'd only have made it worse by operating on him. And maybe they're right, maybe we should have just tried medication, like heparin to stop the blood from clotting, and maybe vasodilators to try to open up the blood vessels."

There was a long silence.

"Peter, we're going to have to hang together on this," said Anselm. "We made the call on the basis of our best judgment at the time, and we have to defend that call, even though in retrospect if we'd known everything we know now, we might have acted differently. Have you talked to your attorney yet?"

"Yeah. Apparently he's tied up with another case

right now, but he's coming down later this week. Why?''

''Our attorneys might want to get together and develop a joint strategy,'' replied Anselm. ''It would make sense, since we're both named in the suit and most of the decisions concerning Bracknell's care were made by one or other of us.''

''I'll mention it when he gets here,'' said Peter, but he didn't seem to attach much importance to the idea.

''My attorney said she wants to talk to you anyway,'' said Anselm.

''*She?*''

''She. And so far she seems like a crackerjack, I'm happy to tell you.''

''Good legs?''

Anselm thought for a second. ''Yes, but that's not what I like about her.''

''Send her over,'' said Peter, his voice suddenly friendly again. ''I'll be happy to tell her whatever she needs to know.''

Anselm put the phone down slowly. Everything about the conversation he'd just had gave him a deep sense of uneasiness.

23

As soon as the last case of the day was over, Lucille Heinz hurried off, leaving her staff to do the routine cleaning-up. She changed as fast as she could, checked her appearance in the mirror over the sink, and hurried out of the hospital. Her car was in the far corner of the staff parking lot, and she almost ran toward it, feeling a growing glow of excitement coursing through her.

She found a space and parked her car outside the hotel where Michael was staying, then went up to the information desk with some trepidation, but luckily she didn't know any of the people working there.

Yes, Mr. Parrett was registered, and they called through to his room while Lucille, holding tightly onto the courtesy phone, waited and listened. There was no answer, although she let it ring a full minute.

"I'll wait," she told the clerk, and sat down in one of the comfortable armchairs in the lobby. After a few moments of feeling exposed and self-conscious, re-hearsing conversations if anyone she knew came in and accosted her, she went over to buy *Glenport Today,* the local paper. Leafing through it, she found a long article with a blurry color photo about a local basketball team, and eventually found a small piece on page two about Denton Bracknell's death. She scanned the paper, thinking what a rag it was. No wonder the local people called it the "Glenport Yesterday."

About forty minutes later, Michael came into the lobby, looking breathlessly handsome in dark pants, a white button-down shirt, an Armani tie, and a loose-fitting Harris tweed jacket. He was walking past Lucille when she said, "Michael!" in a soft voice.

He stopped, stared blankly at her for a second, then smiled and sat down in the chair beside her. "Oh, Lucille," he said, thanking his stars that he remembered her name. "I hope I didn't keep you waiting too long. I didn't recognize you out of uniform," he went on, smiling. "I was talking to the PR person at the hospital, a woman named Erica Barnes." He reached out and touched her hand for a second.

"What did she tell you?' asked Lucille, leaning forward and suddenly suspicious.

"Not much, unfortunately," he replied. His smile was a winner, and he knew it. Lucille could feel her heart beating fast. "Meanwhile," he went on, "I'd like to go up to my room for a quick shower, then we can go out, okay?"

Five minutes later, he was back in the lobby. Lucille had taken the opportunity to go to the ladies' room and put on some makeup, but it was something she rarely did and because of her excitement, she applied it with a heavy hand. So when she stood up as Michael approached, there was something of a marionette about her, with bright red lips, a red spot on each cheek the size of a silver dollar, and her eyes outlined with thick lines of mascara. Michael didn't flinch; as far as he was concerned, she could have looked like the back of a London bus. His job was to get as much information as he could out of her, and anyway he didn't know anybody in Glenport who could embarrass him by seeing them together.

He took Lucille's arm and led her toward the door,

smiling affectionately, knowing that by the time he'd finished with her, she'd be squeezed as dry as a prune of any information he wanted from her.

After a two-minute walk, they sat down in a corner table of the Crossbow, a restaurant close to the hotel and chosen at her suggestion. The menu was impressive, written in French script, with a ribbon across the top corner and backed with deep red textured velvet, but Michael soon found that the food was much less good.

"I guess they shot their bolt with the menu," he said, smiling at Lucille, but she was feasting on him with her eyes and missed the pun.

In the candlelight the garish outlines of her makeup were dimmed, and he found her marginally more attractive than in the brightly illuminated hotel lobby. In any case, he was here on business. He filled her glass again with the house cabernet, and she giggled. "It's lovely," she said, holding it up to the candlelight. "I'm just not used to drinking alcoholic beverages." She opened her eyes wide at him, like a teenager with her first illicit drink.

"You must enjoy living here," he said, smiling. "Glenport's a lovely little town."

"Are you kidding?" Lucille's glass swayed, and her mouth made a little moue. "I hate it. Everybody knows your business here, or wants to. It's New England. Lovely to look at, hell to live in."

"Then why do you live here?" asked Michael. He reached for a cigarette, then remembered they'd been seated in the no-smoking section at Lucille's request. He felt restless and anxious to get his story back to the paper, and wondered how he could end the civilities here and get down to business.

Lucille hesitated, and Michael felt her draw back for a moment. Then she gave him an odd, innocent sidelong glance, and her lip trembled for a second.

Michael got the sudden impression that he was watching a well-rehearsed play.

"My lover died," she said. "He was an officer in the coast guard, stationed in New London."

Thinking that the way she used the word *lover* sounded strange in this context, Michael looked sympathetic, put his glass down, and waited.

"Yes," Lucille went on, holding up the wineglass, her eyes fixed on the bright ruby of the candle through the wine. "He was called at midnight. We were making love when the phone rang."

She looked at him over the top of the glass, as if to gauge his reaction. Reassured, she went on. "It was for a drug bust out at sea. They were to intercept this big sailing sloop about twenty miles off Mystic. . . ."

A tear appeared on her cheek, and Lucille made no attempt to check it. "He was the leader of the boarding party. It was a foggy night, and a shot rang out."

Michael sat back, watching her and trying to keep his face straight.

"They never found his body," she said.

"That's terrible," said Michael. "When did that tragedy occur?"

"Years ago," sighed Lucille. She must have realized that sounded rather vague, so she said, "Exactly five years ago."

"It doesn't sound as if you've ever been able to get over it," he said, his voice brimming with spurious sympathy.

She reached out and held his wrist tightly. "I haven't," she replied softly, staring into his eyes, "not till this moment."

Michael had to cough to cover the hysterical laughter that welled uncontrollably up inside him. Maybe it was the cabernet, he thought, refilling both their glasses to the brim, but he was feeling a sense of de-

tached hilarity, like watching a play that was so bad it
made him laugh.

"Let's get away from that tragic topic," he said,
gazing into her eyes. "Lucille, why don't you tell me
all about Denton Bracknell." He sat back and gave
her his full attention. "From what I've heard, he could
be the most important patient who has ever come into
your hospital."

There was a long silence, and Michael wondered if
maybe he'd cut too fast from Lucille's phantom lover
to Denton Bracknell.

She glanced at him, not sure for a second whether
he was mocking her. Reassured by his attentive expression, she answered. "Well, everybody here knows
about Bracknell because he lives on Carver's Island.
There's a lot of other important people who live there,
you know. Some of the du Ponts, Whitneys, people
like that, but they all keep a very low profile, so we
hardly ever see them."

Lucille twirled the stem of her glass and felt relaxed. All thoughts of coast guard officers cleared from
her mind; she was having a wonderful time. Michael
was so handsome, so sexy . . . and she was sure that
her mentioning being in bed with her lover had turned
him on. She wished the evening would last forever,
but she'd already made up her mind that the best was
yet to come.

"But the Bracknells are more accessible?"
prompted Michael.

"No," replied Lucille, "but his wife's from around
here, and everybody knows her, so there's a sort of
contact through her, if you see what I mean."

Michael nodded.

"So what was the matter with him?" he asked. "We
had a press briefing from a woman called Erica Barnes,
but she didn't say too much." Michael didn't mention

that he'd tried to come on to her but had been rebuffed, smilingly but unmistakably.

"Oh, Bracknell had a blockage in his carotid artery," said Lucille, looking coyly at him through the candlelight. "Didn't they tell you that already, at the hospital?"

"Which side was the blockage?" asked Michael.

"The right." Lucille took a big swig of the cabernet and licked her lips.

"How did his surgery go?" he asked.

"It was a disaster," she replied. "As you could guess from the result. He should never have been operated on in the first place—*I* don't think, anyway, and I have a lot of experience with this kind of situation."

"Why not?" Michael took a sip of his wine. "Surely they would be pretty careful with somebody as important as Denton Bracknell."

Lucille grinned again. "Operations get done for different reasons," she said. Her voice was just a little slurred. "Sometimes it's for medical reasons, sometimes not."

"You were going to tell me about his surgeon, Dr. Harris?"

Lucille smiled and looked at Michael over the rim of her glass. "Yes, I did promise, didn't I? But not now . . . Later, if you're a very good boy."

Her implication was clear, and Michael's stomach lurched with apprehension.

"Why they picked him to come to Glenport, with *his* history," she went on, looking down at her plate, "I'll never know."

His eyes flickered. "His history? Would you like to tell me about that?"

She laughed, a high-pitched, excited laugh that set his teeth on edge.

"Not now," she repeated, waving her glass in front of his eyes, her row of big teeth showing as she smiled.

"Not now, Michael, we'll talk about him *later*." This time her look was so suggestive that there was no room left for doubt in Michael's mind, and he sighed gently to himself. Right from the beginning, when she had brought him into the operating suite, he'd figured it would come to that, anyway.

Michael waited, but Lucille wasn't saying anything more. It was becoming obvious that she was going to stretch it out as long as she could, and parlay her information for whatever she could get.

She leaned forward to give Michael an opportunity to look down her décolleté. "Let's not talk any more about this stuff now," she said. "Let's talk about you." Her eyelashes fluttered and she reached out to touch Michael's hand. "And after we've talked about you," she said, "then we're going to talk about *us*."

When dinner was over and they were walking back to the hotel, Lucille hung on to Michael Parrett's arm and chattered brightly. It was beginning to drizzle, and she unbuttoned Michael's jacket and playfully pulled one side of it over her head. He felt one of her breasts pressing into his side, and for a second he experienced a feeling of mild lust, partly explained by a general feeling of expansiveness related to some of the hints Lucille had dropped during dinner, but the second carafe of wine may also have contributed.

Michael pushed the hotel door open. "Okay, Lucille," he said, laughing. "Try to look staid until we get into the elevator."

They giggled their way across the lobby, but even in her excited condition Lucille kept an eye open for anyone she knew. She didn't mind gossiping about other people, but had an almost pathological dread of being the topic of sniggering conversations in the hospital locker rooms.

Michael fumbled with the room lock, then found he had to press another button at the same time as he turned the key. Finally he managed to open the door, and Lucille ran in, past the little bathroom and the long, counter-like desk, and collapsed on the king-size bed, laughing, and whether it was intentional or not, her skirt rode up almost around her waist. Looking at her chunky, nylon-encased thighs, Michael, even in his euphoric state, felt some confusion about her ambiguous signals. In some ways she tried to appear so virginal, so anxious and apparently inexperienced, but on the other hand she was also suggestive to the point of being crude.

Mentally he shrugged. He didn't have the time or energy to try to figure it out anymore at this point. Quite simply, he felt an urgent need to have sex, she was there and only too willing, and he needed to extract as much information about Dr. Harris out of her before she slipped out of his reach into an alcoholic coma. Michael recognized that he wasn't in the best of shape himself, and the whole thing was going to need some pretty careful timing.

He fell on the bed beside her and slid his hand between her legs, thinking that keeping her thus occupied would give him a few extra moments to consider his *modus operandi*. He was experiencing a complex and unaccustomed combination of desire and disgust, not made easier by Lucille, who started bucking vigorously and panting the moment he touched her. She wrapped her legs around him, and at the same time was scrabbling to pull off her pantyhose with one hand. Her head was drawn back, her eyes fixed somewhere on the ceiling, and Michael wondered if she was lost in some kind of fantasy, maybe with her demon lover from the coast guard, or else she was just too drunk to focus on anything closer.

"Help me," she said, so he sat up and pulled off her pantyhose, which had gathered like brown hobbles around her ankles. Even in his befuddled state it occurred to him that however sexy Lucille's well-fitting panty hose had looked while on, there was something really sordid about her floppy pale white uncased flesh, with shallow pits of cellulite marbling her thighs.

"The lights, Michael," she ordered, struggling with the buttons on her blouse. "Turn off the lights."

"Let's wait till we have our clothes off," he said. He wanted to see what he was getting into, so to speak, and for that Lucille had to be stripped of anything that she could hide behind.

Lucille didn't even hear him. With an impatient gesture she ripped the button off the cuff of one sleeve, and then her blouse was off, sailing into the air with complete abandon. Under the blouse was a heavy-duty bra that looked as if it were made of sailcloth.

Her hands began struggling frantically behind her back, but she was getting nowhere. "Oh, Michael, please," she said in an agonized voice, and she half turned to show a curved back studded with raised brown moles. The bra was held together by a half dozen hooks under moderate tension, and after a moment's hesitation, he undid them, one after the other.

Meanwhile, Lucille was wriggling around, her heavy buttocks flat on the sheets. She reached back and pulled one side of his shirt out of his pants, then grabbed for his crotch, apparently not quite sure what she wanted to get at first.

The last hook was off, and Lucille shrugged the garment off and turned smilingly to him.

"Jesus," he thought, "how old is this woman?" She was slim-waisted, but her breasts were big, white, soft, and floppy, with huge, light brown areolas and flat, almost invisible nipples that faced straight down to the floor. Reddish pink, irregular linear stretch marks extended from just below her shoulders down to the nipples.

She started to undo his shirt buttons with clumsy

fingers, but the garment was from Brooks Brothers and not inexpensive, so Michael jumped up and got out of his clothes standing up. Rarely worried about his virility, he wondered whether he could really get it up for this, but the thought of his coming scoop on the Bracknell case acted like an aphrodisiac, and sure enough, he could. He lay down again.

"Oh, lovely," breathed Lucille, stroking it. "It's beautiful."

Michael lay back, resigned.

"There's a bend in it," she said suddenly. "Is that normal?"

"Damn right it's normal," he said, struggling to sit up. He didn't know whether he could go through with this. He suddenly felt desperate to be out of there and away from this woman. "You were going to tell me about Dr. Harris. . . ."

"Later, darling," said Lucille, fondling him and not taking her hungry eyes off the object of her attention. She leaned forward and giggled. "Shouldn't we practice safe sex, Michael?" She rolled her tongue around his name as if she could taste it.

"You're right, we should," he replied. "I haven't got a condom, so I guess we're not going to—"

"It's all right," she said. She raised her head. Her eyes weren't focusing very well. "I don' care, an' I trust you . . . completely."

"No, no, Lucille, you're absolutely right," he said, trying to sound stern. "We shouldn't risk—"

With one hand Lucille pushed him back down on the bed. She was a strong woman. "And now, don't make me talk with my mouth full," she said out of the corner of her mouth. "Because it isn't polite, and anyway I can't do it."

Five minutes later, desperate to get the whole thing over as fast as possible, Michael rolled over her, and she gave a muffled scream. Unnerved, he propped himself up on his elbows and looked down at her.

"It's my back," she explained. "I have a slipped disc and it can't take any pressure. Here . . ." She rolled over sideways, away from him, then pressed her rump backward toward him. "Try it like this, darling."

Michael stared at her big white behind and felt his gorge rising. "I can't . . ." he whispered.

"Let me help you," she said, and did.

Gritting his teeth, he closed his eyes and thought about Cecelia, a girl with a wonderful body he'd spent a recent weekend in the Bahamas with, and consummated the act as fast as possible.

Then, without any further prompting, she told him all she knew about Dr. Anselm Harris.

"It was Dr. Delafield who got him in," she said, lying comfortably in the crook of his arm. "No other hospital would touch him after that malpractice suit."

Michael shrugged with one shoulder. "Half the doctors in the United States have had malpractice suits," he said. "Big deal."

"Not like this one," retorted Lucille. "Don't you remember it? A year ago, in New York, a politician by the name of Balleterio, something like that."

Michael shook his head, then something lit up in his memory banks. "You don't mean Andy Panneterio, the New York state senator, do you? Jesus . . ."

"Yeah, that's the one. It was all over, on the news, the TV, everywhere. Well, that was our Dr. Anselm Harris when he was working in New York."

"My God," he breathed to himself, already seeing the next day's headlines in his mind's eye. "I remember. We all thought that doc would be out of business forever after that mess."

For the next ten minutes Michael got every bit of information he could think of out of Lucille concerning Anselm Harris, the operation on Bracknell, the problems during the surgery. He also heard the scuttlebutt that Peter and Anselm had been advised by the Washington team not to operate, and that they had just managed to push Bracknell aboard the navy helicopter before he died.

Michael then got up and dressed, and insisted that she leave, in spite of Lucille's begging to stay a little longer.

"Deadlines," he said. "I barely have time to write up my piece about this case, and I have to be alone when I work."

"Can we see each other tomorrow?" she asked once she was dressed again.

"Sure," said Michael, thinking if he never saw her again, that would be too soon. "I'll call you."

"What paper do you work for?" she asked, and then when he told her, she went on quickly, "You won't mention my name, will you? I'd get fired if they knew I'd been talking to you."

"Of course not. Here, don't forget your pocketbook."

As soon as the door was closed, Michael locked it, then picked up the phone, dialed, and started to dictate his report into the computer in the city room of the *New Coventry Herald*.

24

Bob North came in and sat on the visitor's chair in the hospital board chairman's office. For once he looked flustered, and his hair, which usually looked as if it had been varnished onto his skull, was spiking at the sides.

"Close the door, for God's sake, Bob," said Tony irritably, looking up from the newspapers spread out over the desk. Marino was in a thoroughly bad humor; the corners of his mouth were turned down and his jaw stuck out in an aggressive posture. "Did you see this?" He shoved the paper across the desk to his son-in-law. Bob glanced at the headline which read MORE ON BRACKNELL DEATH. Underneath, in smaller letters, it read: "Questions are being asked about the level of medical care given to Denton Bracknell, the president's senior adviser, who died in a helicopter while being transferred to Bethesda Naval Hospital after undergoing surgery at Glenport Hospital. See story p3."

Bob turned to page three, but Tony didn't give him time to read the three-column story. "That's nothing," he said angrily. "Look at this." He tapped the *New Coventry Herald*, lying under the *Glenport Today*.

"Oh shit," breathed Bob. In huge red letters the headline read DEATH DOC IN TROUBLE AGAIN.

"Read it," ordered Tony, his jowls shaking with anger.

Bob obediently started to read. " 'Dr. Anselm Harris,' " he read, " 'the surgeon at tiny Glenport (pop. 22,500) Hospital who operated on presidential adviser Denton Bracknell shortly before his death, could not be reached today to answer questions about a malpractice suit brought against him in New York over a year ago when he was found guilty of medical negligence resulting in the death of Andy Panneterio, a prominent Bronx politician. This fact was well known to the hospital authorities, said a senior employee who insisted on remaining anonymous, and there was strong feeling in the hospital that Dr. Harris should never have been given privileges there. Dr. Harris was—' "

"That's plenty," said Tony, gritting his teeth. "I knew we should never have let him get on the medical staff with a history like that."

"Well, it wasn't my fault," replied Bob. "I told them he wasn't a suitable—"

"Was it you who told the papers about Harris?" Tony looked suspiciously at his son-in-law.

"Certainly not," replied Bob indignantly. "And I know Stefan forbade the staff to talk with the press."

"Well, now that Harris has got us into all this hot water," said Tony, "we have to figure how to get out of it."

"If Peter Delafield hadn't pushed him on the medical staff, Harris wouldn't be here," muttered Bob. "On the other hand, maybe we can make this situation work for us, Tony," he went on, his face clearing. "If the media concentrates on Harris, it'll take the heat off the hospital and the rest of us."

Tony glowered at him. "Bob," he said, "you're an idiot, if you don't mind my saying so." He stood up. "Don't you see that if Harris is in trouble, so are we for letting him join the staff, and for allowing him to operate on Bracknell? Maybe what we need to do is to show everybody how competent he is, all the great cases he's done, what a good thing he is for the community. After all, something like this Bracknell thing could have happened to any surgeon, right? By the way, how come you weren't there during the surgery? Harris called for you several times, didn't he?"

"I'd already left the hospital," replied Bob. "I couldn't stick around and hold his hand all day long."

"You're going to need a better reason than that," said Tony grimly. "Sandy Bracknell's lawyer's going to read those papers"—he poked a thick finger at the tabloid and then at Bob—"and when he's finished digging up all he can on Harris, he's going to hone down on you, you'd better believe it. I can just see the headlines: 'Chief of Surgery Ignores Surgeon's Plea for Help.' . . . Have you been subpoenaed?"

"No, of course not," replied Bob. "I wasn't involved. Why would they subpoena me?"

"Don't be surprised if they find out about your not being available. And for God's sake, if they do find out, don't lie to them, okay?"

"Of course not," replied Bob, sounding shocked.

"Yeah, right," said Tony, grinning. "Of course not."

The phone rang, and Tony picked it up. "Stefan? right, I was going to call you in a few minutes. Did you see the papers? Yeah. Bob's here. We'll be right over."

Tony came into Stefan's office first. His Italian upbringing emphasized respect for elders and superiors, and he would have liked Stefan to stand when he came in, but knew that it would never happen. But the lack of public, visible respect still griped him. Bob North followed him in and they sat down.

"I just had John Kestler on the phone," said Stefan. The newspapers were spread out over his desk too. "He's panicking. He's going on again about hiring a public relations firm to deal with this bad press we're getting."

"Bullshit," growled Tony. "Kestler's just lazy and incompetent, like half the people around this place." He glowered at Stefan. "Anyway, we've got other things to spend our money on than a bunch of public relations people. What the hell is Erica Barnes doing? Isn't that her job?" His normally hectoring voice was louder even than usual; his position as chairman of the hospital board had never taken up so much of his time, and he was getting rattled.

"So what about those newspapers?" Tony asked, pointing at the desk. "Who was the 'senior employee' who told them about Harris's malpractice suit? I thought you'd told everybody to keep their mouths shut or they'd get fired."

"I don't know who it is," replied Stefan. A worried frown and an uneven shaving job made his face even more like a van Gogh portrait. "We can't figure out where it came from, but we're working on it. And when we do . . ." Stefan's ham-like fists bunched. "I can promise you that person will be very sorry he or she opened their mouth."

"Did you notice that those papers gave credit to the *New Coventry Herald*?" Tony felt very pleased that he'd noticed that. "So whoever was covering the story for the *Herald* must be the one who got the stuff about Harris. Anyway, that's somewhere to start."

"I'll ask Erica," answered Stefan. "She should know who the *Herald* reporter is."

"Okay. Anyway, it's time to figure how much damage has been done here," said Tony. "You tell us. Give us a strategic assessment, like they say at the Pentagon."

"Right on," said Bob, nodding his head in agreement, although he wasn't entirely clear about what a strategic assessment might consist of.

Stefan sighed. "It's too early to tell," he said. "But so far, this is what the situation is, as I see it." He raised one finger. "First and foremost, we have that lawsuit to deal with."

"Those goddamn ambulance-chasing attorneys," said Bob angrily. "I bet they were on the phone to Sandy Bracknell the minute the news was out." He shook his head, then patted down the loose hairs. "It's happening more and more these days. Why, last year I had a patient who—'

"Shut up, Bob," said Tony without heat. "I'm sorry, Stefan. Go on."

"As I understand it, Mr. Marino, their main theme is that we were negligent in allowing Harris to work here and do surgery without supervision, especially considering that malpractice suit he was involved in in New York." Stefan sighed, and his broad shoulders sagged with weariness. "They also charge that Bracknell shouldn't have been operated on, that he should have been transferred to a major center, that he didn't have a full workup, that Harris didn't get a neurological opinion or a second surgical opinion before operating—''

"Isn't all that Harris's problem?" asked Tony. "The hospital wasn't involved in how he made his decisions."

"Well, according to our insurance attorney, we're being held responsible for allowing all that to happen. We let Harris on the staff, he screws up, so basically it's our fault."

"Why are they suing all those other people? I don't mean Harris or Delafield, I mean the ICU nurses, people like that?"

"Apparently that's routine, Mr. Marino. It's a fishing expedition to see if there's anything the attorneys can dig up that'll help them. But they're only really interested in going after the deep pockets, and those belong to the insurance companies, including ours.''

"Can we get out of it? Can't our attorneys get the insurers to settle?''

"I'm sure they'll try,'' replied Stefan. "It'll depend on Mrs. Bracknell's attorney, how good he thinks his case is, how much the insurance company offers, and how hungry he is for the publicity that'll go along with a court case.''

"I'm really surprised that Sandy Bracknell is doing this,'' said Bob, sounding aggrieved. "Especially since one time she had something going with Peter Delafield.''

Stefan and Tony ignored the comment.

"What about the autopsy report? And the report from the navy people?'' asked Tony. "After all, we had an agreement with them that they wouldn't put the blame on us, right?''

Stefan grinned wryly. "Yeah, right. We should get the navy report soon. The autopsy report's in already, and we're making copies for the attorneys and for expert witnesses. Meanwhile there are the other fallout problems we have to deal with.''

Bob shrugged. "Nothing as important as the lawsuit. My reading of the situation is that aside from that, the whole thing will be a week-long phenomenon, then everybody will forget about it and we can all go back to work.''

"I don't think so, Bob,'' said Stefan, keeping his irritation under tight control. "The people who really matter to us in this town don't forget that fast, and this whole business is playing right into their hands.''

"You mean Farman?'' asked Tony, and Stefan nodded.

"I've already had their CEO on the phone,'' he said.

"He said their unions are pushing them hard, so they've decided to go ahead with their health facility."

"What's the health facility to do with it?" asked Bob in a blustery tone. "Just because one of our doctors here screwed up doesn't mean—"

"They've been waiting for something like this," explained Stefan patiently. "You know they put us on notice several months ago that they're not happy with the service and care they get here, and they say the costs are excessive."

"That's just nonsense," interrupted Bob loudly. "We have all the people and medical facilities this community needs right here."

"That is not their perception, Bob," replied Stefan equally loudly, and both Tony and Bob stared at him. Stefan's face was flushed, and neither of them had ever seen him this close to losing his cool.

"Bob, you have to understand," said Stefan, getting a hold of himself and speaking in his normal deep, quiet voice. "Just telling them that we think differently isn't going to cut any ice at all. Farman has supported us in the past, given us money when we needed to build a wing or when we needed equipment. They always have given all of their medical business to the local doctors and the hospital. And now, for a variety of reasons, some of which we know about, they've decided to do their own thing." Stefan took a deep breath, amazed that he had to explain all this to Bob, who had as much as anyone to lose. "Anyway, Erica Barnes has developed a good relationship with some of the senior union people, so we're working on that angle."

"Yeah," said Bob, grinning. "Erica should be able to make those guys come around, one way or another."

"We have to do something *positive* to make Farman want to stay with us," Stefan went on, studiously ignoring Bob's comment, but a noticeable hardening of his tone showed his annoyance. "The way it's going, and Mr. Marino knows I'm right, is that by this time next year we'll be out of business as a real hospital, and we'll be relegated to being just an emergency room and a way station for New Coventry Medical Center."

"Or else some private hospital'll come in, cut a deal with Farman, bring in their own docs and staff," said Tony. He grinned unpleasantly at Bob. "Maybe they'll find a job for you working in the emergency room, Bob, or maybe in the laundry."

Bob flushed.

Stefan addressed Tony. "What we have to do, Mr. Marino," he said, "and I've discussed it with their management, is to get the board to authorize money to bring our labs up to date, build a new emergency room with better facilities, develop better outpatient facilities so that their employees don't have to wait around for hours before they get taken care of. I'm afraid, though, that whatever we do will be too little and too late."

"The patients don't have to wait that long in the emergency room," protested Bob, still annoyed. "Why, I've been there when—"

Stefan interupted. "You remember last year, Bob, when they boycotted the hospital for two weeks because of the man who died in our emergency room?"

Bob subsided in his chair. He had been the surgeon on call that evening, and his late appearance at the hospital was partly responsible for the fiasco.

Tony said, "Why don't we tell Farman that we'll put in new equipment and all that stuff in the hospital, whatever it takes to keep them from going it on their own?"

"Because we've gone that route before," replied Stefan. "I used that argument almost a year ago, and the board didn't come through."

Tony hammered his big fists together in sheer frustration. "That goddamn board . . . I just can't get them to do a damn thing. They don't understand what's going on, and they're as tightfisted as if the money was coming out of their own pockets."

"It's not just that," said Bob, for once seeing a chance to get back at his father-in-law. "It's a class thing. *You* can't get anything done with the board because you're not old money or old landed family."

Tony's glower should have frizzled the remaining hairs on Bob's head, but he continued, blithely unaware of danger. "Tony, they made you chairman because you have the money and the interest to do it, but you'll never get their respect or their cooperation."

"Or yours, apparently," said Tony, staring at Bob. "But *that* is a problem I can do something about."

Not wanting their squabble to develop further, Stefan asked them what they were thinking of doing about Anselm Harris.

"Right," said Tony, still glowering at Bob. "That's the next decision we have to make. We have to decide whether it's better to get behind Harris and back him all the way, or else blast him publicly and fire his ass off the staff."

There was a silence while the three men thought about it. Tony's way of putting the question was brutal, but at least it was unambiguous.

"The hospital acted in good faith," said Stefan. "When his name came up for consideration for hospital privileges, we knew about his malpractice history, and everybody had a chance to discuss it. Appropriate questions were asked and satisfactory answers were given. We can't be responsible for everything that happens in this hospital. After all, Harris isn't the only guy around here who's had a malpractice judgment against him."

"We went over his record carefully when he came

here," said Tony, agreeing. "His application had to go through a whole bunch of committees. They all felt that he was well qualified and had been unlucky to lose that malpractice suit in New York."

"Peter Delafield pushed us into accepting him," said Bob. "If it hadn't been for his backing, Harris would never have got privileges."

"The votes were unanimous," said Stefan. "You were on two of those committees, Bob, and you voted for him both times."

"I was pressured," said Bob, his voice rising defensively. "Like everybody else."

"Okay, let's look at the pros and cons of the present situation," said Tony. "What would be the reasons for getting on Harris's side?"

"Consistency," said Stefan. "It makes us look good if we support our own guy when he's in trouble."

"Also it shows we're standing by our decision to give him privileges," said Tony. "If we admit we goofed, we're legally that much more liable, right, Stefan?"

He nodded. "Anything else?" he asked.

Nobody spoke.

"Reasons to throw him out?" Tony pulled out a cigar and clipped the end before sticking it in his mouth and lighting it. His lighter threw a flame six inches long, and Stefan and Bob watched in silence until the cigar was going to Tony's satisfaction.

"When I talked to Farman's CEO this morning," said Stefan slowly, "he told me his unions want us to get rid of Harris right away. It may be just a ploy, but if we move to get him off the staff, it would show that we're taking them seriously. If we combine that with improvements to the hospital, we might be able to get them to put off starting on their medical facility."

"Good thinking," said Bob. "In any case, we can't seriously back a guy like Harris, who has a bad record and who's screwed up again. I suggest we take our lumps, admit we were wrong, but show that we're able to discipline our docs and take decisive action when necessary.''

Tony surveyed his son-in-law without affection. "Bob," he said, "you'd be a lot more persuasive if I didn't know that you're just looking out for yourself. I also know why you went along with Peter Delafield when he wanted to get Harris on the staff.''

"Oh yeah? Why was that?" Bob's occasional efforts to stand up to Tony made him seem ludicrous, and he was uncomfortably aware of that.

"Because your practice was already on the way down. A good proportion of your referrals came from Delafield, and you figured that if you went along with him on giving Harris privileges, you'd still get a bit of the pie, but if you went against him you'd get none.''

"Well, it certainly didn't work out that way," replied Bob angrily. "Since Harris got here, Delafield hasn't referred a single goddamned case to me, unless it was somebody I'd already seen or operated on.''

"Are you trying to make me cry?" Tony took a deep breath. "What I'm failing to get you to understand is that first we have look out for the hospital. If we succeed, then the medical staff and the administration will make out okay. If we do like you're doing, just thinking about your own income and personal reputation, such as it is, we'll all go down the tube together.''

"Right, Tony, of course, I agree, but I still don't see—''

"I know you don't see," interrupted Tony, finally out of patience. "So don't bother trying. From now on, just do what I tell you." He turned to Stefan. "So what do *you* think? Back Harris, or fire his ass out of here?''

"There's one more thing that has a bearing on what

decision we make," said Stefan. "Even before the Bracknell business, the medical staff was divided about Harris. If we throw him out, it might have a good effect on the medical staff's solidarity and morale."

Bob nodded emphatically but didn't say anything, afraid Tony would jump all over him again.

"Then it looks as if Harris is out, right?" Tony looked from Bob to Stefan.

"I guess," said Stefan.

"No question," said Bob.

"Okay, then," said Tony. "What we have to do now is figure out the best way of getting Harris off the staff, and make sure we do it right, every legal point taken care of, so we don't just finish up with another lawsuit on our hands."

"He won't give us any problems," said Bob confidently. "I know his kind. He'll go without a squeal."

25

As usual, Stefan felt relieved when Tony and Bob left his office. He looked on his desk calendar and saw that Erica Barnes was scheduled to come in before her meeting with the Farman union people.

He thought about her for a minute. Erica was good at her job, and did certain tasks involving other people better than he could, because she was local, bright, female, and attractive. Stefan had of course been tempted to develop a relationship with her, because like him, she was single, but Stefan had always been careful to keep business and pleasure at a safe distance from each other, and so far had resisted both his own inclinations and her occasional very tentative flirtations with him. Every so often a small voice suggested to him that if he was smart enough, he could find a way to combine work with pleasure, and that would make him a truly contented man. But all such thoughts had been pushed out of his head by the Bracknell case.

There was a knock on the door and Erica came in, looking great in a red blazer, black skirt, and dark stockings.

"You're going to knock 'em dead," said Stefan. "You look great."

Erica smiled. Stefan hadn't told her anything she didn't know already.

They talked about her assignment for about twenty minutes, then Erica looked at her watch. "I'd better get going," she said. "I'll come right back and tell you how it went."

She knew just how to give a little seductive twist to her body as she walked, and she did so, all the way to the door.

Every few weeks Erica met informally with her opposite number, Andy McKeown, at Farman Industries. Occasionally the representatives of their plant unions would join them. Erica had initiated the meetings a year before at Stefan's suggestion, because of Farman's importance to the hospital and because relations were already strained at that time.

Their meetings were held in the hospital cafeteria, and scheduled in mid-afternoon when not too many people were around.

Andy McKeown was Farman's VP for public relations, and Big John Abrams the main union representative. The day was chilly, and they both appeared in the cafeteria muffled in parkas, Big John lumbering after the quick-footed Andy.

To Erica, waiting for them at a table at the far end of the long room, they both looked very somber, even from that distance.

The men went to get coffee at the dispenser and brought their cups over to the table and sat down, one on each side of her.

After the initial pleasantries, Andy spoke first. "I guess the shit's really hitting the fan with that Bracknell business, huh, Erica?"

"That's what we have to put up with these days," she replied, smiling. "Aren't you guys glad you work in a nice safe industry like Farman?"

Both men laughed.

"I was reading the papers about your Dr. Harris,"

said Big John Abrams. "How the hell did that guy ever get on your staff in the first place?"

"John, you mustn't believe everything you read." Erica's smile was strained. "Dr. Harris has done a wonderful job here, and everybody's been very happy that he's come on board. But sure, right now the hospital's investigating the whole case, and if he did anything wrong, they'll certainly take whatever action is necessary."

"It's a funny thing, Erica," said the union man slowly, "but in this whole Bracknell business, it's Dr. Harris that bothers my members more than anything. It's the idea that this guy was thrown out of New York and finishes up taking care of our people here, like we're getting the medical rejects nobody else wants."

"Management's upset about that too," agreed Andy. "And the theme song around the plant this week is 'Tired of life? Consult Dr. Harris!' "

Big John nodded ponderously. "That's right. And that's why for once we agree with management, Erica," he said. "We've decided to back them on building the medical facility so we can take care of our own people."

"It's settled?" asked Erica.

"Just about," replied Big John. "We have a joint meeting with management tomorrow to ratify the plan in principle. That'll give them the go-ahead. They already have a site selected."

"What do you think your members will get from your clinic that they don't get here?" asked Erica.

"Better care," said Andy simply.

"For less money," added John.

"You're really singing management's song, aren't you, John?" teased Erica. Andy and John stared at her, taken aback, both thinking that any male who had made such a comment would have got a fist in his face.

"That's okay," she went on a little wryly. "You're not alone. I have to sing the management song too."

John shook a cigarette out, remembered the no-smoking rule at the hospital, and pushed the Camel slowly back into the pack. Andy, who had stopped smoking several years before, grinned at him.

"Have you visited any other corporate clinics like the one you're going to get?" asked Erica.

"Yeah, I went to the United Pharmaceuticals clinic in New Coventry about a year ago," replied John cautiously. "Andy came with me. They gave us a tour. It was a pretty impressive place, I must say."

"Sure was," added Andy. "Everything brand-new, clean and modern."

"Did you talk to any of the doctors there?" asked Erica, who had also visited that clinic.

There was a pause.

"Yes, we did," replied John.

"What did you think?" asked Erica.

"Well, to tell the truth, I couldn't quite understand what he was saying," replied John. His chair creaked as he moved in it.

"He was Korean," said Andy. "Seemed pretty agreeable kind of guy, though, didn't you think, John?"

"Sure was."

"And they have to know what they're doing, or they wouldn't be allowed to practice in the U.S., right?"

"The United Pharmaceuticals clinic *used* to employ twelve doctors," said Erica. "The only people they could get to work there were foreign medical graduates. Apparently company clinics are having the same problem all around the country."

Erica leaned back, watching that information sink in. "How would you guys like to be brought there after an accident and you couldn't understand the doctor who's taking care of you and he couldn't understand you? How about if it was your kid, or your wife who got hurt?''

She turned to Andy. ''Is that the kind of doctor you'd like to deliver your child, Andy?'' Erica knew she was on sensitive ground there, because his wife was due in three months.

John and Andy looked at each other.

''Now, this type of clinic typically only handles the really simple stuff,'' Erica went on. ''If there's even a minor complication, what happens? If a patient needs more tests or treatment than the clinic offers, then what do you think happens?''

The ensuing silence was broken by Andy.

''I suppose they'd send them down here.''

Erica shook her head. ''No way. If Farman builds that clinic, this hospital will to all intents and purposes shut down, because half of our business is with you guys and your families. No, for anything beyond minimum care, you'll have to go all the way to New Coventry. If you're really sick, like a pregnant woman having a bad hemorrhage, she'd go by ambulance. It takes a bit over an hour, door to door, unless of course it's icy or foggy.''

The two men looked thoughtful and surprised as they digested this information.

''I guess that your management will accomplish half of what they set out to do, though.'' Erica took a sip of coffee and watched them with her clear hazel eyes.

Andy and John watched her.

''What half?'' asked John. ''What are you talking about?''

Erica said, ''Your management will get their medical costs down, no question. But you guys had better get used to the idea that your members and their families are not going to get *anything* like the quality or depth of service you get here.''

Erica judged her moment, stood up, and went to

refill her coffee cup, and out of the corner of her eye she could see John and Andy huddled in discussion.

When she came back, Andy had a question. "You mentioned that United Pharmaceuticals *used* to employ twelve docs at their clinic," he said, smiling, thinking he could trap her. "Does that mean they've expanded and employ a bunch more docs now, or what?"

"It means that they shut the clinic down eight months ago," replied Erica. "The employees and their relatives refused to go there anymore. They almost had a strike over it."

The meeting broke up soon afterward, and Andy and John went back to their cars and talked earnestly for almost a half hour before driving home.

The day after Lucille's passionate evening with Michael Parrett, she bathed in a hot glow of sexual fulfillment, which was soon replaced by a deep, hard yearning. Michael Parrett was her man, she knew it, she was quite certain. And he was such a wonderful lover, a sensitive, thoughtful, caring person, and obviously deeply in love with her. Lucille felt weak at the memory of Michael on top of her, behind her, growling and thrusting into her. . . .

What she needed to do now, she realized, was consolidate the relationship. It would take planning, she realized that. A man as electrifying and attractive as Michael Parrett wasn't going to give up his freedom without a struggle. In the past Lucille had always failed to get her man to the altar, and each time, after the hurt was gone, she had carefully analyzed the causes of the fiasco. Now, with enough experience and insight into the male mind, she would make it work this time. It had to work; the rest of her life depended on it.

The OR secretary came into Lucille's office.

"Mr. Olson wants you to call him," she said, noting Lucille's vacant, almost dazed expression. "Are you all right, Miss Heinz?"

Lucille stared coldly back to her. "Of course I'm all right," she replied. "When did Mr. Olson call?"

"About ten minutes ago," said the secretary. "Shall I put you through?"

"No, I'll call him from here." Lucille had caught the secretary's expression and instantly wondered if there was any way the woman could have heard about her adventure with Michael. Maybe someone had seen the two of them at the hotel, or while they were having dinner in the restaurant.

"Please come down to my office," said Stefan a few moments later when she returned his call. "Right now, if you don't mind."

All kinds of thoughts rushed through Lucille's mind as she hurried down to the first floor, where the administrative offices were located. Maybe somebody *had* seen them, Stefan was going to haul her over the coals for fraternizing with a member of the press. Maybe it had to do with all the overtime she had accumulated over the past few months, and maybe they'd been checking up on her, or, oh God, she thought, maybe somebody had found the source of the stories in the *New Coventry Herald*.

"Sit down, please, Lucille." Stefan looked up from his desk. There were dark rings around his eyes, and he looked weary and ten years older.

Lucille sat, her knees clamped primly together. Her palms were sweating, and she clasped her hands together in her lap, her pale eyes staring at Stefan.

"I want you to make out a complete report of the operation on Denton Bracknell." He raised his hand when Lucille opened her mouth to protest. "I know it's an unusual request, but I wish to have that report all the same. There are a lot of problems already arising from this case. A lot of questions are going to be asked, and I want to be quite sure that we've covered every avenue, and that the hospital has investigated every source of information concerning the case.''

''What exactly do you want me to write, Mr. Olson? I'm not quite sure what you mean by a report.''

''Well, everything that happened, the times the patient came in and out, his condition, *any problems that arose during the operation, any disagreements with other doctors,* that kind of thing.'' Stefan emphasized the words, and Lucille understood immediately.

''I can do that,'' she said. She stood up, a strange look in her gray eyes. ''When do you want it, Mr. Olson?''

''Today,'' replied Stefan. ''Do it while your memory is still fresh and exact.''

''I'll have it back to you by this afternoon,'' promised Lucille, joyfully realizing that the report would not only be another nail in Anselm Harris's coffin, but also a lure she could use to keep Michael around while she prepared to sink the final hook into him.

26

The next day, Valerie drove back to Glenport, in a way looking forward to her next visit with Anselm and in a way not. There was something disturbing about the man; on first appearance he had seemed in full control of his life and situation, but it was clear that his solid base of professional achievement was crumbling underneath him. Did he fully understand that? Was he just blind to what was going on around him, or was he just putting on a good show of nonchalance while getting his defenses together?

Already Valerie could feel the clouds gathering around him; her instincts and what she had seen and heard about Anselm Harris told her that he was too direct, too uncompromising to be very popular with his colleagues, and she knew what a huge difference that made. A popular doctor who entertained a lot, was respectful to the colleagues who referred to him, who was good-humored, told funny stories, played golf with the local power players, could get away with murder, and Valerie had heard plenty of stories about doctors who had. But a couple of times during their interview, before he got so defensive, it had seemed that there was more to him than met the eye, a quick humor, but the break had closed almost as soon as it opened.

The weather was fine, and the view over the Thames River from the Gold Star Bridge at New London was spectacular. To the right she saw a cluster of white sails, moving slowly like a lazy flock of gulls low on the water. Farther up the river the long, eerie gray shape of a Trident nuclear submarine emerged from the submarine base, shepherded by two ocean-going tugs. They looked like ants towing a dead moth.

Valerie enjoyed the momentary distraction, but when she got back to the humdrum business of driving along I-95, Anselm's case occupied her full attention. She went over all the allegations detailed in the summons. The words *willful neglect, incompetence,* and *professional misconduct* had been featured frequently, and for a moment she felt badly for Dr. Harris. But it wasn't the first time this had happened to him, she thought, and maybe he *had* been neglectful and incompetent. But that wasn't the point, not now. Her job was to defend him, to explain his every action in a way that would show him to be a caring and able surgeon who had done the best he could on his patient's behalf while dealing with an irreversible and incurable situation.

At this point Valerie wasn't trying to build a defense, or even attempting to understand everything that had happened while Denton Bracknell was in Anselm Harris's care. She limited herself to building an empathy with the defendant, an understanding of how his mind worked and what his motivations were. There was an intuitive feeling in the back of her mind that she had to do this first, and let the facts of the case fall into place later. On the other hand, Anselm had got defensive when asked about the non-medical part of his life, and she decided not to ask any more questions that weren't directly related to the case. As somebody had once told her, asking direct questions is the crudest and least satisfactory way of getting the answers you really want.

The traffic slowed abruptly, and for the next fifteen minutes Valerie followed a school bus full of teenage kids, mostly boys, who gathered around the back window and shouted soundlessly, jumped around, and made faces. One of them made a crude monodigital gesture at her. When Valerie stuck her hand out the window and returned it with some vigor, they all disappeared from the window, shocked. With that distraction gone, she asked herself if she was just putting off the hard part, the medical part, by playing around with the easy stuff, like getting to know who her client was. Valerie was already aware that the Bracknell case was very complex, and it would take a lot more time figuring out the best way to defend it, than, for instance, finding who owned a given piece of property in New Coventry.

Valerie's mind went back to Ralph, and she laughed, remembering his expression when he was forced to praise her work at the very moment he so badly wanted to kick her ass into the street. She laughed at the thought, but her fists tightened, knowing that she could take out the pudgy, flabby Ralph any time, and do permanent damage to him without even raising a sweat. Valerie realized that her mind was again slipping away from the task she had set herself. Come on, girl, she told herself, annoyed, keep your mind on your case. There's a lot at stake here, and not only for your client.

But for some stubborn reason her mind wouldn't cooperate, and before she knew it she was at the Glenport exit, negotiating a sharp turn onto the two-lane road that led into the center of the town.

When Valerie came into the office, there was nobody at the receptionist's desk. She pressed the buzzer, and a moment later the door to his office opened and

Anselm came out. Valerie had a fleeting impression that he was quite glad to see her.

"Sorry about that," he said, smiling. "Melanie's mother is sick and I can't find anyone to take her place. Come on in. Would you like some coffee?"

"Thanks, yes." He went off to make it.

When he came back bearing two mugs of coffee, he told Valerie he'd received a copy of Admiral Ellis's report, hot on the heels of the autopsy report, which had arrived the day before. Anselm took them both out of a desk drawer and laid them beside the other documents. The admiral's report was bound, printed, and stamped CONFIDENTIAL in red across the front. To Valerie it had a threatening look, as if the success or failure of her case depended on what lay between its covers.

"Good," she said briskly. "We'll go over it later. Meanwhile, let's go over Mr. Bracknell's hospital admission, how it happened, every detail you can remember up to the time you passed responsibility for him to the navy people."

That took longer than either of them expected. Valerie made voluminous notes and wanted to know every detail of the accident in the corridor, and who was in medical charge at that time.

Then she changed the direction of her questioning. "Do you think you took care of Mr. Bracknell in exactly the same way you'd have treated anyone else with the same problem?" she asked. When Anselm answered affirmatively, she went on, "They're going to go after the fact that you didn't transfer Bracknell immediately. To the best of your knowledge," she asked, "would he have been treated any differently in New Coventry Medical Center? Or in Bethesda Naval Hospital?"

Anselm had thought about that. "No," he said slowly. "No, I don't think so. Of course, the navy people wouldn't agree. They'd say that they have better-trained staff people and state-of-the-art equipment, but basically they would have done the same tests, come to the same conclusion, and—I'm convinced—operated on him. But then things always look different through the retrospectoscope."

Valerie looked up questioningly.

"That's a mythical instrument," he explained, smiling. "Extremely useful but unfortunately only available after the fact."

She returned his smile and felt an unexpected warmth, an empathy with Anselm, and wondered if she would be able to show that kind of gentle humor if threatened with the loss of her livelihood.

Then she picked up Lucille Heinz's report. "Is this normal procedure?" she asked. "Does the OR supervisor write a report on every case?"

"This is the first time I've ever seen that happen," said Anselm. "I suppose it's because it was a case that attracted so much outside attention."

"It's not very favorable, is it?" asked Valerie, after reading the typed sheets.

"No. Lucille Heinz dislikes me for reasons I won't go into now. I'm sure she was glad to get a chance to do this."

Valerie looked at Anselm; she was uncomfortable with the major differences of medical opinion she was uncovering concerning the care that had been given Denton Bracknell. She glanced at Dr. Burton's report, which she had also read. "In fact," she said, tapping the documents, "put together these two reports are rather damning, wouldn't you say?"

Anselm agreed.

Valerie frowned. "How much cooperation are you getting from the hospital?" she asked. "The administrator must have asked for these reports with the knowledge that they would become available to the plaintiff's attorneys.'' She paused, and she tried to figure out what was going on behind Anselm Harris's gray eyes. ''Is there any reason they might be ganging up on you?''

''It's possible,'' said Anselm. He didn't feel this was the time to elaborate. ''There are reasons the hospital might want to get rid of me, but I don't think they have anything to do with this case.''

Valerie shuffled her papers and gathered herself for the possible unpleasantness to come. ''Dr. Harris,'' she said, ''at some point we're going to have to discuss your previous malpractice suit. I think this might be a suitable time, if that's all right with you.''

''No problem,'' said Anselm. ''The papers have already had a field day on that.''

''I'm sure you know that, officially, nobody knows about that case,'' replied Valerie. ''If we come to a jury trial, the plaintiff's attorney can't even mention it unless we make a mistake and it gets admitted into evidence. The problem is that the jury reads the papers too, and even though they're told to disregard something like that, it's often better to bring it out into the open, especially if we can make a rebuttal or at least present a different side to the story.''

Anselm watched Valerie as she talked, and imagined her presenting her case in court. She was wearing a white silk blouse and a beige skirt of thin gabardine. A midnight blue belt with discreet gold trim made a match with her dark hose and shoes. The outfit was simple enough, and probably not too expensive, but it had class, and accentuated Valerie's attractiveness. For the first time since they had met, Anselm was distracted by her physical presence, and had to make an effort to concentrate on what she was saying.

''You want to hear the story?'' he asked. ''Okay, I'll tell it to you, all of it, just the way it happened.''

He sat back in his chair. He had thought about the

case so much that it had lost a lot of its original emotional impact, although occasionally it still made his bowels contract when he thought about it.

"I happened to be working in the emergency room at the Queen's City Hospital one evening," said Anselm. "There was a big fuss at the door, and this guy came in with a whole retinue of people. He was a state senator, name of Andy Panneterio, about sixty years old and very much of a local big shot, supposedly with ties to various mob factions. He knew just about everybody in the ER, most of them by name. Anyway, his driver, who was called Em, for Emilio, had accidentally banged the car door against Panneterio's leg, and although it wasn't much of an injury, the leg didn't look good, with some mottling and his ankle pulses were diminished on that side. I told Panneterio he should have tests and come in for treatment, but he'd had a few drinks, was very talkative, and absolutely refused anything except a dressing on the cut. Anyway, he took a shine to me, told one of his guys to put something in an envelope for me, and that turned out to be six fifty-dollar bills. On the way out, still trying to get Panneterio to stay for tests and treatment, I gave the money back to Em and told him to give it back to his boss once they'd got him home.

"Next day, I got a call from a guy called Joe, who said Andy's leg was all swollen and red-looking. I told him to bring Andy back to the ER immediately, but they never showed up.

"The day after that, Em, Panneterio's driver, the guy I returned the money to and who'd banged Andy's leg with the car door, showed up in the same ER. He was alive but brain-damaged, and his face was bashed to a pulp. Then I got a call from the doctor in charge of the ER at Beth Israel in Manhattan. Panneterio had been admitted in a diabetic coma, and his leg was already gangrenous. The doc was really angry, wanted to know why we'd let him leave the hospital when he was so obviously in serious trouble, and requested a copy of his chart.''

Anselm paused and looked at Valerie. It was important to him that she understood what had actually happened, not what the press had reported. She sat there, her knees together, legs set at a slight angle, looking at him, listening carefully, making notes, not saying anything.

''The records department couldn't find the chart at first, but it showed up a day later, although I didn't see it. Panneterio died, and within days I was served with a malpractice suit, charging negligence in not admitting him to the hospital, not diagnosing his diabetes, not seeing that his leg was pre-gangrenous, and about a dozen other things.''

''Who was the widow's lawyer?'' asked Valerie.

''He was a crook, a guy who worked exclusively for upper-echelon Mafia types. They wouldn't settle, and when it came to trial, they showed that Panneterio's chart had been altered, the implication being that it had been changed by me. They also brought in two nurses who swore they saw me pocket the money, and that I'd told Panneterio that all he needed was a dressing on his leg.'' Anselm smiled grimly. ''One of these nurses wasn't even in the hospital the day Panneterio came in.''

''That attorney, do you happen to remember his name?'' asked Valerie.

Anselm told her, and Valerie wrote it down.

''Your attorney, didn't he get witnesses? Like the ER nurses who'd seen you working on Panneterio?''

Anselm laughed. ''Are you kidding? Maybe you don't know Queens, but no nurse who wants to keep her looks and her job would ever testify against Andy Panneterio's widow. And my attorney . . .'' Anselm's fists bunched. ''He was a drunk,'' he said. ''You could smell his mint breath five minutes before he arrived. Anyway, he'd made up his mind he wasn't going to win this case, so he didn't even try. He didn't even attempt to refute the altered chart.'' His eyes gleamed with retrospective anger and frustration. ''And I found out later the guy was also on the mob's payroll.''

Valerie, taking notes, said nothing more about the suit but instead asked, ''Dr. Harris, have you had any other malpractice suits aside from that one?''

''No. I was briefly named in another one several years back, but they took my name off and anyway the suit was withdrawn.''

Valerie then wanted to go over parts of Bracknell's chart. She looked up from the pad on her knee, working hard to sound in control and confident, but in fact a lot of what Anselm had said, and much of the medical terminology in the report, had gone right over her head. ''But first, as I told you, I'm not familiar with a lot of your medical terminology. You're just going to have to help me when I get stuck, okay?''

Anselm smiled, thinking it much preferable to deal with an attorney who was ignorant than with one who was stupid or a drunk or, like O'Connell, both. Ignorance was a curable condition, whereas the other two were not.

''While Denton Bracknell was on the way over from Carver's Island, Dr. Peter Delafield had advised on his treatment, right?''

''Yes. I didn't hear the conversations he had with the people on the boat. You'll have to ask him.''

''I will. When Bracknell was admitted to the hospital, that was under Dr. Delafield's care, wasn't it?''

''Yes, I didn't see him until—''

''We'll get to that in a moment,'' said Valerie. ''So Dr. Delafield was the one who wrote the admission note, wrote orders, decided who to consult?''

Anselm tapped the chart. "Yes, it's all here."

"Now, if an internist asks a surgeon to see a patient, does that mean he transfers full responsibility to him?"

"No, not if he's just asking for an opinion."

"How about when the surgeon recommends surgery?"

"Then, normally the patient would be transferred to the surgeon's service, and the surgeon would put the original internist on service also."

"By 'on service' you mean the original physician would share the responsibility, make joint decisions with the surgeon about the patient's care?"

"Right. Usually the internist would make decisions in matters that concerned his own specialty, like medications, treatment of associated problems, stuff like that. The surgeon would take responsibility for problems within his own specialty." Anselm could see where the questions were leading.

"I see." Valerie made a notation on her yellow legal pad. She paused and looked directly at Anselm. She had clear green eyes, and he found them distracting. "I've read your notes," she said, "and I got the impression that right up to the time the decision was made, you were reluctant to operate."

Anselm sat back in his chair and put his hands behind his head. He grinned at Valerie, and suddenly he had a boyish, vulnerable look about him.

"I was," he said. "There's no argument about that. But it was ultimately my decision, and I did the operation. Nobody forced me to do it at gunpoint."

Watching him, Valerie wondered if he was fully aware of all the various pressures that had been brought to bear on his decision-making with regard to Bracknell. But she knew instinctively that this was not the moment to discuss it; already she was finding out that Anselm Harris was more complex and unpredictable than he looked or than she had expected. He would need to be handled with care; even now she felt that a poorly judged comment or careless question from her could reverse the good relationship she felt they were building up.

Also, Valerie had always thought of surgeons as technicians; a real doctor would figure out what was the matter with the patient, then if there was no other way out, they'd put a knife in the surgeon's hand and tell him what to do. And in some ways that was what seemed to have happened in Bracknell's case, although Anselm had not grasped the branch she'd held out to him. Apparently he had decided to take full responsibility not only for the operation itself, but for the decisions that had preceded it. Well, that too was something she could work on later.

"Now let's talk about what the navy doctors had to say," said Valerie, picking the bound report off the desk and flipping through it. The text was divided with military precision into sections: a preface, Bracknell's condition on their arrival at Glenport Hospital, the factors leading to the decision to transfer him, events in the helicopter taking him to Bethesda, and finally an analysis of the way the entire case had been handled, first by Drs. Delafield and Harris, then by the navy specialists.

"Let's take the preface first," said Valerie.

In the first ten pages of the report Admiral Ellis discussed the conditions under which he and his team had been asked to see the patient, a word-by-word transcript of the telephone conversations he had had with the hospital administrator, Stefan Olson, Drs. Delafield and Harris, and the instructions the admiral had received from the White House to transfer Denton Bracknell to a naval hospital facility if medically advisable.

"It says here that in his first discussion with you, Admiral Ellis strongly advised against carrying out any kind of surgical operation," said Valerie, tapping the page.

"Right. At the time we had the conversation, I entirely agreed," replied Anselm. "That was before Bracknell had his second attack, when both Dr. Delafield and I felt he'd had another cerebral embolus."

There was a pause, during which he watched Valerie's face. "By that I mean a clot giving up and blocking the flow of blood into his brain." Unnerved that her ignorance showed so clearly, Valerie lowered her eyes. Two faint spots of red appeared on her cheekbones.

"So you felt that the entire set of conditions had changed since the conversation with Admiral Ellis?" she asked, trying to recoup.

"Certainly. You can check the times if you want. In any case, to be perfectly frank, both Dr. Delafield and I took Admiral Ellis's advice with a pinch of salt."

Valerie looked up. Anselm's face was serious, but she thought there might be a hint of humor around his eyes.

"Why was that?" She was surprised; she felt that most doctors would have listened carefully to what the admiral in charge of a prestigious naval hospital would have to say.

"Admiral Ellis mentioned right at the beginning that he was trained as a pediatrician," said Anselm.

Valerie's mouth moved in the faintest of smiles, and she made a note.

"Presumably then, he was taking advice from . . ." Valerie checked the file. "The neurologist, Dr. Neville Sachs, and the neurosurgeon, Dr. Simon Faber, don't you think?"

"They came in later, I think," said Anselm. "What's more, it doesn't refer to either of them in the preface, and as they say in the air force, if it ain't written, it didn't happen.''

Valerie looked up at his tone. If she had had any doubts about his toughness before, they were disappearing fast.

The next part of the report detailed the condition of the patient as they found him when they arrived at Glenport Hospital, together with a list of the tests and procedures that had been performed on the patient.

Anselm agreed that in all important aspects the report was correct, and they discussed that for a while.

After they had gone over every word in the report, Valerie closed it with a thump and thought for a second. There was no point in mincing her words. "It's pretty clear," she said. "They don't think the case was handled correctly while Bracknell was in Glenport.''

"Of course they don't," replied Anselm. "That report was written to make the navy look good and keep them out of trouble. In fact"—Anselm leaned forward, staring hard at Valerie—"even if Denton Bracknell had been taken directly from Carver's Island to Bethesda, there is no question in my mind that he'd have finished up just as dead as he is now.''

Valerie made a quick note, thinking how Norm Hartman would handle that reply.

She glanced at the clock. "Time to go," she said, putting the papers back in order into her briefcase. "I won't be back for a few days," she went on. "I have to set up depositions and talk to potential expert witnesses on your behalf. Next time I'd like to go over the autopsy report, and in more detail the statements by Dr. Burton and Miss Heinz." She stood up and held out her hand to Anselm. "So far I think we're doing just fine, Dr. Harris,'' she said. ''I'll call you.''

Back on I-95 and heading south, Valerie started to sing along with the radio. For some reason she couldn't define yet, she was really beginning to enjoy working on this case.

27

The next morning, Stefan Olson invited Anselm to his office for a conference with John Kestler and himself. Stefan looked grim and Kestler looked uncomfortable.

"Have you been in touch with Mrs. Bracknell, Dr. Harris?" Kestler asked Anselm. "It's very important for all of us to maintain a good relationship with her."

"Actually, my attorney advised me not to talk to her or to anyone else about the case at this time," replied Anselm in mild surprise. "You and my attorney must have gone to different law schools."

Stefan, sitting behind his desk, nodded at Anselm. "I agree with you. Of course, the hospital's in a slightly different situation. I sent a big bouquet of flowers and a personal handwritten sympathy note to her home," he said. "I want to be sure she knows we're on her side and did the best we could for her husband."

"To answer your question," said Anselm, "no, I haven't been in touch with her. But I'm sure that's not why you called this meeting."

"Right, it isn't." Kestler was a large, slow-moving man with a big jaw and a tired, heavy-lidded expression. He had worked at his quiet and lucrative law practice in Glenport for forty years, mainly doing real estate law. He didn't feel at all comfortable in this kind of situation, and he knew there was worse to come very soon. He turned to Stefan, his expression anguished and slack-lipped, a man who knew that he was out of his depth. "Stefan, I wish you'd take it from here. I'm just an old country lawyer, and this kind of thing is outside my expertise."

"I don't know what the two of you are getting uptight about," said Anselm. "We did our best for Bracknell, but he was too far gone to have a chance. There's going to be a lawsuit that's going to waste a lot of everybody's time and money, and when that's over, things go back to normal, right?"

"I doubt it," said Stefan.

"By the way, Dr. Harris," Stefan asked, "I assume you received your copy of the subpoena?"

"Yes, I did. I've also seen the attorney they assigned me. Now could we get on with whatever we're here for?"

"We're getting there." Stefan was feeling tired to the bone. "Our attorneys will be contacting yours concerning the defense of the lawsuit within the next few days."

John cleared his throat. It was apparent that he had been detailed to fire the first salvo. "There was a pretty unflattering article about you in the *New Coventry Herald*, Dr. Harris," he said, looking at some point well above Anselm's head. "I have no doubt you saw it. At some point we're probably going to have to make some kind of statement about that previous malpractice suit you had in New York, and point out that we knew about it and considered it when you applied for privileges here."

"Fine with me." Anselm looked unconcerned. "There's no secret about it, and it's all a matter of record now."

"I wonder who gave the press that information," said Stefan thoughtfully. "The article stated that their source was a senior member of the hospital staff. Do you know of anyone here with any kind of grudge against you, Dr. Harris?''

Anselm shrugged. ''I don't know who gave it. It could have been any one of a number of people. I'm not at the top of *everybody's* popularity list here.''

Stefan gave a wry grin, and John, watching him, grinned too, a moment later.

''I talked earlier to Andy McKeown, the vice-president at Farman in charge of public relations,'' said Stefan. He stood up and paced behind his desk. ''Apparently the union reps read the newspaper articles about you and called for a joint meeting with Farman's executive committee. As a result, Farman states that they're willing to put their medical facility on hold, but on one condition,'' he said.

''What's that?'' asked John on cue.

''That we revoke Dr. Harris's privileges at this hospital immediately.''

There was a heavy silence in the room.

''Why?'' asked Anselm.

''They feel that if you go, it'll put the other doctors on notice and improve the level of service their employees receive. I'm sorry, Dr. Harris. That's what McKeown told me.''

''And if we refuse?'' asked John, to whom nothing seemed obvious.

''Then they'll go ahead with their clinic without any further discussion with us,'' said Stefan.

By now both men were looking at Anselm.

Stefan sighed. ''Dr. Harris, I'm sure you're aware of the problems we're having with Farman Industries,'' he said, putting his hands flat on the desk. ''Farman accounts for almost half of our business, and we can't afford to lose them.''

''You know perfectly well you can't take away my hospital privileges just like that,'' said Anselm, snapping his fingers. "Try it, and you'll have another lawsuit on your hands, plus a court injunction to restore my privileges, so fast you won't even have time to call your own employment agency."

Stefan sighed again and looked at his well-shined black oxfords. "What Farman Industries is saying, Dr. Harris, is that they don't have confidence in our medical staff, and you in particular. I guess they're having second thoughts about their clinic, but they don't want to come back to us without getting some sort of symbolic concession."

"And as it happens, I'm afraid you've become somewhat of a liability to us anyway, Dr. Harris, I'm sorry to have to say this." John stared at the floor.

Stefan looked at Anselm with some compassion, but it didn't stop him from saying what he had to say.

"Dr. Harris, it looks as if we're going to have to make a choice between the hospital's survival and your continuing presence on the staff," he said.

There was a long silence.

"You could voluntarily resign," said John, still looking at his feet. "I've been told you're finished here in any case, so it won't make much difference to you."

"Maybe you could take an indefinite leave of absence." Stefan was kinder; he liked Anselm and wanted to make it as easy as he could for him, but his priorities were clear. "Then once things have quieted down, say in six months, we could review your application again."

Anselm sat back and faced the two men.

"If you think I'm going to volunteer to be your 'symbolic concession' to Farman Industries, you've got another think coming," he said. "I am neither resigning nor will I take a leave of absence, and if you want to pull my privileges, you'd better have a damn sight better case than you have now."

"If that's your final word, Dr. Harris," said Stefan heavily, "you're not leaving us much option."

"Why don't you go home and think about it, Dr. Harris?" urged John. "When you've had time to consider it, I think you'll realize that your leaving the hospital voluntarily at this time would be best for everyone, including you."

"We'll make sure you get good recommendations," added Stefan. "I'm sure you can see it would be very difficult for you to continue here anyway. You'll be much happier with a fresh start."

"We discussed this matter earlier with Mr. Marino, the board chairman," said John, raising his eyes to look at Anselm. "He suggested that we offer you a substantial financial incentive if you decide to leave." He shuffled his feet with discomfort. "To cover moving expenses, loss of income, costs you'd incur setting up again elsewhere, that kind of thing."

"Also," said Stefan, as if he had just thought of it, "with your cooperation in this matter, we'll do all we can to support you in the suit Mrs. Bracknell has brought against you. On the other hand, if you make it difficult for us, we would be forced into the position of being hostile witnesses at the trial."

Anselm stood up. "No way," he said. "I got on the staff here on my merits. You all knew about the lawsuit in New York, and decided at the time that I had acted properly in that case. Now you're panicking and want me out. I suggest that *you* think about the situation some more. If you get rid of me now, it'll make *you* look incompetent, not me."

Anselm got up and without another word left the office.

Stefan sighed, then reached for the phone and dialed the number of Tony Marino's hospital office. Within a few minutes, Tony and Bob North came in and sat down.

When Stefan told them the result of their meeting with Anselm, Bob said, "Okay, then, if he's not going willingly, we put plan two into effect. I'll talk to Erica Barnes." He grinned. "From what I know of her financial situation, I think she'll be delighted to cooperate."

"We're going to have to move fast," said Stefan. "The longer Harris stays on the staff, the more we're at risk."

"You and John Kestler had better go over the hospital bylaws very carefully," said Tony to Stefan. "If we're going to throw Harris out, we have to do it by the book, with due process and all that, or we'll find ourselves in deeper trouble than ever. Harris can get himself a hot-shot attorney who could keep us tied up in legal crap for the rest of our lives."

28

When Erica came to the hospital that morning, she was over an hour late, as her ancient VW bug had once again refused to start. Sometimes she felt that life was getting too much for her, and this was one of the days. Her husband had left her a lot of debts, and Erica's chronic transportation problems made her anxious about her job. Her friends suggested that she get a job in New Coventry or Hartford; with her looks and personality she'd have no problems, they said, but Erica knew that the job market was a lot tighter than they thought. In any case, her family lived in the Glenport area, and she simply didn't want to move.

Coming in from the parking lot, Erica remembered that it was exactly two years since Don's death. She had grieved for two solid months until one chilly Sunday afternoon she piled all his clothes, golf clubs, photographs, and mementos onto the small lawn, everything he had possessed or that reminded Erica of him. Then she emptied a gallon of gasoline over it all and lit the pile.

The flames were still flickering in her head when she saw Bob North hanging around outside her office, apparently waiting for her.

Erica smiled warily at Bob as she unlocked the door,

and wondered if he was going to report her for being late.

Bob's grin suggested that he had other things on his mind, and although she certainly wasn't afraid of him, she tucked herself safely behind her tiny desk while he closed the door. But Bob had come on business— not that he wouldn't try to parlay that business into a little action for himself if the opportunity presented itself, but today business came first.

"How's your VW doing, Erica? I hear you've been having a lot of trouble with it," he said sympathetically.

"It gets me there and back, most of the time," Erica replied, watching him and wondering what he wanted.

"Maybe you should sell your little house and buy a condo closer to the hospital," he suggested.

"Not this year." Erica's smile hardened. She recognized that Bob was teasing her; he knew the state of the real estate market, and that her house in Waterbank wouldn't fetch enough for even the down payment on a condo, never mind what she owed the mortgage company.

"I was just talking to Tony and Stefan," Bob went on, sitting back in his chair, not taking his eyes off her. "Everybody was impressed with the way you handled the media people during the Bracknell fiasco."

"Good," said Erica. "Tell them I could use a raise."

"It could get a whole lot better than a raise," said Bob. "There might be a full-time public relations job opening up here in the very near future."

Erica's eyes flickered in spite of herself.

"Also Tony happened to mention that he could get you a new car on really good terms, without a down payment."

Erica grinned sarcastically. "How about the condo?

Is that thrown in too? And who would stop in for a little light entertainment a couple of times a week? Tony? You? Both of you? How would you like me? In a frilly French maid outfit?'' She shook her head, laughing with disbelief. ''Thank you, Dr. North, but no thanks.''

''Oh no,'' said Bob, trying to look horrified. ''That's not what I meant at all. Nothing like that.'' His face took on a look of concerned gravity and he leaned forward. ''You see, Erica, the hospital's in an extremely difficult situation here as a result of the Bracknell case. I mean with Dr. Harris.''

Bob scratched the inside of his thigh to emphasize his worry, and Erica felt a surge of her old hatred for him, for the way he'd wrecked the life of her friend Hermita.

He explained his proposition. ''You see, Erica, Dr. Harris had one big malpractice suit that we know about,'' he said. ''And we're wondering if he had others that he didn't tell us about. We need to know so that the hospital can be properly protected.''

''Why don't you just ask him?'' asked Erica, sounding naïve and trying to figure what Bob was actually after. ''Dr. Harris is a very honest person, and I'm sure he'd tell you.''

''Well, we don't want to cause him any embarrassment,'' replied Bob, looking away. ''You see, when a doctor applies for privileges at this hospital, he has to declare any and every malpractice suit that has been brought or is pending.''

''What does all that have to do with me?'' asked Erica.

''Well, his secretary is going to be away for at least a couple of weeks,'' said Bob. ''She called my secretary looking for someone to take over temporarily. As you're only part-time here—for now, anyway—and you and Dr. Harris know each other, maybe you could help out in his office during your spare time.''

''And go through his files looking for records of lawsuits?'' Erica's eyes were flashing with contempt.

''The PR job should pay around thirty thousand a year,'' said Bob. ''You'll get an office, a secretary, and of course there's medical insurance, a pension fund, and all the other usual benefits.'' Bob grinned. ''Plus a car allowance.''

Erica pursed her lips and thought quickly about her mortgage, her VW, the way Anselm had talked to her when Bracknell was being transferred, and how he'd turned down her dinner invitation only the day before.

''How long would the contract be for?'' she asked.

''Three years renewable,'' replied Bob promptly.

''And the car?''

''Anything within reason,'' said Bob. ''No deposit, payment over five years, no interest.''

''I want a Le Baron convertible, yellow, with a CD player and leather seats,'' said Erica.

Anselm went back to his office after his interview with Stefan Olson and John Kestler, a knot of anger filling his chest. He wondered whether to call Valerie Morse or whether he should find a second attorney. After all, Valerie had been hired by the insurance company solely to defend him in the malpractice suit, and his problem with the hospital was another matter entirely. But maybe she could recommend somebody . . . His hand was hovering over the phone when it rang.

It was Erica, and her voice was hesitant. ''One of the girls here said you were looking for someone to work temporarily in your office, Dr. Harris,'' she said. ''I've worked in a doctor's office before, and I'd be happy to help out. I'm at the hospital Wednesday and

Friday morning this week, so I can work for you the rest of the time, if that would be of any help.''

Anselm was astonished. "Thank you, Erica. That's very kind of you. . . ." He was about to turn down her offer, but he didn't want to offend her again, and it was really a very thoughtful and generous gesture on her part.

"The agency has someone who can start next Monday," he said, making up his mind, "but until then I could really use some help. Is it okay if I pay you what Melanie was getting? When could you come over?"

"That'll be fine," said Erica, her voice bright. "And I can be over in twenty minutes."

When she arrived, as elegant and pretty as ever, Anselm spent an hour showing her where everything was in the office, how the charts were arranged, and how the filing systems were arranged. Then he went back to his office to call Valerie in New Coventry, but she was in conference. Leaving a message for her to call back, he sat at his desk. There were plenty of things he could do in the meantime to start defending himself against the hospital, like calling the local medical society, and of course, his professional organization, the American College of Surgeons, which he knew had a legal department and would no doubt be ready to help and give advice to members.

A minute later, Erica came into his office holding a mug of hot coffee for him.

"This is rather fun," she said. "I enjoy being your secretary, but I wouldn't want to do it for a living." She put the mug on the desk just as the front door buzzer sounded.

Erica went out and returned a moment later. "Mrs. Gowan's here for her post-op check," she said. "And Neil's here with her. She looks great."

Mrs. Gowan had indeed not only survived, but looked as well as anyone in her physical condition could. She wore a carefully starched checkered black and white blouse with white collars and cuffs, and black pants.

Anselm examined her, noted that her incision was healing slowly, but otherwise she was doing remarkably well.

"There are a lot of people on your side, Dr. Harris," she said as Anselm helped her off the examination table. "Everybody who was a patient of yours, for a start. I wrote a letter to Mr. Olson at the hospital. I know that some of your other patients have done that too."

"Thanks, Mrs. Gowan, it's nice of you to take the time," said Anselm. "I'm sure you read the papers. Mr. Bracknell had a fatal problem and we did the best we could for him. There was a small chance we could save him by surgery, and we had to take it. That's the kind of risks we're trained to take." He smiled at her. "Tell that to your friends."

"That's what Neil and I have been telling everybody." Florence's voice was indignant. " 'Look at me,' I say to them. 'If it wasn't for Dr. Harris, I'd be dead instead of standing here talking to you.' Neil is doing his best for you too, I'm sure you know that."

Neil Gowan was in the waiting room and stood when Anselm came out. He shook Anselm's hand emotionally for a long moment, and there were tears in his eyes.

"It's really terrible," he said. "As soon as we get a really good doctor like you on the staff here, something bad happens to him. Of course, I blame some of the other doctors for a lot of it—"

Anselm cut him off gently, and a few minutes later he showed them both out. Standing at the door, he watched them walk slowly toward the street.

It was a few minutes to five, and Erica was getting ready to leave. "I'm out of here," she said. "I'll see

you tomorrow morning. Shall I bring some doughnuts?''

"Good idea," said Anselm. "Don't forget your keys
to the office. They're on the hook beside the medicine
cabinet. And thanks again for helping out.''

Erica walked back to the hospital, hoping that the
quick charge the mechanic had put into her VW's
battery would be enough to start the car. All she
needed was for it to take her as far as Tony Marino's
dealership, a couple of miles away on Shore Road.
She'd already spoken to the head salesman, and her
new car was waiting.

The Carver's Island ferry was just coming in, and a
great white wash of foam from the stern thrusters
spread and bubbled behind the ship. A row of tractor
tires hanging from the dock creaked and dented when
the stern bumped gently into them, and within a minute the craft was moored and cars were starting to
come off, one after the other like eggs extruding from
a moth.

Sandy Bracknell sat in the line of cars waiting to go
aboard, recognizing the occasional car as it drove off
the ferry, thinking about her last trip across the Sound
with Denton. Now she thought about the house and
what she would do about it, then replayed in great
detail her visit with Norm Hartman several days before.

The car in line ahead of Sandy started to move, and
a deckhand waved at her. She got into gear, the car
lurched over the metal hump and the wheels rattled on
the wide deck of the ferry, and Sandy parked behind
a minivan full of children. Children. She watched them
moving around inside, and the minivan rocked slightly.
A moment later, two little girls came out of the minivan, both dressed very smartly, the younger, about
five years old, in a pink dress and the other in a blue

dress with white cuffs and collar. Very sedately, hand in hand, they walked between the cars to the bottom of the steel walkway and disappeared up toward the passenger deck.

Looking at the girls, Sandy felt a peculiar drawing sensation throughout her body, a stretching of the skin over her face, and a stirring of her insides that lasted only a few moments but left her feeling tense and empty. She had felt that way before when she looked at children, especially babies, and even more after she had learned that she and Denton would never be able to have children of their own. Denton had been terribly disappointed, and after the urologist had shaken his head over Denton's scanty and inactive sperm, he had felt depressed and guilty, although she'd done her best to comfort him.

Sandy got out and joined the line outside the purser's office to buy her ticket. The purser was a tall, good-looking, dark-haired young man she'd seen a couple of times before.

"Hi, Mrs. Bracknell," he said, and hesitated. He had a pleasantly soft voice, uncannily like Jimmy Stewart's. "We were all very sorry about your husband."

"Thanks, Fred," she replied. "Everybody's been very kind." She made an effort to be sociable, and anyway she liked Fred. "Are you still at B.U?" she asked him.

"Yes, it's my last year," replied Fred. He grinned. "Then I can take up unemployment full-time."

Sandy laughed and went back to her car, feeling a mixture of pleasure that people cared enough to sympathize with her, and annoyance that there was nowhere she could go around Glenport, let alone on the island, without being instantly recognized. Well, she thought, it won't last. Now that Denton was dead, she'd soon be forgotten about, and she could revert to her

previous status as a plain, anonymous local woman.
She hoped so, anyway.

At the house, everything was unnaturally silent, as
if the house knew that Denton was never coming back.
Sandy wandered slowly through the rooms. The air
felt close and musty, as if the windows hadn't been
opened for a long time, although she knew that Rose
had come over several times to dust and check that all
was secure.

There was her unfinished painting, the one of the
mermaid. Sandy stared at it almost without recognizing it as something she had done herself, that it was a
part of her, of who she was. Or had been, she thought,
passing into the bedroom. Rose had made the bed and
tidied up the room. Sandy stood in front of the dresser,
touching old, familiar objects with the tips of her fingers, then opened the chest of drawers and pulled a
locked leather-covered box from the bottom drawer.
She opened it with a key from her keychain, took out some
photos, and stared at them for several minutes, almost
hypnotizing herself to relive these happy days. Then
she sighed, put them back, and locked the box. Better
times were coming, she was sure of it. Sandy had already decided to put the house up for sale, move back
to the mainland and then . . . Well, after that, anything could happen.

Lucille was beginning to feel nervous. She hadn't
heard from Michael since their tryst, and he'd forgotten to give her his telephone number. But she knew
which newspaper he worked for and found the number
by dialing New Coventry information. He wasn't there,
and the operator didn't know when he'd be back, but
she promised to give him the message. An hour later,
after the fifth call, she put Lucille through to her supervisor, who frostily said that messages had been left
for Mr. Parrett and please would she not call again.

But Lucille simply couldn't prevent herself from dialing his number, hoping that she might catch him as he came into the press room or whatever they called it. The woman who answered the phone was getting more and more abrupt with her.

The bitch, Lucille thought, she must be in love with Michael too, and was being unhelpful because she resented a competitor. Well, she would show her. In her mind's eye Lucille saw herself coming into the huge press room crowded with desks and busy reporters wearing baseball caps, with the cigar-chomping chief editor in a glass-enclosed office at the far end. In her vision, he looked just like Lou Grant. Michael took her by the hand and led her between the desks, introducing her as they went, then into the editor's office, and . . .

"Mr. Olson's on the line," said the secretary, coming into her office. "The hospital lawyer's there and they want to see you."

"Tell him I'll be down in ten minutes," replied Lucille, flustered. What did they want her for? Maybe they weren't satisfied with her report. She knew that it had been prepared in the heat of the moment, and that she'd written opinions that she had neither the background nor the knowledge to defend. Also her head had been so full of Michael that she couldn't concentrate on anything else.

She unlocked her desk drawer, opened her copy of the report, and reread it. When she finished, she smiled to herself. Although the interpretations were open to question, the facts as she had seen them were correct. The report was carefully written and thoroughly damning. It should certainly take care of Anselm Harris as far as the hospital administration was concerned. She was about to leave the office when the phone rang. She rushed to pick it up.

"Oh, God, Michael," she said when she heard his voice, "I've been trying to reach you all day."

"So I've heard," replied Michael. "And all yesterday and the day before that. What do you want?"

The sharpness of his voice put a sudden fear in Lucille's heart.

"I mostly wanted to hear your voice." She spoke as alluringly as she knew how.

"That's all?" His voice was incredulous. "I thought something new must have broken on the Bracknell case. . . ." He paused.

"I do have something here for you," replied Lucille coyly. "It's a copy of my report on Bracknell's operation."

"Great." Michael's voice was suddenly enthusiastic. "Mark it private, please, and send it here." Michael dictated the address of his paper to her. "Now, Lucille, I'm very busy, so don't call again unless you have something really important to tell me, okay?" Lucille was in the middle of saying how sorry she was when he hung up.

She hurried down the corridor toward the elevators, smiling fondly. She'd so much wanted to ask Michael when they could see each other again, but there just hadn't been time. Poor Michael! He sounded stressed out. It must be such a demanding job, trying to meet deadlines, coping with angry editors. . . . Again a vision appeared in her mind of Lou Grant with his shirtsleeves rolled up, yelling at Michael, and her own anger soared in his defense. She just had to be supportive and understanding, and make him fully aware how totally and unequivocally she was on his side. Only when he understood that could he truly feel the comfort, the peace of mind, the bliss, that would bind him to her forever.

In the elevator, Lucille decided that as soon as she'd finished with Stefan Olson, she would call Michael back and explain it all to him. She could tell from his voice that he was worried about their relationship, and it was only fair to let him know. She smiled, thinking how relieved he'd be once she made it all clear to him.

Anselm got on at the next floor, and Lucille stared at the corner above him, with a sly little grin on her face. She thought about her report, how it would help to send him packing out of Glenport, and with vicious pleasure she remembered the time he'd humiliated her in the instrument room. What goes around comes around, she thought, and she who laughs last laughs longest.

And it was getting better and better. There was some kind of meeting going on in Stefan's office. Mr. Kestler, the hospital lawyer, Tony Marino, and Bob North were there. They asked her a bunch of questions about Anselm's general behavior in the operating room. They wanted to find out whether Dr. Harris's problems in the operating room with Mr. Bracknell's case were isolated instances, or whether they were part of a pattern. Lucille was delighted to tell them of the recurrent difficulties they had had with him, but she was rather vague when asked for specific instances.

"We're just reviewing the situation," said Stefan when she inquired why they were asking.

29

When Anselm got off the elevator, he heard his name being paged and picked up the nearest phone. It was the OR secretary, and she sounded desperate. Frank Abruzzo, the chief of staff, was about to start a case in the operating room, and hadn't been able to find an assistant. Would Anselm help? He agreed to come up. In the last half hour he had heard Bob North being paged several times, then one of the other surgeons, and figured that both had found other, more urgent things to do.

When Frank had first come to Glenport he had been the only trained surgeon there and soon cornered the market. A frugal man, he still drove an old car, worked long hours, and kept his office overhead down by using the hospital emergency room to do consultations and minor surgery in the evenings. Frank, with no interests or abilities outside his practice, had made some unwise investments and lost a lot of money. Now he was still operating, because he was broke, although his diminished abilities were becoming obvious. Nobody wanted to blow the whistle on him because of his long service, but a year ago Stefan had privately asked him always to have one of the other surgeons assisting him when he was doing surgery.

Frank was already scrubbing when Anselm came in.

Still tall, his belly was jammed up against the edge of the stainless steel sink, and the loose tissues at the back of his upper arms flapped as his hands moved against each other.

"Afternoon, Dr. Harris," he said briefly. He didn't look at Anselm.

"Hi," replied Anselm. He turned on the faucet at the next sink and prepared to scrub.

"We've got a new quarterback for next season," said Frank after a long pause. Anselm knew that Frank, an old Yalie, had an obsessive interest in his alma mater's football team. "Boy by the name of Drummond," Frank went on. "Know who I'm talking about?" He stared accusingly at Anselm, who shook his head. Frank pursed his lips. "He's big," he said, "for a quarterback. I mean, not big, well, for a . . ." Frank seemed to lose the thread of his conversation for a moment and stared blankly at Anselm. "What was I saying?"

"You'd just finished saying something about a quarterback," said Anselm. He nodded through the window in front of them at the anesthetist who was putting a mask over the patient's face. "What's this case you're about to do?"

Frank went on staring at Anselm, looking a little confused, obviously making a big effort to collect himself. "Oh. Yes. That's Juniper Manson in there. Old Jerry Manson's daughter. Do you know Jerry? A builder. He twisted a testicle a few years ago, and I had to remove it for him."

Frank started to laugh, a cackling old-man laugh, and dropped his soapy nail brush in the sink. Against the rules, which stated that a fresh, sterile brush had to be taken if one happened to drop, Frank picked it up and started to scrub again.

"Do you know what he said? I mean Jerry Manson? When I told him he was going to lose his testicle?"

Frank almost dropped the brush again, but managed to hold onto it. " 'Well,' he said, 'if I have only one testicle left, does that mean I won't be able to father twins?' " Frank burst out again with his high-pitched laughter.

"What procedure did you say we're going to do in here?"

"Juniper? Gallbladder. Lots of small stones. She's had a lot of trouble with it."

Through the window Anselm watched the scrub tech place a large drape over the patient, an obese young woman with wide, purplish stretch marks on her breasts.

The scrub nurse arranged the top of the drape over the ether screen, then turned to catch Anselm's eye through the window. Soundlessly she asked if he and Frank were about ready to start, and Anselm nodded affirmatively at her.

Moving about the room, crossing over to the corner behind the anesthetist, the circulating nurse was getting IV supplies and equipment for the scrub nurse and the anesthetist. But even then Anselm could feel that the staff was tense; it was common knowledge that they all hated working with Frank Abruzzo.

Frank shut the water off with a twist of his knee and turned away from the sink, hands in the air, soapy water dripping from his elbows.

A minute later Anselm backed into the operating room behind him. Frank was already gowned and pulling on his gloves. As Anselm came into the room, Frank jerked the second glove on too hard, tore it, and had to have it replaced. Everyone in the room could see that Frank was uptight, as he usually was nowadays when he operated. The operating room staff knew that he was working on marginal efficiency, and it made them uptight and nervous too. They knew better than anyone that sooner or later Frank was going to have an accident; as one of them said, working with him was like living in San Francisco and waiting for the big one.

The scrub nurse had draped the patient in the usual way for a cholecystectomy. Today Frank seemed even more tense than usual; he was making sudden, abrupt movements with his hands, his brow had a thin beading of sweat below the line of the paper hood, and his anxiety was making itself felt by everyone in the operating room.

"All set?" he asked, glancing over the ether screen at the anesthesiologist. This morning it was Philip Burton, who had worked with Anselm on Denton Bracknell. Philip nodded affirmatively at Frank, and for a second his eyes flickered over to Anselm with a strange, almost apologetic glance.

Anselm checked the suction apparatus and the electrocautery probe. Frank's hand had a fine tremor when he took the scalpel from the scrub tech. Anselm had noticed the tremor before, but today it seemed more marked.

"Are you feeling all right, Frank?" he asked in a voice low enough so that only Frank could hear.

"Sure, I'm all right. Why do you ask?" His voice was loud, defensive. The beads of sweat were coalescing and tracking down the side of his temple.

"Good," replied Anselm tranquilly. "Just wanted to be sure."

Frank had taken out hundreds, maybe thousands of gallbladders in his time, and he went through the familiar motions mechanically, giving his technique no more thought than an experienced cyclist gives to keeping his balance.

All went routinely until Frank opened the thin membrane of peritoneum that separated the abdominal muscles from the cavity of the abdomen.

To help Frank get exposure of the gallbladder, Anselm placed the flat blade of a retractor below the liver and gently pulled the tissues away from the gallbladder lying under the lower side of the liver. The liver looked and felt abnormal; Anselm asked the scrub tech to hold the retractor for a moment, and he palpated the liver. It was grayish rather than the usual maroon color, and Anselm could feel a large mass in the center of it. Then he felt another, and another, this time on the top surface.

Frank watched him with an annoyed, puzzled expression. "Could we have some retraction, please, Dr. Harris?" he asked brusquely.

Anselm put his hand over the dome of the liver and pushed down. The mass became visible, a whitish growth with a dimpled surface.

Frank stared at it for a moment. "Could we get on with this case, if you don't mind?"

"You want to go ahead and take the gallbladder out?" asked Anselm disbelievingly.

"That's what we're here to do," replied Frank. "Let's get on with it."

"Frank," said Anselm quietly, "what do you think that is?" He pointed with a hemostat at the dimpled area on the liver.

"I don't know. Maybe some kind of . . . anyway, this gal has gallstones and we do know that." Frank pointed at the X rays up on the viewing box.

"Frank, that's a metastatic cancer," said Anselm, shocked at Frank's refusal to recognize that his diagnosis had been wrong. "Don't you think we should try to find where the primary source is?"

"We're here to take the gallbladder out," repeated Frank doggedly. "It's full of stones."

"I'm sure it is, Frank," said Anselm. "But that's not the main problem right now. She's also got a cancer." While he talked, he slipped his hand down under the stomach. Sure enough, there was a big mass situated in the middle portion of the pancreas.

"Here," said Anselm. "Feel it. It's big. Right in the body of the pancreas."

Gently he guided Frank's right hand, which he could feel was trembling seriously now, until it was located in the correct place to feel the main cancer.

Feeling strangely apprehensive, Anselm watched Frank's face, which was now showing a mixture of confusion and fear, and he realized that Frank couldn't appreciate or understand what he was feeling, and didn't have any idea about what he should do. His reflexes, set to do a gallbladder operation, couldn't shift gear to deal with the actual problem they were now facing.

All the life seemed to be draining out of Frank's face. Anselm watched with embarrassed concern as two large tears formed in the corner of Frank's eyes and ran down to be absorbed by the papery tissue of his mask.

"I don't know what to do," said Frank in a hoarse whisper. "You're going to have to finish this . . . Dr. Harris, this is the last operation I'll ever do, and the last time I'll be in here. Now, if you'll excuse me . . ."

Frank put his scalpel down on the drape, turned away, and left the operating room.

The tech looked at Anselm.

"We'll just do a biopsy and close up," said Anselm. "This is an inoperable situation."

Through the window he could see Frank's gowned figure heading for the last time toward the changing room.

30

"I can't believe he wouldn't even consider a financial inducement," said Tony. "Didn't he even ask how much?"

He and Stefan, together with Bob and John Kestler, were still in Stefan's office, Lucille had gone her way, and the atmosphere was like that of a castle under siege.

"No, he didn't. We could have offered him Fort Knox, and it wouldn't have made any difference," replied Stefan. "The guy's tougher than I first thought."

"I was talking to a doc at New Coventry Medical Center about this," said Bob. "What *they* do when they want rid of someone is go back through all the cases he's ever done there."

"What do you mean?" asked Kestler.

"Well, if you go through all the cases of any hospital doctor, especially a surgeon, you can always find lots of stuff that doesn't look right in retrospect," explained Bob. "Tests that didn't get done, wrong diagnoses, stuff like that. If we come up just a few instances, we could have Harris looking very bad very quickly."

"How long would that take?" asked Tony, leaning back and pulling out a cigar.

"Several days, I would think," said Stefan. "But

first we'd need a directive from the quality assurance committee expressing dissatisfaction with the way Harris was handling his cases, something vague like that, but enough to have us start an inquiry."

"No sweat," said Bob. "I'm chairman of the quality assurance committee, and I can call an emergency meeting. I know how those things work. All you need is to get the ball rolling against someone, then nobody wants to look as if they were trying to protect him." He looked at the clock. "I'll get my secretary to call the committee members. If we meet at five-thirty this afternoon, there'll be nobody else around to wonder what's going on."

"Make sure someone takes minutes at the meeting," warned John. "Actually, I'd better come along myself and make sure it's all done correctly from the legal point of view."

"Okay," said Bob. "In the small conference room, five-thirty."

Stefan spoke up. "I'll call the people over at Farman," he said, "and let them know unofficially that we're starting proceedings."

"Good," said Tony. "It'll show them we're serious about working to keep their business."

"Should we tell the media?" asked Bob, his eyes glinting. "Maybe it'll keep them off our backs for a while."

"For God's sake, Bob, of course not," said Tony sharply. "We can't tell them anything about this before we've even started the case review. If anybody asks, Erica can tell them the hospital is presently investigating every aspect of the Bracknell case, nothing more, okay?"

"This should help us with the JCAH," said Stefan. "One of the things they criticized was our ineffective system for disciplining doctors."

''They won't be able to say that once we've finished with Harris,'' said Bob, grinning.

''What else does that Joint Commission want done?'' asked John. ''The hospital can't afford to lose accreditation with them.''

''For one thing, we have to widen the access ramps to the emergency room,'' said Stefan. ''They've threatened to can us on that alone.''

Tony made a movement of annoyance; he didn't want to get into this now. ''Okay,'' he said, ''let's get the architects to take a look at the ER situation, then they can tell us how much it would cost.''

''Thanks, Mr. Marino,'' said Stefan. ''That'll be a good start.''

''Now let's get back to Harris.''

''Right,'' said Bob. ''And on that subject, I hope Erica Barnes will have something to report to us by tomorrow.''

''Are there any other approaches we should be thinking about?'' Tony asked Stefan. ''Right now we're working on Harris's old cases and his malpractice record. Anything else?''

''Dr. Harris has quite a few fans in this town,'' replied Stefan. ''I've had several letters in support of him.'' He paused. ''Next week the *Today* is going to do an article about crime and the Bank Street bums, and show that Harris's storefront clinic just encourages more of these criminal elements to move into town.''

''I don't know how the nurses here'll react if we get Harris off the staff,'' mused Tony. A long ash fell unnoticed off his cigar and fragmented on the carpet. ''I've been told their union is backing him.''

''It's none of the nurses' goddamn business,'' said Bob angrily. ''When the union isn't meddling with stuff that doesn't concern them, they're trying to squeeze more money out of the hospital. In the old days nurses were devoted to their patients, worked for the pleasure of helping people, and didn't think about contracts and overtime and how much money they could make.''

"Yeah, sure," said Tony. He puffed a cloud of cigar smoke in Bob's direction. "You'd like them to be self-less, dedicated, and totally uninterested in financial rewards. Just like you.''

Bob looked at the ceiling, unaffected by his father-in-law's sarcasm.

"We'll get started on Harris," said Stefan. "Once the records people have pulled all of his charts, we can assign a bunch of them to each committee member, and that way we can get through them all without having to discuss each one in committee.''

"Good," said Tony. "So by the time we have the ammunition, we'll know if we want to fire the gun.''

"Well put, Tony," said Bob, smiling at his father-in-law. At this point he knew he was in deep trouble with Tony and was doing the best he could to minimize the damage.

"For the record," said John, speaking after a long, anxious silence. "Make sure this decision post-dates the quality assurance committee meeting you're having this afternoon, okay?''

There was a knock on the door, and Frank Abruzzo came in, looking paler than usual.

"Sorry I'm late," he said.

"You okay, Frank?" said Tony. "Here, take a seat. We've just been talking about how to get Harris off the staff. Any ideas on the subject?''

Frank put his hands on the back of the chair but didn't sit down. "A couple of hours ago," he said, "I was trying to find you''—he pointed at Bob—''to help me with a case in the OR. You didn't answer your page, so I called for somebody else. The only one who bothered to show up was Anselm Harris, and he assisted me.'' Frank paused and looked around the group with his red-rimmed eyes. "He helped me out of a lot of trouble," he said. "So don't count on any support from me against him."

Frank walked out of the office, followed by the astonished gaze of the others.

"I wonder what happened up there," said Bob. "That's the first time I've ever heard him say a good word about Harris."

"Why didn't you answer your page?" asked Tony.

Bob shrugged. "Frank's a senile old fool," he said. "He shouldn't be operating anyway. It's time we put a stop to him too."

Tony heaved his large frame out of his chair with a grunt. "Same time tomorrow," he said to the others in the room. "And every day until we have this situation squared away."

31

Valerie decided to stay in New Coventry to do a computer search for similar cases in the legal literature, and work on finding the best way of putting her defense together. She talked with several people at the New Coventry Medical School and tried to get one of the vascular surgeons to review the case with a view to testifying for Anselm.

"I'm very sorry, Counselor," he told her, "I've already reviewed the case at the request of the plaintiff's attorney, and I will be testifying, but *against* Dr. Harris."

Valerie was beginning to suspect that she had been given an unwinnable case, but pushed that feeling away. No case is unwinnable, she reminded herself, and there were plenty of examples in Americal legal history where apparently hopeless cases had been turned into triumphant victories. All she had to do was find the key, the one fact or circumstance that would change the entire aspect of the case.

By the end of the day, Valerie still had not found the key, and was beginning to think the lock was jammed anyway.

That evening she decided to go and see her brother, Patrick, who was having one of his parties, and stopped off at a wine store to get a bottle of Hungarian

5-*puttonos* Tokay, his favorite dessert wine. Judging by the noise coming from his apartment, the party had been going on for some time, and when Valerie opened the door and let herself in, the sound of music was deafening, with a deep thumping, rhythmic drum sound that Valerie could feel through the soles of her feet.

The apartment was thick with people, mostly young women, hazy with smoke, and loud with conversation and laughter. Valerie coughed when she came in.

Patrick was over by the window in his wheelchair, drinking beer from a can. A very pretty young woman with scarlet pouting lips was sympathetically asking him how he had the misfortune to become paralyzed. Patrick's eyes gleamed.

"I was trying to give myself a blow job," he answered straight-faced, "and then there was this awful cracking noise in my neck."

The young woman's eyes grew big, and she mumbled something about real bad luck, then drifted off to pass that startling piece of information around.

"Patrick, you're incorrigible," said Valerie.

"I was just hoping she'd volunteer to do it for me from now on," he replied, shouting over the noise. On closer examination, Patrick wasn't looking terrific. He'd lost a little weight, and even in the dim light his face was pale, almost waxy.

A cloud of sweet smoke came their way and Valerie coughed.

"You can hear this party half a mile away," she said. "If any of your neighbors calls the police, you'll all get busted."

"All the neighbors are here," replied Patrick. "All the ones within hearing distance, anyway."

The noise was so loud it hurt, and Valerie went to the stereo and turned the sound down a bit, then came back.

"Thanks for the tip about Elliott Naughton," she said. "It saved my skin." She told Patrick what had happened, and he laughed, as always delighted by his sister's ability to get out of tight situations. "What had he done?" he asked. "I mean Stern?"

"Well, one time when Elliott was working at the American Embassy in London, he was called to the police station because some American who had been arrested claimed to be related to the ambassador. . . ."

Dixie came up, wearing a short tight dress with sequins, smiled broadly, and offered Valerie and Patrick a lit joint. Patrick took a long drag and gave it back to her. Dixie offered it to Valerie. "Later, maybe, thanks, Dixie, not now," Valerie said. Already she felt a little high, just from what she'd been breathing since coming in.

Dixie went off to talk to another woman, who turned to look at Valerie. Patrick's coterie of girlfriends was very protective.

"Where was I?" she said. "Right. Anyway, the guy they'd arrested was Ralph Stern. He'd been caught with his pants down, doing something disgusting with a young boy in Hyde Park. The Brits are hot on that particular crime and were going to throw the book at him. Then it turned out Ralph *was* related to the ambassador, a distant cousin or something, and the Brits just put him on a plane the next day and sent him back to the U.S."

Patrick put his head back and laughed out loud. "No wonder he caved in at your meeting," he said. "If that story ever got out, it would be goodbye to any political career for Ralphie."

"Right, but the funny part is that he could just have denied it. The Brits handed over all their arrest documents to the embassy, where they were immediately shredded. So there isn't any evidence anywhere that

Ralph had ever been arrested or charged with anything.''

''I bet he checks up on that,'' said Patrick soberly. ''So watch out. He'll come after you with everything he's got.'' He rocked the wheels of his chair forward and backward a few times and grinned. ''At least you're safe from sexual harassment as far as he's concerned.'' Patrick was looking around for Dixie. ''You know,'' he said, ''the worst thing about being in this wheelchair is you can't look over heads for the person you want.''

Valerie, feeling responsible and sisterly, asked him if he needed anything.

''Money,'' he said in an offhand way. ''That's all.''

She didn't want to get into an argument with him during his party, but then she looked around and realized that she was paying for all this fun. ''Did you get yourself a job yet, Patrick?'' she asked.

He shrugged. ''It's not easy,'' he said. Then his expression became tense, as if a mask had fallen from his face. ''Look, Valerie,'' he said, ''for the last two weeks I've been getting muscle spasms, and I hurt *all the time*, my back, my legs. . . . I'd like to work, I always did, but I just can't concentrate because of the pain. So get off my back, will you? Okay?''

''I'm sorry, Patrick. Have you been back to see the doctors at the spinal center?''

''Those assholes? No way. I'm still trying to find somebody to sue them for me.''

Valerie made a quick decision. ''I'm working on a malpractice case up in Glenport,'' she said. ''I'm defending a doc. He's a surgeon, but he's smart and you'd like him. I'll ask him about your spasms.''

''You're defending a doctor?'' Patrick couldn't believe his ears. ''You, Valerie Morse, champion of the poor, defender of the oppressed, and all that stuff? You've gone over to the other side?''

"Hardly. This guy's a good doc, and got into a situation he couldn't get out of. He was the one who took care of Denton Bracknell."

Patrick's eyes grew bigger. "The guy I read about? The killer doc? Jesus, Valerie . . ."

"I'm going to get him to come down here," she said firmly, without the slightest idea how she would do it. "Then you can see for yourself."

Dixie came back and stood next to Patrick's wheelchair, facing Valerie. She seemed slightly drunk. "I'm worried about your bro," she said to Valerie. "He's been getting a lot of pain in his back and legs."

From behind her, Patrick slipped his hand high between Dixie's legs. The lower part of her body started to move slightly but rhythmically, and her lips parted, although her eyes didn't leave Valerie's.

"It's just in his back and legs," she whispered. "Everything else works just fine."

When Anselm came to the office the next morning, he found a brand-new yellow Le Baron convertible in the driveway, and he parked next to it. The front door opened and Erica appeared.

"Wow," said Anselm, getting out of his Triumph, which looked even older and more battered beside the gleaming Le Baron, "is that yours?"

"Yes. Isn't it a beauty?" Erica came down the steps, her purse slung over her shoulder. "My old Aunt Dorothy died a few months ago and left me enough for a down payment."

"It looks wonderful. I hope you'll take me for a ride in it sometime."

"Anytime," said Erica, "Meanwhile, I'm going over to the hospital. I've put out the charts for your follow-ups, and I did some of the billing. You'll have to check them because I don't know all the Medicare codes."

"No problem," replied Anselm. "You want to leave your car here? This office could use a touch of class."

"I won't be in tomorrow, by the way," she said over her shoulder.

Erica was very thoughtful as she drove slowly toward the hospital. The sky was blue, a cool breeze was coming off the Sound and wafting around her, the Japanese cherry trees were starting to bloom, she was in a new car and had the promise of a permanent job, but at the back of her mind was the thought that she was about to do something terrible to a man she liked and who had never done her any harm.

A half hour later, at a meeting in the boardroom of Glenport Hospital, Erica stood up and announced that she had found the records of another malpractice suit in which Anselm Harris had been cited. She had reproduced it on his office copier, and she handed it to Stefan, who passed the document to John Kestler.

"I can't say I approve of this way of doing things," muttered John, reading the papers. "In any case, this doesn't add up to a hill of beans." He thumbed through the typed pages and summarized them for the people around the table. Frank Abruzzo was there, next to Bob North; Tony sat at the head of the table, and Stefan was on his left. "This was served five years ago in New York," said John. "Apparently Harris was assisting a gynecologist with a hysterectomy. Some time after Harris left the OR, the gynecologist put the wrong size of catheter inside the patient's bladder, and the problems complained of here were due to that. Harris's name was taken off the suit, let's see . . . four days later, and anyway the suit was eventually withdrawn."

"That doesn't matter," said Bob excitedly. "Harris was named in a suit, and he didn't report it in his application for hospital privileges, which makes it a fraudulent application. I think we've got him, right, Stefan?''

"I suppose technically that's correct," said Stefan slowly. "What do you think, John?"

"Technically, yes, I have to agree," said John after a pause. He looked at Bob. "But morally—"

"We're here to deal with *facts*," said Bob.

Abruzzo, who so far had said nothing, stood up. "I think this is disgraceful," he said. "It's certainly possible that Harris made some errors in the Bracknell case, but this is turning into a witch-hunt." He looked around the group with his red-rimmed eyes, appeared to be about to say something else, then changed his mind and walked out. Stefan looked embarrassed, but the others remained stony-faced.

"Silly old fool," muttered Bob after the door closed. "His time's coming."

The meeting ended soon after and Erica left to work in her office at the hospital, hating Bob North with a passion but not feeling too good about herself. She decided to go for a drive downtown in her new car, and that made her feel better.

32

The next morning, Anselm went to his office, made a few phone calls, then picked up the pile of Medicare forms that Erica had filled out the day before and took them over to his desk. He detested this kind of work, and he hoped that whoever they sent from the agency would have a good grasp of how these forms had to be filled out. Even while Anselm was checking the forms, at the back of his mind, lurking like an ugly but wakeful demon, was the case of Denton Bracknell. There had to be some way of getting himself out of this situation, he thought with a mounting sense of desperation, some way to get people to understand that he had done a good job, the best he could. What could he do to show that the tragic outcome had not been his fault? He remembered a saying concerning the difference between Americans and Japanese. When something went wrong, Americans said, "Who can we blame?" and the Japanese said, "How can we fix it?"

Anselm, with his upbringing in a military environment, was not a fan of the Japanese, but they certainly had a point there.

He finished the forms and looked at his watch. Valerie was coming about eleven, in just under three hours, and he felt good about that. He put his elbows on the desk and thought about her, then about the other women in his life. Before Mariana, his relationships had been fun but not particularly profound, and as for Mariana . . . After he'd met her, he had realized what a vast reserve of love he'd built up inside him, but Mariana couldn't accept love any more than she could give it. And then there were her sudden rages, her wild impulsiveness, and her vicious, nasty streak. And her men. Anselm shrugged. What was over was over, and with a sort of relief his thoughts swung back to Valerie. He realized with some surprise that he'd been thinking quite a bit about her since her last visit, and that made him feel a bit silly. He didn't even know anything about the woman; even though he'd established that she wasn't married, she probably was in a long-term relationship with some guy, might even be living with him. For some reason that last idea startled Anselm, and he laughed. For God's sake, he thought, this woman was *hired* to work on his case, and not even by him but by the insurance company. That's who she was really working for, he reminded himself, the insurance company. Not him. But it was clear that Valerie was doing more than she strictly needed to, and behind her businesslike exterior was a genuineness, a warmth, and humor that might grow if they ever got to know each other better. Anselm sat there, happy to be thinking pleasant thoughts for a change, and wondered if Valerie ever thought about him as a person, aside from the case. And if she did, wouldn't the very fact that he was a second-time defendant in a malpractice case make her more likely to despise him as a failure, a bad actor, or at least make her firmly reject any idea of developing a relationship or even a friendship? Anselm had a sudden, very clear physical vision of her, and yes, she was very attractive indeed. He wondered how her breasts would feel,

cupped in his hands, and thought about what it would
be like to make love to her. . . .

The telephone rang. The nurse on B3 wanted to
know when he was coming over, because Juniper
Manson had been asking to see him. Two minutes
later, Anselm was on his way, running with an effortless athletic stride along the tree-lined sidewalk, enjoying the salty air that filled his lungs, and feeling
happy and unaccountably optimistic—and at the same
time concerned about the wide mood swings he was
experiencing.

As expected, Juniper was not doing well after her
surgery. Anselm had seen this type of situation many
times before; patients with advanced but undiagnosed
cancer tended to suffer an acceleration of their disease
after even minor exploratory surgery. The medical literature on that subject was sparse, and Anselm had
often thought of writing a paper on the subject, but
somehow there was never enough time to put it together.

The oncology doctors had seen Juniper a few days
before, and had started her on a course of intravenous
chemotherapy. When Anselm came in, she looked pale
and held a kidney dish listlessly in her right hand,
ready if she needed to throw up.

Anselm sat on the chair by her bed and held her
hand. Juniper had been rather obese when she came
into the hospital, but now her face and eyes were
sunken and yellow, and the skin hung off her previously plump body.

"How are you feeling?" he asked, watching her
eyes. Most people answered "fine" or "good" automatically, but their eyes usually told the truth.

Juniper was more frank. "I feel like shit," she
whispered. "I've thrown up half a dozen times already
this morning. Doc, what's the matter with me? When

I ask the oncology doc, Dr. Leonard, he just says don't worry, everything's going to be all right. But he never stays long enough to really say anything." She looked Anselm straight in the eye. "It really ain't all right, though, is it, Dr. Harris? It wasn't just gallstones like Dr. Abruzzo says, was it?"

Anselm took a deep breath. "No, Juniper, it wasn't." He knew that her tumor was far advanced and that there was no realistic hope of improvement, let alone cure. Her life expectancy was a matter of weeks at most.

"What's this stuff they're giving me, Dr. Harris?" Juniper indicated the small bottle piggy-backed on the main IV. "They told me it might make me sick, but it's a lot worse than that. It makes me feel so awful I want to die. And look at this." She put her hand up, took a handful of her hair, and pulled. It all came out in her hand, and her big brown eyes filled with tears. "I used to have really nice hair, Dr. Harris," she said. "My hairdresser said he'd pay me to grow it and sell it to him. Well, now he can have it for free." Juniper threw the dried-looking handful of hair on the floor. Her white scalp shone through the sparse remaining hair. Another couple of days of chemotherapy and she would be completely bald.

Anselm held her hand gently. "How much do you want to know, Juniper?" He was well aware that some people didn't want to know their diagnoses, nor could they handle the bad news if they were given it.

"Just tell me what's happening," she said, hanging onto his hand. "Tell me the truth"—she managed a grin—"please, and tell it in language I can understand."

Quickly, Anselm went over in his head what he knew about her. Juniper had been married young, left her abusive husband after a year, was now divorced, had no children, and lived with her parents in a large house halfway between Glenport and Mystic. Juniper helped her father with the bookkeeping, and kept house for all of them. That was about it. Not much, he thought, not much to look back on, for a life that was coming to an end.

"I've actually had a great life," she said, as if she could read his thoughts. "Really wonderful." She was tired, short of breath, and had only the strength to speak in short phrases. "Not big things, of course. Like when I was little, I found a kitten down by the hedge, and my mom said I could keep it. . . . I made a little house for it with a pillow . . . inside a shoe-box."

Juniper's hands were pale and lay quite still on the sheets, as if they were already dead. "I always thought a kitten was better than having a baby brother. I wanted to call him Charlie, but Dad got really mad, because of . . . well, you know, Charlie Manson . . . and said that it wasn't a proper cat name, so we called him Ginger. He was so cute. He'd put his two little paws up on the edge of his box and turn his head and look at me . . . with those big serious eyes and big furry ears . . ."

Juniper's eyes were closed now, but she opened them abruptly, as if she'd been in the middle of a dream. "You were going to explain what's the matter with me," she said.

Anselm took her hand again and held it for a moment without saying anything. "You have a tumor," he said finally, trying to make his words not sound like a death sentence. "We weren't expecting to find it, but there it was. In your pancreas and also in your liver."

"Is that like cancer?" asked Juniper.

"Yes, it's a form of cancer," he replied steadily. The biopsy he'd taken at the end of the operation had shown it to be a particularly malignant, anaplastic type of tumor.

"I knew it," she said. "I knew from the way the nurses and everybody look at you and talk to you, like you're not quite human anymore."

Anselm said nothing but just kept on holding her hand with a steady pressure.

"I'm going to die soon," she said after a pause. "Right?" Her voice was quite unemotional.

He cleared his throat, which was feeling very tight, and Juniper, who was watching him, smiled. She didn't need to be told.

"I don't want any more of that stuff," she said, looking up at the small bottle hanging from the IV pole. "Could you take it out, please? And I'd like to go home tomorrow, if you could write the orders."

While Anselm was taking out the IV, Juniper, who had closed her eyes again, said, "Thanks for being so honest, Dr. Harris. That was the nicest thing you could have done for me. Would you talk to my dad, please? He's in the waiting room."

He went out quietly, had a long talk with her father, then went to the desk to write Juniper's discharge orders in the chart.

Feeling a painful tightness in his chest, Anselm got off at the ground floor just in time to hear his name being paged on the loudspeaker system.

He stopped in the small hospital flower shop near the main entrance, and the two blue-rinsed ladies who ran it stopped their talking and stared at him. He asked to use the phone, and while he picked it up, they went on staring at him.

"Oh, yes, Dr. Harris," said Stefan's secretary.

"Mr. Olson wonders if you'd step over to his office if you have a moment."

"Sure," said Anselm. "I'm just down the corridor." He put the phone down, smiled his thanks at the two ladies, and went off. He could feel their eyes watching his back as he walked along the corridor.

Bob North was slouched in Stefan's office, reading a report when Anselm walked in, and he didn't look up.

"Dr. Harris," said Stefan, "please sit down. Thanks for coming." He looked uncomfortable, and Anselm had a feeling that Stefan was about to do something he really didn't want to do.

"We've been going over your entire situation at this hospital, Dr. Harris," Stefan went on, his hands clasped in front of him on the desk. "And a number of things have recently surfaced. In your initial application for hospital privileges here, you stated that the only malpractice suit charged against you was the one in New York concerning the politician Andy Panneterio, correct?"

Anselm nodded, watching Stefan.

"It has come to our notice that you made an incorrect response to that question," said Stefan carefully. "But unfortunately, that's not all. A few days ago there was a meeting of the hospital's quality assurance committee."

He looked over at Bob. "Dr. North, would you like to tell Dr. Harris what transpired at that meeting?"

Bob shook his head, again without looking up.

Stefan sighed. "Well, Dr. Harris, as you know, an internal complaint from one of our own physicians had been lodged with the committee about your handling of the Bracknell case, and it was decided to review that case and all the surgical cases you've admitted since you came here."

"Every single one of my cases?" asked Anselm. He

smiled disbelievingly. "You're going to have one hell of an overtime bill at the end of the month."

Stefan ignored the comment. He was annoyed that Bob wasn't helping him; they had agreed that they would share the unpleasant task equally.

"The QA committee met again last evening," he said. "They reviewed the reports of all the cases and came up with a recommendation."

"And that was?" Anselm was still smiling, but there was no humor on his face.

"This morning the hospital's executive committee met in special session," Stefan went on, ignoring Anselm's question. He had a speech to deliver, and the sooner he got it out the better. "They considered the recommendations of the quality assurance committee and also reviewed the report from the navy doctors concerning your handling of the Bracknell case."

"And?" asked Anselm more sharply. "You're dancing around this like a ballerina."

Bob guffawed.

"They recommend that that your privileges at this hospital be rescinded as of today," said Stefan, feeling like a judge forced to hand down a sentence though he knew the jury was wrong. "I'm sorry. You were given the opportunity some time ago to resign, but you decided not to take it, although that would have avoided the publicity that's likely to come along with this."

Bob finally looked up and smiled at Anselm, an unpleasant, aggressive, triumphant smile.

"Have you read the bylaws?" Anselm asked Stefan.

"Yes, of course," replied Stefan, surprised. If anybody was familiar with the hospital bylaws, surely it was he.

"Well, you may recall that there are only certain

reasons you can use to pull a doctor's hospital privileges," said Anselm. "And you can't do it without a formal hearing, right?"

"Yes, we can," said Bob loudly. "It can be done on an emergency basis to protect patients who would otherwise be at risk. And that's what we did."

"Of course there'll be a hearing," said Stefan hastily. "And at that time, if you wish, you can be represented by an attorney."

"Meanwhile," said Bob, "you can neither use the hospital facilities, admit or treat patients, or enter the hospital without specific permission from the administrator after today."

Stefan, obviously embarrassed, forced himself to finish. "I'd appreciate it if you would complete any outstanding paperwork as soon as possible, Dr. Harris," he said. "Discharge summaries, operative notes, that kind of thing. Do you think you could have these done by the end of the week?"

"I'm up to date," replied Anselm. "I have one patient in the house, who's leaving tomorrow. So I have one discharge summary to do."

"In that case, Dr. Harris, you have permission to use the hospital facilities for those purposes only, for the next week," said Stefan.

Anselm looked at Bob's triumphant expression and suppressed an urge to smash a fist into it.

"I'm sorry, but you realize we're going to have to make a public announcement," said Stefan. "Normally we wouldn't, but because of the publicity associated with the Bracknell case—"

"Sure, go ahead. But let me tell you something." Anselm stepped up to the desk so that his face was a few inches from Stefan's. "You're making a big, dumb, illegal mistake. This hospital's got a lot of hard times coming, and if you think you're going to get out from under by getting rid of me, you're out of your mind.''

"Don't blame us," said Bob, smiling broadly. "We want you to understand that it wasn't Stefan and me. It was a committee decision, certainly not ours. Personally, we're very fond of you."

PART
FOUR

33

Norman Hartman, Sandy Bracknell's lawyer, had been at the game for a long time, and what he didn't know about winning medical malpractice lawsuits probably wasn't worth knowing. Norm looked at his watch. He had two very important meetings scheduled that morning, one with Stefan Olson and the hospital's attorney, and the other with Peter Delafield and his legal representative, and before that he had arranged to meet with Jasmine Wu, the head nurse of the ICU, who had been on duty when Bracknell was admitted. Norman's technique was to name everybody even remotely concerned with a case in the suit, then to call the less involved people and ask if he could have a chat with them. Among his colleagues these interviews were known as fishing expeditions. Some of his warier subjects refused to do so without their lawyer present, but in general, since he was always very pleasant and completely unthreatening, most of them set their mistrust aside and agreed to see him.

Norm gave his secretary a few instructions and ran down the stairs to his car. It normally took him almost exactly an hour to get from his Hartford office to Glenport, and since he wasn't being reimbursed, or wouldn't be until the case was over, he didn't want to waste any time.

Norm felt a sense of exhilaration as he crossed the street to his car. He was already deep into his biggest case ever, one that if successful would make him wealthy for the rest of his life, even if he retired the day after the case was tried. Norman had little doubt about the outcome. The courts in Connecticut had in the past few years been coming down hard on doctors accused in malpractice suits, and this case was as clear-cut as any he'd ever been involved in. He had already lined up medical and surgical experts from around the country to testify against Anselm Harris, and it was clear that he was building an unassailable case. One of his more difficult tasks would be getting the navy doctors to testify, but he was working on ways of getting around that too.

The publicity would be intense, and the more of it there was, the better pleased Norman would be. He was an expert in handling the press and had an excellent TV personality. He always knew exactly what to say in the few moments he was on camera outside a courthouse. Modest, invariably fair, never gloating, he always had a nice word for his opponent. This case would position him as the leading malpractice attorney in the state, and Norman was putting the pieces carefully in place for the magazine stories and TV appearances that would follow. Already he had started having confidential chats about the case over dinner with a few selected friends in the media.

He sat back in the luxurious leather seat and enjoyed the drive. After getting out of the slow Hartford traffic, he turned onto Route 2, a fine, wide highway, and as usual it was almost deserted once he'd got beyond East Glastonbury. The road ahead was clear, and Norman checked his rearview mirror and put his foot down hard on the accelerator. The big BMW leapt forward, and soon the speedometer needle was close to a hundred. Green meadows and trees rushed past, and Nor-

man laughed out loud with the excitement and pleasure of it all. This was a great time to be alive and
healthy, and with a multimillion-dollar suit well in
hand and almost ready to go; the outcome was certain
enough to use as collateral at the bank.

After a few minutes of exhilarating speed, Norm
slowed down and made the rest of the trip to Glenport
at a sedate and legal pace. He didn't spend much time
thinking about what he'd say to Jasmine Wu; interviews of that kind were by now almost second nature.
But his other appointments were going to be a lot more
challenging, and he was still going over every little
ramification in his mind as he parked his car in the
visitors' lot at the hospital.

Norm was by no means handsome, but at a moment's notice he could adopt an expression of sincerity
that in his earlier years as an attorney he had practiced
assiduously in front of a mirror. Now it came naturally, and with the defendants he intended to let off
the hook, he was in addition as kind and compassionate as anyone could be.

He waited for Jasmine at the door of the cafeteria,
where he had arranged to meet her during her break.
When the tiny nurse appeared, dwarfed by the other
nurses with her, she looked at the man in the dark suit
with apprehension, but he greeted her with such
friendliness that she soon relaxed.

"Here, I hope these are the kind you like," he said,
setting a plate of doughnuts in front of them. "I hate
to take your time away from your patients, really I
do."

Norm's smile was so earnest and so full of sincere
concern for her that Jasmine felt flattered and smiled
shyly back at him.

He sat down and picked up a doughnut. "I know I
shouldn't eat this," he said, and his smile enveloped

her in a warm glow, "but I couldn't have a figure like yours even if I never ate another doughnut in my life."

Jasmine laughed, a tinkly oriental laugh. The idea of this great big man with her tiny waist seemed very funny to her. Norm looked at her wedding band. "I'm trying to guess how many children you have," he said. "One, I bet."

"Three, actually," replied Jasmine. She hesitated, then took a photo out of her bag and passed it over, watching his face. He was entranced by the children's beauty and obvious intelligence, and she was totally won over.

He handed the photo back.

"This is a really sad business about Mr. Bracknell," he said after a suitable pause. His tone took on a somber tone. "It's a tragedy for everyone, for the patient, his wife, even for the doctor who, I hate to say it, was the cause of the problem." He leaned over confidentially. "I'm sure you heard that he got into real major difficulties at his last job. It's a crying shame that he was ever allowed to come here"—Norm paused to look around the dingy cafeteria—"and disrupt this fine hospital and destroy its reputation."

Jasmine mumbled something. Dr. Harris had always been nice to her, but this Norm Hartman was obviously saddened and angered by what had happened, and seemed sincerely upset that Anselm Harris had brought shame and disgrace to the hospital and, by extension, to the entire community.

He then asked about her involvement in the case, which, as he already knew, was minimal. While he listened intently, Jasmine nervously told him about Bracknell's arrival in the ICU, how he'd started to convulse, then she had called a code on him.

"Well, I can see now that I got the story wrong," he said, smiling admiringly at her when she finished. "You are obviously a most valuable resource to this hospital," he went on. "Your very prompt reaction obviously saved his life on that occasion. You should feel very proud of *your* part in the case, and I hope that you have been given credit by the administration." Norm hesitated. "I have to tell you, Jasmine, that on the basis of this conversation, I'm seriously considering withdrawing your name as a defendant in the suit. What I might do, though"—he paused but didn't take his bright eyes off hers—"because you are a most impressive young woman, is maybe have you testify for us. . . . We'd be happy to pay any expenses for time off work, that kind of thing." Somehow he made it sound as if he was doing her a big favor, and she said she'd be happy to testify if he thought it would help.

Norm smiled, but from the look on his face Jasmine could see there was something still bothering him.

"Jasmine, I feel I've really got to know you, so I'm going to ask you this rather personal question." He leaned forward confidentially. "How would you say Dr. Harris is liked here in the hospital?"

"Pretty well," she replied, relieved that his question wasn't really personal. "The nurses like working with him, but of course with this case, there's been a lot of talk. . . . Some people really don't like him, but they're not . . ." She was trying not to tell tales out of school, but there was something easy about him that encouraged her to say just what she thought. "Well, he doesn't always get along with the other doctors," she explained, "and some of them are jealous of him." Jasmine looked at the floor. "Like Dr. North, for instance, and of course everybody knows the OR supervisor doesn't like him."

"That's Miss Heinz, isn't it?" asked Norm, who had done his homework. He made a mental note to make appointments to interview both Dr. North and Miss Heinz.

He glanced at his watch. "Jasmine, I know you're pressed for time. Do you know of anything else about Dr. Harris that could have, well, upset people at the hospital? I don't know, maybe personal things . . ." He let the question hang in the air.

This time he drew a blank, although that question often produced results, sometimes enough to change the entire development of a case. But of course Dr. Harris had been at Glenport for only a year, probably not quite long enough for people to get a good handle on him aside from evaluating his professional competence.

Jasmine had to go back to work, and Norm, well pleased, walked down the corridor toward the administrative offices. Tall but self-effacing, he was now an inoffensive-looking man whom nobody noticed. His mind raced ahead to the interviews he was about to conduct with Stefan Olson, Peter Delafield, and their respective legal advisers. Unlike his meeting with Jasmine, these meetings would have a most important bearing on the overall strategy of the case.

34

Maybe it was because Valerie was feeling so many pressures on her, but she was a trifle crisp with Anselm when he arrived fifteen minutes late for their meeting at his office.

She had punctually arrived a few minutes early, and noted the new car in the driveway. Erica showed her in and made coffee for her. Valerie sat and read the *Law Review*, and at the same time she watched Erica with some curiosity. She didn't look like a secretary, and Valerie wondered if she was a girlfriend of Anselm's, standing in while Melanie was away.

Once he arrived, they got down to business immediately and discussed the navy report in detail, then went back, step by step, over what Valerie called "the chain of command": who was calling the shots and who was making the crucial decisions regarding Bracknell's care.

A few hours later, they took a coffee break.

"You have a new secretary?" asked Valerie when the door closed behind Erica.

"Erica? No. She works at the hospital and is very kindly helping me out this week."

Valerie had seen the way that Erica looked at Anselm, and couldn't figure it out. They didn't have a romantic attachment, judging by their body language.

Erica did seem to like him, though, which made sense, otherwise she wouldn't be there. But Valerie thought she saw something chilly, almost calculating in her expression.

Valerie reached for her briefcase and pulled out a file. She had other things to think about besides Anselm's clerical arrangements.

"I've been trying to get expert witnesses to testify for you," she said, opening the file. "I've pretty well gone through the list of top-echelon specialists in New Coventry, Boston, and Hartford."

"Who did you get?"

"Nobody so far. I'm trying to get a list of members of the Society of Vascular Surgeons."

Anselm put his mug down and went to the bookcase. "Here's the yearbook," he said, giving her a small blue booklet. "Every name's in there."

"Are you all right?" she asked, watching him. "You seem very . . . quiet this morning."

"I'm a very quiet person," he said, noticing that he was standing very close to her. The knot in his stomach tightened, and he wondered if this was a good time to tell her that his hospital privileges had been withdrawn. No, he decided; he'd tell her later. He stepped back. There were too many other things to think about right now.

Then they went back to work, analyzing the points made in Dr. Burton's report.

An hour later, Anselm looked at his watch. "I'm sorry," he said, "but I have to go downtown now."

Valerie looked at him in surprise. "Can't you go later? You have a deposition tomorrow, and I want to go over that with you."

"Sorry," he said, "but there are people waiting for me." He eyed her contemplatively, then smiled. "Do you want to come? I can promise you it'll be interesting."

"What are you going to do?" Valerie wasn't sure that she wanted to get involved, but she was curious.

Anselm stood up. "Trust me," he said. "I do a clinic for street people every week. Neil Gowan, the pharmacist, owns an empty store downtown that he lets me use."

Erica came in to say she was leaving, and ten minutes later, Anselm and Valerie were trundling down Manitauk Avenue in the blue Triumph, with the top down and his medical bag in the space behind his seat. The sky was clear, and the crisp air made them both feel like a couple of kids going on a picnic. Valerie's hair blew in the wind, and Anselm watched her out of the corner of his eye. Now that she wasn't concentrating on her work, she seemed to have a different kind of beauty, a smile that was twice as open, plus a freedom in her expression that showed a capacity for relaxation and enjoyment that he'd only suspected before. He wished he'd met her under different circumstances.

They drove downtown, and he found a parking place at the far end of Main Street, near the railroad station and the ferry terminal.

There were already four men and a couple of women outside the store, leaning against the wall or sitting next to a pile of their sad belongings. While Anselm was unlocking the store, Valerie noted that the window was so dirty that passersby could barely see inside.

A man got up from where he was sitting on the edge of the sidewalk and came over, teetering on his thin legs. Valerie fought an urge to edge away from him; he was thin, hollow-checked with a straggling beard and a glazed expression, and emanated a powerful odor of urine and liquor.

Anselm got the door open. The store was bare ex-

cept for a table and three wooden chairs, and the floor
was gray with dust.

"Sit down, Mal," Anselm told the man, who had
followed them in. Mal almost fell into one of the
chairs, his head sank down on his knees, and his arms
hung down, red knuckles touching the floor.

Valerie, who still hadn't quite figured out what was
going on, hung back, instinctively repelled by this man
whom she'd have walked around without another
glance if she'd seen him in the street. She felt uncomfortable and almost afraid to talk to him, and for the
first time she realized how much ordinary people shut
themselves off from people such as Mal. Out of the
corner of her eye she could see Anselm watching her,
appraising her responses.

"Okay, Mal, roll up your pants and let's see how
that leg's doing."

Mal didn't move.

"Valerie,' said Anselm, "if you'd sit in the other
chair and put his leg up on your knee, then I can get
a look at it." He handed her a green surgical towel to
protect her skirt.

Valerie hesitated, thinking that if she did what Anselm asked, she'd stink for the rest of the afternoon
and have to send her entire outfit to the cleaners. Anselm waited, watching her, and she could sense that
he was putting her through some kind of a test. She'd
told him about her work for Legal Aid; now he was
going to find out if she was serious about her desire
to help poor people, and if she had the guts to get her
hands dirty doing it.

Valerie pulled up the chair, reached down for Mal's
leg. He was wearing old, cracked shoes without socks,
and his brown ankle looked like bones covered with
parchmenty skin.

She took hold of his leg. Startled, and used to re-
sponding to sudden attacks from prowling teenage

kids, Mal raised his head and kicked out. His foot hit her chair and almost knocked Valerie off it.

"Take it easy, Mal,"said Anselm, putting out a hand to steady her. She got her balance back and quickly pulled down her skirt, which had ridden up around her thighs. She had wonderful legs, Anselm noted in a brief parenthesis, remembering Peter's question about her.

"I'm going to pick your leg up so I can look at it," he told Mal. He grasped his ankle, placed it on Valerie's knee, then pulled up the frayed pants leg. Valerie almost threw up. A large red-rimmed ulcer was leaking fluid that now trickled in an irregular gray-brown stream onto the towel. Anselm cleaned the ulcer with hydrogen peroxide, which fizzed and made a white froth when it hit the infected area. He put a layer of brown betadine ointment on the ulcer, covered it with a gauze dressing, and attached the whole thing to his leg with adhesive tape.

Valerie had never seen anything like this before, and looked over at the half-open door. Four people had come in and taken up stations against the wall. A young woman sat on the floor, holding a baby. None of them paid any attention to Mal, just remained there, immobile, looking into space.

"Okay, Mal, that's it," said Anselm cheerfully. He pulled Mal's pants leg down over the bandage. "Who's next?"

"Why don't you send him to the hospital?" asked Valerie in a low voice. "And aren't you going to tell him how to take care of that . . . horrible thing?"

"He'll never go to the hospital," he replied. "For one thing, it makes him too nervous to be in a place full of people. As for how to take care of it, I'll be surprised if he even has a bandage on it next time we see him."

Through the store window behind her, Anselm saw

a police car come slowly around the corner and park on the opposite side of the street. Two policemen were in the vehicle, and the sunlight flashed for a moment on the driver's dark glasses.

The young woman got up from where she had been sitting and came over slowly toward them, bare feet splayed, holding the baby in the crook of her arm.

"Hi, Helen," said Anselm as she sat down. "How's the boy doing?" The baby's eyes were dull and hollow-looking. "He's had a lot of diarrhea," she said. "But he's okay now." She undid the single functioning button on her shirt and opened it. Her breasts were heavy and pendulous, with blue veins coursing across the top of them. There was a large swollen, inflamed-looking area just above her right nipple.

"Oh boy," said Anselm, "when did that happen?"

"Five days," said Helen. Her voice was flat, and Valerie figured her accent placed her from the Boston area. "The kid's hungry, and he really chews on my tit."

Anselm thought for a moment. This was beyond what he could properly do without proper facilities. Here there wasn't even running water, but he also knew that Helen would never come to his office, and would rather die than go to a hospital for treatment.

"It's an abscess," he said. "I don't like doing it here, but it needs to be opened."

Helen shrugged, and Valerie felt her stomach tighten up. Was Anselm actually going to do surgery on this woman right here in the storefront? The woman who had come in with Helen came up and took the baby. He didn't make a sound.

The operation took only a few moments. Anselm pulled on a pair of latex gloves, put another green towel under Helen's breast, took a little syringe, and squirted some Xylocaine into the skin over the dome of the abscess. It must have been excruciatingly painful, and

Valerie winced as she watched, but Helen didn't even flinch. Then, with a scalpel in one hand and a bunch of gauze sponges in the other, Anselm pushed the pointed end of the knife deep into the top of the abscess. Valerie shut her eyes tight. When he withdrew the blade, a gush of greenish pus came out, tinged with bright red blood. He held the sponges over the incision, but they were quickly saturated and some pus leaked out onto the towel.

While all this was happening, a train had come in the station a few yards away, accompanied by a clatter and ringing of bells when the crossing gates came down. About a dozen people came off the train, mostly men carrying briefcases, and walked past the storefront. Not a single one looked in, or gave a glance at the people waiting outside, and their self-absorbed lack of interest made Valerie feel suddenly indignant.

The two policemen got out of their car and crossed the street. They came into the store and leaned back against the door, watching.

"Get me some more sponges," ordered Anselm, who couldn't reach them without releasing pressure on Helen's breast. Valerie got the packet of sponges and handed it to him, astonished by what he had done.

"Shouldn't this be a sterile procedure?" she asked. "Couldn't she get infected?"

"She already is infected," said Anselm, taking out a long rubber drain and picking up one end with a curved hemostat. "That's why I opened that abscess, and that's what the pus is all about. Now open that drain pack, please. Don't touch the inside, it's sterile." He pushed the rubber drain into the hole left by the abscess. "If I didn't put in a drain," he explained, "the skin would close up and the abscess would reform in a few days." Helen's rather flat, blank face had shown neither emotion nor pain throughout the procedure.

"Hi, Doc," said one of the cops, a young, good-looking man with a small mustache. He sounded very uncomfortable.

"Hi, David," replied Anselm, looking up. "You want to give us a hand here?"

"No, he doesn't," said his partner, shorter, stockier, with very short dark hair and a cold look in his eye. "You can't do this kind of stuff here, Doctor," he said. "This place ain't licensed as a hospital or clinic. You're committing a breach of the peace."

"This is the only place these people can get any medical care," replied Anselm calmly. "Sure, I'd rather to do it in a better facility, but they won't come to the hospital. You both know that."

"Doc, I'm really sorry, but we have to ask you to move out of here," said David. "That's unless you can show us a license to make such use of these premises. It's a city ordinance, and we have to go by that."

"I've still got those people to take care of," said Anselm, looking at the half dozen people still outside.

The second cop, obviously on a short fuse, took a step forward, but David put a restraining hand on his arm.

"Please, Doc," said David, "just pack up your stuff and get out of here. Otherwise we'll have to arrest you."

"You don't have to do anything of the sort," said Valerie, speaking up for the first time. "We're not causing any disturbance. Has a citizen's complaint been filed? Who sent you here?"

The cops stared at her as if they hadn't noticed her presence before. "Who's she?" asked David, pointing at Valerie.

"This is Ms. Valerie Morse," he said. "*Attorney* Morse."

"Jesus Christ," said the second cop disgustedly,

"you can't even move in this town without bumping into one of them."

David said, "Look, Doc, this time I'm just going to give you a warning. We're going back to the car, and we'll be back here in about half an hour. Be out of here by then, okay?"

"We should be finished in about twenty minutes," said Anselm. "Thanks for stopping by. If you ever get a breast abscess, you know where to come."

David grinned. His partner scowled.

In fifteen minutes, Anselm had dealt with the rest of his patients, the last one a thin young man with purplish lesions on his face who was wheezing and coughing so badly he could hardly walk. The friend who came with him didn't look much better. Valerie had never seen anybody who looked so sick.

"He's in real bad shape," said Anselm when the two men had left. "There's really nothing I can do for him, and he knows it. He and his buddy live in an abandoned sewer pipe section over by the Watertown Mall."

"What was that on his face?" asked Valerie.

"Kaposi's sarcoma," replied Anselm. "He has AIDS and pneumonia. He's sworn he's never going into the hospital again."

"What's going to happen to him?"

"He's going to die," replied Anselm. "Within a week or two, I would guess." His voice was calm, but Valerie could see how frustrated he was not to be able to do anything for the man.

Anselm put the old dressings and other garbage in a plastic bag, closed it, and gave it to Valerie to carry back to the car. He put his equipment back into the medical bag, which he lugged back with him.

"You owe me to get this skirt cleaned," she said as they got back into the Triumph.

"Consider it your personal contribution to the suffering masses," he replied.

It was close to four o'clock, and the afternoon was glorious. It was unseasonably warm, there wasn't a cloud in the sky, and a faint breeze moved the bright new leaves on the trees. If ever there was a day to be in a little convertible with the top down, this was it. They didn't speak on the way back to his office; for one thing, the engine made a lot of noise and conversation would have been difficult. Also, Valerie was silent because for the first time she had seen Anselm in action, diagnosing, making decisions, even operating, with a calm efficiency and humanity that gave her a totally different idea of who he was. Valerie was astonished and very, very impressed. She was surprised at the strength of the feelings she was developing for him, and realized that she would have to be very careful. Anselm Harris was a client, and attorneys were not supposed to get emotionally involved with clients.

"Thanks for helping with my clinic," he said as they got out of the car. "And thanks also for scaring off the fuzz."

The tone of his voice made her look sharply at him. He was pulling his heavy bag out of the back, and he seemed to have changed; a great sadness seemed to have overtaken him, replacing the assured, competent attitude he had shown earlier, and Valerie felt an almost irresistible urge to take him in her arms and comfort him.

When Anselm came into the office, lugging his heavy bag and followed by Valerie, the phone was ringing and he went to answer it. To his surprise, Frank Abruzzo was on the line.

"That Erica Barnes," said Frank in his gruff voice, "isn't she working part-time in your office?"

"Yes, she is," replied Anselm, surprised.

"I think you should know that she turned you in,"

said Frank. "She told the committee about some malpractice suit you were named in, in New York, one that came to nothing. She must have taken the record from your files."

Anselm was stunned. Then he sat down at his desk and started to laugh. There wasn't much else he could do.

Valerie watched him from the doorway, wondering what could be making him laugh in that strange way. "Shall I make us some coffee?" she asked.

Anselm raised his head. "No," he said. "I'll tell you what we're going to do. We're going to get in the car, stop off at the deli down the road, get us a bottle of wine, then we're going to drive up to Mystic for a picnic by the river."

35

There was a new feeling in the air between Valerie
and Anselm when they set off, an intensity that was
sharpened by the clear sky and the urgent signs of
spring all around them. To Anselm it was like a temporary truce, a space between the clouds when he
could forget all about the hospital, Bracknell, everything.

Valerie felt the same way, leaving her anxieties about
her job, Ralph Stern, Patrick, even the case of Anselm
Harris, behind her as they sped across the long bridge
over the Thames River.

On the way up to Mystic, while on a causeway across
a wetlands area where new green rushes were pushing
aside last year's gray, faded stalks, Anselm suddenly
slammed on the brakes and pulled off onto the grassy
verge. They bumped to a halt and he said, "Did you
see him?"

Valerie, who had been jolted hard against her seat
belt, didn't have the slightest idea of what he was talking about, and shook her head.

"A blue heron," he said, his eyes gleaming. "A
beauty. Don't open the car door, climb out over the
top. And keep as quiet as you can."

Anselm hopped out, and Valerie followed, glad she
wasn't wearing a tight skirt.

They went under a wire fence and crept quietly down through scrubby stands of sedge and sea lavender, around clumps of round-leafed bayberry bushes and spike grass, toward the place Anselm had seen the bird. Valerie, close behind him, caught her foot on a branch and almost fell, and he turned and caught her hand. They walked for a few minutes, slowly, unable to see more than a few feet ahead of them. She had visions of getting lost, sinking into the swamp, and disappearing forever, but he was sure-footed and had a naturalist's ability to move around without noise or fuss. Behind them, a semi roared by on the highway, an incongruous, distant intrusion. They came to a small clearing, and he stopped and listened. The only sound they heard was the buzzing drone of a few winged insects and, far away, the roar of traffic. Valerie was very aware of his physical presence, his closeness, and felt excitement and tension growing through her entire body.

He pressed her hand. "Look!" he whispered in her ear. She followed his gaze, and between thin white birch trunks she saw first the dappled blue and white reflections of the sky in a shallow pool of water, then, with a shock, the tall, stooped, elegant figure of a great blue heron, outlined in white by the sunlight, standing on one long and skinny leg by the water's edge, immobile, waiting.

Anselm crouched in the long grass and gently pulled her down beside him so that they would be almost invisible to the bird.

"He's huge," she whispered. Indeed, the crane-like bird was about four feet tall.

Suddenly the great heron moved and pushed himself up into the air with all the strength of his stalk-like legs, wings flapping noisily, ungainly in his first moments of flight. He swung over the trees, an awesome gray-blue shape and passed over their heads like a vast prehistoric pterodactyl, wings hissing, legs trailing, making a deep, harsh, petulant croaking noise, annoyed at being disturbed, and disappeared over a stand of alders.

Anselm had his arms around Valerie. "That's the second great blue I've seen this year," he said softly in her ear. "But this is the one I'll remember for the rest of my life."

The feeling between them was too strong for either of them to resist now. The ground felt soft and welcoming as they sank onto it, and it smelled of spring and peat moss and the sea, and they lay there for a while, locked tightly together, unable to get close enough to satisfy the need that rose in both of them, but rejoicing in the intimate feel and shape and outline of their bodies and the sense of sharing in the passion that now enveloped them. Gently, Anselm undid the buttons of her blouse, and then she felt the touch of the cool, liberating air on her breasts, and then they were naked and easy and free, and laughed and touched each other with a curiosity and delight for a few moments before passion hit them again and they came together.

They stayed there almost an hour, with the tall salt hay grasses and cattails swaying above them, the smell of the earth and the feelings of spring, by turns tender and fierce, catching them up in a tsunami that washed away everything else in the world.

36

It was cold and getting dark by the time they got back to Glenport. The soft top on the Triumph wouldn't latch shut, and Valerie had to hang onto it to keep it from blowing away.

"You have a deposition with Norm Hartman tomorrow," she said firmly, her teeth chattering as they pulled up outside his office. "I'm sorry, but you're still my client and I have to be certain you're prepared."

"I've done this before," Anselm growled. "I know what to say to him."

"Right. And I'm more interested in what you *don't* say to him," replied Valerie. "I'm too cold to argue, so please, just give in without a fight, okay?"

"Fine," said Anselm. "But we're not doing it here. Let's go to my house, order ourselves a pizza, and do it in a civilized way, in the safety and comfort of a hot tub."

He did a U-turn in the street and three minutes later pulled up outside the garage of his house.

Ten minutes later, they were in the hot tub, hidden from the neighbors by a high hawthorn hedge.

"The first rule," said Valerie, retreating to the opposite side of the tub and keeping everything below her neck decorously beneath the gently steaming surface, "is to say the least possible. *Never* volunteer information, however trivial it may be.'' She looked over at Anselm, who had followed her example and was submerged except for his head. ''Remember,'' she went on, ''everything you say will be gone over carefully by a team of people whose job it is to destroy you.''

''One of the things that worries me about you, Valerie,'' said Anselm, ''is your cynicism. Where is your belief in the ultimate goodness of men? Or women?'' he added, not to sound overly sexist.

''I'm talking about attorneys,'' she replied. ''And as you've noted, most of us ain't even human.'' Her foot accidentally brushed his leg, and that interrupted her concentration for a moment.

''What's the second rule?'' asked Anselm. He pulled a dead leaf out of the water and flicked it over the side.

''The second rule is, *always obey the first rule.*''

''Is there a third?''

''Yes. The third rule is *tell the truth.* If you don't remember something, say so and stick to it. If you don't know, say so and stick to it. Don't let them lead you into statements that you wouldn't have made without their prodding. You can refuse to answer questions, but the judge may insist later that you answer them. It's better to answer vaguely than not at all, because no answer draws attention to the question—''

''My God, Valerie, you're up to about ten rules and I wasn't taking notes. Would you repeat them?''

Before she could answer, Anselm turned on the blower, and noisy bubbles started to rise until the entire surface of the water was like a boiling caldron. Valerie sighed. Her voice couldn't be heard over the noise, and anyway the pedagogic urge had left her. They came together in the middle of the tub and stood up, tense with desire, locked in each other's arms.

After an indeterminate number of minutes, Anselm glanced over her shoulder and saw the pizza boy hanging over the back gate, holding the box in front of him, watching, his jaw slack with astonishment.

Twenty minutes later, sitting in terry-towel robes at the kitchen table with an empty pizza box between them, Valerie caught him glancing at the clock.

"Do you have to go?" she asked, reluctant for the evening to end. "I suppose you have to do evening rounds at the hospital."

Anselm shook his head. "Actually, I don't." He was looking grim again. "They decided I was a menace to my patients, and today they pulled my privileges at the hospital. So aside from a few follow-up patients I see here in the office, I'm unemployed."

Valerie was astonished. "Who is 'they'? Did you have a hearing?"

" 'They' are the hospital administrator and the chief of surgery, working through the surgical quality assurance committee and the executive committee," said Anselm, trying to sound nonchalant.

"Do you have an attorney?" she asked. "I mean, aside from me?"

"No, I don't. I was going to ask you about that."

"Well, does the hospital have one?" Valerie knew perfectly well that even the smallest hospital had an attorney, and her question was rhetorical. She just wanted to make the point.

"Yes. Actually, he was at the first meeting a week or so ago, when they tried to get me to resign voluntarily from the staff."

Valerie thought for a moment. She didn't want to get involved in legal proceedings that weren't directly related to the malpractice suit, but if the hospital showed its lack of confidence in him in such an obvious way, it might well hurt Anselm's chances of winning the suit.

"Do you have a copy of the hospital bylaws?" she asked him.

"I keep it on my bedside table," he answered lightly, but she wasn't amused, so he went on. "There's one in my study. I'll get it." He stood up, went up a flight of stairs into the room he used as an office, closely followed by Valerie, who was curious to see where he worked at home.

While Anselm rummaged around in a desk drawer, Valerie looked around. The room had been a bedroom in a previous existence, with a central window overlooking the front yard and the street. A desk with a computer console occupied most of the opposite wall, next to a low bookcase filled with journals and textbooks. On the wall above the desk were several framed class photos, one of a track team with a young Anselm looking coolly out at her. A stack of stereo equipment stood in a corner, with one small red light gleaming. Valerie walked over to the bookcase and looked at the two framed photos on it. One was of a good-looking air force pilot in his early or mid-thirties, helmet in hand, standing in front of his jet, and another of the same man, with a rather grim-looking but well-built young woman standing on the front steps of a house, eyes narrowed from the sunlight.

"My parents," said Anselm. He handed her a small blue-bound volume. "Here's the bylaws. Latest edition."

Valerie looked at the index, then turned to the section dealing with hospital privileges, withdrawal of.

"Did you have any patients in the hospital at the time your privileges were rescinded, Anselm?"

"No. I had one, Juniper Manson, but I'd already written her discharge orders. I didn't have a single other patient there at the time," replied Anselm.

"Then it doesn't seem to me that they had any right to withdraw your privileges on an emergency basis," said Valerie. "It's quite clear. Section 3 (5)." She showed it to him. "It states clearly that they can only be withdrawn to protect the interests of patients considered to be at risk.''

"Like if I came into the operating room drunk," said Anselm. "I know that. I told them they were acting illegally. I can't imagine why John Kestler, who's their attorney, allowed them to do it."

Valerie made what sounded like a snort.

"I've talked to him," she said. "John Kestler is basically a real estate guy, and all this stuff is way beyond him."

She paused, thinking, not entirely sure that she was doing the right thing. "I'm going to file an injunction," she said. "You'll get your privileges back within a couple of days, pending a formal hearing"

Anselm raised his eyebrows. "Are you sure I shouldn't get another attorney to do that?" he asked. "I don't want you to get into any trouble with the insurance company. They're the ones who are paying you."

"Don't worry about that," said Valerie, thinking fast. "This may actually work out in our favor. The injunction'll put the hospital on notice that they can't push you around. Second, if we decide to make it public, it'll make them look like a bully, and that's certainly not what they want."

Valerie took a deep breath, and the corners of her mouth moved with excitement. Another idea had just come into her mind, but she decided that it wasn't the time to discuss it with Anselm, not yet.

They were getting chilly in their robes, so they went back into the hot tub and made love again. Valerie left soon after, taking the little blue volume of hospital bylaws book with her back to New Coventry. In the car, the warm, loving, excited feeling she'd had all afternoon and evening gave way to a feeling of uncertainty and concern. The legal code of ethics wasn't as strong as the medical one, but she knew that it was very much frowned on for attorneys to develop intimate relationships with their clients. Not only was it a breach of ethics, she realized, but a most dangerous situation that could lead to all kinds of trouble. "Back off," said the calm voice of reason inside her head. "Get out of this situation with Anselm. What'll happen when you lose the case? What is he going to think about you then?"

As she drove onto the ramp leading to I-95, she realized, with a little shiver of mixed delight and apprehension, that it was maybe too late to worry about it.

37

As part of the preparation of her case, Valerie was discussing the overall strategy with her resident expert, Dexter Milne. They had come to the question of how to deal with Anselm's previous malpractice suit.

"I'd try to stay away from it," said Dexter. "You'll have to prevent it from being admitted as evidence, and that's not going to be easy, because Norm'll do his damnedest to get it in. I know you think your client got a bum rap on that one, but if it's admitted, the judge isn't going to let you reopen the case. Your client was found guilty, and that's it."

Dexter broke off. During their conversation Valerie had felt he was ill at ease, and now he was looking at her with a concerned expression.

"Do you really know what you've bitten off here, Valerie?" he asked. "I mean, this case is really loaded. The guy you got as an expert witness—every attorney in the malpractice field knows him. They call him the 'schlock doc.' Of course, you couldn't have known that. And you're not going to get any help from the navy doctors. My guess is that they are all being coached right now, and by some of the smartest lawyers in Washington."

Valerie sighed. "You know, Dexter," she said, "I still can't figure why Andrew gave me this case. I don't have the expertise, and even if he wanted me to work on it, he should have put somebody like you in overall charge.''

Dexter chewed on his lower lip, hesitant to continue. Then he said, ''Look, Valerie, this is what really happened. As you well know, Ralph Stern was adamant about wanting you out, and naturally enough, Andrew didn't want to offend him. His solution was to give you a no-hope case. If you lose it, then they can fire you because you didn't handle it right, whatever. If against all the odds you win it . . .'' Dexter grinned faintly. ''Well, Andrew told Ralph that if you do win it, it'll prove you're such a hot-shot attorney that he'd better swallow his bile and be thankful to have you on board.''

''How do you know this, Dexter? Or are you just guessing?''

''I'm not guessing. Andrew asked me to look over the case before he spoke to you. I read it, made a bunch of phone calls, and reported back to him. I had to tell him I didn't think there was a snowball's hope in hell of winning it.''

They looked at each other silently. ''I'm sorry, Valerie,'' said Dexter. ''Really.''

Valerie walked back to her office feeling that everyone's gun was loaded and pointing at her. But then the Dr. Kasper case had been a no-hope situation too. There *had* to be a way to defend Anselm Harris successfully, in spite of the odds. There had to be something out there, something they had both seen but not recognized as the key to the case. It was certainly going to take all her time and every scrap of energy she possessed, not to mention creative lawyering, but she had plenty of the first two and knew herself to be pretty good at the third.

A little later, while going over the transcript of Anselm's first deposition, she decided to rent a small apartment in Glenport for a week or two. It would avoid the daily two-hour commute and make it easier to talk to the different people involved in the case. Also, it would give her more time to spend with Anselm.

Lying in bed that night, she missed him, and as she gradually became more sleepy, her hand reached between her legs and soon she was wriggling luxuriously in a sweet, warm, and moist fantasy before finally going to sleep.

"I'll walk over with you," said Anselm. "I wouldn't want Peter to be caught by surprise."

Anselm and Valerie hadn't seen much of each other since their picnic, and both felt that that afternoon had been spent in a dream world they'd inhabited briefly, and they weren't quite sure how to get back into it.

"He won't be," murmured Valerie. "I made an appointment."

Peter's office was a couple of blocks farther down the same street, and the short walk in the crisp spring air, the blossoming chestnut trees along the sidewalk, reminded them that life wasn't just subpoenas, citations, and depositions.

The office was larger and more modern than Anselm's. Also much busier. There were patients waiting for blood tests and X rays, others sitting in comfortable chairs in the waiting room. Nurses in white uniforms walked soundlessly across the carpeted floor. There was an atmosphere of well-to-do comfort about the place.

Peter was in his office, said Denise Beckwith, his secretary, a middle-aged woman with unusually short, muscular arms. She wore a loose-fitting maroon dress and a large silver and onyx pin with matching earrings.

"Doctor Harris!" she said, smiling up at him. "It's

so nice to see you. And this must be Miss''—she checked the daybook in front of her—"Miss Morse.''

"Right. She's my attorney.'' He turned to Valerie. "Denise here is an old friend.''

"Dr. Harris operated on me last year,'' she said to Valerie. "He's the best surgeon in this town.''

Valerie noticed how defensively she spoke, as if she expected Valerie to disagree with her.

Peter came out of his office. Valerie saw a tall, confident, good-looking man, immaculate in a fresh white coat.

Anselm made the introductions and went back to chat with Denise Beckwith for a few moments.

Valerie followed Peter into his office. It was a fine room with chrome and white leather furniture, big windows, a large, framed David Hockney behind the desk, and an opulent Chinese rug over the white carpet. A tall, surrealistic figure made of strips of shiny metal, possibly representing a woman with her child, stood in the corner. The office was much more luxurious than Valerie would have expected.

She took a small portable tape recorder out of her purse. "I don't want to do a formal deposition now, Dr. Delafield,'' she said. "I'd just like to ask you a few questions about the Bracknell case, if you don't mind.''

"Sure.'' Peter sat back, relaxed and at ease. "Be my guest.''

Valerie's mind went back to Anselm, under such stress and fighting for his professional life, and she resented the contrast.

"I assume you know that I'm also being sued, and the hospital, too,'' Peter went on.

"Yes,'' replied Valerie, "I read the subpoena. I'm not surprised. It's customary for plaintiff's attorneys to sue everybody and anybody connected with such a case, then dismiss charges if they turn out to be groundless.'' Not that that will happen to you, she thought. You're as involved as Dr. Harris, maybe more so. While she talked, she was trying to gather an impression of the man in front of her. Calm, collected, he seemed quite in command of everything, and in addition there was a certain aura about him, an assurance that she recognized. Peter Delafield was the kind of man who made many, many women fall desperately in love with him. And she didn't fail to recognize the interest that he was showing in her.

"Now, if we can get started . . .'' Valerie put the tape recorder on the glass-topped desk and switched it on. "If you'd say your name to identify yourself for the record, please, Dr. Delafield. Good, thank you. Now I'd like you to think back to the events of the fourteenth of April this year. Please tell me what your relationship was to Denton Bracknell at that time.''

"Well, he was my patient,'' replied Peter, watching her with a well-suppressed twinkle in his eye. "I'd known him for a couple of years, and I guess he relied on me for his medical care. He didn't think much of the government doctors in Washington, or so he told me. Anyway, since he was pretty important to the nation, I had to take specially good care of him, with a complete physical every six months or so. He had bronchitis this winter, then some minor blood-pressure problems. He'd had some minor hardening of the arteries for some time, but nothing too bad.'' He smiled at Valerie, obviously thinking about other things.

"So until this episode, to your knowledge he was in good health?'' She checked the meter to make sure the tape was recording.

"Right. The first I heard about his being ill was when Mrs. Bracknell called from Carver's Island. Apparently Denton had just come in from Washington, complained of a headache, and went to have a nap. When she came to see how he was feeling a couple of hours later, she couldn't rouse him, called the island fire department, and they took him over on Alec Ponting's boat because the fog was too thick to use a helicopter.''

Valerie tapped her pencil on the legal pad in front of her, but so far the only thing she had written on it was Peter's name.

"Was Mr. Bracknell taking any medication at the time?'' The evening before, with Dexter Milne's help, Valerie had made notes of the questions she needed to ask, and now she referred to the list. "For his blood-pressure, for instance?''

Peter shook his head. "No. I'd had him on a ten-day course of Ceclor for his bronchitis, but that was weeks before, in January. Let me make quite sure . . .'' He flipped through the office chart on the desk. Valerie noticed that Mrs. Bracknell's office chart was clipped to the back of her husband's. Both charts were thin, she noted, and that suggested to her that both the Bracknells had been pretty healthy. "No, he wasn't taking anything else,'' confirmed Peter, closing the chart.

Valerie's next questions concerned Bracknell's condition when he first examined him at the dockside before his transfer to the hospital. "At what point did you consult Dr. Harris?'' she asked.

"I asked him to stand by when I heard what had happened,'' said Peter. "From what they told me, it sounded as if he might have had a stroke, and sometimes these are caused by blood clots that travel inside the bloodstream into the brain.''

After her coaching from Anselm and Dexter, she was now well versed in the traveling tendencies of blood clots. She nodded.

"Once he was in the hospital, were you able to confirm that diagnosis?'' she asked.

Peter explained about the ultrasound test that confirmed the partial blockage in the carotid artery leading to the head.

"In the navy report, they mentioned that the hospital's ultrasound equipment was not the latest model," said Valerie. "In fact, the word they used was *obsolete*."

Peter moved in his chair, not at all perturbed. "It certainly isn't the latest model, nobody's contesting that. But it was quite adequate to give us the information we needed."

He put his hands on the glass surface of his desk, winked at Valerie, and spoke directly into the recorder. "Just because at Bethesda Naval Hospital they have the most modern gadgets with all the latest bells and whistles doesn't necessarily mean they practice better medicine."

Valerie smiled. There really was something very engaging about Peter Delafield.

"After you requested Dr. Harris to see Mr. Bracknell in consultation, did he think he should operate?"

"No, not at first, and nor did I. The question at that time was whether Bracknell was well enough to be transferred to another hospital such as New Coventry Medical Center or Bethesda, and we both strongly opposed such a move."

"Then after the tests showed the presence of the clot and the patient had a sudden relapse, you changed your mind and decided that he needed to be operated on?"

Valerie had carefully prepared the wording of that question, but Peter was ready for her, and his slightly bantering expression vanished. He looked fixedly at her.

"I didn't make that decision, Counselor. I'm just an internist. As I'm sure you know, the final decision to operate has to be made by the surgeon on the case, and only by him."

"Of course." Valerie shuffled her papers. "But am

I correct in stating that after reviewing the new facts of the case, and with your knowledge of what the cause of Mr. Bracknell's problems were, you advised him or encouraged him to do the surgery?''

Peter paused, taking in the language Valerie had used and taking his time composing his reply.

"We discussed the findings," he said carefully. "And I agreed with his opinion about what was causing Bracknell's problems. I also basically agreed with him about what needed to be done." He spoke with pointed emphasis and tapped his fingers on the glass desktop to stress his words. "But Dr. Harris was the only one who could decide whether it was surgically appropriate and feasible."

Valerie knew that she would get no further with Peter on this tack; she had tried to get him to take the responsibility for making the crucial decision to operate, and she had failed.

After going in some detail into the results of the tests and the reasons why the operation had been carried out, Valerie saw Peter looked at his gold Rolex.

"I have to go and do my rounds," he said. "I'm sorry. I was quite enjoying this."

He came around the desk and stood looking down at Valerie, who was putting away her tape recorder in her briefcase.

"I know you still have a lot of stuff you want to go over, Counselor." He hesitated, and now that he was physically close to her, she could feel the strength of his attractiveness.

"Tomorrow's Saturday," he said. "How about if you and Anselm came sailing with me and Susan tomorrow? We can have a good time and get the rest of this stuff over and done with at the same time. How about it?"

Valerie thought quickly. It seemed like a great idea, for that way she and Anselm could spend most of the

day together, and there was still some material she
needed to cover with Peter before she went ahead with
the formal deposition. And even if they didn't get much
work done, she loved sailing and didn't often get such
an opportunity.

"If it's all right with Dr. Harris, it's fine with me,"
she said. "And I can tell you now I'm a pretty darn
good crew."

"Great. I'll call Anselm while you're on your way
back to his office. If he can make it, we'll leave about
eight, after I've finished early rounds. We should still
get some of the morning offshore breeze." Peter's enthusiasm was so obvious it made Valerie smile. "We'll
go over to Block Island, have lunch there, maybe a
swim, then come back later in the afternoon. Bring a
sweater, because it can get a bit chilly on the water in
the evenings. And of course sneakers, but since you're
an experienced crew I don't need to tell you that, do
I?" He grinned at her in a playful, flirtatious way, and
Valerie laughed back at him in a way that told him not
to get his hopes up.

She walked back to Anselm's office, going over the
interview of the past hour and a half in her mind. Peter
hadn't seemed arrogant, just supremely confident. He'd
made it clear that the surgical decision had been made
by Anselm, and the knowledge that he too was being
sued apparently didn't bother him one bit. She smiled
at the remembrance of his voice; he seemed to have
absolutely no questions about his own ability, his
decision-making, or his physical male attractiveness.
Peter Delafield seemed a lot more flamboyant than
Anselm, but then, as she told herself a touch defensively, substance wins over style, every time.

When Valerie came back to Anselm's office, he was
just putting down the phone.

"You certainly made a big hit over there," he said,
smiling. He was very happy about the invitation to go

sailing, which he interpreted as an olive branch held out to him by his old friend.

"After we come back from sailing tomorrow, Anselm," she said with a touch of hesitancy, "would you mind coming down to Milford with me? I'd love for you to meet my brother, Patrick."

"Sure," he said readily. "We could all go out for dinner if you like."

Valerie explained about Patrick's accident, his stay in the spinal unit in New Coventry. "He's having a lot of muscle spasms," she said, "and he refuses to go back to see the neurologists at the unit."

"I don't know much about spinal injuries," said Anselm. "But I know someone who does. Sure, let's go there after the sail."

"Great. Thanks. Meanwhile," said Valerie, looking at her watch and gathering up her papers, "I'm outa here."

38

The next morning Valerie woke up with a start, and it took her a second to remember that she was in her little furnished Glenport apartment. The travel alarm on her bedside table showed seven-fifteen, and Anselm had said he'd come by to pick her up at seven forty-five.

By the time the door buzzer sounded, she was ready, wearing a striped navy blue and white shirt, white shorts, and a pair of nifty-looking Topsiders she'd bought the evening before on sale at the Warwick Mall. She checked herself quickly in the mirror. She looked pretty good. On the way to the door she laughed to herself, remembering once when she was a teenager and all dressed up for a party and waiting for her date to pick her up. When he arrived and was standing looking at her in gawky admiration, her little brother, Patrick, had come up and whispered in her ear, "You look like a castaway sailor's wet dream."

She opened the door and Anselm stopped on the step, taking in her outfit.

"Wow," he said appreciatively, "you look terrific. I'm going to have to shoot Peter with a tranquilizer dart."

"Don't just stand there," she said, pleased. "Come in. We just have time for a cup of coffee."

Anselm looked good, in his usual understated way. He was wearing a brown-and-white-striped rugby shirt with khaki shorts. He looked different, more relaxed. Valerie could not avoid seeing how well his clothes showed off his hard body, and for a second she saw him again, naked and glistening in the hot tub.

"What's Susan Delafield like?" she asked. In the short space of time since her picnic with Anselm, she had developed a strange new feeling, a wary alertness about the other women who knew Anselm.

"Nice," he said. "Pretty. Actually, she used to be super pretty. They've been married about ten years."

Valerie poured the coffee, thinking that she'd find out soon enough what Susan Delafield was like. As a professional woman who spent a lot of her time working with men, Valerie was always interested in how the male mind worked, and their responses to such questions was a clue. A woman would have gone into more detail about how Susan looked, how she dressed, whether she was friendly, got on well with the other doctors' wives, or liked a drink, or had reorganized the garden club, or whatever."

"Sugar and milk?"

"No sugar, thanks."

They talked briefly about driving to Milford after the sail, and Valerie was beginning to think it maybe wasn't such a good idea after all. Patrick had not been enthused the evening before when she suggested the visit. Anselm, on the other hand, seemed quite happy about the idea. "We'll go in your car, though," he said, "unless you want to hold onto the top all the way again." They both laughed, but something had arisen in the air between them, just a slight feeling of discomfort, enough to keep them from touching. Valerie wondered if she was taking unfair advantage of his expertise by asking him to go to Milford with her. It would have been smarter to ask him later, she realized, after the sail, when she could better judge the situation.

They drove down to the dock in Anselm's car, for which Valerie was developing a real fondness. It was noisy, the seats were close together, and they were both acutely aware of each other's presence, her long, smooth, tanned leg separated from his hairy, muscular one only by the short stick shift. Valerie put a hand gently on his thigh.

"Tell me some more about Susan," she asked.

Anselm was negotiating a sharp corner and didn't say anything for a moment. He took it accurately and they roared along an almost deserted Wharf Street toward the waterfront. "Susan used to be a nurse," he said. "From the Midwest somewhere. She's bright, religious, but rather depressive and gets easily overwhelmed when things aren't going her way. She hasn't made any real friends here. I think that being married to a doctor doesn't quite measure up to her expectations. And of course Peter . . ." Anselm glanced at Valerie. "Well, I guess he gives her a run for her money."

Peter was standing at the dock, looking very elegant in a thick white cable-knit sweater and twill pants. His hair, dark blond and wavy, blew in the breeze. Anselm and Valerie walked along the floating wooden dock, which creaked and swayed slightly with their weight.

"Wow, that's some boat," said Valerie, taking in the long, glass-smooth blue hull, the low, elegant lines of the cabin, the tall single mast with a radar antenna high up above the shroud spreaders. She glanced at Anselm out of the corner of her eye. "I know doctors are all stinking rich, but this boat must have cost a fortune."

"It's French," replied Anselm, returning Peter's wave and ignoring Valerie's comment. "A Dufour, I think he said."

"Welcome aboard," said Peter. He gave Valerie a

hand and she stepped on the deck and Anselm followed.

"Aren't we supposed to salute the quarterdeck or something?" asked Valerie, smiling at Peter and appreciating the quality of the boat. "She really is a beauty."

Peter laughed, showing a set of perfect teeth. "We're about ready to go. It's going to be a great day."

At that moment a woman's head, tightly covered with short red curls, appeared in the hatchway. Then the rest of her body emerged, tall, thin, a bit angular, graceful in a lithe, athletic way.

"And heeeeere's Susan," said Peter, sounding like a game-show host. She was wearing a bright red shantung silk jacket with gold threads radiating through it, over a gray one-piece swimsuit. She was pretty, as Anselm had said, but Valerie could see that her looks were fading fast. She had big, dark blue eyes set in a freckled face, and the thin black lines of mascara made her eyes look even bigger. Her face and limbs were still young, but with the fine lines that appear so soon with that kind of pale, sun-intolerant skin.

"Coffee's hot if anybody would like some," said Susan after the introductions. The aroma of fresh coffee had followed her out through the hatchway.

Anselm and Valerie followed her down into the cabin, unusually spacious and luxurious for a sailboat. Susan showed them where the head was, then stowed their bags in the forward cabin. The gimballed coffeemaker was on the draining board of the ultramodern galley.

They could hear Peter's feet padding on the deck above their heads. "He's checking everything out before we leave," said Susan. "He's a very careful sailor."

There was something in her tone that made Valerie

glance sharply at her, but her expression hadn't changed.

They all took their coffee up on deck, each mug imprinted with the boat's name, *Docstar,* in tall blue letters on one side, and on the other a picture of the boat heeling over under full sail.

"Anselm," said Peter, looking around, "if you'd like to cast off the forward lines, Valerie and I can handle the one at the stern."

Susan positioned herself behind the shiny metal wheel, and in the brief moment when the boat was free, just before Anselm and Peter jumped back on board, she grinned at Valerie. "What a temptation to take off and leave those guys behind on the dock!"

At the harbor mouth, Anselm and Valerie pulled the genoa jib out of its bag and clipped it onto the stay while Peter, squinting in the sunlight, cranked the sail up from the base of the mast. The sky was clear, with a few feathery trails of high cirrus to the east, and the breeze was strong enough to make the boat heel hard over when the big genoa filled. A few moments later, they had the mainsail up and winched in tightly against the wind, and they could feel the full power of the sails straining against the drag of the water. Peter took the helm and Susan went below to switch off the engine, and now the only noise was a faint hissing from the wake behind them and the sound of the wind in the rigging.

"Would you like to take the helm for a while?" Peter asked Valerie.

"Sure." She moved behind the wheel and grasped the stainless steel rim.

"Keep her on this heading," he said, sitting beside her. "Zero-nine-zero degrees, due east."

It took a few minutes for her to get the hang of it, but it wasn't very difficult. Anselm had gone forward and was sitting in the bow, enjoying the sun and the wind, and Susan was in the galley.

Valerie noticed that Peter was sitting very close to her, and she couldn't move away without letting go of the wheel. It was a good ploy, she thought, half amused and half annoyed, and she wondered how often he'd used it. But she knew exactly how to deal with him.

"Let's talk business," she said, keeping an eye on the compass. "Yesterday you told me that you'd kept a pretty close watch over Denton Bracknell, with a physical exam every six months. But the autopsy showed he was riddled with arteriosclerosis. How come you missed it?"

Out of the corner of her eye, she saw a momentary flash of surprise and annoyance on his face. "Arteriosclerosis isn't something that shows up like a cancer or pneumonia," he said. He moved away from her slightly, enough so their legs weren't touching, and she grinned delightedly to herself. Her method had worked again. "It's hard to diagnose until something occurs to block the arteries, the way it happened with Denton Bracknell." Peter went on, "In any case, we did know he was arteriosclerotic, from seeing the blood vessels in his retina and a couple of other indicators. We knew that all along."

There was a heavy silence, broken by Anselm, who came back from the stern and sat on the transom next to Peter, comfortable again in his company, and watched the wake bubbling under the stern. "How fast are we going?" he inquired.

"Not as fast as I'd like," replied Peter with a sidelong glance at Valerie. He grinned, his good humor restored by his own witticism. "Just over six knots." He pointed at the indicator fixed to the bulkhead.

A herring gull appeared just behind the boat, a few

feet above the water, watchful, maintaining a precise, effortless distance.

"I think I'll go help Susan in the galley," said Valerie, standing up. She smiled sweetly at Peter. "Thanks, Peter, that was fun. Maybe we can talk some more about Mr. Bracknell later."

"Talking about Bracknell," said Anselm after she had gone below, "Peter, you remember when Bracknell came in, and he was waking up but still confused, how cold his hands and feet were?"

On the port side, a powerboat was coming toward them at a fast clip, and Anselm could hear the thud as it came up out of the water and slapped down hard on the next wave.

"Hold tight," said Peter, getting ready to take avoiding action. The boat passed just a few yards away, two scantily clad girls sitting dangerously on the bow, without life jackets, screaming with excitement.

"Goddamn bathtub jockeys!" he shouted after them. He turned back to Anselm. "Those morons should be exterminated," he said. "I tell you, Harris, one of these days, I'm going to buy an Uzi, then I'll come out here and spend an afternoon mowing those suckers down." He took a deep breath. "What was it you were saying?"

"About how cold Bracknell's hands and feet were," said Anselm.

"You and Valerie," said Peter, shaking his head. "You have just one topic between the two of you." He laughed. "Yeah, sure I remember about Bracknell. What about it?"

"I've got a second deposition with Sandy Bracknell's attorney next week. I was going over the clinical findings, and in retrospect I couldn't figure that out. I mean about his coldness. And he was sweating a lot too."

Peter turned to raise the lid on the cooler beside

him, keeping the other hand on the wheel. "Beer or Coke?" he asked. "Help yourself."

Anselm could see that Peter was not particularly anxious to talk about Bracknell, but after opening a can of Heineken, Peter decided to humor his friend. "Those patients are often like that," he said. "It must have been some kind of vascular spasm, I suppose, or maybe an endocrine response to the stress. Who's doing the deposition? Norm Hartman?"

"Yes. You know him?"

"I have to do one with him on Tuesday," said Peter. "Goddamn waste of time."

The sail to Block Island took an exhilarating three hours. The wind was brisk, from the north, and they made good time to the narrow channel into the Great Salt Pond, where they dropped anchor between Champlin's and the New Harbor, and had lunch on deck.

"Isn't this great?" said Peter, spreading his arms wide to include the sand, the shore, the little houses, and the lighthouse on the point. "We should do this more often," he went on, smiling at Valerie. "Would you like to come back when you're finished with this case?"

"Sure," she said enthusiastically. "I'm sure the three of us could come some weekend. That would be just wonderful, thank you."

Peter stared at her for a moment. "Did you say the *three* of us?"

"Sure. Anselm, of course, and Patrick."

"Who's Patrick?" asked Susan. "Your boyfriend?"

"My brother," replied Valerie. "He was paralyzed in an auto accident, but you could swing his wheelchair on board with a winch, right, Peter?"

Peter bit hard into his egg and salami sandwich. "I guess so," he said, but he didn't meet Valerie's cool and amused glance.

It was getting dark by the time they got back to

Glenport, and Peter suggested they all go to a restaurant for dinner, but both Anselm and Valerie demurred, without saying anything about going to Milford. It was none of Peter's business. As they were saying goodbye, Susan held onto Valerie's hand. "Could we have lunch?" she asked. "Just you and me?"

"Sure," replied Valerie readily. "How about Monday? I'll be in Glenport all day."

"Great." Susan seemed relieved. "The Pirate's Lounge, at twelve?"

"I'll be there," promised Valerie.

39

The evening air was chilly, but Anselm didn't put the top up on his TR6 and they drove out through the gates of the marina, kicking up a cloud of dust as he slid the car around the sharp corner. Outside her apartment they exchanged cars, and by the time they got onto I-95, it was dark. Anselm was very quiet, and although Valerie was very aware of him again at such close quarters, she realized that although they had just spent the entire day together, they hadn't had a single moment when they felt close.

And now a distance had sprung up between them, like a sudden chill wind on a warm summer's day, leaving both of them unnerved and a little apprehensive. It had started the moment he appeared on her doorstep that morning, and although he had climbed out of his car feeling he couldn't wait to see her, they had had the same simultaneous sense of emotional withdrawal. On the boat, with other people and other things to talk about, they had enjoyed each other's company, but now that they were physically together again, the sense of emotional distance returned, more pervasively. The feelings of just a few days before, that romantic, exciting, wonderful feeling when they had wished the day would never end, was like the distant memory of a dream.

Anselm looked straight ahead as Valerie drove fast along the road, and she watched him out of the corner of her eye. The highlights on his face moved as the streetlights swept by, curiously changing his expression. One moment, with his jaw and chin sharply outlined, he looked aggressive and determined, and the next, when the light struck his face less harshly, he seemed more vulnerable and pensive.

It didn't take long to get to Milford. The lights were on in Patrick's apartment, and for a second Valerie wondered if he was having another of his parties, but the place was quiet. She and Anselm walked along the path, not touching each other, not saying anything.

Patrick was in his wheelchair, sitting by the window, and did not look happy to see them. After Valerie had introduced Anselm, Patrick ignored him and glowered at his sister. "I've been trying all week, and I can't find a single attorney willing to sue those goddamn doctors," he said. He turned his head and stared at Anselm with studied nonchalance. "Maybe I should talk to the guy who's suing you."

Outraged with her brother's rudeness, Valerie opened her mouth to scream at him, but Anselm calmly pulled out one of his cards, wrote quickly on the back, and gave it to Patrick.

"Here," he said. "The guy's name is Norman Hartman. I don't know his address, but it's in Hartford and should be in the phone book. He's supposed to be pretty darn good." He cracked a faint smile. "I'll be happy to recommend you to him."

Patrick stared at him, and Valerie stifled a laugh.

After a moment Patrick's face broke into a broad grin. "What would you guys like to drink?" he asked.

Valerie made three gin and tonics.

"Your sister says you're having problems with muscle spasms," said Anselm, after they'd been chatting for a while.

"I'm having one right now," said Patrick. "In my leg. Shit, that really hurts." He grimaced and put his hand on his right calf.

Anselm pulled the blanket off Patrick's knees, checked the condition of the muscles, and started to massage the back of the calf. "Actually, having cramps there could be a good sign," he said after working on it for a couple of minutes. "It shows that there are probably still some functioning nerve connections there."

"Great," said Patrick. "How can I fix it?"

"Well," said Anselm in his deliberate way, "yesterday afternoon I called my friend Paul Bruckner, who's a neurologist at New York Hospital. He suggested this new drug." Anselm reached into his pocket. "Luckily I have a friendly local pharmacist, and he'd just received some samples. Here." He put a small package on the table. "Take one of these every morning on an empty stomach, and the cramps should be gone within twenty-four hours."

They stayed and talked for another hour, then Anselm and Valerie got up to leave.

Patrick rolled his wheelchair to the door with them. "Thanks for the pills," he said to Anselm. "Next time you come, you don't need to bring her."

"Good luck with Norm Hartman," replied Anselm, grinning.

Valerie took his arm as they walked back to the car. As he opened the driver's side door for her, she kissed him. "Thanks, Anselm. That was really so nice of you to—"

"It was a pleasure," said Anselm, smiling but cutting off her thanks.

He kept his eyes closed for the first part of the drive back to Glenport. Valerie didn't know whether he was doing this out of tiredness or because he didn't want to talk.

She was glad of the time to think; she was beginning to realize how deeply involved she was with Anselm, but was feeling very insecure about him. Was she just another conquest to him? She remembered what various people had said to her about his effect on women, and it had certainly worked on her and then some. Looking over at him, all relaxed right next to her, she thought, darn it, he isn't even aware of the emotional impact he makes. She was sure he didn't do it on purpose; maybe it was endorphins, attractant substances invisibly exuded from a person . . . or was that pheromones? Whatever it was, she decided, Anselm Harris sure had them.

Valerie wondered what this lawsuit was really doing to his psyche, his self-esteem. Maybe he was an entirely different person when he wasn't under this kind of strain. Maybe . . .

Anselm opened his eyes. He was wide awake and alert, and Valerie wondered if he had been like that all along.

He watched her for a moment, looking at her profile and feeling a heartache he hadn't expected.

"Valerie," he said, "I think we may have made a mistake by getting involved."

Her hands tightened on the wheel, but she said nothing.

"You're defending me in a lawsuit that's probably going to finish my career as a surgeon," he went on. "You're a very clever and competent woman, Valerie, and you have a great future ahead of you. Getting seriously involved with me would just drag you down too, and I don't want that to happen."

Valerie felt tears coming into her eyes and wanted to say, to scream, that it didn't matter, she loved him, they'd get by somehow, he'd get work somewhere, that this sorry business wouldn't be the end of the world for him, and in any case she was going to win that case. But she said nothing, because she knew he was right.

"I hope you'll continue to be my attorney," Anselm was saying. "I've got great faith in you. If anyone can do anything, I believe that you can."

Valerie nodded miserably, turned the corner to his street, and suddenly they were there, stopped outside his house.

"Would you like to come in for a drink?" he asked her.

"I don't think so, Anselm," she replied, feeling sadder than she ever remembered feeling before. "But thanks for the offer, thanks for being so nice to Patrick, thanks for the sail. . . . Thanks for . . ."

Valerie found she couldn't speak, and turned her head away until Anselm was out of the car. When the door closed, she pulled away with a squeal of tires, and the tears in her eyes made it difficult for her to see where she was going.

Anselm had been home only a few moments when the phone rang. It was Mariana, and she wasn't in a good mood. And she sounded as if she'd been drinking more than usual.

"I hear you've managed to get yourself in trouble *again*, Anselm," she said. "Even up there in that remote hole you live in. You must have a special talent."

"What do you want, Mariana?"

"Well, darling dearest Anselm, I was thinking that you must be needing me terribly, all alone up there, stuck in the back of beyond, without a friendly face within a hundred miles. . . . You see, baby, in addition to my feelings for you, which are *para siempre* undiminished by time or distance, there was a conspiracy at the agency, and I was fired last week. They did it just like that, the fuckers, without warning. And just because . . . well, you don't need to hear all that.

And I don't have any money. It's all gone. *All gone.*"
Her voice went up in a familiar crescendo. "Goodbye,
money. I never cared for you anyway. . . . Mum and
Dad are in Australia for six months, and I hate Manhattan anyway, so I'm going to come up to your lovely
Glenport and cook for you and take care of you, and
poison or shoot all those miserable, nasty people
who're giving you a hard time."

"Thanks a lot, Mariana, but that won't be necessary," replied Anselm patiently, wondering how he
could head her off. "As a matter of fact, I already have
somebody here to do all those things . . . and more."

"Oh dear," said Mariana, quite unfazed. "That just
makes one more person I'll have to kill. I can't guarantee to stay very long, but I'll see you when . . ."
She was still talking when she hung up. Anselm, oppressed by a feeling of sadness and responsibility for
her, and the certain knowledge that the woman he had
once loved was rapidly disintegrating, hung up a few
seconds later. He knew that one of the things that had
kept her from going off the deep end was her job, in
which she had taken great joy and huge pride. And
now that was gone too. Anselm looked at the phone,
wondering who he could get in touch with who could
help her. But there was no one. Mariana had no
friends.

On Monday morning, Valerie drove directly to Anselm's office, spoke briefly to Paula, the secretary sent
by the agency, pulled out her papers, and put them on
Anselm's desk. To look at her, immaculately turned
out and features all composed, one would never have
guessed the turmoil inside her heart. When she saw
him, it took all of her courage not to turn and run.

"You've got a new secretary?" she asked.

"Paula's from the agency," he said. "You remember Erica?" He had forgotten to tell Valerie about Er-

ica's espionage, and in retrospect he made it sound
rather funny. "You did see the car, didn't you?" he
asked her, who nodded. "She certainly chose the right
color." Anselm watched her, an ironic twinkle in his
eyes.

Valerie blinked; she had no idea what he was talking
about.

"Her car's yellow, remember?" he said. "And yellow's the color of betrayal and treason." Anselm was
looking rather pleased with himself. "I'd have thought
that as a lawyer you'd know that." He glanced at her
writing pad. "Didn't you know that's why legal pads
are yellow?" He grinned at her with that endearing
smile, as if they were still as close as they'd ever been.

Valerie had a sudden desire to throw something
heavy and hard at him.

"That's what you get for allowing women you don't
know to come into your life," she replied. "And yellow's also the heraldic color of smartasses." She
looked at him, not certain why she was feeling so aggressive toward him. "Anyway, let's get back to business. I need your help with some stuff in the autopsy
report that I don't understand." She pulled the bound
volume from her briefcase. "But on the brighter side,
you'll be happy to know that I managed to get a date
for depositions from the navy doctors."

Anselm didn't look particularly impressed. "Great,"
he said. "What about the autopsy report?"

"There's a paragraph at the end that says something
about the carotid artery constricting around the ob-
struction." Valerie had marked the place with a yellow marker. "It says that could have triggered the
whole sequence of events."

"Right. I suppose that fits in pretty well with what
Peter said. . . ." Anselm thought for a minute. "All
of Bracknell's blood vessels were constricted, and that

also explains why he had such cold hands and feet when I first saw him.''

"Okay, thanks," said Valerie, writing his answer on her legal pad. "If you're satisfied with that explanation, so am I."

She sat back in her chair and looked at him. "You know, Anselm," she said slowly, "there's a time in most legal cases when deals are cut. It's like a pause in the action at some particular time in the proceedings. Then all of a sudden you get deals between the attorneys, the attorneys and the defendant, witnesses, everybody. Everything gets rearranged, things settle down, then everybody goes back to work."

"So?"

"I feel that the time for deals is approaching. I feel it in my bones."

"What you're feeling in your bones is probably early arthritis," said Anselm. But there was a gentleness in the way he spoke and looked at her that told her that he wasn't having an easy time of it either.

Later that morning, Valerie tried to reach Peter, but according to Denise Beckwith, his secretary, he was spending a lot of time at the hospital and in meetings with his lawyer, and she was vague about when he would be available to see her.

Valerie checked her watch and put her papers away. "I'm off to lunch," she told Anselm. "I have a hot date."

He was working at his desk and looked up for a second. "I know," he said. "I was there when you made it."

Valerie had the feeling that his reaction would have been different if her date had been with, for example, Peter rather than with his wife, Susan.

Anselm was very busy. He'd taken several reference books down from the shelves, piled them on his desk, and was thumbing through them with such concentration it made Valerie smile. She could imagine what he'd looked like as a medical student.

"What are you doing?" she asked.

Anselm glanced up at her; there was something in his expression, a mixture of excitement and perplexity that intrigued her. "I'm doing some research," he said. "But so far all I'm getting is more confused."

Susan was already at the Pirate's Lounge, sitting at one of the picnic tables overlooking the water, when Valerie arrived. It was just warm enough to eat outside, and they lined up to get a big bowl of steaming New England clam chowder and a handful of oyster crackers.

Valerie could see that Susan was distressed about something but didn't know quite where to start. So Valerie made conversation, got her to laugh a couple of times with stories of her law practice, until Susan took a deep breath and said, "Valerie, I wanted to talk to you because I feel I can trust you, and quite honestly there isn't anybody else around here I can talk to."

She was wearing a yellow polo shirt with a bright silk scarf. Her wrists were thin, almost bony, and her hand kept moving all the time. The rings on her fingers seemed large, as if they had been made for a much bigger person.

Valerie nodded encouragingly but said nothing. She took a spoonful of the thick, spicy soup, while Susan watched her with a nervous, uncertain expression.

"It's Peter," she said. "I don't know what to do about him." Again she hesitated, looking hard at Valerie, trying to anticipate how she would respond to what she was going to say. It wasn't too late to back off and just enjoy lunch.

"You were on our boat," said Susan, making up

her mind. "You saw it. It cost a fortune, and costs a fortune to keep up. You saw his car. He didn't buy it new, but it still cost over a hundred thousand dollars. Valerie . . ."

Valerie saw the tears brimming and looked away, embarrassed. She put her hand on Susan's thin arm. "Try some of the chowder," she urged. "It's really good."

Susan pushed her bowl away. "I think he's going broke," she said. "He owes money all over the place, and there isn't enough coming in from his practice to cover it all. And he keeps on spending, buying stuff."

Valerie was astonished. Usually it wasn't difficult to tell when people were in financial difficulty, but Peter had seemed so relaxed and confident, and his office practice was so obviously busy, that it would never have occurred to her that he was in that kind of trouble.

"How about selling the car? Or the boat?" she asked.

"We could give them back to the banks, I guess," replied Susan. "But it wouldn't help much. They already own most of everything we have."

"Have you guys ever spoken to a financial counselor? They can be really helpful."

"Peter would never do that," replied Susan. "He's far too proud. The first thing they do is take away your credit cards, right?" She tried to grin. "Can you imagine Peter watching some clerk cut up his platinum American Express card?"

Valerie had a few more suggestions, but none of them seemed to fit the bill. Going through bankruptcy court would be absolutely the last resort for Peter, but from the sound of it, Susan obviously felt that they were heading fast in that direction.

Over mugs of hot coffee, they chatted about other things, and Valerie, who had started off feeling sorry for Susan, was really getting to like her. Susan was modest, with a sharp, unassuming, but novel way of looking at things that Valerie responded to instantly.

The weather was turning cold, and Susan shivered.

"Let's go," said Valerie, pulling her jacket around her shoulders. "You want to do this again some time soon? I guess I won't be staying in Glenport much longer, but maybe we can meet halfway between here and New Coventry if you like."

There was something about Susan's expression that made Valerie stop.

"There's something else bothering you, isn't there, Susan?"

"Yes, there is." She put her chin up and looked with a kind of defiance at Valerie. "I'm sure you've already figured out that Peter likes women. A lot. He's probably had a crack at you." Susan paused. "You're just his type. But quite aside from his little affairs, I'm sure that he's really in love. I don't know who the woman is, but I feel certain Peter's going to leave me for her."

Valerie tried to be comforting, but there really wasn't much she could say. As she drove back to Anselm's office, for some reason that she couldn't pinpoint, the image of the beautiful, ambitious, but unprincipled Erica Barnes kept flitting through her mind.

40

Back in the office, Anselm was still hard at work and obviously not inclined to chat, although Valerie would have liked to talk to him about her lunch with Susan. Instead she checked the list of people she had to talk to. One was the OR supervisor, Lucille Heinz, and judging from the report that had become part of Valerie's documentation on the case, she would be a hostile witness.

Valerie made an appointment to talk to her at two that afternoon, and she walked over to the hospital a few minutes early. At the entrance she saw Peter going out with Stefan Olson and a couple of other men she didn't recognize. With them was a tall, slim, sad-looking man with black hair and bright eyes, carrying a big legal briefcase. Valerie instantly recognized Norm Hartman from the description Dexter Milne had given her. They were all laughing together, and when Peter saw her, his smile faded for a second. Then he waved before going off toward the parking lot. For no better reason than her intuition, Valerie felt that whatever they were all laughing about was not going to be good for her client.

A time for deals. That's what she'd told Anselm, and now she had a feeling that the other people involved in the case were busy making them, only she hadn't been dealt a hand in this particular game. She found her way through the corridors up to the operating suite. Lucille was in her office, and her hostility was almost palpable from the moment Valerie stepped in. Lucille's pale gray eyes, long nose, and pale, unaccented face and absence of makeup, together with the white nurse's cap on her head, gave her a strange, cloistered look. She couldn't look more dead if she were a fish lying on a marble slab, thought Valerie, smiling a greeting, watching Lucille's immobile face.

"I don't want to trouble you by asking you to make a deposition now," said Valerie after introducing herself and shaking Lucille's reluctant hand. She was still hoping she could turn Lucille into an ally. "I'd just like to go over your interpretation of some aspects of the operation that Dr. Harris performed on Denton Bracknell."

They went over Lucille's report. Valerie had taken the precaution of discussing it, sentence by sentence, with Dexter Milne the day before.

"You said here that Dr. Harris ignored the instructions of Dr. Burton, the anesthesiologist, to stop the operation," she said.

"Correct," said Lucille, staring at her. "The patient's blood pressure had fallen to dangerously low levels. Any responsible surgeon would have abandoned the operation and closed up immediately."

Looking at Lucille's tight, censorious lips, Valerie caught herself feeling sorry for her. There surely couldn't be much joy in this woman's life.

"Don't you think that was a matter of judgment, Miss Heinz?" she asked gently. "Dr. Harris was in charge of the case, not Dr. Burton, and he decided on the basis of his experience and expertise that it would be wiser to go ahead and complete the operation."

"Right," said Lucille, her gray eyes smug. "I'm

sure that's exactly what he did. And look what happened.''

Valerie went over a few more points, but didn't spend much longer with Lucille. If the case came to trial, and Valerie was beginning to hope that it wouldn't, Lucille could severely damage her client. But Valerie felt that Lucille was so obviously hostile to Anselm that with skillful questioning, her attitude might be turned to his advantage. It wouldn't be as good as having a strong case, but at this point there didn't seem to be much else she could do.

When Valerie left, Lucille went back to work on the next month's schedule, but had only been at it for a few minutes when a secretary from the personnel department came up, knocked on her door, and gave her an envelope with her name on it. The girl was wearing a broad smile that seemed to Lucille to be totally inappropriate. She snatched the envelope, scowling angrily at the messenger. Worse still, the girl let out a half-stifled giggle on the way out, and Lucille made a mental note to call her boss and complain about her impertinent behavior.

Lucille ripped the envelope open and pulled out a curled, typewritten sheet that had apparently come in on the hospital fax machine.

It was from Michael, and Lucille started to shake as she read it. In it he told her that he was grateful for her help, and that the information she had given him on Dr. Harris had been most valuable, not only to him but to the public, which had a right to know about the physicians they trusted with their lives. However, the repeated phone calls she had been making were intolerable, and he hoped that this letter would be enough to put an end to them without his having to take further action.

For a full minute Lucille found that she couldn't breathe. She crumpled the letter in her hand and

banged her forehead repeatedly on the desk in a frenzy
of despair. Then it occurred to her that Michael could
never have sent such a letter. It was a forgery, of
course, probably written by the woman who answered
the phone, the jealous one who'd been so unpleasant
to her. She sat up. Michael had to learn about this.
She was reaching for the phone when it rang. It was
Donna Forrest, Stefan's secretary. Mr. Olson wished
to see her immediately.

Lucille ran down the stairs, running away from the
letter as much as toward Stefan's office.

Donna looked up from her typing, eyed Lucille up
and down, then told her to go straight in.

Stefan looked up from his desk and glowered at her.

"Sit down," he said. He held up a copy of the fax
she had just received. "I take it you got this," he said.

"Yes, I did," she replied, her words coming out so
fast she was gabbling. "It's a forgery. I was just about
to call Michael and tell him—"

"It isn't," replied Stefan. "I was talking to Mr.
Parrett just before you came in."

Lucille's mouth opened, and she wanted to scream
and scream, but no sound came out.

"I will accept your resignation now, Miss Heinz,"
he said, after reminding her that she had been specifically forbidden to discuss the Bracknell case with
anyone on pain of dismissal.

He pressed his intercom button. "Donna, do you
have that letter? Good. Bring it through, please."

Lucille signed it. She would have resigned anyway.
The thought of everybody in the hospital looking at
her and giggling behind her back made her almost
vomit right there on Stefan's desk.

When Valerie got back to Anselm's office, there were
several message slips waiting for her in Paula's rounded
handwriting. Anselm was still working at his desk. He

hadn't stopped for lunch; in fact, he was so engrossed in what he was doing that the thought hadn't even crossed his mind. He had made a lot of notes and was now going through the bound navy report. As he read through the immaculately printed document, at the back of his mind he had a feeling that a faint, flickering light was glowing at the end of the tunnel. The feeling was inexplicable, and certainly didn't come from the report, which was as damning as anything that had so far come up in the case.

Valerie watched him for a few moments, then came around the desk and put a hand gently on his shoulder. After all, just because they were working on the same case didn't mean they had to act like strangers. "Do you have a minute to talk about Lucille and her report?" she asked.

Anselm stood up and turned to face her. "Sure," he said. They were standing very close, and the tension was unbearable. "I'll be very glad when this case is over," he said very quietly.

"Me too," said Valerie, but she had a numbing intuition that when the case was over, their relationship would be over too. Anselm seemed quite confident that they were going to win the case, but Valerie, who saw the weight of evidence and momentum against them, had no such illusions. At this point she felt that the best she could do was minimize the damage to both the insurance company for which she worked, and to Anselm.

He raised his hands, put one on each side of her face, and kissed her on the lips, briefly but with a tenderness that almost brought tears to her eyes.

"Now," he said, "we can talk about Lucille Heinz and her report."

Every fourth Wednesday, as part of her public relations job, Erica Barnes met with the three women who ran the nurses' union in the hospital, Marylou Larsen, the president, Gloria Kantrowitz, the secretary, and Pat Mooney from the ER, who was treasurer. It was generally recognized that they formed a tough trio; they had been called variously the three musketeers, the triple threat, and the three bitches from hell. Pat Mooney was without question very attractive, and the other two were no slouches either, but no one ever thought of calling them the three graces. They didn't like Erica particularly because they all thought that she was out for herself, too aggressive and ambitious, and certainly overly insistent and greedy about men, but they recognized that she was capable and very smart, and since Erica had often been helpful to them, they kept their feelings to themselves.

Marylou Larsen came in a few minutes late, as usual. She was petite and always immaculately dressed, unusual for a pediatric nurse who continually ran the risk of some kid throwing up over her. Gloria glowered when Marylou came up. "For chrissake, Larsen," she said, "why can't you ever be on time? Just once in a while? D'you think we peons don't have anything else to do?"

"In your ear, Kantrowitz," said Marylou sweetly. "I've been up to the elbows in diarrhea all afternoon. I don't need any more shit from you."

"Right," said Erica. "Now we've got the courtesies over . . . Pat, what's happening with that ER reconstruction project?"

"Believe it or not," replied Pat, "it's getting off the ground. The architects have been prowling around—there's one called Siggie, with the cutest buns—anyway, they're going to redo the access ramp for a start, then they'll start on the ER itself. They're presenting the overall plans to the board next Thursday morning." Erica made a mental note, and an idea lit up in her head like a light bulb. Thursday would be the perfect day for it.

Marylou was struggling to get the top off her coffee container, and a small jet shot out and landed on the front of Gloria's uniform. "Sorry, Gloria." Marylou was genuinely apologetic. "I don't know why they make these lids like that." She picked up a napkin and moved to wipe the coffee stain off Gloria's chest.

"Get away from me," said Gloria, knocking her hand away. "You always manage to get stuff all over everybody else but never on yourself."

"Okay, guys, let's keep this show on the road," said Erica. "We have contract negotiations coming up in a month. Is there anything I can do to help?"

"We need more nurses," said Gloria.

"More clinic secretaries," said Pat. "I spend half my time answering the phone and running to the pharmacy. And I come expensive."

"Like you, Erica," said Marylou, as demure as ever. They all grinned, including Erica.

"You did a great job with the Farman people about their clinic, Erica," Marylou went on, to take the bite out of her last comment. "I heard you scuttled it, like singlehandedly?"

"They hadn't really thought it through," replied Erica.

"I'm glad Anselm Harris got his privileges back," said Pat, looking hard at Erica. "We decided to back him to the max at the last meeting, did you know that?"

"There have been rumors," admitted Erica.

Marylou, always in there with the personal questions, asked innocently, "Erica, did you ever get anything going with him? I mean personally?"

"Not exactly," said Erica in a flat voice.

"Good," replied Marylou pointedly. "Peter wouldn't have liked that, would he?"

"Somebody said you were spending a lot of time with Bob North," Pat said, joining in. "We all thought you hated him."

"Would you guys lay off?" said Erica good-humoredly. "We're not here to talk about my personal life."

"And here he comes," said Gloria, looking over Erica's shoulder. "Dr. Wonderful."

Bob North saw them and came over, all smiles. "How're you girls doing?" he asked, putting both hands on the back of Erica's chair. "Taking care of all the problems of the hospital?" His eyes were on Erica, and he wasn't thinking about the problems of the hospital.

Gloria and Marylou watched in surprise when Erica turned in her chair and smiled up at Bob. They knew she despised him, and normally she would have completely ignored him.

Erica moved her hips slightly in her chair. "There's nothing much we girls can do just by ourselves, *you* know that, Dr. North," she replied, blinking her eyelashes at him.

Bob looked puzzled for a moment, then his eyes lit up. "Right," he said, smiling broadly at her. "Well, I'm sure we can discuss that subject another time." He hesitated for a second, as though he expected to be asked to join them, then he said, "Well, I'd better be getting on my way. Now y'all be good, girls, and if you can't be good, be careful!"

Stony-faced, the four of them watched his receding figure.

"Asshole," said Gloria, making a hissing noise between her teeth.

"Motion seconded," said Marylou, "and passed unanimously. . . ." She looked curiously at Erica. "I think. What's with you, Barnes?" she demanded. "I thought you hated him worse than any of us."

"That's what I thought too," said Gloria, who had also turned back to stare at Erica. "When you smiled at him like that, I almost threw up."

"Relax," said Erica, looking as contented as a cat finishing up the cream. She hooded her eyes for a second and made a pouty, spoiled face. "There are circumstances that can make a girl change her mind about a guy, right, y'all?"

41

It wasn't until two days later that Valerie was able to get an appointment to see Peter Delafield. Denise Beckwith was very apologetic, and from the tone of her voice Valerie got the impression that she'd been told to put Valerie off as long as possible.

When she finally got to see him, Peter seemed less ebullient and outgoing than usual, and he wouldn't meet her eyes when he shook hands. When she started her questions where they had left off the last time, to her surprise he answered in an evasive manner, and when she brought up the subject of Anselm's discussions with Sandy concerning the operation he was planning to do, he shook his head and said that he had no recollection of Anselm's mentioning it to him.

Valerie watched him, trying to figure out what was going on.

"By the way," she said casually, "what's the name of the attorney who's defending you? I'd like to go over a few things with him or her. We need to coordinate the case between all the defendants."

Peter moved uncomfortably in his chair. "Actually, I don't have an attorney, Valerie—not now, because I'm not a defendant anymore," he explained. "My insurance company's attorney decided to settle. I didn't

ford. Barry had developed a severe crush on he
ing her visit and had repeatedly asked her out
She explained to him what had been happ
that as far as she knew, Anselm was no
fendant in the case.

"I've been thinking about it," s
we discussed it at our group d
terday morning. The consens
should settle."

"They're asking for
erie, "and under th
they'll settle for
"Settle it fo
already be a
has ever
is a lot

uld see that he knew, and that the matter *had* been discussed, no doubt in considerable detail.

Valerie stood up. "Thanks for all your help," she said, making no effort to hide the sarcasm in her voice. "Dr. Harris is really fortunate to have a friend like you." She was infuriated not only by his conduct but also because she'd been totally outmaneuvered by Norm Hartman.

By the time Valerie got back to Anselm's office, she had the feeling that the situation was slipping away from her fast, so she called Barry Buonacotti, a vice president of the Professional Insurance Company. He was in charge of all medical malpractice cases insured by his company in Connecticut. When she had first been given the case, she had gone up to discuss it with him in PIC's palatial company headquarters in Hart-

dur-
since.
pening, and
w the sole de-

aid Barry. "In fact,
visional meeting yes-
us at that time is that we

wenty-two million," said Val-
e circumstances, I don't suppose
uch less."

five, Valerie," he said. "That would
huge settlement, the biggest this company
made, and to him a sure five million dollars
better than a long shot at twenty-two million."
I'll talk to him," she said after chewing on her
ower lip for a moment. "Is that your top figure?"

"Up to eight, top *max*," replied Barry. "But you should be able to do it for five. Even that's going to seriously affect our divisional profit figure for this year."

Valerie was very doubtful that Norman Hartman would go for five million, or even eight, but on the other hand, it would cost him a lot of time and money to take the case all the way to court, and the outcome could never be certain.

"I'll give it my best shot," she said.

"Good," he said. "When will you see him?"

"Today, if he's available," she replied, feeling that today was already too late. Norm Hartman's game plan was now obvious. He'd settled with Peter Delafield and the hospital, presumably for a lot of money, and narrowed his case down to one defendant. Now Norm could focus all his energy and resources on where he had the strongest case, and of course that was against Anselm Harris.

"Then why don't you come over here after you've seen him?" Barry was saying. "You can tell me how it went, and there's a great new French restaurant I'd like to take you to. It just opened near the civic center."

Valerie hesitated for just a fraction of a second. She was going to be in Hartford anyway seeing Norm, and the alternatives to dinner with Barry were either going home to New Coventry or grabbing a bite at one of the local restaurants in Glenport.

"Thanks, Barry, but not this time. Maybe next week." And maybe not, she added to herself. Barry was a really nice guy, and there was no point antagonizing him, especially at this juncture in the case, but she didn't think that she could bear to spend an entire evening with him.

Norm Hartman sounded as if he was expecting her call. "Sure, come on up, Counselor," he said. "I was in Glenport only a couple of days ago. If you'd called then, we could have met for lunch."

Yeah, sure, thought Valerie. I know you were here, you son of a gun. And I know why. "I'll be there in about an hour," she said.

Her trip to Hartford took longer than it had taken Norman, because her car was not in as good shape, and she had been driving it hard for the past few weeks. Above fifty miles an hour the motor made an unpleasant knocking sound and the whole vehicle vibrated.

Hartman's office was somewhat less luxurious than Andrew Collier's in New Coventry, but still quite splendid.

He stood up when Valerie came in. "Nice to meet you, Counselor," he said, looking her over with some curiosity. "I've heard lots of nice things about you."

Norm was in his late fifties, from the look of him. He was expensively well dressed in a dark business suit, probably bought at Barney's in New York, she thought, with a black-and-white-striped silk tie with a thin red line between the stripes. His clothes, expensive but loose in the Armani style, had the effect of making him look even more lanky and funereal. Norm's eyes, which could be so gentle and compassionate, now had their natural expression: observant, hard, and unforgiving.

"So what can I do for you?" he asked after they had sat down in his office. The wall behind him was covered with framed diplomas, a certificate of service as an assistant DA in the Bronx, a youthful photo of him with Bobby Kennedy, and yellowing photos of his college crew. Suspended above the diplomas was a long oar fitted to a wooden frame on the wall.

"I've had instructions from my insurance company to settle with you on the Bracknell case," she said bluntly. "I don't agree with them, because I think we have a winning case, but I guess I have to do what I'm told."

"Great," said Norm, smiling sadly. "I'm sure you know that the hospital and the other defendants have been wise enough to follow that course."

"For how much?" she asked casually, but he merely grinned and waved a deprecating hand. It was clear that he hadn't personally lost any money over the arrangement.

"I've been authorized to offer your client up to five million dollars," said Valerie. "This is far more than my company has ever settled out of court for, and I personally think it's grossly excessive, but there it is. I'm just obeying orders. Five million dollars. It's on the table."

Norm's contented expression froze, as Valerie knew it would.

"Counselor," he said in a voice full of hurt and outrage, "I hope you didn't come all the way up to

Hartford just to waste my time and yours.'' He took a deep breath. ''We're not talking here about a simple malpractice case, as I'm sure you're well aware,'' he went on, staring at her as if she didn't have any idea of whom or what she was dealing with. ''We are talking about the *death,* the unnecessary death of one of the most important citizens of these United States.'' His voice rose. ''The defendant, a man with a history of proven malpractice, has been blatantly negligent to a degree quite unknown in my experience—''

''Come on,'' said Valerie impatiently. ''Let's get down to business. I'm sure the company would up the ante a bit if they were pressed real hard.''

''I know most of the guys at Professional Insurance,'' he said, ''and I've played golf with Barry Buonacotti a few times.'' Norman recovered the intiative fast, and he was apparently not too put out by being halted in the full flow of his oratory. ''My guess is that Barry told you to offer five, up to a max of eight, right?''

Valerie didn't answer.

Norm stood up. ''On the basis of my twenty-five years of experience in this field,'' he said, his smile indicating that he knew exactly how long she had been in the same field, ''I expect to get well over twenty million for my client from a jury when this case comes to trial,'' he said. ''The issues are so clear, and your client's guilt is so obvious and blatant, that I believe this is going to become a landmark case that will find its way into every legal textbook in the country.''

He put his hands together, as if he were doing his final summing up for the jury. ''So I would be failing in my duty to my client if I accepted anything less than sixteen point five million dollars. That low figure, you understand, would be making a huge allowance for the court charges, the cost of expert witnesses, and all the other heavy expenses that we would otherwise incur.''

''That figure is totally out of line,'' said Valerie dismissively. ''And please don't think you're the only one with the expert witnesses. Anyway, no Connecticut jury has ever awarded anything like such an amount in any medical malpractice case—''

''I'm well aware of that, Counselor,'' he said smoothly. ''The biggest award to date was exactly four point eight million, just two years ago in New Coventry, in a case of brain damage to a newborn child, the only son of a devoted Puerto Rican couple. The reason I know that is because I appeared for the plaintiff.''

''Well, if you want to slug it out in court,'' she said, trying not to show her desperation, ''we'll be ready for you. I can promise you that we'll pull out every stop there is, and maybe a few more.''

Norm uncoiled himself from behind his desk. ''Please don't try to frighten me, Counselor,'' he said, smiling tolerantly. ''Thanks for stopping by. And you can tell Barry Buonacotti that as always, we remain open to any reasonable offer.''

Valerie stifled the totally unreasonable suggestion that sprang to her mind, and she tried not to feel that she had been humiliated by this arrogant, self-satisfied son of a bitch.

But there was no energy in her step as she walked back to her car. Dexter Milne had been right in his first analysis of the case. It was a no-win situation, and one of the implications of that was that once again she'd be out looking for a job, and probably soon.

42

While Valerie was on her way back from Hartford, and Paula, the agency temp, had already left for the day, the phone rang and Anselm answered it. Denise Beckwith was on the line.

"Could I see you, Dr. Harris? Just for a minute?" Denise was sounding flustered and apologetic.

"Of course. Come on over, I'm still in the office. Are you sick?"

"No, it's not that. . . . I'll tell you when . . . I'll be there in a couple of minutes. Thank you, Dr. Harris."

She arrived soon after, looking pale and very nervous, and Anselm sat her down in his office and offered her a cup of coffee.

"Oh no, thanks, Dr. Harris," she said. "I'm so nervous already I'm just about jumping out of my skin."

Anselm sat at his desk and waited.

"I wanted to talk to you when you were over at our office the last time," she said, "but there were too many people around, and anyway . . ." She looked embarrassed. "I just had one thing to tell you until this morning," she went on, "but now I have two."

Anselm looked as encouraging as he could.

"The reason I'm telling you this," she said, "is

because you were so good to me when I was sick. My sister Rose said if it hadn't been for you, I would never have pulled through.''

Anselm had an instinct not to interrupt her, and didn't.

"Well, yesterday after lunch, Dr. Delafield called all the office staff in and said we weren't to talk to you or Miss Morse or anybody about Mr. Bracknell, or about you, and he was looking at me when he said that, because he knows you're special to me.'' Denise shook her head, blushing slightly. "It's really a shame. I always thought he was your best friend, I mean Dr. Delafield. But that wasn't what I wanted to talk to you about."

She picked her purse off the floor, pulled out a tissue, and blew her nose, obviously gathering her strength for the revelation she was about to make.

"A few days after Mr. Bracknell died,'' said Denise, "Sandy Bracknell came to the office to see Dr. Delafield.'' From the emphasis on Sandy's name, it was clear that Denise didn't like her. "Well, I had to come into his office to get him to sign something. I do that all the time, well, you know how much paperwork there is with Medicare and all the insurance forms."

Anselm wanted to get back to his research, and was beginning to feel a little impatient with Denise, but he nodded encouragingly and tried to look attentive.

"Well, as I said, I came into Dr. Delafield's office with this form. I suppose I didn't knock, but then I don't always knock, because you have to understand I'm in and out all the time.'' She gave him an anxious look as if she were hoping he would tell her, it's okay, Denise, you did the right thing.

Anselm said nothing. Denise's voice grew noticeably jittery. "When I came in, not thinking about anything except the form he had to sign, well, there they were."

"Dr. Delafield and Mrs. Bracknell?"

"Yes. They were both standing there, and *he had his arms around her*!" Denise's voice was so full of shocked indignation that Anselm had difficulty suppressing a laugh.

"Doesn't Dr. Delafield ever hug his patients?" Anselm asked gently. "I do. I hugged you when you were my patient, don't you remember?"

"Yes, I suppose so, but that was different."

"Couldn't he have been giving Mrs. Bracknell a hug to comfort her? Because she'd just lost her husband in such a tragic way?"

"Maybe, yes, but at the time I thought it was different. Yes, I suppose . . ." To Anselm's astonishment her eyes filled with tears. "I've been so worried. I didn't know what to think."

"That's not what's really bothering you, is it, Denise?" he asked gently. He came around the desk and gave her a big hug, to emphasize that it was quite ethical for a doctor to do that with a patient. His gesture released a flood of tears, and Denise spent the next ten minutes telling him about the problems with her sister Rose, who had been the Bracknells' housekeeper ever since they bought the house, and would be unemployed after Sandy Bracknell sold the house, and felt too old to go looking for another job. Rose cried all the time when she was home, and Denise didn't know what to do.

Anselm comforted her as best he could, made some suggestions about who Rose might talk to about getting a job.

Denise finally dried her tears and went home. All the poor woman needed was someone to talk to, thought Anselm, but it had been devoted of her to risk her job warning him about what was going on in Peter's office. Anselm shrugged to himself, sighed, and went back to work, but as he went painstakingly through the pile of textbooks, journals, and specialized articles, making notes on the pathology and clinical findings of carotid vascular disease, at the back of his mind he saw Peter gathering his office staff and telling them not to talk to him or Valerie. That was hardly the action of a friend, although no doubt it was Peter's attorney who had suggested that course of action, but it made Anselm feel slightly sick, then angry.

As he worked, another set of images came to him, images that he tried to dissolve before they developed, images of a clear New England sky with a great blue heron flying low overhead, followed by images of an embroidered white blouse coming off and flying into the high grass, a lithe, smooth body that stopped at the stiff, loose waistband of her jeans, as incongruous as a statue of Aphrodite fitted with pants, the heart-stopping first look at the splendid breasts that Valerie had so unself-consciously revealed. Then images of a gloriously unrestrained, supple body pushing up at him, straining joyfully against his. . . .

Sweating, Anselm sat back and looked at the phone, aching for Valerie in a way he couldn't even have imagined.

It rang and he grabbed it, but it was Mariana. Her voice was a soft cooing that he recognized as belonging to her craziest phases. "Anselm, you have hurt me so much that at this point I simply don't have any compunction for you anymore."

"I think you mean compassion," said Anselm tersely. "What can I do for you?"

"I've met the *nicest* young man," she said. "He's actually as nice as I once hoped you would be . . . actually, nicer, far far nicer than anything you could inspire to in your wildest imaginings, asshole of my heart."

"Wonderful," said Anselm, deciding to let the second malapropism pass. "I hope you'll be very happy together."

"We will. And I'm becoming a writer. With his help. We're writing this story together."

Anselm looked at his watch. "Yes? What about?"

"You," said Mariana, a triumphant note in her voice. "It's going to be the true story of my life with Anselm Harris, the Killer Doctor. It's going to be a lead story in the newspapers next Sunday," she said. "Please look for it. All the brutality, the disappointments, the agonies I've suffered with you—"

"The *brutality*?"

"Even on the very day our divorce was made final," said Mariana, her voice slurring more as she spoke. "Don't you remember, throwing me down the court steps. . . . I'll never forget that, and the way you bared your teeth at me with such hatred. . . . Luckily Michael helped me get a copy of the emergency room record from the hospital."

"Michael? Is that your new boyfriend's name?"

"Michael Parrett. He's one of the great investigative reporters of our generation." Mariana's voice rose, as it usually did when she was in this frame of mind. "And when I compare him with you, you loser, you pig, you monster, you abuser of women—"

Quietly, Anselm put the phone down.

Valerie sat looking at her phone and wondering whether to use it when it rang. It was Anselm, asking if she would like to go out for a drink. He sounded tense, but she didn't really want to go out again.

"Why don't you come over here instead?" she asked, delighted to hear his voice. "I must tell you, I'm feeling the way you sound." She had been intending to open another bottle of red wine and get bombed all by herself.

A few minutes later, Valerie heard the unmistakable

sound of Anselm's TR6. The motor died outside her window. She felt unaccountably nervous and glanced around the small apartment to be sure she hadn't left any underwear or shoes around.

Anselm came in with a bottle tucked under his arm. He put it on the sideboard. "I'm glad you didn't go back to New Coventry tonight," he said simply. "And I want to tell you, I'm just very glad to see you."

"You look as if you'd had a tough day," said Valerie, picking up the bottle and examining the label. "Is this scotch? I've never heard of this brand."

"The Macallan," he said. "It's a single-malt scotch, the best one I know. I got it from a patient who owns a liquor store in Mystic."

His voice sounded subdued, almost shaky, and Valerie turned her head to look at him. "Are you feeling all right?" she asked.

Anselm took a deep breath. "To tell you the truth," he said, "I'm not all right. I've been thinking about you, and how we were, and what's going to happen with us, because . . . I know that if we lose this case we lose each other." He swallowed. "I'm also feeling scared that if we lose I won't be able to practice medicine, and I don't know what else I could do. There isn't anything else I *can* do. I've been either in med school, in residency, or in practice ever since I was twenty, and being a doctor is all I ever thought about." He sat down heavily on the couch.

Valerie pulled down the folding shelf on the sideboard and took out two tumblers.

"Here, Doc," she said. "Do you want to pour the Mac whatever-it-is, or would you rather I did?"

Her matter-of-fact tone made Anselm look up. He smiled at her.

"I'd better do it," he replied, getting up. "It would be foolhardy to let a mere woman pour liquor of this quality."

"Shall I put on some music?" asked Valerie, standing carefully away from Anselm. She knew what would happen if she got too close to him.

"Not for me," he said. "I want to talk to you, and I can't listen to music and concentrate at the same time."

"You sound like LBJ's description of Jerry Ford," she said. "Except that was about walking and chewing gum at the same time, if I remember rightly."

Nothing more was said until they each had a half-filled tumbler. Valerie's suggestion to add water or ice was vetoed by Anselm on the grounds that it would ruin the subtle flavor.

They sat on the couch and touched glasses. He wanted to say, "To us," but instead he asked how Patrick was doing.

"You made quite a hit there," she replied. "And those pills you gave him worked like a charm. He's even forgiven me for representing you."

"What happened between him and his doctors in the spinal unit?" asked Anselm. "Why does he hate them so much?"

"He was there for almost ten weeks," she said. "On the neuro intensive care unit, then on the spinal injury unit. His doctors always came in a half dozen at a time, they were always too busy to talk to him or to me, and when I finally insisted on being told what was happening, they spoke over my head in that condescending way and used jargon I couldn't understand. After somebody told them I was an attorney, they wouldn't talk to me at all. Patrick got very upset with all that, and what was worse than anything, they didn't do him the slightest bit of good, and the bill was out of this world. I'm still paying it. In fact, Anselm Harris, if it wasn't for that, you wouldn't have the privilege of having me as your attorney. Maybe we'd never even have met." She paused for a moment, watching his face. "And even if we had, I wouldn't have had anything to do with you because I don't like doctors. Present company excepted."

There was a pause while they both considered that.

Anselm said, "You can't blame the neuro people. With that kind of injury, there's not usually much anybody can do."

"That's the point." Valerie took a swig of the Macallan. It was smooth and peaty and lit a slow fire all the way down to her stomach. "If there wasn't anything they could do, why did they waste all that time and energy? And all that money?" She felt herself getting worked up again and looked challengingly at him.

"I'm sure they did their best," said Anselm, beginning to feel warm and conciliatory. "It takes time before they can be sure that the damage is irreversible.' His eyes were more interested in Valerie than in what he was saying. She was wearing a plain black dress with a V-neck that didn't reveal much, but even so there was something unbearably sexy about her. "Anyway," he went on, looking away, "I'd like him to go down to see Paul Bruckner at New York Hospital. Paul's done some extraordinary things with people with spinal injuries. I didn't tell that to Patrick because I didn't want to get his hopes up. But I talked to Paul again this afternoon, and he'll be happy to see him."

Valerie was touched by his concern, and the Macallan was making her feel great. She thought for a moment how nice it would be simply to go over and sit in his lap, and . . .

"Anselm," she asked, "how did you get that name? Every time I say it, I feel like I'm reading a verse out of the Bible."

Anselm took a big drink of scotch and didn't reply until it had finished making its fiery way down. "The only Anselm I've ever heard of was Archbishop of Canterbury in the eleventh century,'' he said. ''He liked to have things his own way, and kept having big-time arguments with a guy called William Rufus, who happened to be the king of England at the time, and Anselm lost. So although everyone knew he was in the right and a good man, Anselm finished up being disgraced and exiled.'' He grinned. ''Actually, my mother saw the name in some women's journal when she was pregnant with me. If I'd had the choice, I'd rather have been called Bill, or Joe, or something easy like that. My father's name was Frederick. I wouldn't have minded being called Fred.''

There was a brief silence while he thought about his father, and she contemplated the similarities between the careers of Anselm the archbishop and Anselm the surgeon.

''You were telling me that you don't like doctors,'' said Anselm, surprised that he was pursuing the subject. But he felt an easiness in talking with Valerie that almost invited discussion of touchy topics.

Valerie, now feeling brave and reckless, found the words for a deep-seated anger that she had never allowed to surface before, and certainly not with Anselm. She took a big breath.

''Well, I'll tell you what my basic gripe is, and a lot of people feel the same way. It's not about any particular doctor, it's about doctors in general. Like everybody else, we were brought up to think of doctors as special people, sort of superhuman maybe, people who held the secrets of life and death in their hands, and who put their patients first, before money, before their families, before everything.''

She paused, watching to see his reaction, but he just watched her with a curious, intense expression. ''You see,'' she went on, ''the way people felt about

them gave doctors a special kind of responsibility.''
Now she was choosing her words with care, for she
sensed that she was treading on thin ice. ''But now
you look around and see lots of doctors who just
want to get rich, who've become nothing more than
businessmen, who cheat the system, prescribe medication people don't need, do unnecessary operations . . .''

Valerie raised her hand when she saw Anselm was
about to interrupt. ''Let me finish. When people see
that, it gets them really worked up. If it was used-car
salesmen or politicians doing that kind of stuff, everybody would shrug it off because they expect it. But
when doctors do it, people feel they've been betrayed,
and then they want revenge.''

Anselm put his tumbler on the low table. If she
wanted to do battle, that was okay with him. ''Come
on, Valerie,'' he said, ''you're just spouting the malpractice lawyers' party line, and you know it. Most
doctors are good, honest, hardworking people, and it's
the lawyers who are destroying medicine and making
millions at the same time with their lawsuits. In America we used to have the best system of medicine in the
world, but just look at what the lawyers have done to
it.''

He got up to refill his glass. ''Do you want some
more?'' he asked. ''We've still got half a bottle to get
through.''

Valerie was so anxious to get her message across
that she didn't even hear him. ''Anselm, if you want
to understand what's going on, if you want to understand why you were sued, and why you wouldn't have
been sued twenty years ago, you have to understand
what people are thinking now, today. You're the one
who's getting hurt here, and it's not because Sandy
Bracknell wants to destroy you. The whole ball game
is different. The game's still playing, but the field

tips up and down, and the rules change all the time.''

Anselm spilled a little of the precious Macallan and tried to pick it up on his finger.

''What do you mean, the rules change? People don't change, and their illnesses don't change much either.''

''Anselm, I don't think you're listening to me. What I'm saying is that if you don't go by the new rules, you get nailed, and that's exactly what happened to you.''

He came back and sat down, this time closer to her, thinking, shut up, Valerie, stop talking and come and hold me, put your arms around me. . . .

But she kept going, because she knew that was the only way to keep her feelings at bay. ''Aside from all that, Anselm, when you were taking care of Denton Bracknell, you forgot one thing that as a physician you absolutely cannot forget, especially when you're taking care of important people.''

''Like what?'' He tried to concentrate on what she was saying. ''What did I forget?''

''You forgot that you have to protect your ass, first and foremost. And that's exactly what you didn't do, and that's why you and I are sitting here right now.''

''I suppose you're right,'' said Anselm. ''I guess when all that was going on, I was thinking more about Denton Bracknell's life than my ass.''

''Exactly. You did what you should have done as a doctor, but not what you should have done as a potential defendant.''

Very slowly, to give her time to retreat if she wished, Anselm put his hand out and touched Valerie's cheek with his fingertips, so tenderly that she closed her eyes to fix the memory of it.

''I've been wanting to do that all evening,'' he said.

Valerie, feeling that every muscle in her body was trembling, managed to say, ''Good. Me too. And if you're staying, there's a new toothbrush for you in the bathroom.'' She was trying to sound cool, but her voice shook and she didn't resist when he put his arms around her.

43

Sandy Bracknell had put her Carver's Island house up for sale, but as the agent told her, the property market was severely depressed and she couldn't expect to get more than a fraction of what they had paid for it. But Sandy wanted to make a clean break and told her agent to sell it for whatever she could get.

Today she was going over to the island to put the place in order; Max, the old gardener, was coming over to cut the grass, do some weeding, and trim the bushes around the property, and Rose was coming in to help her get the inside of the house tidied up and ready to be viewed.

Sadly, Sandy had already sold her two fine horses to a Long Island stud farm, and she hadn't been able to hold back her tears when the big horse trailer slowly turned at the end of the drive and disappeared in the direction of the ferry terminal. The sailboat was gone too, on consignment to a yacht brokerage in Stamford.

Wondering if this was the last time she would ever come to the island, Sandy followed a new Mercedes off the ferry, waved at Alec Ponting, who was waiting for someone in his blue Range Rover, and drove along the dusty road, lined by carefully tended flower gardens, with tall pink and red hollyhocks curling over the tops of the high hedges. It almost felt like summer now, and Sandy wound the windows down to catch the unique fragrance of the island, a compound of cut grass, flowers, and the tangy smell of the ocean.

Five minutes later, she turned into the drive, and the dust raised by the car caught up with her before dying quietly down into the roadway.

Rose was in the kitchen, putting new paper on the shelves in the closets.

"Hi, Mrs. Bracknell," she said, turning around. She had the family look of the Beckwiths, rounded, pink-faced, and with the same thick, short arms as her sister Denise.

"Max is in the greenhouse," Rose went on. "He's fixing some glass panes that got broken in the last storm."

"Good. I'll go upstairs. There's a bunch of things I want to take back to the mainland. Shout if you need me."

Upstairs, the bedroom smelled musty, and she opened the big windows. The wind coming off the ocean billowed the gauze curtains, and Sandy stood there, looking out over the ocean. The air was clear, and she could see a single sloop a couple of miles offshore, its genoa set, leaning hard into the wind. Beyond it, the horizon was misty and indistinct, a sign that the weather might be changing.

Sandy went into her old studio adjoining the bedroom. The white sheets were still on the floor, and the painting of the mermaid was still there on the easel, still unfinished, still as sad.

Impulsively, Sandy picked up a palette knife from the box on the front of the easel and slashed the painting from the top all the way to the bottom, then across. Then she ripped the torn canvas from the frame and stuffed it into the garbage basket.

Breathing hard, she went back into the bedroom, opened the closet where she kept her clothes, and pulled an inlaid wooden box from the top shelf and put it on the dresser. Just one look, she thought, then she would get down to work. There was a lot to do.

Taking the key from her purse, she opened the box and was looking at the photos when she heard a crash outside, a man's shout, and a second later a terrible sound of smashing glass.

She dropped the photos on the dresser and ran down to the back door. She knew that the noise had come from the greenhouse, about twenty yards from the house. Rose was ahead of her, her arms waving with the unaccustomed effort of running.

Around the corner they saw Max, his body inside the greenhouse, his legs outside, tangled in his step-ladder. Broken glass was everywhere.

Rose helped Sandy to lift him out, taking care not to cut him any more on the projecting shards of glass.

"I'm very sorry," Max muttered. The left side of his face was gashed and bleeding profusely. His right forearm also was cut, and bits of broken glass were all over his shirt and pants.

They sat him on the grass, and while Sandy tried to apply pressure to stop the bleeding, Rose ran back and returned with a clean dish cloth that Sandy applied to his face.

Sandy thought quickly. "I'll take him down to Nurse Nelligan," she said to Rose. "You're going to need to have that stitched, Max," she said, smiling reassuringly at the old man. He was looking dazed and didn't reply.

"Do you think you can get to my car? Here, hold the cloth tight against your face, like this."

With Rose on one side and Sandy on the other, they raised him up and walked slowly around the house to where Sandy's car was parked.

"Call Davina Nelligan and tell her we're coming," Sandy told Rose as they helped Max into the passenger seat. The cloth was already soaked, and blood was dripping down his jaw and onto his shirt.

"Right," said Rose, and then in a quiet voice, "I hope she's sober."

Sandy ran in to get the keys, then she was in the driver's seat and driving off. The nurse's house was a good fifteen minutes away, on the other side of the ferry terminal, and Rose hoped that Max wouldn't faint from loss of blood. But he was a sturdy old man, and in his day had survived worse accidents.

Rose waited until the car had disappeared, then hurried back inside the house to phone Davina Nelligan. She figured Max would have to go over to the hospital on the ferry after Davina temporarily fixed him up.

Rose was so shaken that she walked right past the phone in the hall and went upstairs to use the one in the master bedroom. Davina was in, her voice sounding slurred as usual, but she promised to take care of Max as soon as they got there. Still shaking from the shock of the accident, Rose closed the windows and was about to go back downstairs when she saw the open box and the photos.

She walked back to the dresser and looked at the one on top. Astonished, she picked it up, then sat on the embroidered bench and looked at the others.

A few moments later, Rose got up and went slowly down the stairs, holding on to the banister, feeling sick and still shaking. When she called her sister Denise, she used the hall phone.

Valerie spent a good part of that morning with Dexter Milne, going over strategy.

"My guess is that this is how Norm Hartman is going to put his case together," said Dexter in his careful way. "First . . ." He raised his index finger, like a schoolteacher making a point. "First, he's going to say that Bracknell should have been transferred immediately to a hospital with better facilities. He's going to bring in transportation experts who'll tell the jury that it could have been done with no problem. And the administrator of New Coventry Medical Center is on record as having offered to send up a special fully equipped ambulance to Glenport to pick him up. Still, you might be able to handle that. For one thing, it was a day with very dense fog, and it would have taken a lot longer than just an hour to make the trip."

Valerie nodded.

"Second," Dexter went on, "he's going to say that Glenport Hospital was not adequately equipped or staffed to do this kind of procedure. And that may be a problem. It certainly doesn't have the most modern equipment. Norm will focus on that for sure."

"Actually, Dexter, I found that the equipment they used in this case is roughly comparable to that of several similar hospitals in the state. Not so for a lot of their other diagnostic hardware, but we don't need to discuss that."

It had taken Valerie a lot of time, several phone calls to the Joint Committee for Accreditation of Hospitals, the American Hospital Association, and talks with hospital administrators and purchasing agents around the state to establish that simple-sounding fact.

"Good point," said Dexter, nodding his approval. "Also," he went on, "you have documented that similar carotid surgery has been successfully performed at Glenport Hospital before, and that it's neither uncommon nor beyond the normally expected skills of a surgeon who's had the training Dr. Harris has."

Valerie listened carefully to Dexter's comments; he had a lot of experience, but even more important, he knew the legal players. He was showing Valerie that one key to a successful defense is to know how the mind of the prosecuting attorney worked, and to make an educated guess about which direction he would try to take the jury.

"I see one great opportunity to refute a lot of what the navy doctors are alleging." Dexter put the palms of his hands together and looked at Valerie in a concerned, paternal way. "And that's the incident that happened in the corridor when Bracknell was being taken to the helicopter, when he stopped breathing and they didn't have a laryngoscope or an endotracheal tube with them. At that point, even though they were still physically in Glenport Hospital, the navy people had already assumed responsibility for Bracknell. You could certainly make a case that *they* were the ones who were careless and ill-prepared."

Valerie sighed. "Right. But I need Dr. Delafield's testimony on that, and he refuses to talk to me. If I subpoena him, he'd be a hostile witness and Norm could turn that to his advantage when he got him on cross."

Neither of them said anything for a few moments. Then Dexter pushed his reading glasses up onto his forehead, sat back in his chair, and rocked to and fro a couple of times. "Valerie, what Norm's really going to get you on is Dr. Harris himself," he said. "Norm's going to try to make him look like an idiot, an incompetent fool who took on a case that he simply wasn't equipped to deal with. He'll point out to the jury that Harris didn't even realize that Bracknell should have been transferred to a major center. He's going to say that he essentially killed the patient with unnecessary surgery, as an ego trip or for the money, and that he isn't fit to be trusted with the lives of other people."

Dexter took a deep breath. He didn't like doing this, but the sooner Valerie realized what she was up against, the better. "Norm will go all out to destroy his character and his credibility," he went on. "He's going to try to show him up as a man who doesn't get on with his colleagues, an incompetent trouble-maker.''

Valerie winced, and Dexter stared at her. "You're not getting attached to this guy, are you?" he asked.

"I believe in him," replied Valerie, covering up her momentary confusion. "I think he's a good doctor who's getting a really raw deal. And not for the first time either," she added, thinking about his previous case. "He's been steamrollered by the system," she went on. "He's a good guy, but not fully aware of half the nasty stuff that goes on in the real world. He's like Candide, and although he tries not to, he works on the basis that people are basically good and trustworthy.''

"Well, at least Voltaire made Candide come out all right," said Dexter with a rare grin. "It's an interesting idea: if you don't see or recognize the horrors, it means they don't exist.''

"Yeah. I'm sure that's the philosophy you base your practice on," replied Valerie, laughing. Then her expression became serious. "Maybe it's a pity, Dexter, but nowadays, people like Anselm Harris need to have people like me to get them out of trouble.''

"We've all got to earn a living, I guess," he replied shortly. "Anyway, let's get back to your case. Do you know yet who the judge is going to be?''

"Mort Gold," she answered. "I understand I didn't exactly hit the jackpot by getting him.''

"He's a loser." Dexter shook his head. "I know him. His family's got money up around Glenport, and they put him through law school. He couldn't make it in private practice, so he got a judgeship. Anyway, that's the luck of the draw. He's one of those Jewish liberal guys. . . ." Dexter frowned, trying to recollect something. "That's right. He got into the papers a few years back because he put a teacher who'd been molesting kids for years on probation instead of in jail, because he didn't think the victims had really suffered that much.''

Dexter's glasses fell back down on his nose, and Valerie didn't know if he'd done it on purpose. "But in your kind of case," he went on, "you might as well know that Gold does not care for doctors. Luckily he's not very smart, so if you plan it carefully, you might goad him to say something unwise and get a mistrial out of it.''

"I'd hate to make that my first line of defense," she said. Her stomach was tied up in a knot of anxiety. Dexter was making it abundantly clear that he stood by his original evaluation that it was a no-hope case.

"Look, Valerie," he said, "I don't know if you have anything up your sleeve that you haven't told me about . . .'' He paused for a second, watching her, but she shook her head.

"Then I don't see how you have any hope of winning this case," he said bluntly. "The only thing you can do at this point is concentrate on damage control, and try to minimize the size of the judgment against your client.''

Feeling sad and defeated, Valerie got up and put her papers back in her case.

"By the way," said Dexter, "I understand that Ralph Stern is really out for your blood. I don't know if there have been any new developments. . . .'' He paused fractionally, but Valerie just went on methodically packing her papers. "Anyway," went on Dexter, "because of that, and remembering the circumstances under which you were given this case, if I were you I think I'd start circulating my resumé. We'll miss you.''

Dexter took his jacket down from behind the door and put it on. With one hand on the doorknob, he turned to Valerie. "Valerie, I'd like you to know that I personally think you are a fine lawyer, and could have done very well here. If I had any say in the matter, I assure you that you'd be staying.''

She had to force herself to get into her car and head out toward Glenport. With a feeling of dread she realized that she hadn't even told Anselm yet that the hospital had settled, and that his best friend, Peter, had also settled. And somehow they had to respond to the fact that Norm Hartman, having disposed of the others, was now gearing up for his assault on the one remaining defendant.

44

On Tony Marino's orders, Galbraith and Wilson, the hospital's architects, had put together a hurried plan to bring the emergency room into compliance with the Joint Commission's guidelines. In order to avoid getting in everyone's way, Tony had further ordered them to give their presentation to the board of managers at eight o'clock that Thursday morning at a time when the ER would normally be quiet.

The presentation was to be given in the small auditorium next to the ER so that the board members could then inspect the actual site with the architects.

Erica, always a careful dresser, prepared herself with special care that morning. Eyes, hair, face, nails, all got careful attention, especially the nails, painted a striking shade of crimson. She wore a pretty silk blouse with lots of little buttons down the front, not her best one but certainly good enough, and an insubstantial black lace bra just visible underneath the blouse.

The board members started to gather a few minutes before eight. The architects had been there already for a half hour setting up the sound system and projector. Frank Abruzzo was there, wearing a suit and long collar tips on his white linen shirt. Stefan appeared, large and purposeful, looking very much in charge and cheerful, as if something had happened to rejuvenate him. Then Tony walked in wearing a loose-fitting gray suit with a tasteful mauve and blue silk tie. As always, Bob North trotted alongside him, short, pink, and shiny in a glistening sharkskin suit, looking, as Peter had once whispered to Erica, like a pig on casters. Bob saw her helping the architects and quickly came over to lend a hand.

"Sit near the back," she told him in a quiet, intimate voice, without looking directly at him.

Bob's eyes almost came out of his head. "Yeah, sure, Erica," he whispered. "Of course."

He went immediately to sit down in case somebody else sat in the back row, and for the next five minutes he hugged himself with delight at his good luck. Erica Barnes! Finally!

The architects started off with their presentation, which was scheduled to last about twenty minutes, after which the entire group would go outside to inspect the condition of the present ramps.

When the lights dimmed and the projector started to show a computer simulation of the proposed ramps from various points of view, Erica appeared silently beside Bob. She put a hand on his thigh, and Bob quivered. "Come with me," she whispered. "Don't make a sound!"

Like two wraiths they slipped unnoticed out of the room, and Erica led him to the room normally used by the on-call emergency room doctor. It contained a bed, a desk with a lamp and a telephone, and at this time it was unoccupied. Erica turned the bolt in the door.

"Come and sit here beside me, Bobby my boy," she said, going over and sitting on the bed.

Astonished and excited beyond anything he could remember, he sat down beside her. He felt hot and loosened his collar.

The auditorium was on the other side of the wall,

and they could hear the architect's droning voice quite clearly.

"You look hot, Bobby baby," murmured Erica, nuzzling his neck. "Why don't you slip off your jacket?"

Bob stood up, his knees shaking with uncontrollable excitement.

"And your pants too, while you're at it, honey," said Erica. "Quietly now, Bobby, and hurry because we don't have much time."

His hands were shaking so much he had trouble unfastening his belt, and she obligingly helped him.

"Sit, Bobbolino," she said softly, and when he had sat beside her, his shirttails covering the top of his white legs, she said, "Bobbinski, would you like to see my breasts?"

Bob gulped and nodded. With a swift movement Erica tore her blouse from the top down, sending buttons flying across the room, and with the same movement ripped her bra, tearing the strap. And there they were, her gorgeous, creamy breasts swelling out at him, and Bob almost came in his underwear.

"Take a good look," said Erica, smiling. "A real good look. I want you to know that I'm not doing this just for me, but mostly for my friend Hermita. You remember Hermita, sweetheart?"

Bob went pale, blinked, and stared at Erica, confused, trying to figure out what she meant.

Then she brought her right hand up gently and raked it hard down the side of his face, her sharpened nails drawing four red trails of blood. At the same moment she screamed, a terrifyingly loud and piercing sound. Bob jumped up, petrified, his hand going to his face, already covered in blood.

"Please, for chrissake, Erica!" he said, but she kept on screaming, and a moment later someone rattled the door and shouted. "What's going on in there?" A lot of other voices were heard outside. "Open this door!" With a sob of terror, Bob recognized Tony's voice. A heavy shoulder crashed against the door, hard, but the door was strong and held fast. Bob, in total shock, huddled down on the bed, his hands over his ears. Erica kept on screaming and pointing at the door, and Bob, terrified out of his skull, stood up obediently and went over to open it.

About ten people erupted into the tiny room, led by Tony, who took one look at the trouserless Bob and the distraught Erica, caught Bob by the back of the neck, and threw him sprawling flat on his face into the corridor. Erica, almost fainting, fell into Stefan Olson's sympathetic and outraged arms.

Somebody got a blanket from the ER and put it around her shoulders, and Stefan led her off, still sobbing unrestrainedly, to recover in his office.

White and shaking like a leaf, Bob got up and went back into the room to get his trousers. Tony was waiting grimly for him and closed the door. They didn't reappear for a good ten minutes, and when the door opened and Bob came out to face the small but hostile group that had collected, he knew that it was all over for him, professionally and personally, here in his hometown of Glenport.

Anselm had spent many hours working on the problem, and he hadn't really come up with anything that fully explained it. *Harrison's Textbook of Medicine* lay open in front of him, and books on pharmacology and neurology were piled up on each side of the desk. He had made several pages of notes in his meticulous script, but nothing was coming together, nothing that made any sense.

Had Bracknell had a fever when he first came into the hospital? Anselm turned to the first few pages of the well-thumbed Xerox of Bracknell's hospital chart.

Nothing really, half a degree perhaps, but with all that had been going on with him at the time, a half-degree fever didn't really mean anything.

Anselm had checked all the reference books he could lay his hands on, then cross-checked with his own excellent memory banks, but the clinical picture that Denton Bracknell had presented simply didn't seem to jibe completely with the textbook cases. He had read and reread the sections on stroke and on carotid artery blockages and embolism. Certainly most of the symptoms fitted the diagnosis that he and Peter had made, and of course that had been confirmed at the autopsy, but the vasoconstriction, or spasm of the arteries, that had seemed to have been part of his problem simply wasn't mentioned in any of the books, and there didn't seem to be any other cause he could put a finger on.

The other finding that didn't jibe was Bracknell's high pulse pressure, which, as he had explained to Valerie, meant that there was an abnormally high range between the highest and lowest blood pressure.

Anselm slammed the textbook shut and sat back in his chair, feeling the beginnings of a headache coming on. He'd even considered poisoning as an outside possibility, but of course the navy people had done a toxicology screen and it had come up negative. Of course, there were all kinds of weird syndromes that populated the textbooks of neurology, describing in great detail the findings when various parts of the brain were damaged by clots or tumors or injury, and Anselm had read through all of them, except for those that occurred only in childhood. He found nothing to help him.

In desperation he again read his and Peter's admission notes, thinking there might be something he had missed, something in the sequence of events that might give him a clue to these unusual findings.

Bracknell had had no symptoms until after he was

home, complained of slight dizziness, then a headache. So far, easy. He'd just got out of a helicopter and had presumably experienced the usual pressure changes during the flight, he was known to have arteriosclerosis, or hardening of the arteries, and that combination was quite enough. Then he had taken some headache pills and gone to bed. Maybe, thought Anselm, maybe he was on some other medication and that had reacted badly with the headache pills. He knew that he'd checked it before, but he did it again. In Peter's writing, "taking no other meds" was scrawled at the end of his admission note, and that was crystal clear. And Peter was Bracknell's family doctor and would know better than anyone. Sandy had also mentioned that Denton wasn't taking any medication, and if he'd been taking a heart medication such as digoxin, it would have showed up on the blood tests.

Anselm stared at the pages, willing them to tell him if there was anything there he should have picked up. The only thing he didn't know for sure was what kind of headache pills Bracknell had taken, and Anselm almost gave up right there. Neither aspirin, Tylenol, nor any of the common proprietary pills he knew of had that kind of side effect.

He looked at the clock, tempted to call it a day, leave, go and spend the evening in a bar, anything to get away from the frustration of chasing a wild goose that in any case could never lay a golden egg for him.

"Okay," he said to himself, "one last try." He picked up the phone and dialed Peter's office number. Peter would think he was crazy, but at least he could fill in the last possible gap in the case. The line was busy. A minute later, Anselm tried again, but it was still busy.

"Screw it," he said out loud, getting up from his chair. His leg cramped, and he stretched, feeling as if he'd been sitting there for a week.

Valerie came in, looking unusually glum.

"Tough day at the office, dear?" he asked, smiling.

"Yeah." She flopped down in a chair. "I don't know what your day's been like, but I feel like I'm the messenger who's going to get killed because she's bringing bad news."

"What's a little more bad news?" asked Anselm, but he could feel his stomach contracting in anticipation.

"You remember when I went up to Hartford to see Norm Hartman? The day of the night we drank that bottle of Macallan?"

"It's indelibly engraved in my memory," he replied, watching her intently.

"I went to see Norm on the instructions of my insurance company," said Valerie slowly, looking Anselm squarely in the eye. "Not because I wanted to, but because they told me to." She paused, her insides tightening. "They figured it would cost them too much if we went to trial, and wanted me to settle the case."

Anselm's eyes grew bigger. "You're telling me *now*? How come nobody asked me about it? Don't I have any say in the matter?"

"Anselm, it's an accounting decision," she replied. "If you read your policy, it will tell you that it's the insurer's decision whether to fight the case or settle, and it's their decision alone. I know it sounds crazy, but you don't have any say in the matter at all. The insurance company's interest is to get out of the case with the least cost to them, and they're not very interested in who's right and who's wrong. If they feel there's a good chance of losing, they'll do their best to settle, and if in doing that your reputation gets hurts, that's just tough." Valerie looked at his stricken face, and her voice softened. "I'm sorry, Anselm, but you know that I have to tell it to you the way it is."

"So how much did it cost the insurance company? To settle, I mean?"

She stretched out a hand and put it gently on his arm. "I wasn't able to settle," she said. "They were asking much more than the insurers were willing to pay. I'm afraid we're going to have to go through with the trial."

Anselm digested that. "I'm not entirely surprised," he said. "When are you and the hospital's and Peter's attorneys going to get together?" he asked. "Aren't we going to need to develop a common defense strategy? I told that to Peter a couple of days ago," he went on, "but he didn't seem to think it was important. I hope his lawyer does."

Valerie put her hands together in her lap. Her palms were sweating. "Anselm, get ready for this. The hospital has settled out of court with Norm. I also found out that your good friend Peter has done the same thing."

There was a long silence. "Peter did that? Without even mentioning it to me?" Anselm flushed a deep red. "When?"

"Earlier this week. I don't know exactly, but I saw Peter and Stefan Olson and Norm Hartman and a bunch of lawyers outside the hospital a couple days ago, and they all looked as if they'd just done a deal."

"How much did they settle for?"

"I don't know. Norm wouldn't tell me, but I'd guess it was a substantial amount, in the millions, for sure."

"So where does that leave us? I mean me?"

"It leaves us alone," replied Valerie, and the tone of her voice made him look up.

"Does that make any difference? I'm still being sued, whatever happens with Peter or the hospital, right?"

"Yes, it does. They can now focus all their attention and energy on you, and it also means that now you won't get the support you might have had from either Peter or the hospital or the other defendants who have settled."

Anselm's eyes narrowed. "Why not?"

Valerie sighed. She was astonished that a man who was clever enough to get through medical school and a surgical residency program could be so naïve about his fellow doctors, and about what was happening in his profession.

"They'll never admit it, Anselm, to you or anybody else," she said patiently, "but you can be sure that Norm Hartman cut a deal with them. 'I'll allow you to settle,' he told them, 'on the understanding that from now on you stay out of it. Don't talk to or in any way help the one remaining defendant.' And that, of course, is you."

"I don't believe it," he said loudly. He gripped his coffee mug hard. "Peter would never agree to that. For God's sake, Valerie, he and I were in med school together, we were best friends there and we've been best friends ever since. He rescued me and got me privileges at the hospital here when I truly had no other place to go; surely that proves it. Doesn't it?" He looked challengingly at her. "Maybe the hospital made that kind of a deal, I wouldn't be surprised. But not Peter. *No way.*" He said it with such conviction that Valerie hesitated to go on. But she felt she had to.

"Anselm, if Peter hadn't done a deal with Norm, he'd still be a defendant," she said. "You have to understand that. Of course, it's quite possible that his attorney forced him into it," she went on, realizing how weak that sounded.

Anselm's entire body seemed to be freezing up as Valerie's words ate into him, syllable by syllable.

"Well," he said finally, in a voice that put a sudden chill of fear into Valerie, "I'm going to have me a little chat with Peter Delafield about all this before the night is much older."

45

Peter wasn't at the office, which wasn't surprising, considering the hour, so Anselm called him at home. Susan answered. "He's not here," she said. "Did you try paging him?"

"No, I didn't," replied Anselm grimly. "I actually want to talk to him in person, not on the phone."

"He's probably at the hospital, then," said Susan in a flat voice. Anselm knew that she spent a lot of evenings alone.

"If he happens to call or come home, would you tell him I need to see him? Yes, tonight. It's important. Thanks, Susan."

Valerie, listening, was alarmed by Anselm's tone of voice.

When he grabbed his coat and made for the door, she jumped up and said, "I'm coming with you."

He hesitated for a second. "Okay," he said. "But my conversation with him is going to be private."

It was chilly in the TR6, and Anselm pushed the car hard until they came to the lights near the hospital. They were red, but there was no traffic, so he gunned the car through, then turned with a squeal of tires into the parking lot. He came to a halt outside the ER, jumped out, and walked fast into the hospital.

"No," said Pat Mooney, "I haven't seen him. Anyway, he's usually finished and long gone by this time."

Anselm called the hospital operator. Dr. Delafield had signed out about seven, over an hour before.

Back in the car, Anselm sat very still for a minute, thinking.

Valerie said nothing. She was beginning to get cold.

"His boat," said Anselm suddenly. "That's where he is."

Five scary minutes later, he pulled up in the marina parking lot. It was quite dark, and only when his headlight scanned across the lot did he see the red Lamborghini parked inconspicuously in a far corner. As the vehicle swung around, Valerie caught a momentary glimpse of another car parked some distance beyond it. The only thing she could say about it for sure was that it was yellow, but that was enough to make her gasp. She glanced at Anselm, but he didn't appear to have noticed. It took a couple of minutes of walking in the dark to get where the boats were; they passed a couple of buildings, then a huge mobile boat lift loomed up in front of them, blacker than the sky behind it, its empty canvas straps hanging over a dark pit. They saw no lights until they came to the end of the dock, which was closed off by a small wire gate. The marina beyond it was crowded, mostly with sailboats, and their rigging sang and tinkled in the light breeze. There was not a soul around. Bare light bulbs every twenty feet or along the marina gave only a faint illumination. A cat meowed somewhere in the darkness.

Anselm was about to yank the gate open and march into the marina when Valerie put a cautioning hand on his arm. "I think Peter might have somebody with him," she said.

That stopped Anselm in his tracks, but only for a moment. They walked down the center walkway with boats on either side of them, big boats with radar and inflatable dinghies across the transom, small boats with tiny open cabins, rolling much more in the current than the larger ones. Aside from the noise in the rigging high above them, silence reigned, an expensive, cossetted silence that had its own eeriness. For no reason both Anselm and Valerie found themselves walking on tiptoe, unwilling, almost afraid to disturb the quietude.

Peter's boat was in its usual place, tied up at the far end of the dock. Like the others, it was shrouded in darkness and silence, and if Anselm hadn't seen the Lamborghini, he would have turned back at that moment and gone to look elsewhere.

"Look!" whispered Valerie. A tiny crack of light had appeared between two curtains in one of the windows next to the dock.

Anselm stepped forward silently and put his face as close to the crack as he could. Through it he could see the main stateroom, the radio and radar instruments above the navigator's desk, and the big double bed that came together in the middle of the cabin when the bunks were slid out. In the bed, or rather on top of it, locked in a complicated embrace and doing things that made Anselm's mouth drop open in astonishment, were the naked bodies of Peter Delafield and Sandy Bracknell.

Anselm and Valerie drove back toward his office in total silence. His expression was strange, and for a moment she was afraid of him, of what he might do.

As he drove, his mind was going at top speed, and a lot of questions were weaving, intertwining, cancelling each other out, and the earliest glimpse of enlightenment was starting to filter through his unwilling brain.

He drove straight past his office and came to a halt

outside the Manitauk pharmacy. It was ten minutes
from closing time, and there was no one in the store
except Neil Gowan.

The doorbell clanged as they came in, and Neil hurried out of his raised dispensary area when he saw
them. "How's it going, Dr. Harris?" he asked anxiously before Anselm could say anything. "My mother's doing real well, and that's thanks only to you."
He was an emotional man and couldn't prevent himself. He wiped a tear from his eye.

Anselm was icy calm now. "Neil, the Bracknells
always used your pharmacy, didn't they?"

"Sure," he said. "Everybody on the island does,
because they don't have a pharmacy there. Sandy's
parents still come here. When she got married and
went over to the island, she still came here."

"Neil, do you happen to know what kind of headache pills Denton Bracknell was using?"

"Headache pills?" He shook his head, but an odd
look came into his eyes. "No, Dr. Harris," he said,
"but now you mention it . . ." He motioned to them
to come with him back to the dispensary. They followed him up the high step into the well-lit area behind the counter. Neil opened a door into a small room
where he did his accounts and attended to his other
business matters. There was a small desk and two
chairs for visitors.

Neil pulled a heavy ledger out of a file drawer and
opened it on the desk. In it were computer printouts
of all the prescriptions that had been filled, with the
date, the patient's name and address, the type of medication and recommended frequency of use, and the
name of the doctor who had made the prescription.

He flipped back several pages and motioned to Anselm to look at it with him. "Here we are," he said,
"March. It was around the fifteenth . . ." Neil turned

one more page and pointed with an unsteady finger at an entry near the middle. "There."

Anselm read the entry out loud. "Fifteenth March, Mrs. Sandy Bracknell, Post Office Box 125, Carver's Island. Ergotamine tartrate 2mg tablets, times 20. Take one for migraine as directed. Prescribing doctor, Dr. Peter Delafield, Glenport."

A deep, horrified anger started to build in Anselm. He looked at Neil. Ergotamine was a powerful medication prescribed only for the most severe migraines. "Did Sandy have migraines, Neil?"

"Well, Dr. Harris . . ." He was now sweating profusely, and his tan looked yellow. "The only reason I'm mentioning this is that I've known Sandy Bracknell ever since she was a child, and I'm quite certain that she'd never had a day's migraine in her life."

"Let's make quite sure about the ergotamine," said Anselm. "Do you have a *PDR* handy?"

Valerie's eyes went from Neil to Anselm and back, wondering what on earth this was all about but sensing that something cataclysmic was in progress. Neil reached for the well-worn blue-covered *Physician's Desk Reference* on the top of the filing cabinet, put it on top of his ledger and flipped through the pages.

"Look under 'Contraindications,' " said Anselm softly.

"You read it, please, Dr. Harris," said Neil. "I don't have my glasses."

". . . Must be used only in prescribed dosage," murmured Anselm. "Can cause gangrene . . . The drug is specifically contraindicated in cases of arteriosclerosis, where it can cause arterial spasm leading to strokes or other vascular complications."

Neil sat in his chair and put his head between his hands. "I know I should never have given it to her," he said.

"Neil, can you make me a copy of this ledger entry?" asked Anselm urgently. "Now?"

Neil looked up. "Sure," he said. "It's all in the computer. I'll make a printout for you." He put the *PDR* back on the top of the filing cabinet and went over to the table with his computer equipment. He pressed a few buttons and within a few seconds a long perforated sheet came out of the printer. "That's my new laser printer," he said in a lifeless voice. "You can select from fourteen different fonts."

"I want you to sign this," said Anselm, taking a pen out of his pocket and giving it to Neil. "Write: 'This is a copy of the daysheet.' Stamp it with your pharmacy rubber stamp. Now sign it with today's date. Good. Thank you, Neil."

Anselm was in a cold, calculating rage. All the different implications of this sheet of paper started to come together in his head. Of course, the fact that Sandy Bracknell had the ergotamine pills didn't prove that these were the headache pills that she'd given her husband, but Anselm also knew that even at this late date, there were tests that could detect minute amounts of the drug in the autopsy material. It wasn't a drug that would be picked up by the usual toxicology screening techniques they had used on Denton Bracknell. Very clever, that Peter.

"Dr. Harris, I have a feeling all this is going to cost me my pharmacist's license."

Anselm came back to the present and looked at Neil in surprise. "Why? You filled the prescription, just the way you were supposed to. You followed the doctor's orders. It's not your job to know if Sandy suffered from migraine or not."

"But I did know. When you're a pharmacist, you know how healthy your customers are." Neil gulped. "Like I said before, I've known Sandy since she was a young girl. Believe me, I checked it out. The only other record that I had of her getting medicine was when she was seven and had an ear infection. That's aside from the contraceptive pill she's been on for the last three years, and that was also prescribed by Dr. Delafield.''

Anselm drew in his breath and Valerie looked at him. "You remember in Bracknell's chart," he said quietly, not looking at her, "under 'Family History,' Denton had non-viable sperm on two consecutive tests."

He turned to the pharmacist, who was sweating and looking utterly miserable. "Neil, put that ledger in the safe, keep it there, and swear to me that you won't talk to anybody, not a single soul, about this, okay?"

Neil swallowed, promised, and Anselm and Valerie left.

"Let's go to your place," said Anselm. "We have a lot to do, and we don't want any interruptions."

46

Valerie opened the door to her apartment, put on the light, and they took off their coats. Her teeth were chattering with cold, and they went into the kitchen to make some coffee. Anselm opened his jacket and folded it around her. In spite of the cold outside, he was as warm as toast, and she got as close to him as her shivering body could get. After a minute, she stepped back. "That was very nice," she said, "now would you do me a favor and explain what all that business in the pharmacy was about? What's ergotamine?"

Anselm was still sorting things out in his head and didn't answer immediately.

Could Sandy Bracknell suddenly have developed migraines? Though unlikely, it was certainly possible, but even if she had, it would have been unheard of for Peter or any other doctor to prescribe such a powerful medication before trying other, less toxic substances first.

"If you wanted to pick a drug that would kill a person with severe arteriosclerosis," he said, "ergotamine would be a good bet. What it does is make the circular muscle around the arteries contract, and if the arteries are already narrowed, that can cause a complete blockage, which is of course exactly what happened to Denton Bracknell.''

He struck his fist into the open palm of his other hand. ''Why didn't I think of it?'' He glowered at Valerie.

''Don't waste your time worrying about it,'' she said. ''Keep talking.''

''There are two factors here,'' said Anselm slowly. ''One is seeing Peter having sex with Sandy, and then this ergotamine business. . . .'' He tapped the pharmacy printout. ''Separately, these two items probably wouldn't amount to much. But together . . . Valerie, do you realize what we may be dealing with?''

''Yes,'' she said. ''This may be turning into a murder case.''

''I think we're going to need some help on this,'' he said. ''Let's first go over everything we know up to now, so we're sure we haven't missed anything.''

A half hour later, Anselm was about to call the Glenport police department when he remembered Marlin Foster, the FBI agent who had come up from New Coventry when Denton Bracknell was admitted.

''Is this something the FBI would deal with?'' he asked Valerie.

''Bracknell was a federal employee at the time of his death,'' she replied. ''So I think they have the option: if the FBI wants the case, they take it; otherwise they pass it on to the local or state police.''

It took Anselm a few minutes to get the number of the FBI office in New Coventry. He talked to the duty officer, who wouldn't give him Foster's home number but said he'd get him to call back.

The phone rang, loud and imperative, five minutes later and Anselm picked it up.

It was Marlin Foster, and yes, he remembered Dr. Harris well.

"There's been a major development on the Bracknell case," Anselm told him, "and I think it's become a matter for you guys. No, it can't wait till tomorrow. Can you come to Glenport? It would make more sense than us coming down there, for a number of reasons."

He listened for a few moments, then put the phone down. "He'll be here in an hour," he told Valerie.

Marlin Foster was on the doorstep in exactly fifty-five minutes.

They filled him in on the developments, showed him the computer printout, and told him what they had seen.

Foster was not immediately impressed.

"Before we can be sure a crime was committed here," he started cautiously, "we need to try to put these items in perspective. Can you guys help me put this whole story together?"

"We can try," said Anselm.

"Okay, let's start off with motivation," said Marlin. "What's in it for Mrs. Bracknell and Dr. Delafield?"

"As I understand it," said Anselm, "they had a more or less public affair for a couple of years before she met Denton Bracknell. He was married, of course."

"You think she married Bracknell with something like this in mind?" asked Marlin.

"I have no idea. But judging from what we saw, and the fact she's been on a contraceptive pill all this time, they didn't abandon their affair just because Sandy got married."

Marlin thought about that. "I hope you guys are not building your case on that premise," he said. "She's a widow now. She could have simply started up again with Dr. Delafield."

"We're not building any case," said Valerie. "All

we're doing is telling you what we've found. If there *is* a case, you're the one who's going to build it."

"Do you have any soda?" Marlin asked her.

"On the back of the refrigerator door," she replied. "Help yourself."

Marlin heaved himself out of his seat with a sigh. "Okay, we've covered the love part," he said over his shoulder. "How about the money? *Follow the money* was Deep Throat's advice, so it should do for us."

"According to his wife, Susan, Peter's about broke," said Valerie. "He has debts everywhere, for the boat, their house, his car. If this really was a plot between Sandy and Peter, he could pay off everything and they could live quite nicely for the rest of their lives on the money they got from the suit."

" 'Quite nicely' is right," said Anselm. "No wonder Peter seems so relaxed about everything. If all went reasonably well, Sandy could expect maybe twelve million dollars out of this case, including money from settling with the hospital and Peter's insurance company, and subtracting Norm Hartman's cut. If she puts that in Treasuries at eight percent, they'd make almost a million a year in interest alone."

"Anselm, you're better than Clever Hans," said Valerie, smiling.

"Who?" asked Marlin.

"Clever Hans was a horse who could count," she replied.

"Tell me the medical part, Dr. Harris," said Marlin, popping the soda can open.

Anselm did so, and the agent took notes in a tiny notebook.

When Anselm finished, Marlin was a lot more impressed. "How do you put all this together, Counselor?" he asked Valerie.

"Well," she said, "my guess is that the story starts a couple of years ago when Sandy and Peter were a hot item. She married Denton Bracknell hoping she and Peter could get something out of it, who knows, money, deals . . . Denton was already a very big shot. I would guess that Peter was the one who saw the potential in a malpractice suit, and Anselm Harris was the perfect fall guy. He had a recent notorious malpractice suit, so he was already a setup. Peter managed almost singlehandedly to get him on the staff at the hospital here, and Sandy and he just bided their time. A foggy day presented the perfect opportunity and they took it.''

''Why a foggy day?'' asked Marlin.

''Because then there was nowhere for Denton to go except Glenport Hospital,'' replied Valerie. ''Once he was admitted, it was up to Peter to keep him there, and he did that very effectively. He resisted a lot of pressure to transfer him.''

She turned to Anselm. ''Peter also convinced you to operate on him,'' she said. ''And he knew that the problems were from the ergotamine, not from a clot, and so he also knew that the surgery would probably be fatal, right?''

Anselm nodded.

Marlin addressed him. ''Dr. Harris, would you say, thinking back, that Mr. Bracknell showed signs of ergotamine poisoning when you first saw him?''

Anselm shut his eyes. ''Yes, Bracknell showed the classic picture, although at the time it was the last thing I would ever have thought of,'' he said. ''His hands and feet were icy cold, his pulse was thready. The ultrasound test showed more narrowing of the arteries than on the old films. Even the autopsy report mentioned the constricted arteries, but it never occurred to me that it could have been from ergotamine.'' He shook his head. ''I can't believe that I saw every one of those signs and missed them all completely.''

"Couldn't those signs have been caused by his having a stroke?" asked Valerie.

"Maybe some of them, but still . . ." Anselm shook his head. "The thing is that in arteriosclerosis, ergotamine is *known* to be a really lethal drug. I tell you, if he really planned this all out, our friend Peter is absolutely brilliant." His lips tightened. *The perfect fall guy,* Valerie had called him.

"Can we test Bracknell's body for ergotamine?" asked Marlin.

"I'm not a toxicologist, but I think so. I believe they can detect tiny amounts, so if it's there, they could probably find it in the organs they still have in Bethesda."

"So we wouldn't need to exhume his body."

"Right."

Marlin stood up, took a tiny electronic address book out of his pocket, went to the phone, and dialed a number with a 202 prefix. "Ergotamine is what we're looking for," he said after a long pause. He spelled it out. "Sure, there should be plenty of tissue left to test. We do not want to dig him up unless we absolutely have to."

"What do you think?" asked Valerie when he came back to the table.

"They said they can find ergotamine even in a small sample of tissue, and they're going to do the test as soon as possible." His gaze went from Anselm to Valerie. "So far, you've pretty well convinced me," he went on. "But we're going to need a lot more in the way of proof. There's a couple of things to do tonight before we can all go to sleep."

"If we can get Peter's office files on the Bracknells," said Anselm, "we can find out if Sandy ever complained of migraine. If she did, there would be a record of other, simpler remedies he'd have tried before using ergotamine. Then there'll be the report on Denton's sperm in his file.''

''That'll be for starters,'' said Marlin. ''But first I have to talk to my boss. Valerie, do you mind if I use your phone again?''

47

"I think we should just burn them," said Denise Beckwith. "There's no point keeping that . . . *dirt*." Her sister Rose was sitting beside her in their Glenport home, having come back from the island on the last ferry. They were both sitting up very straight and eyeing with distaste three photos laid out in front of them on the dining room table, all of Sandy Bracknell and Peter Delafield in various sexual poses.

"I agree we should get rid of them," said Denise. "They can only cause trouble. Why can't you just put them back?"

"The house is closed up," replied Rose. "And anyway, she'll have taken the box with her."

"Won't she miss them?" asked Denise, reaching down to stroke their tabby cat which was prowling around her legs.

"I don't think so," said Rose. "There were lots of them. I only took three from the bottom."

"But why take them?" asked Denise. "You could just as easily have told me about them."

Rose hesitated. "I don't know," she said. "I was so shocked. Doing things like that when she was married to poor Mr. Bracknell. He's lucky he's dead, I suppose."

Denise sat quietly for a moment, her eyes thoughtful. "That means I was right, that time I saw her with Dr. Delafield in the office," she said. She stood up, a determined look on her face. "I'm going to call Dr. Harris. He'll know what to do."

Two days later, at eleven o'clock in the morning, an angry and surprised Norm Hartman appeared outside Judge Mort Gold's chambers. Valerie was already there.

"What the hell is going on here?" Norm asked her. His tone was soft, but there was so much fury in his voice that a spray of droplets shot out of his mouth with the words.

"All I can tell you now, Norm," she replied calmly, "is that this has become a criminal case." And she refused to say another word until they went into chambers, where Judge Gold, tall and lantern-jawed, greeted them.

"First, I'd like to protest this meeting, Your Honor," said Norm. "No proper notice was given, and I only came here on your direct order—"

"Maybe Attorney Morse will explain why this meeting was necessary," said Judge Gold, looking curiously at Valerie.

"I want to have the case of Bracknell versus Harris thrown out," said Valerie, ignoring Norm's indignant snort. "I have evidence to show that a serious crime may have been committed in direct relation to this case."

"Your Honor, this is outrageous!" exploded Norm. "There is absolutely no precedent—"

"Let her get on with her story," interrupted Gold. He turned to Valerie. "I'm warning you right now, Counselor, this had better be good."

"It's better than good, Your Honor," replied Valerie crisply. She showed him the printout from the pharmacy and passed it to Norm, who seemed to swell up with rage. "What are you trying to prove with this?" he asked after glancing at it. "This doesn't mean a damn thing! So my client has migraines, what does that prove?"

"She doesn't have migraines," said Valerie softly. "She never did. And nor did Mr. Bracknell."

That was too much for Norm. "Are you a doctor now or what? How can you have the—the gall to say such a thing without any kind of evidence?"

"The FBI checked Dr. Delafield's records early yesterday morning," replied Valerie. "He had been her doctor for over five years, and there was no mention in the office chart of any headaches or any other illness, let alone migraines. Also . . ." Valerie took a deep breath. "The central FBI lab yesterday confirmed the presence of toxic amounts of ergotamine in Mr. Bracknell's body tissues."

Norm was severely shaken, but was still thinking fast, and countered that Bracknell could have developed a headache in Washington and got the medication from a friend.

When Valerie produced the photos, Norm almost exploded. "I can't believe this," he screamed. "You're presenting material stolen from my client as evidence? Your Honor, this is not only illegal but totally unethical. As soon as we got out of here, I will contact the Connecticut Bar Association and start proceedings. . . ."

Judge Gold let him go on for a few minutes, then said to Valerie, "Those photographs could have been taken years ago, surely. How can you put a date to them?"

"I asked the same question earlier this morning," she replied. "I talked to the head of the biggest film-developing lab in New Coventry. There's a new system called DX coding that's used for automatic cameras to tell the speed of the film. This has only been in use for the last year, and this film was equipped with it.''

That was the death blow for Norm, and his already pale face went gray.

''The case has been taken by the FBI rather than the local police because Bracknell was a federal employee on government business at the time,'' Valerie went on, speaking calmly, although she could feel the fierce pounding of her heart. ''The New Coventry office is handling it, and Agent Marlin Foster is in charge of the investigation. He said he'd be glad to confirm this with you if you wish, Judge Gold.''

''Well, I guess that's it,'' said the judge, looking quite amazed. He stood up. ''Since the case is now under criminal investigation, Mr. Hartman, I'm sure you are aware that you can neither start nor continue with a civil suit until after the criminal component has come to trial or has been settled. The case of Bracknell *versus* Harris is therefore adjourned, *sine die*. Thank you both.''

Valerie and Norm walked out of the chambers together. Norm was silent and angry. He had just lost the biggest case of his career, although only a couple of days before, he could have settled it for more money than he'd ever seen in his life.

He stopped and turned to face Valerie. ''Counselor,'' he said, his voice as calm as if he'd just lost a dollar at backgammon, ''I have information in my possession that you should have, now that this has become a criminal case.'' He paused, looking hard at her. ''When I first took this case, I checked out the principal defendants, who at that time were Dr. Harris and Dr. Delafield. I used, as I always do, the Malone detective agency. They're expensive but good.'' He sighed. ''At that time Dr. Delafield was a principal defendant. Terry Malone found that he and Mrs. Bracknell had stayed together overnight in several hotels and motels in the Glenport area within the last year. When Malone came up with this report, we had already settled with Dr. Delafield, so I had no interest in his activities.''

Norm pushed his hand deep into his pockets and smiled thoughtfully at Valerie. "So you see, Counselor, you didn't even need those photos. If you like, I'll send you the file on Delafield.''

"Thank you, Norm," said Valerie. "That's most generous of you.'' An idea came to her and she smiled at him. "Did you find out anything like that about Dr. Harris?" she asked casually.

"Nope." He grinned again, this time more spontaneously. His spirits were coming back; there would be plenty of other cases to win. "Only the stuff about his malpractice case in New York. I read the transcript, and between you and me, he got screwed.''

Judge Gold came by. "Anyone for coffee?" he asked them.

"If you're buying," said Valerie, and the three of them crossed the street to the coffee shop opposite the courthouse.

48

Later that day, Stefan Olson and Tony Marino met in Stefan's office. The news of the murder investigation had spread through the community like wildfire, and everyone had his own theory and her own story to tell. The only thing the stories had in common was that Dr. Anselm Harris had been made the scapegoat for a vicious crime, and people were very angry about it.

Tony was looking rather shaken, and they talked about the case for a while.

Then Stefan led the conversation where he wanted it to go. "I met yesterday with the top management people at Farman," he said. "They've finally deep-sixed the idea of their clinic because their union people changed their minds and withdrew their support. It was our Erica who convinced them. She showed them what had happened to other company-owned health clinics in the area."

"*Our* Erica?" said Tony, staring at Stefan. "I tell you, that girl's becoming an expensive proposition, what with her full-time job here, a nice new-car deal with me, and now the business with my fool son-in-law."

"She's certainly earned her keep as far as we're concerned," said Stefan, trying not to show the new enthusiasm he felt for her. "Anyway, I believe that this is exactly the right moment to get Farman seriously involved with this hospital and cut a deal with them.''

Tony took out a cigar, looked at the tip, but didn't light it.

"I talked to Bruce Lord at Farman this morning," Stefan went on slowly. "He said that he's prepared to join the board of the hospital."

"Bruce would? Personally?" asked Tony disbelievingly. "Or would he just send some deputy?"

"Personally. Not only that, but they're prepared to put up a substantial sum to re-equip the lab and X-ray departments, and for the ER, whatever it takes to bring us into compliance with the JCAH."

"What's the price tag?" asked Tony. "I mean, what do we have to do in return?"

Stefan took a deep breath. "We have to reorganize the way we run this hospital," he said. "We'll need to build satellite clinics and develop a more responsive attitude to the needs of the community. Erica—''

"We need a new chief of surgery," said Tony, who seemed to be going off in his own direction.

"Bruce Lord is pushing to give Anselm Harris that job," said Stefan, who hadn't wanted to get to that quite yet. "He knows all about his Bank Street clinic and thinks it's wonderful. 'Good for the hospital's image as a caring institution,' he said.''

Tony shrugged. At this point he didn't care who was chief of surgery.

"We also need a new hospital attorney, one who's more up to the job than John Kestler," Stefan went on. "But the main thing Farman is insisting on is an entirely new board of managers."

"*Entirely* new?"

"Yes, sir. Bruce Lord already has a list of people he wants to be on it."

Tony was paying attention now. "That's ridiculous,'' he said sharply. ''Who the hell does he think he is?''

''They've got us by the short hairs, I'm afraid,'' said Stefan, who had spent the past two weeks working hard to make this situation come about. ''Farman's our biggest source of patients, the Bracknell business has shown everybody how deficient we are at the hospital, and a lot of people feel that the board simply hasn't been doing its job.''

''We can change that,'' said Tony defensively. ''I've got my own plans to reorganize the board.'' He stared aggressively at Stefan, lit his cigar, and puffed a cloud of smoke in his direction.

Stefan pushed a copy of the local newspaper across the desk, folded to display the second page. ''I don't know if you've had a chance to read this,'' he said.

Tony held the paper out at arm's length. '' 'Glenport Hospital in Peril,' '' he read, and then looked over at Stefan. ''What's this shit?'' he growled. Stefan said nothing, and Tony read on in silence. The article detailed the problems the hospital had had with the JCAH, and the various deficiencies that had led to the threat of losing accreditation.

Tony started to read aloud again. '' ' ''The only hope is a complete restructuring of the hospital,'' said Farman CEO Bruce Lord to the city's Rotary Club meeting at the Sherada Hotel yesterday. Lord emphasized his readiness to work with Stefan Olson, the hospital's president, who also spoke at the meeting.' '' Tony paused and glowered for a second at Stefan.

''They're already putting on the pressure,'' said Stefan. ''And it could get a lot worse. So far we've kept that incident with Erica and Dr. North quiet, but if the papers ever got hold of that''—Stefan's expression was sympathetic as he went on—''they'd make a meal of the fact that Dr. North is the son-in-law of the chairman of the hospital board, which would explain why there hasn't been a full investigation into the matter.''

Stefan shook his head at the viciousness of the media and took a deep breath. ''You know, Mr. Marino, quite honestly, at this point it would be better for everybody if the entire board resigned now, including you, rather than wait for a public outcry to force them out.''

Tony bunched his fists, stared at Stefan, who stared calmly back. They looked at each other for several seconds like two china dogs on a mantelpiece, while Tony's mind scrabbled for a way out. Then he got up and walked toward the door. He stopped halfway, turned, and deliberately dropped his cigar on the floor. He put his foot on it and twisted it, still lit, into the carpet.

''I knew we should never have hired you, you goddamned Swedish meatball son of a bitch,'' he said.

Erica was in the outer office, sitting on the edge of Donna Forrest's desk, chatting, swinging her elegant legs and filing her nails, when Tony stormed out. He stopped dead when he saw Erica, who stood up very deliberately, went to the door to Stefan's office, and pushed it open without knocking. She turned and gave Tony a wink that was so lewd and suggestive that he stepped back in astonishment. It wasn't until the door had softly closed behind her that Tony, suddenly feeling sick with anger, realized how diabolically he had been set up.

About the same time, Anselm and Valerie were sitting on a bench outside the Whaler Inn. The weather was warm and a breeze came up off the Sound, just strong enough to blow the corners up on their paper napkins. In the distance they could see the irregular blue-gray mass of Carver's Island, clearly visible, looming up out of the water.

They sat close together on the bench and sipped beer.

Anselm was quiet and thoughtful, and Valerie, who was feeling utterly elated, asked him what he was thinking about.

"Peter," he replied simply. "He was my good friend for such a long time. It feels like there's been a death in my family."

Valerie held tightly onto Anselm's free hand and said nothing.

"I wish I could do something to help him," he continued, staring out over the water.

Valerie, not by any means as forgiving, felt a now familiar mild irritation at Anselm's soft-hearted attitude. "I'm more interested in helping *you*," she said. "And to that end, we're going to reopen that malpractice case back in New York. I think I know just how to go about it."

"No, you're not,' said Anselm, shaking off his sadness about Peter. "Somebody else may, but you won't. There's that little question of legal ethics. . . ." He put his arm around her shoulder and held her close. "As of this morning, Valerie Morse," he said, "you are no longer my attorney, and I'm shortly going to take full advantage of that fact."

About fifteen miles away to the northeast, a great blue heron stood motionless in the curve of a shallow, marshy inlet, near a group of five stunted alders. A patch of sunlight slid along the ripples and illuminated the bird in gold and white. He shook his feathers out for a few moments to absorb the warmth, then took off and swung low over a clump of bayberry bushes, slowly gaining height as he went.

Make Room For Great Escapes At Hilton International Hotels

Save the coupons in the backs of these ⓓ Signet and ⓢ Onyx books and redeem them for special Hilton International Hotels discounts and services.

June

REVERSIBLE ERROR
Robert K. Tanenbaum

RELATIVE SINS
Cynthia Victor

July

GRACE POINT
Anne D. LeClaire

FOREVER
Judith Gould

August

MARILYN: *The Last Take*
Peter Harry Brown &
Patte B. Barham

JUST KILLING TIME
Derek Van Arman

September

DANGEROUS PRACTICES
Francis Roe

SILENT WITNESS:
*The Karla Brown
Murder Case*
Don W. Weber &
Charles Bosworth, Jr.

2 coupons: Save 25% off regular rates at Hilton International Hotels
4 coupons: Save 25% off regular rates, <u>plus</u> upgrade to Executive Floor
6 coupons: All the above, <u>plus</u> complimentary Fruit Basket
8 coupons: All the above, <u>plus</u> a free bottle of wine

(Check *People* Magazine and Signet and Onyx spring titles for Bonus coupons to be used when redeeming three or more coupons)

Disclaimers: Advance reservations and notification of the offer required. May not be used in conjunction with any other offer. Discount applies to regular rates only. Subject to availability and black out dates. Offer may not be used in conjunction with convention, group or any other special offer. Employees and family members of Penguin USA and Hilton International are not eligible to participate in GREAT ESCAPES.